WHAL

Christopher Mitchell is the author of the The Magelands and Masters & Makers fantasy series. He studied in Edinburgh before living for several years in the Middle East and Greece, where he taught English. He returned to study classics and Greek tragedy and lives in Fife, Scotland with his wife and their four children.

BY CHRISTOPHER MITCHELL

THE MAGELANDS ORIGINS

Retreat of the Kell
The Trials of Daphne Holdfast
From the Ashes

THE MAGELANDS EPIC

The Queen's Executioner
The Severed City
Needs of the Empire
Sacrifice
Fragile Empire
Storm Mage
Soulwitch Rises
Renegade Gods

THE MAGELANDS ETERNAL SIEGE

The Mortal Blade
The Dragon's Blade
The Prince's Blade
Falls of Iron
Paths of Fire
Gates of Ruin
City of Salve
Red City

City Ascendant
Dragon Eyre Badblood
Dragon Eyre Ashfall
Dragon Eyre Blackrose
Dreams of Kell
God Restrainer
Holdfast Imperium
World's End

The Magelands Dominion

Serpent Dominion
Demon Witch
Death Seer
Blood Burden
Kin Strife
Tempest's Edge
Creator of Worlds
Palace of the Almighty
Sapphire Throne

Masters and Makers

Fall Seldom Kings
The Making of Abigone
Whalebone King
Lies the Prince

Cover Design by Sasha Almazan and Gene Mollica, G&S Cover Design Studio. LLC.
Maps by Irina French

Brigdomin Books Ltd
First Edition, January 2025
ISBN 978-1-915978-51-6

ACKNOWLEDGEMENTS

I would like to thank the following for all their support during the writing of Masters & Makers - my wife, Lisa Mitchell, who read every chapter as soon as it was drafted and kept me going in the right direction; my parents for their unstinting support; Marilyn Hopwood for reading the books in their early stages; James Aitken for his encouragement; and Grant and Gordon of the Film Club for their support.

Thanks also to my Advance Reader team, for all your help during the last few weeks before publication.

THE WORLD OF THE MASTERS & MAKERS

Selected Notes on the World of the Masters & Makers

Yearl – Once the centre of the Elestian Empire, Yearl is now a province of the Sanctian Empire. Its capital of Elestia remains the largest city in the Central Provinces.

Jallin – A small client kingdom to the north of Yearl. Not formally part of the Sanctian Empire, but the realm has a defensive alliance with that empire, and its policies are strongly influenced by Sanctos.

The Great Forest – This forest once covered most of the Central Provinces, but many areas have been cleared for timber. Extends over the northern portion of Yearl, and the western half of Jallin.

Upper Down – A small mountain realm between the old Northern Provinces and the old Central Provinces of the Elestian Empire. Historically part of the Duchy of Down, it gained independence with the collapse of the Elestian Empire, splitting away from what became the kingdoms of **Greater Down** and **Lesser Down**. Upper Down sits astride one of only three passes through the mountains, but its most significant attribute is that it remains the last realm still governed by Masters and Makers.

The Elestian Empire – Sometimes referred to **the First Empire**, the Elestians governed vast tracts of the continent for almost a thousand years. Ruled by an elite aristocracy of Masters and Makers, it eventually collapsed after prolonged rebellions and uprisings. Its collapse led to widespread massacres of Masters and Makers, reducing their numbers until few were left alive. The old calendar system ended upon the death of the last Emperor, and the years are now dated from this momentous event. ***The Making of Abigone*** begins in Year 108, i.e. one hundred and eight years since the fall of the Elestian Empire.

The Sanctian Empire – Centred around the island of Sanctos, the Sanctian Empire arose from the ashes of the Elestian Empire. Sometimes referred to as **The Second Empire**, the Sanctians have been re-conquering many of the old provinces, and re-uniting them under its rule. The Sanctians view Masters and Makers as wicked and blasphemous, and have pledged to hunt down and execute the last remaining survivors.

The Westlanders – Hailing originally from the great plains to the west of the old Northern Provinces, the Westlanders swept through those provinces following the collapse of the Elestian Empire. Seen as a primitive, violent people by the citizens of the old Central Provinces, the Westlanders are hated and feared. Known for their worship of the three moons as much as for their raiding and brigandage, the Westlanders are unrivalled in warfare.

Klef Mordain – A large port city on the eastern coast of the continent, north of the mountains that divide the old Northern Provinces from the former Central Provinces. Once the foremost port of the Elestian Empire, Klef Mordain has recently been annexed by the Sanctian Empire, following the assassination of its ambassador to the city.

Masters – Men who possess the ability to transmute elements.

Makers – Women who possess the ability to summon objects.

NOTE ON THE ELESTIAN CALENDAR

This calendar was devised during the rule of the Elestians, and is used in all lands that were provinces of that empire.

The world has three moons – the Big Red Moon (King Aloth), the Silver Moon (Queen Ninia), and the Little Red Moon (Prince Logar); and the months are organised around the orbit of the largest of these – the Big Red Moon, which goes around the world once every 33 days. Hence, each of the eleven months contains 33 days – creating a Solar Year of 363 days (with no Leap Day required).

Each month is named after one of the Emperors or Empresses of Elestia.

In the Elestian Calendar, each year begins on the 1st day of Pomana. The below list of months details the corresponding dates upon Earth. These dates are a rough guide only, as a year on the world of Elestia and Sanctos contains two fewer days than a solar year on Earth.

- Pomana– corresponds to 21 March to 22 April
- Saluna– corresponds to 23 April to 25 May
- Ara– corresponds to 26 May to 27 June
- Considera– corresponds to 28 June to 30 July
- Tempora– corresponds to 31 July to 1 September
- Desira– corresponds to 2 September to 4 October
- Lamenta– corresponds to 5 October to 6 November
- Minula– corresponds to 7 November to 9 December
- Quoma– corresponds to 10 December to 11 January
- Regula– corresponds to 12 January to 13 February
- Nova– corresponds to 14 February to 18 March

DRAMATIS PERSONAE

Refugees from Klef Mordain

Princess Abigone, Aunt of King Alfgang VI (19)

Prince Mor Dennahelm, (Denny) Son of Mor Galthide (19)

Lothar, Commander in Mountain Rangers

Annalise, Lady-in-Waiting to Princess Abigone

Fyenna, Former Head of the Makers' School (47)

Mor Galthide, Former Prince of Geathan (47)

Eshia, Graduate Maker (19)

Raewyn, Former Student Maker (17)

Stanza, Former Student Maker (15)

Reath, Former Student Maker (14)

Nyli, Former Student Maker (14)

Constans, Former Student Master (17)

Aplin, Former Student Master (16)

Marlow, Former Student Master (15)

Salus, Former Student Master (14)

Ignatius, Former Student Master (14)

Amery of Yearl, Lawyer

Loryn, Notary

Sanctian Expeditionary Force

Princess Safina, (Saffie) Granddaughter of Emperor Antonio (20)

Zola, Captain in the Offices of Purgation

Aldo, Lieutenant in the Imperial Army

Marco, Lieutenant in the Offices of Purgation

Elestia

Lord Commander, Chief of Offices of Purgation in Yearl

Steppen

Hemming, Former Pirate, Master, Whalebone King of Steppen (67)

Ragnvald, Hemming's Eldest Son, Master (30)

Einar, Hemming's Second Son (27)

Erling, Hemming's Third Son (25)

Magnus, Hemming's Fourth Son, Master (17)

Colette, Hemming's Second Wife, Mother of Magnus (36)

Lord Matteo, Sanctian Agent for Steppen

Westlanders in Steppen

Duggan, Young Slave

Aisly, Young Slave; Duggan's Sister

Johan, Former Leader of a War Band

Station on Yearlian/Jallian Frontier

Werven, Lieutenant in Yearlian Militia

Journeying from Upper Down

Duke Walter, Duke of Torrent, Regent of Upper Down, husband of Princess Kilbride (27)

Count Sebastian, Member of the Emperor's Imperial Court

Dietar, Lieutenant in Mountain Rangers

Otto, Sergeant in Mountain Rangers

The World of Masters & Makers
The Westlands
Northern Provinces
Desert
Upper Down
Klef Mordain
Lesser Down
Estral
Greater Down
Campsie
Anster
Guran
Central Provinces
Jallin
Yearl
Osbruck
Elestia
Mylos
Anster
Dibain
Nessos
Aubruk
Subnestia
The Thousand Lakes
Sanctos
Western Colonies
Ocean
Geathan
Ocean
Southern Provinces
Road
Town
Ocean
N
W
E
S

CHAPTER 1
THE OFFICES OF PURGATION

Elestia, Yearl, Central Provinces – 9th Day of Minula 108

Saffie turned away as the prisoner screamed.

'Give me the name of the man who told you this,' said the Lord Commander.

'I don't know his name – I swear it!' cried the prisoner.

The Lord Commander nodded to the hooded agent standing next to him. The man turned the wheel a notch, tightening the pressure on the prisoner's ankles. Saffie heard what sounded like a bone cracking, and the prisoner screamed again, his cries echoing off the damp walls of the cellar; then he passed out, his head lolling forward onto the iron frame to which he had been shackled.

'Do we need the name?' said Captain Zola. 'The prisoner has already confirmed what we had suspected, my Lord Commander.'

'If I am to dispatch an expeditionary force into the wilds of the Great Forest,' said the Lord Commander, 'then we need to be sure. The evidence this man has provided is not enough. All he has given us are a few tales and rumours. We require someone who has personally seen the Whalebone King.' He glanced at Saffie. 'There is another delicate matter we have to consider, Your Highness – the location of this so-called king lies across the border in Jallin. I do not wish to spark a diplomatic incident with our neighbours; therefore, our evidence must be solid.' He gestured again to the agent. 'Relieve the pressure on the prisoner's ankles, then revive him.'

The hooded man inclined his head. He turned the wheel, and the iron bar pressing against the prisoner's legs moved back an inch, displaying the discoloured and swollen flesh where the bar had been. The agent withdrew a small vial from a pocket, then he prised off the lid and placed it under the prisoner's nose. The captive's eyes jerked open with a start, then he grimaced in pain.

'Let us return to the reason you are here,' said the Lord Commander. 'You were overheard talking about a suspected Master dwelling in the Great Forest, and yet you neglected to report this to the correct authorities. For this lapse, your freedom, and perhaps your life, are in my hands. If I tell this agent to release you, you will be released. If I tell him to execute you, you will be executed. There is nowhere to run, and no one is coming to save you.'

'You Sanctian bastards,' the prisoner groaned.

'Come now; do you long for more pain?' said the Lord Commander. 'I am trying to be reasonable. Give me some answers, and you will be back with your family this evening.'

The prisoner said nothing.

'Tell me more about the individual who told you that the Whalebone King was a Master,' said the Lord Commander. 'I know you can do better than *a man from Jallin that you met in a tavern*. What was the man's occupation? What is the name of the tavern? What did the fellow look like? How old was he?'

'He works on the river barges,' the prisoner said. 'They delivered their cargo of silver to the merchant bank yesterday. He didn't tell me his name.'

'Had the barges come directly from the silver mine?'

'I think so. The man told me that he saw the Whalebone King executing several slaves, with nothing more than a few muttered words.'

'And what happened to these slaves? Be specific.'

'Their faces turned green, then they fell down dead. The king had their heads removed, and then he placed them onto spikes by the front of the temple.'

'What temple?'

'There is an ancient temple to the spirits next to the silver mine; or so the man told me.'

'That detail is true, my Lord Commander,' said Captain Zola. 'I have interviewed bargemen who have confirmed it.'

'But none of these bargemen have ever spoken of the so-called king using his Master abilities in front of an audience?'

'That is correct. Perhaps the Whalebone King has become complacent.'

The Lord Commander turned back to the prisoner. 'And the name of the tavern?'

'The *Black Bull*,' gasped the prisoner.

'I want that tavern raided within the hour, Captain Zola,' said the Lord Commander; 'and I want everyone inside the building brought here as soon as possible.'

The captain saluted. 'Yes, my Lord Commander.'

'Take Her Highness with you,' said the Lord Commander, 'but be sure to keep her safe.'

The captain nodded, then he gestured to Saffie. 'Ma'am?'

Saffie eyed the Lord Commander. 'Thank you for allowing me to be present at the interrogation,' she said.

The Lord Commander smiled. 'As you are joining the Offices of Purgation, Your Highness, I thought it best that you got a small taste of our work here. Stay close to Captain Zola when you are out and about in the city; he will keep any harm from coming to you.'

Zola escorted Saffie out of the dank chamber, and they ascended a flight of stairs to the ground floor of the large palatial building. Workers were busy unloading crates from a line of wagons by the main doors, while a huge portrait of the emperor was being removed from a wall.

Saffie frowned.

'That painting is destined for the governor's new residence, ma'am,' said Captain Zola, 'which is, naturally, the old royal palace. It's the largest portrait of the Most Exalted Emperor Antonio in Elestia, and the governor wishes to place it in the main reception hall of his new home.'

'Then we shall need to order a new one,' said Saffie.

'The Lord Commander has already done so, ma'am,' said Zola. He smiled. 'A few months ago, the Offices of Purgation had to work out of a single room in this building – now, with the governor moving into the palace, the entire place is ours.'

'Do the Offices of Purgation need such a large building?' said Saffie. 'Exactly how many Masters and Makers are living in Yearl?'

'More than you would think, ma'am, and certainly more than we would like. Also, you must remember that our responsibilities cover more than Yearl alone. We also oversee the activities of the sub-offices in every neighbouring province. The main problem is that, with a little cunning, rogue Masters and Makers can blend into a civilian population. If they never use their wicked abilities, then they can be very hard to track down. Another problem is that a few unfortunates do not even realise they are Masters and Makers. In the bad old days, Elestian priests would routinely test all youths living in the Central Provinces, but that habit fell out of practice over a century ago. Can you imagine living your whole life without realising that you happened to be a Master or a Maker?'

Saffie narrowed her eyes. 'How could that be possible? How could one not know?'

'Just a moment, ma'am,' Zola said. He turned to a pair of young Sanctian army officers. 'I need the two squads on duty to accompany myself and the princess to a tavern by the river front.'

'Which tavern, sir?' said a lieutenant.

'The *Black Bull*,' said the captain. 'We are to bring all occupants of said tavern back here for questioning. We shall require covered wagons, but there shouldn't be any need for shackles. Bring the wagons round to the rear of the building, and we'll set off from there.'

Saffie's attention drifted away as the three officers continued to discuss the details of the forthcoming operation. She walked up to where the enormous portrait of Emperor Antonio was being lowered slowly to the marble floor. A thick rug had been laid out to protect the gilt frame, and over a dozen workers were labouring in silence. Saffie gazed into the eyes of the painted emperor. The artist had been generous in his depiction. He had retained the stern gleam in the emperor's eyes, but had removed all traces of his cruelty.

'Step back, girl,' one of the workers shouted at her. 'Get out of our way.'

Captain Zola broke off his conversation, and hurried over. He gripped the worker's collar with one hand, and slapped him across the face with the other.

'How dare you?' Zola cried. 'You should be strung up for such impertinence.'

The workers stared at him.

'Do you know who this is?' Zola went on. 'You were addressing Her Highness Princess Safina, daughter of Prince Vincenzo; granddaughter of the Most Exalted Emperor Antonio.'

The workers cried out and fell to their knees, their heads bowed. The one in Zola's grip whimpered, his palms raised in supplication.

'My apologies!' he cried. 'I didn't know! I'm sorry!'

'Don't apologise to me, you worthless wretch,' said Zola; 'apologise to Her Highness.'

He released the worker, who fell to the marble floor and prostrated himself before Saffie. He crawled towards her, his face lowered, then he raised his hands.

'Your blessed Highness,' he sobbed; 'please forgive me.'

Saffie gazed down at him. Her main inclination was to tell everyone not to be so stupid – did they think she had been mortally offended by a single offhand remark? On the other hand, it was her first full day in the city of Elestia, and her first morning in the Offices of Purgation, and perhaps she needed to make an impression. She knew what her grandfather would advise in such a situation, but Saffie felt that a grisly execution was a step too far.

'Flog him,' she said. 'Four stripes.'

'I would recommend ten, Your Highness,' said Zola.

'Four will suffice.'

Zola clicked his fingers, and a squad of Sanctian soldiers rushed over. They took hold of the worker's shoulders, and hauled him to his feet.

'Have this man flogged in the public courtyard,' Zola said. 'Four lashes, for disrespecting Her Royal Highness.'

The soldiers dragged the man away.

'Everyone else,' said Zola, 'back to work.'

The workers averted their gazes and resumed their job of lowering the giant portrait. Zola gestured to Saffie, and they began walking towards the rear of the building.

'We shall travel to the *Black Bull* in an unmarked carriage, ma'am,' he said, as though nothing untoward had taken place. 'The Offices of Purgation have several we can use.'

Saffie nodded. 'What will happen to that man after he has been flogged?'

Zola eyed her. 'He will likely be taken to the hospital, ma'am.'

'Ten lashes would have killed him.'

'Indeed, ma'am,' said Zola; 'but four will still send a message to the others. Everyone will know the price of disrespecting a princess of the empire.' He opened a door for her, and they passed into a hall at the rear of the building, where two squads of soldiers were preparing their equipment. 'I wasn't aware that you had spent time with the navy, ma'am,' Zola said.

'And how would you know that, Captain?' she said.

'You said *stripes*, rather than *lashes*, ma'am. The last time I heard that I was on board a frigate.'

'I spent a year as a junior lieutenant with the navy patrols,' Saffie said.

'And now you are with the Offices of Purgation, ma'am?'

'The Most Exalted Emperor likes his grandchildren to receive a rounded education.'

'If you have been at sea, ma'am, then you might not have heard the latest news from Klef Mordain.'

'I am aware that it has fallen to our forces. I was told this when I arrived in Yearl.'

'But, ma'am, are you aware of the rumours regarding your noble cousin Prince Mor Dennahelm?'

'I know that his father abducted him nearly two years ago.'

'The prince was seen in Klef Mordain, ma'am. He was in the company of a rogue Maker who assassinated the Sanctian ambassador, along with dozens of soldiers and civilians. She brought the entire building down.'

'What are you implying?'

'Nothing, ma'am. I am merely quoting from the official report. Witnesses suggest that Prince Mor Dennahelm pretended he was married to this Maker so she could gain access to the embassy. Furthermore, his body was not found in the ruins, and no one has seen the prince since.'

'Was the Maker apprehended?'

'No, ma'am. She remains on the loose. The report also mentioned something about her identity that I find hard to believe. Apparently, she is none other than Princess Abigone from Upper Down – the same Princess Abigone who destroyed the cannon belonging to the Most Illustrious Prince Valentino.'

'What was a princess of Upper Down doing in Klef Mordain?'

'The report's authors believe she was attending a secret school to train rogue Makers, ma'am. They also believe that she fled by sea. Our flagship, the *Bitter Respite*, was sunk in the local waters of Klef Mordain, along with two frigates. Needless to say, the Lord Commander greatly desires to apprehend this Abigone. If she passes through the Central Provinces, she would make a very fine prize. We have spies watching the roads leading north to Upper Down, in case she tries to travel to her home.'

They stopped by the rear doors of the building, and watched as the two squads of soldiers readied four large, covered wagons. Horses were hitched to the front of the wagons, and the soldiers began to clamber aboard.

'If, however,' Zola went on, 'the fugitive princess happens to be in the company of Prince Mor Dennahelm and his father Prince Mor Galthide, then we suspect that they may be travelling towards Geathan.'

Saffie smiled. 'Denny was never even remotely interested in Geathan. He used to mock the place. I very much doubt that he would be going there, and I find it simply unbelievable that he would associate with a disgusting Maker.'

Zola turned to face her. 'Is it at all possible that Prince Mor Dennahelm was hiding the fact that he was a Master, ma'am? Is it even remotely possible?'

'It is utterly inconceivable,' said Saffie, 'and I would appreciate it if you would refrain from spreading such a vile rumour.'

'Of course, ma'am. The Lord Commander insisted that I pose you the question, and I apologise for any offence it may have caused. Shall we board our carriage?'

Saffie inclined her head, and they walked down the steps into the rear courtyard. Zola led her to a plain-looking carriage, and then he helped her climb up into its comfortable interior. Zola said a few words to the two soldiers on the driver's bench, then he joined Saffie inside the carriage and closed the door.

Saffie gazed out of the window as the carriage led the four wagons through the iron gates and into the wide, clean boulevards of central Elestia. Her shock at Zola's words had been suppressed, but her thoughts ran wild under her calm demeanour. Could it be possible? Could Denny be a Master? It sounded like a nightmare made real. She had been good friends with Denny on Sanctos and, of course, they had known each other since they had been infants. The imperial family contained sixteen cousins – seven grandchildren of the emperor, four grandchildren of Prince Valentino, and another five grandchildren of Princess Carla. It had been the emperor's will that all sixteen siblings and cousins were trained together from an early age, and they had undergone all manner of hardships in each other's company. She had been on Sanctos when Mor Galthide had kidnapped his son, snatching him from a palace one grey morning, and spiriting him away. The other cousins had been devastated, and Princess Volena – Denny's poor mother – had been distraught and almost hysterical. The imperial navy had been dispatched to Geathan, but no trace of the reluctant prince and his son had been found there; and then Denny had supposedly turned up in Klef Mordain? Why would he have gone there? The obvious answer was also the most ridiculous – that he had travelled to the great northern city to attend a school for Masters, just as Abigone had done, but for Makers. How else could they have met? No. It couldn't be true, and yet it tapped into Saffie's worst fears about her own life. For well over a year, she had been having recurring dreams that she was a Maker – dreams that had chilled her blood with horror. She wasn't a Maker, of course, but the dreams had left her weary and terrified. Were the dreams the real reason for her volunteering to join the Offices of Purgation? She had wanted to leave Sanctos, but she could have chosen almost any job in the empire – had she chosen to hunt Masters and Makers due to her repressed fears and guilt over her nightmares?

Her eyes hardened. She found it hard to express how much she loathed Masters and Makers. If Denny was one, then she would gladly wield the sword that ended his life, no matter how much she had loved him in the past. They were disgusting, cursed creatures; barely human, twisted by their evil blasphemies into walking abominations. She recalled what Captain Zola had earlier mentioned – that some people might spend their lives *not knowing* that they were a Master or a Maker. What nonsense. They all knew. No one with that amount of evil within them could not know.

Their carriage turned towards the river that ran through the centre of Elestia. The city had over a dozen elegant bridges, all with high arches to accommodate the busy traffic on the river. Saffie glanced at the view as they passed over one of the bridges. There was no doubt that Elestia was a fine city. It was larger than any on Sanctos, and its central districts were full of monuments and buildings that were testament to the power of the old Elestian Empire. One thing it was missing was the presence of any new buildings. Unlike the capital city of Sanctos, which resembled a building site due to the amount of new construction being undertaken, Elestia looked old. It was grand and elegant, but its glory was fraying at the edges.

The carriage took a left turn after the bridge, and descended to the docks that ran along the banks of the river. They came to a halt by a row of ancient-looking taverns, and the four wagons parked behind them on the road. Saffie gazed out of the side window and saw the *Black Bull*, a shabby, three-storey building that seemed as though it might topple over at any moment. Captain Zola signalled to the two soldiers up on the carriage's driver's bench, and one of them blew a whistle. Soldiers began climbing down from the four wagons, then they piled into the tavern.

'Of the twenty-seven people detained from the *Black Bull*,' said Captain Zola, 'we have identified six with Jallian accents, my Lord Commander. Should we have the others released?'

The Lord Commander gazed out of the bay windows at the view of the city. 'Not yet. Have the six Jallians been isolated from the others?'

'They have, my Lord Commander. We have put them in the storage chambers in the cellars for now.'

'Work will soon begin on converting the basement into a decent prison,' said the Lord Commander. 'We shall require a large holding cell, several individual cells, and a few rooms in which to conduct interrogations. The plans are being drawn up by the army. For now, though, the storage chambers will have to suffice.' He glanced at Saffie. 'Would you like to be present when we question the Jallians, Your Highness?'

'I would, yes,' said Saffie.

'We shall try the gentle approach, I think,' said the Lord Commander. 'The men and women we have detained are not criminals; they are merely assisting us with our enquiries.' He turned back to the captain. 'Shall we?'

They left the room and descended a flight of stairs into the basement. Armed soldiers were guarding the folk who had been dragged out of the tavern in one of the main cellars, and several locals eyed the Lord Commander with a mixture of fear and suspicion. Captain Zola led the Lord Commander and Saffie to a low-ceilinged passageway, where a row of smaller cellars was located. Each little chamber had one occupant, and all were being guarded by Sanctian soldiers.

The Lord Commander peered into the first chamber. An old man was sitting on an upturned crate, his gaze on the stone floor.

'Not him,' said the Lord Commander. 'Our prisoner gave me a description of the bargeman while you were visiting the *Black Bull*. He is younger, with short hair and earrings.'

They walked along the passageway, and the Lord Commander looked into each chamber in turn. He came to a halt at the fifth room, then he nodded to Captain Zola and they entered. Saffie squeezed into the tiny chamber after them. Inside, a man was sitting on the floor, rubbing his eyes. He glanced up when the others entered, and scowled at them.

'I was bloody sleeping when your damn soldiers pulled me out of bed,' he said, his Jallian accent clear. 'What is all this? I've broken no laws.'

'I apologise for the inconvenience,' said the Lord Commander; 'we are grateful for your cooperation.'

The man rolled his eyes.

'We have a few questions,' the Lord Commander went on.

'I thought you might,' the man said. 'Is this about the silver mine in the Great Forest?'

The Lord Commander and Captain Zola glanced at each other.

'Why would you ask that?' said Zola.

'It's bloody obvious,' said the man. 'You work for the Offices of Purgation, and they only have one job. You want to know if what I was saying in the tavern last night is true.'

'Well, is it?' said the Lord Commander.

'Every damn word,' said the man. 'The Whalebone King is a filthy

Master, and I saw him kill three Westlander slaves with my own eyes. You need to go up there, and sort that bastard out.'

'Would you be willing to write a statement about everything you witnessed?' said Zola.

'I would, if I could write.'

'You can dictate it to one of our secretaries,' said the Lord Commander. 'Let me ask again – are you absolutely certain? You clearly saw this so-called *king* use Master powers?'

'I did. I happened to be in the wrong place at the wrong time, and he didn't know I could see him. The temple by the mine is bloody enormous, and it's easy to get lost. I turned a corner and saw Hemming, and he...'

'Who?' said Zola.

'Hemming,' said the man. 'That's the name of the Whalebone King. Did you not know that? Anyway, I saw him and his four sons, and they were leading a group of his nasty mercenaries. Shower of bastards, that lot. The mercenaries had hold of three Westlander slaves, and Hemming insisted on being the one to execute them. I think he might have been drunk.'

'What was their crime?' said Saffie.

The man glanced up at her, as if noticing her presence for the first time. 'I have no idea, miss. The lives of the slaves in that place are cheaper than dirt. One of them probably looked at Hemming the wrong way, or something like that. Hemming raises his hand, and the Westlanders scream; though not for long. Their skin turned a shade of green, and they fell to the ground. After a couple of minutes, Hemming had the mercenaries behead the slaves, and that was when I made myself scarce. I could hardly wait to get out of that damn place. To think – that bastard has been hiding up there for nigh on thirty years.'

The Lord Commander smiled. 'And now we have him.'

'Why did you not report this to the authorities when you arrived in Elestia?' said Zola.

The man laughed. 'I only got here yesterday, and then we had to unload the barges, and wait for hours to get paid. I didn't even know that the Offices of Purgation had opened up in the city.'

'It's fine,' said the Lord Commander. 'None of that will be held against you. In fact, you will be handsomely rewarded as soon as you have dictated every detail you can remember. You have been of great service to the Sanctian Empire.'

'Fair enough,' said the man. 'Are you going to arrest the bastard?'

'We shall certainly endeavour to make sure he answers for his crimes,' said the Lord Commander. He turned to the soldiers in the passageway. 'Take this man upstairs, and ensure that he has food and drink made available to him; then send in a secretary to record his statement. As for the others, release them all, and give each one a purse of ten sovereigns for the inconvenience they have suffered this morning.'

The soldiers bowed, then two set off.

The Lord Commander walked out of the chamber, then he led Saffie and Zola back up the stairs to his office. A broad grin split his features, and he rubbed his hands together.

'We shall need to send a strong force up the river,' he said. 'I want you to handle this personally, Captain.'

'It would be an honour, my Lord Commander,' said Zola.

'I wish to accompany the captain,' said Saffie.

The Lord Commander's smile faded a little. 'I'm afraid that is out of the question, Your Highness. It would be far too dangerous for a lady of your position.'

'That is not up to you, Lord Commander,' she said. 'I cannot influence your policy, but my most exalted grandfather has given me the freedom to choose the terms of my service.'

'The Most Exalted Emperor would not approve of you putting yourself in grave danger, Your Highness.'

Saffie smiled. 'Wouldn't he? It sounds exactly like the kind of thing he would do. If you wish to confirm this, I would be happy to write a letter to His Imperial Majesty, telling him that you are hindering my work here. Then we can await his reply together.'

The Lord Commander narrowed his eyes. 'That will not be necessary. You can go. However, before you leave with Captain Zola, I would be grateful if you wrote another letter, stating that it was you who took the decision to travel into the Great Forest; in case anything untoward were to occur. It is my earnest hope that no such letter will be required, but one must be careful.'

'One must,' she said. 'I will write the letter for you, and I take full responsibility for my actions. You will have nothing to fear if I am slain in the forest; I will make sure of that.'

The Lord Commander frowned, then he glanced at Zola. 'Guard the princess with your life, Captain.'

'I will, my Lord Commander.'

'As for this Hemming creature,' the Lord Commander went on; 'bring me his head.'

CHAPTER 2
THE FOREST'S EDGE

South-Western Jallin, Central Provinces – 11th Day of Minula 108

'Desire you a throne, fair Abigone?' said Mor Galthide. 'Return to Upper Down, if that is your wish, but there you will remain a princess. Go instead to Geathan, and you shall be a queen.'

Abigone stared out from the tavern veranda at the banks of the river. On the far side, by the wooden piers and wharf, men were busy loading a long row of barges in the afternoon light. Beyond that, the dark edge of the Great Forest began; a forest that spread over more than a quarter of the land that had formerly been the Central Provinces of the Elestian Empire.

Did she want a throne? Abigone wasn't sure. Part of her wanted to go back to Upper Down, but she knew that she had lost any realistic possibility of returning to her old life. She glanced at the faces of the survivors from the Makers and Masters schools of Klef Mordain. Lady Fyenna had gathered them together to discuss their next destination, but Abigone had kept her mouth closed. For twenty-two days, they had been travelling; putting hundreds of miles between them and the fallen city. During that time, Abigone's sole desire had been to get away, and she had been putting off the decision that Fyenna had decided to force upon them.

'I wish you would stop badgering Abigone, Father,' said Denny.

'You're not the only one,' muttered Lothar.

'Have I uttered a lie?' said Mor Galthide. 'Scorn not my attempts to persuade the fair Abigone to choose the correct path.'

'We are not going to Geathan,' said Lothar. 'Even if we ignore the near impossibility of trying to stir up a successful rebellion; how would we get there? By land? That would take us weeks of trekking through the Great Forest, only to find our way blocked by a mountain range. And if we tried to go by sea, the Sanctian navy would stop us long before we reached the shores of Geathan.'

'Shameful words,' said Mor Galthide. 'Have we not made it this far? The border of Yearl lies only a few days by wagon to our south; we could be in Subnestia by the end of Minula.'

'At the risk of repeating myself,' said Amery, 'I feel obliged to point out that I cannot enter Yearl. If I did so, and was arrested, I would be hanged. I am exiled for life.'

Mor Galthide shrugged his enormous shoulders. 'You would not be arrested, young Amery,' he said. 'Why would anyone even notice that you had entered Yearl? Pick for yourself a false name, and hide in the wagons until we leave Yearl behind. If that response satisfies you not, then go your own way. You are not beholden to us, nor we to you. To be frank, I doubt we will have much need for a lawyer once we reach Geathan.'

'Can I go back to my room?' said Ignatius. 'I don't care where we go. We can't return to Klef Mordain, and we can't stay in the Central Provinces. Just pick a destination, and I'll come along.'

'Remain here,' said Fyenna.

Abigone watched as the Head Maker glanced at everyone sitting round the long table.

'We summoned you together for a reason,' Fyenna went on. 'It has been a hard journey since we were forced to sell the *Little Ghost* and continue onwards by land. Our three wagons have been essential, but they keep us divided, and we have had few opportunities to sit down in one group to discuss our future – a future that affects each one of us.

We have but two choices, as far as I can see – turn north and seek shelter within the realm of Upper Down; or turn south and embark upon a long journey to Geathan.'

'I say Geathan,' said Constans. 'The damn Sanctians took everything from us, and I want to see them pay for their crimes. Hiding in Upper Down will achieve nothing, even if Princess Kilbride allowed us to stay.'

Mor Galthide smiled. 'You make a good point, lad. Kilbride has a reputation for cunning, but she will not wish to risk the safety of the realm she governs. It would take but one stray word, and news of our presence in Upper Down would be winging its way to the ear of Emperor Antonio. There will be threats, an ultimatum, then war. Would Kilbride thank us for bringing these troubles to her doorstep?'

Stanza raised a hand.

'Speak, girl,' said Mor Galthide.

'There have already been a few stray words,' Stanza said. 'Reath was talking loudly earlier today, and she was overheard by more than one person.'

'Shut up, you little telltale,' said Reath.

Fyenna frowned. 'What was said?'

'She was talking about Abigone and you, ma'am,' said Stanza; 'about how your Maker abilities could kill anyone who tries to stop us. Two old men by the riverbank were listening, and I saw a woman glance up at us. This was after you had forbidden us to mention anyone's name, or what we were doing here.'

Reath clenched her fists. 'I will break your nose if you don't shut your mouth.'

'Is this true, Reath?' said Fyenna.

'Those people had no idea what I was talking about,' Reath said. 'They looked at me because I was shouting, not because of what I was saying. No one here knows anything about what happened in Klef Mordain.'

'But they will be aware of the name of Princess Abigone,' said Amery. 'That does it. We leave tomorrow, regardless of our destination.

If word spreads that Abigone is here, this place will be crawling with Sanctian soldiers.'

'I am inclined to agree,' said Fyenna; 'but first, we shall allow everyone to state their opinion regarding our ultimate destination. Come the dawn, we shall leave this town, and be long gone before any Sanctians get here. The nearest garrison is over forty miles away; there is no need to panic.' She looked at the faces of the young students. 'Mor Galthide thinks we should go to Geathan; while Lothar believes we should travel to Upper Down. Constans has already voiced his opinion, so we shall begin with you, Raewyn.'

The seventeen-year-old girl looked up. 'I will follow you, my lady,' she said. 'I don't know what the best course is, but I trust your leadership.'

Constans narrowed his eyes at her, but said nothing.

'I agree,' whispered Eshia. 'I don't want to have to decide. I will follow Lady Fyenna.'

'You have a powerful little voting bloc of three, my lady,' said Mor Galthide.

'So it seems,' said Fyenna. 'Amery; what do you think?'

'It has to be Upper Down,' said the lawyer. 'There is no alternative.'

'Marlow?'

The fifteen-year-old boy frowned. 'I don't want to go anywhere near Subnestia again, but I will, if Denny thinks we should go to Geathan.'

'Does anyone else here think the same?' said Fyenna. 'Are there others who will follow Denny's lead?'

Aplin raised a hand.

'I will follow my cousin's lead,' said Salus. 'If Constans goes to Geathan, then I will follow him.'

'Excellent,' said Mor Galthide. 'That makes six votes for Geathan; nine, if Lady Fyenna's bloc joins us.'

'That is only the case if Denny himself wishes to go to Geathan,' said Fyenna, 'and he has yet to state his opinion. Denny; what say you?'

Denny stared at his empty plate.

'Speak, my boy,' said his father.

'What would we do when we reached Geathan?' said Denny.

Mor Galthide rubbed his hands together. 'Let me allay a few concerns, for I know some of you deem me rash,' he said. 'Put simply, we are not ready to begin an uprising against the Sanctians, so we shall not be bringing any attention to ourselves, not at first. Here is what I propose. Hills dominate the southern parts of Geathan, and there are valleys and villages too remote for the Sanctians to patrol. That is where we shall hide. We shall reopen the secret schools, and lessons can continue in peace, while we nurse our strength and bide our time.'

'Princess Kilbride would also allow the schools to reopen,' said Lothar.

'Would she?' said Mor Galthide. 'Say you that with any certainty?'

'Let us ask Abigone what she thinks about it,' said Fyenna.

Abigone eyed the others. 'My sister will help us,' she said.

Lothar grinned. 'See?'

'I hadn't finished,' said Abigone. 'Kilbride will help us if we turn up in Torrent, but she will not be pleased about the position into which we will have placed her. If the Kendril Wall still stood, the realm could ignore any threat from the south, but the wall has gone, and Upper Down lies defenceless. The Sanctians would discover our location, and an army would be dispatched.'

'Then you choose Geathan, my fair lady?' said Mor Galthide.

'The journey to Geathan is fraught with danger,' said Abigone. 'We would have to travel through Sanctian territory for hundreds of miles, and then try to find a ship to take us onwards – a ship that would have to sail past Sanctos.'

'The western extremity of Sanctos is closer to Geathan than many here might think,' said Denny. 'It would be far easier for the Sanctians to send forces there than it would be for them to dispatch another army all the way to Upper Down.'

'Which is why I suggested that we remain hidden in the southern valleys, my son,' said Mor Galthide. 'The Sanctians would not discover our presence; whereas, we would be easily noticed within the bounds of Upper Down. It is a tiny realm, is it not; with but two towns?'

'That is probably true,' said Denny.

'What about your claim to the throne?' said Constans. 'That's the crux of the matter. Do you want to be king of Geathan, Denny?'

Denny glanced at his father, then at Abigone. 'No.'

'No?' said Mor Galthide. 'You strike my heart with a cruel blade, son. No? Your forebears would weep and rend their clothes over such a word. The oppressed masses of Geathan would cry out in their pitiful agonies, wondering what they had done to deserve such an ignoble heir.'

'Let him speak,' said Abigone. 'Denny, would you care to explain your reasons?'

'The people of Geathan have suffered enough,' said Denny. 'The last thing I want to do is bring another war to their shores.'

'You sound like a coward,' said Constans. 'The Sanctians are trampling all over your homeland, and you would prefer to do nothing.'

'Am I a coward?' said Denny. 'My words may speak of peace, but everyone here has witnessed my actions.'

Reath laughed. 'You're the opposite, Constans. You talk a lot about courage, but you whimper like a baby whenever any real fighting starts.'

'What do you think we should do, Reath?' said Fyenna, before Constans could say anything else.

'Me?' said Reath. 'I reject both choices. I want to go back to Nessos.'

'Me, too,' said Nyli. 'Can Reath and I please go home?'

'Let it not be said that I am incapable of compromise,' said Mor Galthide. 'We shall place the question of rebellion and the claim to the throne to one side. Instead, I offer peace and security within the high valleys of southern Geathan. On the way there, we shall pass by Nessos, and allow Reath and Nyli the chance to return to their family.'

'What about me?' said Stanza. 'If we went to Upper Down, we would have to pass through Greater Down first, and that's where my family lives. I want to go home, too.'

'Then we divide,' said Amery. 'Some of us go north, the others south. Who thinks we should go to Upper Down? Let's have a show of hands.'

Amery raised his right arm. Next to him, Loryn frowned, and did the same, followed by Lothar and Annalise. Stanza gazed at Fyenna, then slowly raised her own hand.

'You lose,' said Mor Galthide. 'There are eighteen of us here, and five is not a majority.'

'Who wishes to go to Geathan?' Amery went on, lowering his arm.

Mor Galthide's arm shot up, followed by that of Constans and Salus.

Amery smirked. 'Is three a majority, Mor Galthide?'

Denny sighed, and also raised his hand. Marlow and Aplin glanced at each other, and did the same.

'Six seems more than five, does it not?' said Mor Galthide; 'or is my arithmetic faulty?'

Abigone eyed Denny. 'I thought you said you didn't want to be king of Geathan.'

'I don't,' he said, 'but we could hide more easily in Geathan than we could in Upper Down. The schools could reopen, and we would be safe. I agree with what you said about your sister. Princess Kilbride would not thank us if we arrived in the Kendril Gap with regiments of Sanctian soldiers at our heels.'

Abigone bit her lip, then she also raised her hand.

'Seven!' cried Mor Galthide. 'For this, Abigone, you have earned my eternal thanks.'

'Make it eight,' said Ignatius, as he raised his hand. 'We should stay together. I don't want us to split up.'

Mor Galthide nodded, then he turned to Fyenna. 'My lady,' he said, 'your vote for Geathan would win the day, for Eshia and Raewyn have pledged to follow you.'

'You are asking the impossible,' said Fyenna. 'The only way to reach Geathan is by ship, and yet you have told Reath and Nyli that we could simply divert to Nessos on our way to your homeland. Such a thing is beyond the realms of credibility. Nessos lies more than a hundred miles from the ocean, on the far side of the Great Forest. Were we to travel there, we would have to double back on ourselves, all the way to Subnestia, to find a ship.'

Mor Galthide scowled, but said nothing.

'Furthermore,' Fyenna went on, 'Upper Down might be small, but it lies amid a range of tall mountains. There will be hidden valleys where we could reopen the schools without becoming a hindrance to Princess Kilbride. Is that not so, Lothar?'

The former Mountain Ranger nodded. 'It is indeed so, ma'am. I know every goat track through those mountains, and I could devise a route that would take us past the Kendril Gap without being observed. We could hide the young Masters and Makers in a remote location, and then some of us could descend to Torrent to let Princess Kilbride know.'

'She would still be angry,' said Abigone.

'She is not the only regent, Your Highness,' said Lothar. 'Lord Walter would also have a say. If it turns out that both are opposed, then we simply move the secret school beyond the borders of Upper Down.'

'Into Westlander territory?' said Constans.

'Technically, that would be true,' said Lothar, 'but the Westlanders would have no reason to trek around the high mountain passes; and, once they learned that Masters and Makers were there, they would stay clear. That way, Princess Kilbride could deny everything to the Sanctians.'

'This is ridiculous,' said Mor Galthide.

'How so?' said Fyenna. 'My priority is the safety of the students from Klef Mordain, not the future of Geathan. Upper Down is far closer to our present location than your homeland, and the journey there would be much easier. I vote for Upper Down. If Raewyn and Eshia are in agreement, then that makes it eight votes apiece.'

Everyone turned to Reath and Nyli.

'Why are you staring at us?' said Reath.

'Because you are the only two not to choose either Upper Down or Geathan,' said Abigone.

Constans rolled his eyes. 'We cannot leave such a decision to these two.'

'Hush, lad,' said Mor Galthide. 'Allow the girls to speak their minds.'

'We've already spoken,' said Reath. 'Nyli and I want to go to Nessos.'

'Choose between Upper Down and Geathan,' said Constans.

Reath pulled a face at him. 'No.'

'Then we divide,' said Amery. 'The eight who voted for Upper Down should go there, and the others can attempt to reach Geathan, via Nessos.'

'No,' said Fyenna. 'We must stay together.'

'Why?' said Amery.

'Thirteen of our number are either Masters or Makers,' Fyenna went on. 'That represents the last hope for our kind upon this continent. If we split up, then the Sanctians will hunt us down, one group at a time. Only by staying united and by keeping up our lessons, can we survive.'

'Then I plead with you to change your mind, my lady,' said Mor Galthide. 'Venture with us to Geathan. Yes, the journey will be long and hard, but the reward will be all the greater when we arrive. Have I not already pledged to put aside any thought of rebellion? If you choose Geathan, then I shall not bring it up again for two years – you have my solemn word.'

The veranda fell into silence as four waiting staff walked out from the tavern's main building. They began to collect the empty dishes and plates, then Nyli got to her feet.

'I need to go to the bathroom,' she said.

'Are we done?' said Ignatius.

'We have yet to reach a decision,' said Fyenna.

Ignatius lowered his gaze as he stood. 'Then it's like what Mister Amery says, ma'am. We each choose our own path.'

Some of the others got to their feet.

'Think on it overnight,' said Fyenna. 'We shall defer our final decision until we sit down for breakfast. And, do not leave the tavern – is that understood?'

There were a few murmured agreements, then the veranda started to empty. Abigone remained next to Denny and Fyenna, as most of the others walked into the main building.

Mor Galthide stood. 'I shall go for a walk,' he said. 'I assume I am allowed to leave the tavern, my lady?'

Fyenna eyed him, but said nothing. As soon as Mor Galthide and the serving staff had gone, she turned to Abigone and Denny.

'How can I change your minds?' she said. 'Abigone, don't you long to see your home again?'

Abigone nodded. 'I would very much like to go back to Torrent, ma'am,' she said, 'but I don't want to live in a cave in the mountains. I have to accept that I might never be able to have a normal life in Upper Down again; not if the Sanctians are aware of what we did to oppose them in Klef Mordain. Geathan offers a fresh start.'

'But it is an impoverished and backward place,' said Fyenna. She paused again as several waiting staff returned to collect the remaining dishes.

Abigone got to her feet and walked over to the railings of the veranda. The sun was setting over the Great Forest, while the dock labourers were still hard at work loading the long line of barges.

'Where does that river go?' she said.

She glanced back at Fyenna and Denny, but both shrugged.

'It goes deep into the Great Forest, ma'am,' said a young waiter.

'And then?' said Abigone.

'Those barges deliver supplies to a silver mine, ma'am, and then they are loaded with the silver that pays for it all.'

'And then they return here?' said Abigone.

'No, ma'am,' said the waiter. 'The currents are too strong, and the barges can only go downstream. After the mine, the river cuts south through the forest, until it reaches a larger river, which flows through the centre of Elestia. That's where the silver is unloaded, in the old imperial capital.'

Abigone narrowed her eyes. 'Elestia? Do the barges take passengers?'

The waiter shook his head. 'No, ma'am. They might occasionally take new servants, workers or guards to the mine, but never passengers. If you're heading for Elestia, you'd be far better sticking to the roads.'

The staff picked up the last of the dishes and walked into the building.

Fyenna glanced at Abigone. 'It was worth asking,' she said, 'though I happen to agree with the waiter. If your heart is set upon Geathan, then there are easier routes to choose than through the Great Forest. At the same time, though, Yearl is now a formal province of the Sanctian Empire, and even the roads would be dangerous. Jallin has not yet joined the empire, and neither has Greater Down. The way north comes with less risk.'

'There will still be Sanctian garrisons along the way,' said Denny.

'Did I say the journey would be without risk?' said Fyenna. 'Yes, we will still have to pass a few outposts of the Sanctians, but far fewer than on the road south. Listen to me; you two possess much influence with the other students. I beg you to consider Upper Down, in order to keep us together. If you change your minds, then Aplin, Marlow and Ignatius will fall into line. Constans and Salus will surely not go alone with Mor Galthide to Geathan; in fact, Mor Galthide would be forced to accompany us north. Please – think it over.' She stood. 'I will leave you two alone to ponder my words. The future of Masters and Makers is at stake; ponder carefully.'

Denny joined Abigone by the railing as Fyenna disappeared back into the building.

'What should we do?' Abigone said.

Denny took her hand. 'Going to Upper Down feels like postponing the inevitable,' he said. 'Both you and I are probably known enemies of the Sanctian Empire after everything that happened in Klef Mordain. The Sanctians will have ransacked the Maker school by now, and they will be aware that it was you and I who slew their ambassador. Knowing that, we cannot impose ourselves upon your sister's hospitality. We would achieve nothing but the imperilment of your realm.'

Abigone watched as a few lamps were lit by the banks of the river. The sun had set behind the unending forest, and the air was getting cooler. Winter would be upon Upper Down by the time they reached the small mountain realm, and that would mean heavy snow and frozen ground.

'Is it warm down in Geathan?' she said.

'So I am told,' said Denny. 'I have never been there, but most of it lies further south than the isle of Sanctos, and its winters are very mild. My father has even talked of deserts. I assume Upper Down will be cold?'

'Yes. That wouldn't be a problem if we were living in the palace in Torrent, but Lothar's idea of us hiding in the mountains would be unbearable. We would likely freeze up there.'

Denny eyed her. 'So it comes down to the weather?'

'I am trying to be practical,' she said. 'Perhaps if it was spring, then I might consider Upper Down, but we have a long winter ahead of us.'

Several members of staff walked out on to the veranda.

'Apologies,' said one, 'but this table has been reserved for a large party of merchants, and we are going to have to ask you to step indoors.'

Abigone and Denny walked off the veranda, and entered the bar. It had filled up since they had passed through on their way in, and a raucous collection of river workers, peasants and merchants were drinking red wine from large pewter mugs. A few glanced at Abigone and Denny, who both kept their mouths shut to avoid betraying their accents. They reached a door, stepped through, and ascended a flight of wooden stairs to where their rented rooms were located. Despite being betrothed, Mor Galthide and Fyenna had strict rules about Abigone and Denny's sleeping arrangements, and they had been placed into separate rooms. They paused at the top of the stairs.

'Who are you in with tonight?' said Denny.

'I'm sharing with Raewyn,' said Abigone. 'You?'

'Marlow. I wish...' He smiled. 'Do I need to say it?'

'If Fyenna and your father have their way, we'll be waiting until we are married,' she said.

'Maybe we could find somewhere quiet?'

Abigone raised an eyebrow. 'Inside this tavern? I don't want to spend our first time together worrying about being interrupted by drunken Jallian peasants.'

A door opened, and Mor Galthide peered out. 'I thought I recognised your voices,' he said. 'Linger not; go to your rooms.'

'Abigone and I are both nineteen, Father,' said Denny.

Mor Galthide shrugged. 'You know the solution – get wedded. Until then, besmirch not your family names. Go on; I am watching you.'

Abigone rolled her eyes, then she and Denny kissed, before they separated and walked to their different rooms. Raewyn was sitting on her bed when Abigone entered their sleeping quarters. A small lamp had been lit, and its light was flickering off Raewyn's face.

Abigone closed the door, and sat on a chair next to her own bed. 'Did you hear Mor Galthide?' she said.

'I heard him,' said Raewyn. 'I don't know why you and Denny don't get married.'

'And what chance have we had to do that? We've been on the run for twenty-two days. Why don't you and Constans get married?'

Raewyn glared at her. 'I don't want to talk about Constans. He would rather follow Mor Galthide than ask me what I want to do. He keeps talking about all of the brave things he intends to do to fight the Sanctians, but he forgets...'

Raewyn paused, and put a hand to her face.

'He forgets what?' said Abigone.

'He forgets that it was you, me and Lady Fyenna who slaughtered all those sailors on the *Bitter Respite*. He has never asked me how I feel about what we did; never. Yet he talks about killing those two soldiers in the harbour of Klef Mordain as though he was the hero that day. I'm so tired, Abigone, and the guilt is making my stomach ache. Do you feel bad about what we did?'

Abigone thought about lying, but decided against it. 'No,' she said. 'Those sailors were trying to kill us. They got what they deserved.'

Raewyn turned away from her. 'You are so cold.'

'Maybe.'

Raewyn slipped her legs under the blankets. 'I'm going to sleep.'

Abigone watched her for a moment, then she leaned over, extinguished the lamp, and undressed for bed.

Abigone was awoken by the bedroom door being swung open. She opened her eyes, and saw Fyenna standing in the dim light of morning.

'What's going on?' said Raewyn.

'Have either of you seen Reath and Nyli?' said Fyenna. 'Or Salus and Ignatius?'

'Not since we ate dinner yesterday,' said Raewyn.

'Get up, both of you. At once.'

'Why?' said Abigone.

'Our four youngest students have gone missing,' Fyenna said. 'I need you to help search for them. Get dressed while I look in the other rooms, then come downstairs. Mor Galthide is already outside, combing the area.'

Fyenna closed the door. Abigone and Raewyn glanced at each other, then they got out of their beds. Abigone pulled on a pair of warm leggings, her head groggy from the patchy sleep she had experienced in the uncomfortable tavern bed.

'Those stupid little brats,' Raewyn muttered, as she laced up her boots. 'They will have gone off for a walk, and now Fyenna is having a breakdown.'

'I thought Salus was sharing a room with Constans,' said Abigone.

'He was, until Constans complained about it. Aplin and Salus swapped rooms.'

Abigone slipped a long dress over her shoulders, and placed her feet into her shoes. There was no mirror in the room, so she pulled her hair back and tied it with a ribbon. She and Raewyn stepped out of their room. Denny and Marlow were crouching by a door further along the hallway, examining the lock.

Abigone and Raewyn walked over to see what they were doing.

'Someone forced open Reath and Nyli's door last night,' said Denny.

'Are you sure?' said Raewyn.

Denny gestured to the doorframe. 'The bolt ripped through the wooden beam meant to hold it in place, as though the door was kicked down.'

'I didn't hear anything,' said Abigone.

'No one did,' said Marlow.

'What about the boys' room, where Salus and Ignatius were sleeping?' said Abigone.

'I don't think they locked their door,' said Denny. 'There are signs of a struggle in their room, but their door was undamaged.'

Raewyn stared at him. 'You mean they haven't just gone for a walk?'

'I think someone snatched them,' said Denny, as he and Marlow stood.

They hurried downstairs, and found Amery and a few others standing by the empty bar.

'It's not safe here,' Amery said. 'We need to leave. Someone has been watching us; they know who we are.'

'Calm down,' said Lothar. 'They took the four youngest students; they didn't care about you.'

Fyenna and Stanza appeared at the bottom of the stairs.

'I have searched every room,' said Fyenna. 'Our four missing students are not in the building.'

'I heard a noise last night,' said Annalise, 'but I paid no attention.'

'What kind of noise?' said Fyenna.

'Perhaps a door being slammed?' said Annalise. 'I assumed that someone was returning drunk from the bar.'

A door to the outside opened, and Mor Galthide strode inside, his hair and shoulders wet from the morning rain. The Geathan warrior was still limping from the injuries he had sustained in Klef Mordain, but his face betrayed no pain.

'Well?' said Fyenna.

'I bear news,' Mor Galthide said; 'grim news. The river barges have all departed the docks, but not before several porters witnessed a small number of extra passengers being bundled on board.' He gestured to another man, who was standing outside. 'Enter. Tell them what you told me.'

The man walked into the tavern, his eyes downcast.

'Speak, before I slap you about the head,' said Mor Galthide.

'I was coming off duty last night,' said the man, 'and I noticed the barges setting off earlier than usual; they usually wait for dawn, see? I asked around, and a porter told me that four new recruits for the silver mine had been found at the last minute. Young they were, he told me. Two boys and two girls. The porters were paid a little bit extra to make sure the barges got underway without any more delay.'

'Did you see them with your own eyes?' said Fyenna.

The man shook his head.

'Can we follow them on foot?' said Lothar.

'No, sir,' said the man. 'The way is only passable by boat.'

'Our alternative destination is now out of the question,' said Abigone. 'If four of our friends have been taken down the river, then we are going to follow them.'

'I will not go into the forest,' said Amery. 'The only way out leads to Yearl, and... need I say more?'

'You and Loryn are welcome to go your separate way at this juncture,' said Abigone. She glanced at the others. 'Does anyone object to this course of action? Lady Fyenna?'

The Head Maker shook her head. 'Not if the lives of the younger ones are at stake.'

Abigone glanced at Lothar, who frowned.

'I will go where you go,' said the tall Mountain Ranger.

'Why would anyone take four children to a mine?' said Annalise.

'The silver mine is always looking for young recruits,' said the local man, 'but no one from round here ever volunteers.'

'Are there any barges for sale?' said Fyenna. 'We need to leave as soon as possible.'

'I will make enquiries, ma'am,' said the man.

'Then do so,' said Fyenna. 'You know where to find us.'

CHAPTER 3
DEEP WITHIN

Steppen, Great Forest, Jallin, Central Provinces – 19th Day of Minula 108

'Why are you so fucking useless?' said Ragnvald. He placed his feet up onto a chair, and inhaled from a long clay pipe. He leaned his head back, and a cloud of acrid smoke came from his mouth. It hovered above him in the candlelight, and one of the slaves coughed. Ragnvald lowered his gaze back to his half-brother Magnus. 'Try again. Rock to silver.'

Magnus looked at the heap of rocks sitting on the low table in front of him. He tried to empty his mind of all thoughts, but there were too many distractions, and the smoke from his brother's pipe was making his eyes water. He raised his hand.

'Take this rock,' he said, 'and in its place put silver.'

Nothing happened.

Ragnvald shook his head. 'When are you going to admit that you were lying, you sack of shit? You're not a Master; you just said that to please the boss. Wait until he finds out. He'll kick your arse into next week.'

'I wasn't lying,' said Magnus. 'I changed wood into metal. It's only happened once, but I did it all the same.'

'You're talking shite, boy,' said his older half-brother. He took another draw from the pipe, then he frowned, and gazed at Magnus. 'Are you needing a smoke to calm you down?'

'Can you use your Master abilities when you've been smoking that stuff?'

Ragnvald shrugged. 'I can't remember the last time I tried.' He held out the pipe. 'Here; give it a go.'

Magnus took the pipe, but held it away from his body. He sniffed the smouldering end, and grimaced.

Ragnvald shook his head. 'Is there something wrong with you? Smoke the fucking pipe.'

Magnus placed the other end to his lips and inhaled. He immediately started to cough, as though he was choking, and Ragnvald snatched the pipe from his hands before he could drop it. Magnus retched, his head spinning, and one of the Westlander slaves laughed.

Ragnvald turned to the slave. 'Find that funny, did you? Do you enjoy mocking my family?'

The slave straightened his back, his smile gone. 'No, sir.'

'Fucking prick,' said Ragnvald. He raised a finger and pointed at the slave. 'Bone to wood.'

The Westlander slave screamed in agony, then he fell to the floor, convulsing. His movements started to slow, but his cries continued. The other slaves averted their gazes, and one of the younger ones began to tremble. Ragnvald watched the dying slave for a few moments. The Westlander's cries quietened, until nothing was coming from his mouth but a low rasping gargle, then he fell silent.

'Forty seconds,' said Ragnvald. 'Forty seconds of pure agony. That's a lot more satisfying than the old *water to salt* trick. With that, they're dead in under two seconds; this way, they actually suffer.'

Magnus said nothing.

'Back to you, Magnus,' said Ragnvald. 'Show me rock to silver.'

Magnus swayed, the contents of the pipe having numbed many of his senses. He stared at the heap of rocks, his vision blurry.

'Take this rock,' he slurred, 'and... and in its place put silver.'

A fragment of rock split off from the side of a boulder with a crack, then it fell to the floor. Magnus's eyes widened, then Ragnvald leaned forward. He reached out and picked up the piece of rock that had fallen, and stared at it. On the fractured side, tiny lines of silver were threaded through the stone.

'I told you I could do it,' said Magnus.

'You did,' said Ragnvald. 'That was a shite effort, but there's definitely silver in here. Not much, but it's there. We'd better show this to the boss.'

'I'm not sure my legs are working.'

Ragnvald laughed. 'You know, little brother,' he said, 'until I saw that silver, I had always believed that your whore of a mother had fucked some peasant, and had then passed you off as the boss's son. Looks like I was wrong.'

Magnus clenched his fist and swung it at Ragnvald, but the older man leaned back out of the way, and Magnus fell to the floor, off balance.

'It was a joke, you little prick,' said Ragnvald, laughing. He reached out and pulled Magnus to his feet. 'Just a joke. Swing at me again, and you'll be losing a few teeth.'

Magnus staggered as Ragnvald placed the fragment of stone into a pocket. Ragnvald led his half-brother out of the room, and they climbed a set of rock-cut steps up onto the roof of the temple. The entire building had been carved out of the cliff face, and was a maze of slender towers, pinnacles and narrow bridges, with over a hundred chambers hewn from the solid rock. Ahead of them, the largest of the five waterfalls was tumbling down from the cliffs, and the water was glistening in the sunlight. At the base of the waterfall, the river course divided into dozens of smaller channels, along with artificial pools and basins. Some of the channels went under and through the temple, before issuing out to coalesce on the far side back into a single river. Beyond that, there was nothing but forest for hundreds of miles in every direction. Beech trees dominated, but there were ash and oak, along with darker patches of fir and pine. Magnus gazed out at the ocean of green. He had been born in the Temple of Steppen, and the Great Forest was all he had ever known.

Ragnvald cajoled him onwards, and they ascended to a higher section of the flat roof, where their father was reclining in the midday sunshine, surrounded by his old cronies and a few heavily-armed mercenaries. Sitting on his lap was a young Westlander slave, and she was feeding dried raisins to the older man.

Ragnvald bowed his head. 'Boss,' he said, 'prepare to be astonished.'

The man looked up. Upon his brow sat his old crown, formed from yellowed strips of whalebone. His gaze went from Ragnvald to Magnus, from his oldest son to his youngest.

'Why is the boy staggering?' he said.

Ragnvald mimed puffing from a pipe, and their father laughed.

'Well,' he said; 'astonish me.'

Ragnvald reached into a pocket and withdrew the fragment of rock. He held it out for his father, who took it.

'What am I supposed to be looking at?' he said.

'Do you see those tiny traces of silver running through the stone, boss?' He pointed his thumb at Magnus. 'He did that. It's true. He's a Master. A shite Master, but a Master nonetheless.'

The old man pushed the slave from his lap and got to his feet, his eyes wide as he stared at the small flecks of silver.

'He was only able to do it after a smoke,' Ragnvald went on, 'but I guess he wasn't lying.'

The old man grinned. 'Two of my boys are Masters,' he said. 'From now on, Magnus, you will be practising every day. If you end up half as good as Ragnvald, I'll be a happy man. What do you have to say for yourself?'

Magnus swayed. 'I can see two of you, Father.'

The old man frowned. 'Don't call me that. To you, boy, I am *Your Majesty*, or *sir*; *sir* will do. Or even *boss*. This is the realm of the Whalebone Crown, and you are a fucking prince. We have standards to uphold.'

'Sorry, sir.'

'That's better.'

Ragnvald gestured to a slave. 'There's a body downstairs in my quarters. Clear it away.'

The slave bowed and hurried off.

'What body?' said the Whalebone King. 'Who have you killed now, Ragnvald? If it was another girl, I'm cutting your access to the women's quarters. There are barely enough to go around as it is.'

'It was a man, boss. A Westlander. He laughed at Magnus, so I turned his bones into wood.'

'Wood, eh?' said his father, looking interested. 'How did that work out?'

Ragnvald smiled. 'Forty seconds of excruciating pain, boss. It was a joy to behold.'

'We should cut the bastard up, to see what he looks like on the inside.' He pointed at a slave. 'Go after the other one, and bring the body up here. I'm in the mood for a dissection.'

A robed man stepped forward. 'Might I have a word, Your Majesty?' he said in a Sanctian accent.

The Whalebone King sighed. 'What is it now, Matteo?'

'You are already running grave risks by openly discussing the fact that you and your eldest son are Masters, Your Majesty,' said the robed Sanctian. 'With the addition of Prince Magnus, that risk has only increased. I worry that word will reach Jalburg, or even Elestia. Now that Yearl is a formal member of the Sanctian Empire, there will be agents from the Offices of Purgation based there, and we are not all that far from the Yearlian border.'

The Whalebone King waved his hand in Matteo's face. 'We have been here for thirty-one years, and you are the only damn Sanctian I have ever seen in Steppen. You're worrying over nothing.'

'All the same, Your Majesty,' said Matteo, 'I counsel extreme caution.'

'You're only concerned about what will happen to you if the Sanctians discover how corrupt you are,' said the Whalebone King.

'That may be so, Your Majesty,' said Matteo, 'for if you fall, I will certainly fall with you. The Sanctians will see me as nothing more than a traitor.'

Ragnvald laughed. 'You *are* a fucking traitor, Matteo,' he said. 'But, thanks to the boss, you are a very rich traitor, so keep taking the money and shut the fuck up.'

The two slaves appeared on the roof, carrying the body of the Westlander that Ragnvald had slain. The Whalebone King gestured to a low table, and the slaves deposited the body there, and stepped back, their gazes lowered.

The Whalebone King extended a hand. 'Knife.'

A soldier handed the king a sheathed blade.

'Let's open this bastard up,' said the king, a gleam in his eyes, then he lowered the blade, and began slicing into the Westlander's flesh.

'Might I be excused, sir?' said Magnus.

His father the king looked up. 'No stomach for it, eh, boy?'

'It's not that, sir; I've seen plenty of dead bodies. Smoking that pipe has made me hungry, that's all.'

'Off you go, then,' said the king. 'And remember – practise. Two hours every day until you can kill a man from fifty paces.'

Magnus bowed his head, turned, and walked away, as his father got to work on the corpse. He had lied about being hungry; in truth, the pipe had made him nauseous, and he had no desire to witness a body being cut into pieces. It wasn't that he had no stomach for it – as he had told his father, he had seen plenty of dead bodies in his seventeen years. The Temple of Steppen and its neighbouring shanty settlement were host to all manner of violent episodes, and torture, beheadings, and random executions were a way of life. The mercenaries beat, raped and murdered the slaves with impunity, and, if anything, the Whalebone King's old cronies from their seafaring days were worse. Some of the things Magnus had witnessed had lived with him for years, seared into his brain. He wondered if life in Steppen was normal, then he remembered what his mother had told him about her old life, before she had been stolen from her family's farm in Jallin. His thoughts went to his mother as he descended the steps back into the narrow passageways of the temple. He had been avoiding her in recent days. Her anger and frustration with how her life had turned out could make her uncomfortable to be around, and yet, she was the only person in Steppen that Magnus loved.

He made his way through the maze-like passageways until he reached the guarded quarters where several dozen of the most valuable women of the settlement lived. Two bored-looking mercenaries were on duty by the sturdy oaken door, and they smirked at Magnus as they unlocked it to let him pass. The door was locked behind him, and he entered a large rock-cut chamber, lit by a series of barred slit windows close to the high ceiling. Half a dozen women were sitting on low wicker couches, and a few glanced up with anxious expressions, then they relaxed when they saw who it was.

'Colette,' said one, 'your boy's here.'

'Sit, lad,' said another.

Magnus took a spare seat, then a woman in her thirties emerged from another doorway. She stared at Magnus, and took a few steps forward.

'I am not sure if I have forgiven you,' she said to him. 'You shouted at me the last time I saw you.'

'I'm sorry, Mother,' he said.

'Did the old bastard send you here?' she said.

'I thought it was time to pay you a visit,' he said. 'How's life?'

Colette rolled her eyes. 'We are slaves – prisoners, held in the grip of a madman who calls himself a king – and you ask how my life is going? My life ended the day I was snatched from my father's fields. Whatever this miserable existence might be, it isn't any kind of life.' She sat down across from him. 'Tell me about your life, instead.'

'Does the lad want some tea?' said an older woman.

'He can make his own tea,' said Colette.

'Come now,' said the old woman; 'compared to the usual visitors we get in here, your son behaves like a gentleman. He's a credit to you, Colette. Tea, lad?'

'Thank you, yes,' he said.

The older woman got up and left the chamber via another entrance.

'Your life,' said Colette; 'tell me about it.'

'Something happened to me a few days ago, Mother,' he said. 'I turned some wood into metal.'

The chamber stilled, and every eye turned towards him.

'But when I tried to do it again,' he went on, 'I couldn't, and no one believed me. They thought I was lying to impress Father.'

Colette snorted.

'So, today,' Magnus said, 'Ragnvald told me that I had to prove my claim, or else... well, he wasn't specific about what might happen to me.'

'That man is nothing but a beast,' said Colette, and a few of the other women murmured their agreement.

'Anyway, I did it,' Magnus said. 'It wasn't much, but I managed to change a tiny amount of rock to silver.'

'The king might start to favour you again, Colette,' said another woman. 'You gave him a Master; the king can't ignore that.'

'What makes you think I want him to favour me in any way?' said Colette. 'I don't want that vile bastard anywhere near me.' She turned back to Magnus. 'Well done, I suppose. Are you pleased?'

'Father was pleased. Matteo seemed worried.'

'Lord Matteo is a snake,' said Colette. 'How I wish the Sanctians would find out what he has been doing here. He is supposed to be an imperial agent, but he has done nothing but take your father's bribes to keep his mouth shut about what happens in this forsaken place. Anyway, I asked if *you* were pleased.'

'I don't know. I think I was quite happy to remain unobtrusive. Some days, I was close to believing that Father had almost forgotten who I was. Now? He wants me to practise for two hours every day. He'll be keeping a closer eye on me.'

'That is very true,' she said. 'Do as he says, for now. Perhaps, if your Master abilities improve, you might be able to strike down those who have done this to us. That would make me very proud, son. Turn their blood into salt, and I will spit on their corpses.'

'You're going to get us into trouble, Colette,' said another woman.

'I won't say anything,' said Magnus.

The older woman returned with a cup of tea in her hands. She offered it to Magnus, and he took it.

'Thank you,' he said.

'There is something else I want to talk to you about, son,' said Colette.

'Yes?'

'If you are a Master,' she said, 'then your privileges will increase. Is that a fair assumption?'

'I'm not sure.'

'Ragnvald does whatever he pleases; everyone knows this. That is partly because he is the eldest son, but it is also because he is a Master. Your other half-brothers Einar and Erling are treated like dirt in comparison, but even they are allowed to talk to the Jallian bargemen who deliver our supplies. Perhaps you might be, too.'

'Why would I want to talk to a bunch of Jallian bargemen?'

'Isn't it obvious? Those bargemen are the only contact that Steppen has with the outside world. They come here once a month, unload their supplies, load up with silver, and then travel downstream to Elestia. If I was to write a letter, then perhaps you could pass it to them.'

'What kind of letter?'

'One that describes exactly what is taking place up here; one that details how many of us were stolen illegally from our homes. I am a citizen of the Realm of Jallin, and it is against the law for any citizen to be enslaved.'

'That wouldn't help all of us,' said a Westlander woman. 'According to your law, because I am a foreigner, then it's all right to enslave people like me.'

'Ahh, but I will add information about Hemming, making it clear that our pretend king is a Master. The Sanctians won't stand for it.'

'My father makes up his own laws,' said Magnus, 'and this is his kingdom.'

A few of the women shook their heads at him.

'Your father is nothing but a renegade, Magnus,' said Colette. 'This land belongs to Jallin, and he has usurped power over this part of the Great Forest.'

'If that's true,' he said, 'then why haven't soldiers from Jallin come here to take it back?'

'I don't know for certain,' said Colette, 'but I could hazard a guess. We are deep within the forest, hundreds of miles from the city of Jalburg – very difficult terrain to take an army over. I would also guess that Hemming uses the silver to bribe officials in both Jallin and Elestia – silver that prevents them from becoming too curious about what goes on here. Look how easily Lord Matteo was corrupted. That greedy oaf is the very man who is supposed to be overseeing the silver mine on behalf of the Sanctian Empire, and yet he does nothing to help us.'

Magnus shook his head. 'I will not be giving any letter to the Jallian bargemen. They are also bribed with silver, and I don't trust them. They would go straight to Ragnvald or my father, and tell them what I had done.'

'Some of the bargemen must have good hearts, son.'

'Maybe, but how would I find them? And what actual proof do we have that my father is a Master?'

'We have all witnessed him kill.'

'So it would be our word against his. And, no offence, but you are a slave, and the testimony of a slave counts for nothing.'

Colette simmered with anger. 'I refuse to accept that we are powerless. I refuse to resign myself to this awful life. Do any of us here deserve this fate? And we are the lucky ones. If we disobey orders, or anger our *betters* in any way, then we are sent down to the women's quarters in that horrible shanty town, where the mercenaries can treat us however they please. We all know what happens to the poor girls sent down there.'

The chamber fell into silence, and Magnus began to feel uncomfortable. His father and brothers had always taught him that women were little more than property, to be used and abused by the men who owned them; protected if they behaved, and punished if they caused any trouble. He sensed the women in the chamber looking at him, but he was unable to meet their eyes.

'I should go,' he said, getting to his feet.

Colette gave him a wry smile. 'Well, at least you didn't shout at me this time, son.'

'Thank you for the tea,' he said to the older woman, then he turned and walked to the door.

The two mercenary soldiers on duty allowed him to pass through the entrance, then they locked the door behind him. Magnus walked through the twisting passageways of the huge temple, and came to his own small suite of rooms. He had been given a little apartment when he had turned sixteen the year before, but it was in an out-of-the-way location within the temple, far from the royal court where his father lived in sumptuous luxury.

Magnus lay down on his wicker bed. It creaked beneath him, as he turned on to his back to stare at the carved stone ceiling. His mother had talked about the Realm of Jallin and the Empire of the Sanctians, but they were just names to him; names without any tangible meaning. In the depths of the Great Forest, only one rule applied – his father's. Bargemen came and went, and new slaves and mercenaries would occasionally appear, but, apart from that, the Temple of Steppen seemed as though it was the most isolated spot in the world. Would an empire care if a few slaves had been taken illegally? If the rulers of the empire were anything like his father, then the answer was clear.

No one was coming, because no one cared.

Magnus awoke from his afternoon doze when someone kicked the side of his bed. He opened his eyes and saw the face of Einar leering down at him.

'What do you want?' said Magnus.

'Get on your feet, you little prick,' said his half-brother. 'The king is here.'

Magnus's eyes widened, and he shot out of bed and stood on the smooth stone floor.

Einar laughed, then he moved to the side, and King Hemming walked into the room. He eyed the few possessions that were lying around, then his gaze fell upon his youngest son.

'This is my first time in your apartment, Magnus,' said the Whalebone King. 'Very nice.'

Magnus said nothing.

'I heard you were in the women's quarters earlier today, lad,' the king went on. 'That was a little presumptuous of you, was it not? Did you think that, just because you are a Master, you would be allowed to select a whore as your companion, eh?'

'I was visiting my mother, sir,' Magnus said.

The king's expression darkened. 'Why the fuck do you keep visiting that bitter old hag?' he cried. 'If she hadn't given me a son, I would have handed her over to the mercenaries years ago. Did she rant about how awful I am? Did she blame me for all of her troubles? She is lucky to be alive. I should have known better than to snatch a woman who can read and write – they always cause the most difficulties.' He shook his head at his son. 'Do you know your problem, boy? You are too soft-hearted. Slaves aren't real people, and we captured them fair and square. They have no rights. If they are loyal and faithful, then they are allowed to remain alive; if not...'

Magnus remained quiet.

'All the same,' his father went on, 'as my son, and as a Master, you are indeed entitled to a bed companion. However, we are running a little low on young slave girls, as you probably witnessed for yourself when you visited their quarters. Most of that lot have been here for twenty years or so. In a perfect world, I would simply go out raiding for more, but the Jallian army seems to object to such practices, and I don't want to draw any unwanted attention towards us. The only alternative is to buy legal slaves, most of whom are ignorant Westlanders – savages, in other words. They are expensive, and young, female Westlanders cost even more. Matteo reckons it will take an entire month's worth of silver to purchase ten such girls, and we will have to wait for weeks to get them. You will need to be patient; unless you are willing to make do with an older whore for now. Well?'

'An older woman would twist him round her little finger, boss,' said Einar.

'Not if he breaks her in properly,' said the king. 'Lack of food, lack of sleep, a few beatings – that sort of thing usually does the trick.'

'Can I think about it, sir?' said Magnus.

'No,' said the king. 'I need an answer now; else, I will assign the ten new Westlander girls to others, and you will have to do without.'

'Then I accept, sir. I will take one of the new slaves when they arrive.'

The king smiled. 'Good lad. Have you practised your Master abilities since I last saw you?'

'No, sir.'

'Then do it now,' said the king. 'I want to see a steady improvement over the coming months. Is that understood?'

'Yes, sir.'

The Whalebone King gave his youngest son a smile, then he turned and walked out of the apartment. Einar lingered for a little longer, his gaze on Magnus.

'Did your mother say anything about me?' he said.

Magnus shook his head.

'What did she say about the king?'

'Nothing.'

'You're lying. If I find out that she's been stirring up trouble again, I will cut out her tongue. What do you say to that, boy?'

Magnus kept his gaze lowered and his mouth shut. Einar was ten years older than him, and had beaten him up on many occasions.

Einar laughed. 'You are weak. If it weren't for the fact that the king protects you, then you wouldn't last a single day in Steppen.'

Magnus remained silent. Einar started to look bored, then he snorted and walked out of the apartment. Magnus sat down on his wicker bed.

He hated his half-brothers and, though he found it hard to admit it, he hated his father as well. Despite the beauty of the pools and waterfalls, Steppen had killed any hope Magnus felt about the future. But what could he do? If he rebelled against his father, he would be ground into the dirt. If he tried to flee into the forest, he would die of starvation long before he reached civilisation, if such a place existed.

He gazed at his hands. If he could develop his Master powers, then he might have a chance. He imagined slaying his father and his brothers, and the loathsome mercenaries, then rescuing his mother and escaping from Steppen. He would turn his father's blood to ice, and he would watch him die. And then, maybe, he would be free.

CHAPTER 4
DUKE OF TORRENT

Jalburg, Jallin, Central Provinces – 20th Day of Minula 108

'Sixteen?' said Walter, as he lifted the mug of ale to his lips. 'The emperor has sixteen damn grandchildren?'

Sebastian laughed. 'No, Walter; there are sixteen cousins – the grandchildren of the emperor, his brother Prince Valentino, and his sister Princess Carla. Two of the sixteen are my own children – Caterina and Salvatore.'

Walter narrowed his eyes. 'And you are married to Princess Carmen, yes? And she is?'

'My wife is the daughter of Princess Carla. She's the emperor's niece, in other words.'

'It's too complicated,' Walter said.

'You will need to have it memorised by the time we arrive on Sanctos, my friend.'

Count Sebastian gazed at the entrance to the private booth where they were sitting in the large tavern. Two of his knights were ensuring that no unwanted visitors disturbed them, and two of Walter's Mountain Rangers were also there, keeping an eye on the busy crowds inside the tavern.

'Where is that whisky we ordered?' Sebastian said.

'It's possible that they don't stock any,' said Walter. 'We are in the land of wine, unfortunately.'

'This is the biggest tavern in the entire city, Walter.'

'I'd hardly call Jalburg a city. It isn't much bigger than Torrent and Twinbrook combined, even if it is the capital of Jallin. Anyway, will all sixteen of these royal cousins be on Sanctos when we get there?'

'That is highly unlikely,' said Sebastian. 'They were kept together when they were younger, as it was the intention of the emperor that they all underwent the most rigorous training regime. I myself had a small hand in that – I used to train some of them in how to correctly use a sword. However, half of them are in their twenties by now, and the older ones may have been posted to various provinces and so on. One of them most definitely won't be on Sanctos – Mor Dennahelm.'

'Odd name,' said Walter.

'His father is Mor Galthide, a former prince of a southern realm, and one must assume that he had a hand in naming the lad, just as Princess Hygilt's mother is named Hygla. The emperor has a penchant for finding exotic spouses for the imperial household. A prince from this kingdom, a princess from that realm. Only a few of us, such as myself, are actually natives of Sanctos. Have you finished that ale?'

Walter glanced into his empty mug and nodded.

'What ho!' cried Sebastian to his knights. 'Find us a serving boy or girl; at once. Duke Walter is thirsty.'

One of the knights bowed, then he walked into the crowded part of the tavern.

Sebastian eyed Walter. 'Why are you grimacing, my friend? Do you dislike being called a duke? You are a duke, whether you like it or not. The Duke of Torrent.'

'I don't feel like a duke. I wish Kilbride hadn't thought of it.'

'Your wife is a wise woman,' said Sebastian. 'Granting you the vacant duchy was a masterstroke. You have to remember that you are married to the next-in-line to the throne of Upper Down. If something terrible was to happen to young Alfie, may the spirits preserve him, then Princess Kilbride would become queen; and any consort of a queen should be at least a duke. Furthermore, old chap, the imperial court on Sanctos values such things. You will be treated with more respect as a duke; believe me.' A gleam came into his eyes as he glanced at Walter. 'And your unborn son or daughter will inherit the duchy; there is that to consider.'

Walter stared at the surface of the table.

'Do not be downcast,' said Sebastian. 'You will be back in Upper Down in time for the birth of your first child.'

'I doubt that,' said Walter. 'If I knew why the emperor wishes to talk to me, then I might be more sure.'

Sebastian regarded him. 'You are not a stupid man. Why do you think a regent of Upper Down has been summoned to Sanctos?'

'To renegotiate our treaty?' said Walter. 'Here's what I imagine happened – Valentino returned to Sanctos with his sixty broken cannon and a treaty, and the emperor's head exploded in rage. He sends out a new ambassador, relieving you of your duties, and demands that a regent appears before him. Half of me thinks he's going to throw me in jail as soon as I arrive.'

'I was never a serious long-term prospect as an ambassador to your realm, Walter. I am a soldier, not a diplomat.'

The knight returned with a young serving boy, who was carrying a tray.

'Is that whisky?' said Walter.

'Yes, sir,' said the boy. 'It's the only bottle in the entire town, sir. The tavern owner sent me out to purchase it from a friend of his.'

'Good lad,' said Sebastian. 'Please thank your employer for his diligence and service. There will be a generous tip for you at the end of the evening. Now, set out two glasses, and leave the bottle with us. Oh, and bring us more ale, there's a good fellow.'

The boy placed the bottle and the glasses onto the table, then he bowed and hurried away. Walter picked up the bottle and glanced at the tattered old label.

'Does its provenance satisfy you, Walter?' said Sebastian. 'Is it from a distillery of which you approve?'

'I can barely read the label, it's so old.'

'Old is good, yes?'

'Yes, until it becomes too old.' He opened it and filled the two glasses, then he slid one to Sebastian.

The count took a sip. 'I'm no expert,' he said, 'but I like it.'

Walter also took a sip, then he smiled. 'This will do. Is it wrong of us to sit here getting drunk while there are so many troubles in the world?'

'I don't know what you mean,' said Sebastian. 'There are no major conflicts, the Westlander raids into the Central Provinces have ceased, and the peaceful rule of the Sanctians continues to spread.'

'Like it spread into Klef Mordain?'

Sebastian gave a gentle shrug. 'That city will flourish under our rule; mark my words.'

Alcohol may have loosened Walter's tongue a little, but he suppressed any desire to tell Sebastian what else he knew about Klef Mordain. He and Kilbride had kept the fact that they had sent Abigone there a secret from the count. Walter considered Sebastian to be a friend, but he was also a Sanctian, and it was better that he did not know anything about the existence of any schools for Masters and Makers.

'Besides,' Sebastian went on, 'how else should the empire have reacted to the brutal assassination of our ambassador there? The government of Klef Mordain was being very difficult. They absolutely refused to enter any kind of peaceful negotiations with us. Just think – with that city absorbed into the empire, we shall control the merchant fleet that plies the great ocean. One day, I would like to cross the ocean for myself, to see if the tales are true. Giant, man-eating lizards; covens of witches that dwell in caves up the mountains; you know, that sort of thing.'

'I'm only interested in securing the future of Upper Down.'

'Yes, well, Walter, your outlook is somewhat parochial. This is your first time in Jallin, is it not?'

'I have never been further south than Greater Down.'

'Then you are in for a treat. Yearl, as you know, has recently been annexed into the empire, and is now a full province. We shall be stopping off at Elestia on the way south – now, there's a city worthy of the name. I am very much looking forward to showing you the sights.'

Walter refilled their glasses. 'You never say much about your generation,' he said. 'You always talk about the imperial cousins, but rarely about their parents. Who should I watch out for on Sanctos?'

'Crown Prince Mikel is the heir to the throne,' said Sebastian, 'but he and his most exalted father have not been seeing eye to eye for some time.' He glanced at the knights, then back to Walter. 'You did not hear that from me, of course,' he whispered. 'The emperor's second son died many years ago, and his third son Prince Vincenzo is High Admiral of the Sanctian Fleet. Princess Isabella is unmarried – she is a priestess. In fact, she is the highest-ranked priestess in the entire empire. If you think the emperor hates Masters and Makers, wait until you meet her. The emperor's final surviving child is Princess Volena, the mother of Mor Dennahelm. Do you know what – I think I will write it all down for you.'

'What about your own children?'

Sebastian smiled as he sipped more whisky. 'Caterina is my pride and joy – clever, beautiful, and afraid of nothing, while Salvatore – what a boy! I couldn't be prouder. He will be joining the army soon, when he turns eighteen.' His features darkened a little.

'Is something wrong?' said Walter.

Sebastian leaned in close. 'The emperor has some rather... odd ideas about who my children should marry, Walter; just as he has the same odd ideas about some of the other cousins. For example, he intends to marry off Prince Vincenzo's daughter – a young lady by the name of Safina, to the son of Prince Stephano, my wife's brother. This is despite the fact that they are cousins.'

Walter frowned. 'You have just described the family ties that exist between myself and Kilbride. We also share a great-grandfather.'

Sebastian looked a little embarrassed. 'Ah. Yes. I see what you mean. Hmm. I suppose that this custom has been slow to reach Sanctos. In past times, no one upon my homeland would have ever considered intermarriage between cousins, even if they are second cousins, as is the case with you and Princess Kilbride.'

'Is the emperor going to marry your children off to their second cousins?'

'He has Prince Marcello in mind for my dear Caterina, but I don't know what he has planned for Salvatore.' He frowned again. 'I only discovered that my daughter was betrothed when the new ambassador of Upper Down informed me.'

'Can she refuse?'

'Only if she wishes to incur the emperor's wrath. Let's just say that such a course might be unwise.'

'What do you think the emperor will demand when I see him?'

'That, I cannot say.'

'Make a considered guess.'

'Very well, though this is mere speculation. Firstly, I imagine that the Most Exalted Emperor Antonio will insist that Upper Down purges itself of all Masters and Makers, as a necessary precondition for any treaty.'

'Then the talks will get nowhere, because I am not prepared to make any such concession.'

'Why not? Princess Abigone is no longer in the realm, and it will be years before anyone knows if the boy-king has any abilities.'

'And what if he does? What if King Alfgang the Sixth turns out to be a Master?'

'By that point, you will have plausible deniability. You simply claim the truth, which is that you didn't know. After all, you cannot foresee the future.'

'Yes, but wouldn't the emperor insist that he be removed from the throne?'

Sebastian gave Walter a wary smile, and leaned in even closer.

'Do not repeat this to anyone, Walter, but the emperor is an old man, if you get my meaning; and many of those in the line of succession do not share all of his views.' He leaned back again, and drained his glass. 'More whisky?'

Walter nodded, and Sebastian refilled the glasses.

'A toast to the emperor,' Walter said, raising his glass; 'but I forget – what age will His Imperial Majesty be on his next birthday?'

Sebastian raised his own glass. 'His Majesty's birthday isn't for another month or so, and he will be seventy-two.'

'To the emperor's health,' said Walter, then he drank from the glass as he pondered Sebastian's veiled words. They had ten years or so before Alfgang's potential abilities would become evident. Would the emperor be dead by then?

'And to a long reign,' said Sebastian.

'At last!' cried a voice.

Walter and Sebastian turned, and saw a man and a woman pushing their way through the crowded tavern towards their private booth. The two knights raised their arms to block their way.

'Amery?' said Walter. 'What in the name of the spirits are you doing here?'

'Looking for you, Lord Walter, what else?' said Amery. 'The entire town of Jalburg is aware that you and Count Sebastian are in this tavern.' He tried to get past the knights, but they pushed him back. 'I need to speak to you alone, Walter,' Amery went on. 'It is very important.'

'I remember you,' said Sebastian. 'You were the lawyer who helped draft the treaty between the empire and Upper Down, yes?'

Amery inclined his head a little towards the Sanctian. 'Yes, my noble count; that was me.' He turned back to Walter. 'Please; I very much need to speak to you.'

'Should I remove this person from the tavern, my lord?' said one of the knights.

'Wait,' said Walter. 'I'll speak to him. Please excuse me for a moment, Sebastian.'

The count narrowed his eyes, but said nothing.

Walter got to his feet, and then realised how drunk he was. He swayed slightly, then made his way past the knights and the Mountain Rangers to where Amery was standing next to a young woman.

'Right,' said Walter; 'what do you want to talk about?'

Amery glanced around. 'Not here. We need to go somewhere private.'

Walter raised an eyebrow. 'Outside? There's nowhere quiet in here, and I could do with some fresh air.'

'He's drunk,' whispered the young woman.

'That is very true,' said Walter. 'Well spotted. Imagine finding a drunken person in a tavern, eh? What's the world coming to?'

The woman frowned, then Amery led them through the crowd and out of the tavern. The night air was chill and crisp, and the sky was clear. Walter smiled up at the sight of two of the three moons. The Little Red Moon was full and setting to the west, while the Big Red Moon was just past full, and was shining overhead. Its light was dimming the stars, and Walter savoured its beauty.

'Those Mountain Rangers have followed us outside,' muttered Amery.

'What?' said Walter.

Amery gestured to the two Rangers.

'That's just Otto and Dietar,' said Walter. 'They follow me everywhere.'

'What part of *alone* did you not understand?' said the young woman.

Walter laughed. 'Is this your woman, Amery? How the fuck did you manage that?'

Amery rolled his eyes. 'Lothar used to say something similar.'

'How is the big bastard, eh? Is he in Jalburg, too?' said Walter. He frowned as he remembered something. 'Wait a moment – have you come from Klef Mordain? Is, uh…' He eyed the two Rangers. 'Step back a few paces, lads.'

The Rangers inclined their heads and walked back to the tavern entrance, from where they kept an eye on Walter.

'Is Abigone all right?' Walter whispered.

'We think so,' said Amery.

'You *think* so?' said Walter.

'We haven't seen her or Lothar for nine days,' Amery went on. 'She was perfectly well back then.'

'Where is she now?'

'There is so much to tell you,' said Amery, 'that I'm not sure where to start.'

'Did you find the secret school?'

'Abigone attended the school for Makers for several months,' said Amery, 'but we were forced to flee when the Sanctians arrived. We stopped when we got to Jallin, because we couldn't agree where to go next. I wanted to go back to Upper Down, but several of the others wanted to go to Geathan.'

'Where?'

'Geathan, Walter. Have you heard of it?'

'I can't say that I have.'

'It doesn't matter. It's a long way away; that's all you need to know. Anyway, while we were arguing about this, some river men snatched the four youngest students from right under our noses, so Abigone and the others went after them.'

'Slow down,' said Walter. 'There are other students?'

'Several. The youngest ones are only fourteen, and so the others felt obliged to attempt to retrieve them.'

'But you didn't?' said Walter. 'You couldn't have known that I was travelling south; are you saying that you abandoned them?'

'I am exiled from Yearl. I will be hanged if I go back there.'

'Were the children taken to Yearl?'

'Well, no. They were taken into the depths of the Great Forest, to a silver mine. It does lie close to the border of Yearl, though.'

'You never have been very brave, have you, Amery?'

'That's not fair,' said the young woman.

'Are you ever going to introduce me to this young lady?' said Walter.

'Of course, sorry,' said Amery. 'Walter, this is Miss Loryn of Klef Mordain. Loryn, this is Lord Walter of Upper Down.'

'It's Duke Walter now,' he said.

'Is it? Are you the Duke of Ridden?'

'Hector's oldest boy is the Duke of Ridden. I'm the new Duke of Torrent.' He laughed. 'Can you believe that? I got Stefan's duchy. Kilbride thought it would be a good idea. I guess she didn't want to get married to a commoner.'

Amery's eyes tightened. 'You married Princess Kilbride?'

'I have, and she's expecting our first child. Damn it, I wish I was still in Upper Down. I'm only here because the emperor demanded that a regent go to Sanctos. I'm probably going to get a stern telling off about the treaty we signed with Valentino.' He laughed. 'Do you have any legal advice?'

'Can we please get back to talking about Abigone?' said Amery. 'She may require your assistance.'

'Why? Doesn't she have Masters and Makers from the school to help her?'

'Most of the students are hopeless. They are children, Walter, and the Great Forest is a dangerous place.'

'I'm sure Abbie knows what she's doing.'

Amery glared at him. 'Is that what you are going to tell Princess Kilbride? Are you going to inform your new wife that you had the chance to help her sister, but you turned it down? Tell me – what was the purpose of sending Princess Abigone to the secret school in Klef Mordain?'

Walter frowned. 'Um...'

'It was so she would be able to protect Upper Down,' Amery went on.

Loryn shook her head. 'This is a waste of time. *Duke* Walter is clearly too inebriated to be of any use. Perhaps we should try again in the morning, when he has sobered up.'

'Give me a moment,' Amery said, his attention still on Walter. 'Duke of Torrent,' he went on, 'were you aware that Princess Abigone intends to travel not to Upper Down, but to the fallen realm of Geathan? This is, of course, if she makes it out of the Great Forest alive. Isn't it your duty to try to persuade her to return to Upper Down?'

Walter stared off into the distance. Part of him wondered if it would be better to allow Abigone to seek her own path in the world; without her presence in Upper Down, he could truthfully claim to the emperor that he knew of no Masters or Makers living in the small realm. If she was there, then Antonio might demand her arrest, or worse, her execution. At the same time, he dreaded having to inform Kilbride about what he had learned. What would she want him to do? He wasn't sure. Besides, Kilbride and Upper Down lay hundreds of miles to the north, and Walter would have to reach his own decision.

'Do you know the location of the silver mine?' he said.

Amery smiled. 'No, but I do know how to get there. There is a large village by the edge of the forest, which lies on the banks of the River Antiago. That river flows all the way to the mine, and then it turns south towards the city of Elestia. The river is how one travels to the mine, and the river is also the only means by which one can leave it. I can give you detailed instructions on how to reach this village. You will need gold, in order to hire a few bargemen. I assume you have plenty?'

'How many days will this diversion add to my journey?'

'I am not entirely sure. Perhaps a month, altogether. Do you have a date by which you need to appear in Sanctos?'

'The emperor said *as soon as practicable*. There was no date.'

'Excellent. Then you will do it?'

'And what will you be doing?'

'We... are currently unsure about our next move. We were travelling up to Campsie when we heard that you and Count Sebastian were staying in Jalburg for a few days. Would I be welcome in Upper Down?'

'I don't see why not, but Upper Down would become a dangerous place to be if I persuade Abigone to go there. The emperor will react badly to her presence in the realm. If you are after a quiet life, then I recommend you look elsewhere. Do you have rooms in Jalburg?'

'We have rented quarters in a small tavern,' he said. 'It isn't as fancy as the one where you and the count are staying, but it will suffice.'

'Come back in the morning with a map that shows the location of the village,' Walter said.

'Is this your way of saying that you will help Abigone?'

'I guess it is. Now I have to find a way to tell Sebastian. It was nice to meet you, Loryn. I will see you in the morning.'

Walter turned and walked back towards the tavern entrance. Otto and Dietar followed him into the crowded building, and they made their way to the private booth, where Sebastian was talking to a man in an apron.

'Ah, there he is,' said Sebastian. 'This is Walter, Duke of Torrent. Walter, this man owns the tavern.'

The owner bowed low. 'It is a great honour to have you both staying under my roof.'

'Thanks for the whisky,' said Walter, as he sat.

'It was nothing, my lord,' said the man. 'I hope you enjoy your stay. If there is anything you need, anything at all, please let me know.'

Sebastian eyed Walter as the man walked away.

'I need to make a small adjustment to my plans,' said Walter, as he picked up his glass.

'I thought you might,' said Sebastian. 'The emperor will be displeased if you refuse to travel to Sanctos.'

'I'll get to Sanctos,' said Walter, 'but I might take another month or so.'

'I see. And where would you be going?'

Walter shrugged.

'I understand the need for discretion, my friend,' said Sebastian, 'but consider this – I may be able to help you. I can tell the emperor that you are on your way, but he will want to know the reason for this delay.'

'I can't tell him the reason.'

'Ah.'

'And if I tell you, and then the emperor asks you, you will feel obliged to give him an answer. I'm not blaming you for this, but you are married to the emperor's niece. You can hardly lie to him.'

'Indeed.'

Walter drained his glass. 'All right – here is what I am going to say. Don't ask me to explain myself any further – this is all you are going to get out of me. There has been a possible sighting of Princess Abigone, and I need to investigate it. I'm going to a silver mine in the Great Forest, and I should make it to Elestia within a month or so. From there, I'll travel south to catch a ship to Sanctos.'

'A silver mine?' said Sebastian.

'Apparently. By the time you reach the emperor, Abigone will no longer be there.'

'Are you going to help her?'

'I am going to *investigate*. She is a co-regent of Upper Down, isn't she? She might have an opinion regarding our treaty with the empire.'

Sebastian raised an eyebrow, but said nothing.

'Will that satisfy His Imperial Majesty?' said Walter.

'I cannot say for sure. I might wait for you in Elestia, so that we can coordinate our... version of events. Ask for me at the governor's residence. I can send a letter to the imperial court on Sanctos, informing them of the delay.'

'Why would you wait for me?'

'Because, Walter, I sense it would be unwise for you to travel to Sanctos alone. I am not only your travelling companion; my presence by your side deters any of the more enthusiastic sections of Sanctian society from doing you any harm. There are those who believe that they would please the emperor by bringing him your head.'

'Would he be pleased?'

'Quite possibly. Upper Down defied the armed might of Sanctos, and made a fool out of Prince Valentino. The emperor's anger might well be unshakeable. It would be prudent if we entered the imperial court together.'

'You would put yourself at risk for me?'

'When I call you *my friend*, do you believe that I am merely being polite? No, Walter, I have staked my reputation on the treaty that brought the conflict between Upper Down and the empire to an end. I put myself at risk as soon as I added my signature next to Prince Valentino's. According to the new ambassador to your realm, the illustrious prince is currently being blamed for the failure of the operation to subdue Upper Down. If Valentino falls out of favour with the emperor, then so shall I.'

Walter said nothing.

'Go after Abigone, my friend,' Sebastian went on. 'Do what you need to do, and then I shall meet you in the city of Elestia when you are ready to travel to Sanctos. Do we have a deal?'

Walter refilled their glasses. 'We have a deal.'

CHAPTER 5
MUTUAL MISTRUST

Great Forest, South-Western Jallin, Central Provinces – 23rd Day of Minula 108

'Why isn't this river busier?' said Abigone, as she sat on the deck of the slow-moving barge. 'If it goes all the way to Elestia, then why isn't there more traffic?'

'I have been wondering that myself,' said Denny. 'It must be faster and cheaper to ship goods downstream, than it is to carry them by road.'

One of the nearby bargemen rolled his eyes. He was using a barge-pole to keep the vessel from getting too close to the river bank, but it was clear that he had been listening to Abigone and Denny.

'Why do they always do that?' whispered Abigone.

'They're keeping something from us,' said Raewyn, who was sitting close to them, 'and I don't like it.'

Denny glanced up at the bargeman. 'Is that true?'

'You're paying this crew to take you downstream, young sir,' said the bargeman, 'not for a guided tour.'

'Why isn't the river busier?' said Abigone. 'There must be a reason.'

'There is, young miss,' he said.

The others waited, but the bargeman said nothing else.

'Well?' said Raewyn. 'What's the reason?'

'There are several.'

'Yes?'

The bargeman smiled and glanced away.

'Stop playing with them,' said another bargeman, who was sitting at the rear of the vessel with his hand on the tiller. He glanced at Abigone and the others. 'I'll tell you why this river is so quiet. You said it goes all the way to Elestia, and that's true, but no barge can get there by water alone.'

'Why not?' said Abigone.

'The Menjano Step,' he said; 'a great line of cliffs that runs for over two hundred miles from east to west. The cliffs are hundreds of feet high, and the ground drops away on the southern side. In other words, this river becomes one giant waterfall, with rapids and rocks.'

'Then how shall we get to the silver mine?' said Denny.

'The boats are lowered down by cranes. The mine is at the bottom, where several rivers coming from the north converge. If you like waterfalls, then you're going to love Steppen.'

The other bargeman laughed.

'Steppen?' said Abigone. 'I haven't heard of this place.'

'It's the name of an ancient temple next to the mine,' said the man by the tiller. 'The Whalebone King lives there.'

'Who?'

'He's the... owner of the silver mine. A charming fellow. You're going to love him, too.'

Denny frowned. 'Why is he called the Whalebone King?'

'Because he has a crown made of whalebone. He claims he killed the whale himself, back when he was the captain of a squadron of pirate vessels. They used to roam the coastal seas by Campsie and Yearl, or so the story goes. Then the Sanctian navy arrived, and started blowing them out of the water. Old Hemming – that's his name – decided to cut his losses and move inland; only, he brought many of his crewmates with him. Over a hundred, by all accounts.'

'Should we be telling them this, skipper?' said the man wielding the bargepole.

'I don't see the harm. They're going to find out soon enough, ain't they?'

'Do these former pirates work in the silver mine?' said Abigone.

The two men laughed.

'I fail to see how that was funny,' said Abigone.

'The old pirates don't do any of the actual work, young lady,' said the man by the tiller. 'They live off the proceeds, but they haven't done an honest day's toil since they arrived in Steppen. They have slaves for that. And mercenaries, who guard the slaves. It's a very profitable set up.'

'It is illegal to enslave citizens of the Central Provinces,' said Denny. 'The four children that were taken are all citizens.'

'Then why didn't you report it to the town militia, boy? We ain't stupid. You're on the run from something, or someone; otherwise, you would have informed the authorities.'

Fyenna appeared on deck. 'Say nothing more to these men,' she said. 'There is no need for them to know our business. I want you three to come below for a moment; we need to talk.'

Denny, Abigone and Raewyn got to their feet, and followed Fyenna down into the main cabin, where the others were all sitting. Fyenna closed and barred the hatch. Abigone took a seat on a wooden bench, while they all waited for Fyenna to speak.

'I shall be honest with you,' Fyenna said; 'I do not trust the bargemen. They have had dealings with the silver mine before; the same silver mine that appears to have abducted four of our number. I believe that the bargemen would not hesitate to betray us. If offered money, they might sell us to the same people who stole Reath, Nyli, Salus and Ignatius. We must be vigilant at all times.'

'I agree with every word,' said Lothar. 'The bargemen could easily be in league with the silver mine. They know we decided not to tell the militia about what happened in the village; they probably think we're easy marks.'

'I look forward to proving them wrong,' said Mor Galthide; 'and the sooner the better. What say we dispose of them? It takes little skill to punt a barge; we do not need them.'

'I am inclined to agree,' said Fyenna.

'You can't be serious,' said Eshia. 'Are you saying we should murder five bargemen who haven't harmed us in any way?'

'Better safe than sorry, lass,' said Mor Galthide. 'Call it a pre-emptive strike. We should kill them *before* they can do us harm.'

'We have been on this barge for nine days,' said Constans, 'heading deeper and deeper into the Great Forest. Why has no one brought this up until now?'

'I decided to mention it because we do not have much further to go, Constans,' said Fyenna. 'In perhaps another day or two, we shall be arriving at the silver mine. If we are going to act, then we need to formulate a plan.'

'Did you hear what the tiller man told us about the cranes?' said Abigone. 'We are going to come to a large waterfall, and the boat will be lowered down the side of a cliff. At the bottom is a temple, where a king lives.'

'He is not a real king,' said Fyenna; 'he merely calls himself one. And yes, we could hear your conversation from down here. Why do you think I closed the hatch? If what the bargemen said is true, then we cannot trust anyone at the silver mine. I am old enough to recall the days when pirates terrorised the coastline south of Klef Mordain. To give credit where it's due, the Sanctians did a fine job of cleaning up the seas. Such a fine job, in fact, that when they announced they were sending warships to Klef Mordain to combat piracy, most folk in the Central Provinces probably believed them. If there are a hundred former pirates dwelling near the silver mine, then we could be in for a fight. If it turns out that they are encouraging others to steal slaves for them, they are hardly likely to hand back our missing children without a struggle.' She glanced at Abigone. 'We may have to be ruthless.'

'Our tactics can be simple,' said Mor Galthide. 'Those who can fight shall protect the Masters and Makers, allowing them to deal with any hostile forces we encounter. Who do we have that can kill from a distance?'

'There's me,' said Fyenna, 'Eshia, Abigone, Constans and Raewyn. Our fighters are Mor Galthide, Lothar and Denny. That leaves four who can do neither.'

'That makes me feel as though I am a burden upon the others,' said Annalise.

'I can fight,' said Marlow.

'You are too young,' said Fyenna. 'I will not place a fifteen-year-old into the line of battle.'

'We should arm the boy all the same,' said Mor Galthide; 'and the other one – Aplin. How old are you, Aplin?'

'Sixteen,' said the boy.

'Can you fight?'

'Against slavers?' said Aplin. 'Yes.'

'He hates slavers,' said Stanza, 'because his mother was a slave.'

'That's nobody's business,' snapped Aplin.

Abigone frowned. 'Is that true, Aplin?'

The boy turned to stare out of a small porthole.

'His mother was a Westlander,' Stanza went on. 'She was captured after the battle of Hader Pull.'

'You mean there were Westlander slaves in Klef Mordain?' said Abigone.

'Very few were still alive by the time you arrived in the city,' said Fyenna; 'but yes. It was perfectly legal, though that is not to say that I approved. Westlanders are not citizens; they are foreigners, and the Corse allowed those captured in that battle to be enslaved. It is what they would have done to us, had they won.'

'If his mother was a slave,' said Raewyn, 'then who was his father?'

'Can you all please shut up?' Aplin cried. 'I don't want to talk about it. My mother... she...'

'She loved you very much,' said Fyenna. 'She would be very proud of the man you are becoming.'

'I didn't know any of this,' said Denny. 'I'm sorry, Aplin. You should know that Emperor Antonio, for all his many faults, despises slavery. He is determined to eradicate it from every province of the empire.'

'The Elestian Empire was also opposed to it,' said Constans.

'That's true, in theory,' said Denny; 'but the Elestians turned a blind eye to many abuses in this area. For a bribe, local courts would often strip ordinary people of their citizenship, allowing them to be enslaved. The Sanctians have put an end to that corrupt practice.'

'I grudgingly admit the truth of that,' said Mor Galthide.

'The final century of Elestian rule brought shame to every Master and Maker,' said Fyenna. 'The last emperor owned thousands of slaves, many of whom had lost their citizenship in the manner described by Denny. Very well, Aplin, if you wish to fight, you can fight.'

'Aplin and I can protect Stanza and Miss Annalise, ma'am,' said Marlow.

'What is your weapon of choice, Marlow?' said Mor Galthide.

'I'm handy with a knife, sir.'

Lothar shook his head. 'It pains me to hear us talking about arming children, but we might have to get our hands dirty if we're going to come out of this intact.'

'You and I should be training them, Lothar,' said Mor Galthide. 'We are the only ones here with military experience, with the notable exception of Lady Fyenna; though her martial skills differ somewhat from ours. My son has also been trained. It should be we three who kill the bargemen.'

'We can't murder them because they *might* be planning something,' said Denny.

'Thank you for saying that, Denny,' said Eshia. 'I'm glad that someone apart from me possesses an ounce of morality.'

Abigone narrowed her eyes at Eshia, but said nothing.

'Why don't we wait a little longer?' said Denny. 'We can do as Lady Fyenna suggested, and remain vigilant. If the bargemen attempt to betray us, then we act. Can we agree to that?'

'I would rather we retained the element of surprise,' said Mor

Galthide. 'If we strike first, we could kill those five Jallians in a few minutes. If we wait until they betray us, they will expect resistance.'

'What are we turning into?' said Eshia. 'If we do this, we shall be as bad as our enemies. Is that what you want? We will have proved the Sanctians right – that Masters and Makers are violent and cruel people who kill anyone who stands in their way. Those five Jallians probably have families, and yet you would make widows of their wives, and orphan their children, over nothing but an unfounded suspicion.'

The cabin fell into silence.

'Very well, Eshia,' said Fyenna; 'we shall take the advice offered by you and Denny. We shall wait. For now, we shall return to the deck, and pretend that this conversation never happened. Be civil to the bargemen, but not over friendly, and tell them nothing about who we are or why we are here. Keep your eyes and ears open, and report anything suspicious to myself, Mor Galthide or Lothar.' She walked to the hatch, removed the bar, and opened it wide, letting in the fresh air. 'Dismissed.'

Abigone and Denny climbed back up onto the long, narrow deck. The man by the tiller glanced at them, then turned to gaze downstream, his eyes on the river. Abigone stared into the thick forest on either side of the waterway, then she looked up at the strip of blue sky overhead. Noises were coming from the forest – the sounds of birds, she imagined. Apart from that, the stillness seemed complete.

A few of the others ascended from the cabin, and the deck filled with the refugees from Klef Mordain. A strange, uncomfortable silence hung over the vessel. Abigone tried to think of something to say, so that the bargemen wouldn't get suspicious, but her mind went blank, and the silence lingered on.

One of the bargemen laughed. 'Look at the guilty expressions on their faces,' he cried. 'What were you all doing down there, eh? Plotting something?'

'I don't think they trust us, mate,' said the man by the tiller.

'You would be right,' said Mor Galthide. 'Can you give us a reason to trust you, men of Jallin?'

'How about, we could have killed you all while you slept at any point over the last nine days, big guy?' said the tiller man. 'Or, we could have killed you, and the other guy who looks like a soldier, and done whatever we pleased with the rest of you. We haven't done either of those things.'

Mor Galthide narrowed his eyes.

'Who cares what they think?' said another bargeman. 'Let's just earn our wages and take them to Steppen. What happens to them after that is none of our business.'

'I don't like this,' whispered Abigone. 'They're hiding something.'

'I think you might be right,' Denny whispered back, 'but I don't think it's about them; I think it's something about Steppen.' He gazed down the river. 'What are we walking into?'

A spear skittered across the deck, then a bargeman cried out and fell, splashing into the muddy waters of the river.

'Everyone down!' yelled the tiller man. 'Brigands on the northern bank!'

'Get below deck,' Fyenna shouted.

An arrow whistled past Abigone's face, then she and Denny took shelter behind the only raised cabin on the deck. Another bargeman fell, an arrow striking his right leg as he was ushering the students down the steps into the lower cabin. The only person still standing out on deck was Mor Galthide, who was beating his chest and yelling abuse into the forest as more spears and arrows flew past him.

'We have no cargo!' the tiller man shouted into the forest, his hands cupped by his mouth. 'There's nothing to steal, you stupid bastards!'

The crouching bargeman at the front of the vessel cried out in alarm. He turned to the tiller man.

'Obstruction ahead, skipper!' he yelled.

The barge began to slow, then it bumped up against something. The rear of the craft kept moving, and the vessel began to turn, until its left-hand side was up against the obstruction the bargeman had mentioned. A picket line of wooden stakes had been hammered into the shallow bed of the river, creating a barricade that was holding the barge in position. There was movement in the forest, then a long wooden gangway was lowered, its far end slapping down on the deck of the barge. Several armed men ran out from the forest. Their boots clattered over the gangway, but Mor Galthide was waiting for them, a sword in his right hand. He hacked down the first brigand with a vicious swing of the blade, then he rammed the tip of his sword into the second brigand's waist.

Lothar ran up next to him, a crossbow over his shoulder. He crouched by Mor Galthide's side, gripped onto the end of the gangway, and heaved it up. Another brigand fell into the river, then Lothar dropped the end of the gangway into the water, and two more fell off.

'I was having fun, Lothar!' Mor Galthide said.

A spear struck the front of the barge by Mor Galthide's feet. In response, the Geathan prince jumped into the river, the water coming up to his waist, then he waded towards the shore, his sword raised. The current pushed him towards the row of wooden stakes, and he used them to guide his way. Arrows flew past him, then he reached the bank, roared out a battle cry, and disappeared into the forest. Moments later, the hail of spears and arrows ceased, and an uneasy quiet fell over the barge. The three brigands who had fallen into the river appeared by the shore, hauling themselves out of the mud. Lothar raised his crossbow, aimed and loosed. A bolt hit one of the men square in the back, and he fell face first into the mud.

Abigone raised her hand as she eyed the other two, but Fyenna gave her a stern look. Denny grabbed a spear that had fallen onto the deck, then he stood and threw it, and it hit one of the other brigands in his side. The last brigand by the muddy banks fled into the forest, and the tiller man slowly got to his feet, his eyes on the trees.

'Start pulling those stakes out!' he shouted.

Two of the bargemen jumped into the river, and examined the stakes.

'We need rope, skipper,' one of them called out.

At that moment, the body of the bargeman killed by a spear floated up against the barricade and came to a halt. The others stared at it for a moment, then the tiller man threw a coil of rope down to the two in the river.

'Help me,' the tiller man said to Lothar. He glanced at the others, and pointed at Denny and Constans. 'You two lads, get over here. As soon as my men have secured the ropes, start pulling the stakes out. We need to get this boat moving again.'

'We will not be leaving our colleague behind,' said Fyenna.

'Did I suggest that?' said the tiller man. 'We're leaving no one behind. We'll keep a couple of stakes in place until your friend is back on board.'

'Where is he?' said Stanza, her eyes on the forest.

The tiller man helped Denny, Lothar and Constans as they heaved on the ropes tied round the stakes. The first one came free, and Denny and Constans fell back onto the deck.

'Keep going,' said the tiller man. 'Untie the rope and throw it down to the lads in the river.'

Abigone walked over to Fyenna, who was gazing into the forest.

'Thank you for stopping me, ma'am,' she said.

'I know that it seems unfair,' said Fyenna. 'You and I could have killed every one of those brigands in a few seconds, and yet we had to stand back and let others do the fighting. Even if we are wrong, and the bargemen are reliable, we cannot afford to let them know who we are.'

Mor Galthide appeared by the banks of the river. He was covered in blood and mud, and he was holding three severed heads by their hair.

'I have solved the brigandage problem,' he said, his eyes gleaming.

'If you have any strength left, big guy,' said the tiller man, 'help us get the last of the stakes out.'

Mor Galthide tossed the three heads into the bushes, then he waded into the river. He reached the remaining stakes, then he took hold of one as he braced his feet, and ripped it out of the riverbed.

'That'll do,' cried the tiller man. 'Get back on board.'

Denny and Lothar helped Mor Galthide and the two bargemen back onto the deck, then he and Constans pulled on the ropes tied to one of the last posts. It came free, and the barge began to drift downstream again. The tiller man ran back to the rear of the vessel, and corrected their course, then two bargemen leaned over the side, and hauled their dead comrade up onto the deck. They laid him flat on his back and covered him with a blanket, then Lothar and a few of the others gathered round the injured bargeman. Lothar gripped the arrow with both hands, and drove it through the man's leg, then he snapped off the barbed tip, and pulled out the shaft. The bargeman grunted, his face grimacing in pain, then Lothar tied a strip of fabric round his thigh, and the bleeding slowed.

'You've done that before,' said the tiller man.

'Once or twice,' said Lothar. 'No artery was hit. Your man should live, if the wound doesn't get infected.'

Lothar took off his outer coat, rolled it up, and placed it under the injured man's head.

'Keep an eye on him,' he said to Stanza, who was crouching nearby. 'The bleeding should stop soon. If it doesn't, come and get me.'

'One dead, and one injured,' said the tiller man. 'I'm going to need a couple of volunteers from among the passengers to help with the punting.' He eyed Denny and Constans. 'You lads have proved useful; will you take the first shift?'

They both nodded, and then they took up their positions by the rear of the vessel, while the two fit bargemen went to the bow.

'What do I do?' said Constans, as he picked up a bargepole.

'You keep us from colliding with the bank, lad,' said the tiller man. 'The current can be strong, and there's always the risk that we'll drift to one side or the other. If you see that happening, use the pole to push us back out into the middle of the river.'

Mor Galthide sat down on the deck, his clothes smeared in browns and dark reds.

'Do you trust us now, big guy?' said the tiller man.

Mor Galthide eyed him, but said nothing.

'How frequent are these attacks?' said Abigone.

'It depends how many barges are in a convoy,' the tiller man said. 'Large, well-armed convoys are rarely attacked. Those bastards probably saw us a few days ago, and raced ahead to prepare the stakes. They must have thought we were an easy target.'

'Ignorant were they of my presence on board,' said Mor Galthide. 'They will not have a chance to make the same mistake.'

The tiller man rolled his eyes. 'Who are you? Actually, I don't want to know. The sooner you are off my boat, the better.'

Abigone sat down close to where Denny was standing.

'What is Steppen like?' she said to the tiller man.

He eyed her up and down. 'A young woman like you shouldn't be going to a place like Steppen; that's all I'll say.'

'What choice do we have?' said Abigone. 'Four of our friends are being taken there against their will. They're only fourteen years old.'

'Then, as cruel as it might sound, I would have mourned them as already dead, girl. No one who goes into that place comes out alive.'

'You do,' she said. 'The bargemen pass through all the time.'

'No, we don't. We unload our supplies after the cranes have moved our vessels down the side of the cliff, then we pick up the silver and punt round the edges of the temple – we never go inside. Your four friends are gone.'

'I refuse to accept that.'

'Clearly. It's a shame, though – a group of young folk like you? You'll be eaten alive.'

'Why are you trying to frighten us?' said Raewyn.

'Because it's not too late. There is a path through the forest that leads down the cliffs without you having to go into Steppen. It's a dangerous route, but it's the one I recommend.'

'Why are you telling us this now?' said Abigone.

'I was greedy, and I wanted the gold you were paying for this trip,' he said. 'But now? After seeing the way you lot dealt with those brigands, I'm starting to feel sorry for you. We'll run close to one of those paths I was talking about around sunrise tomorrow morning. If you like, I can drop you off there.'

'That might not be such a bad idea,' said Denny.

Abigone narrowed her eyes at him. 'I can't believe you just said that.'

'I'm not thinking of abandoning Reath and the others,' Denny went on, 'but this other way might allow us to sneak up on Steppen. We would be able to avoid the cranes, which I am guessing will be guarded.'

'You guess correctly,' said the tiller man. 'There are usually about thirty or so mercenaries up by the cranes, along with a few dozen slaves who operate the machines. We all have to step onto dry land, then the barges are searched before the cranes lower them down to the ground below. In other words, if we reach the cranes, and you're still on board, there will be no way to escape.'

'How difficult is the climb down the cliffs if we take the other path?' said Abigone.

'It's not too bad if you're fit and strong,' he said. 'Unfortunately, girl, not all of your party are fit and strong.'

Abigone chewed her lip, then she glanced at Fyenna, Mor Galthide and Lothar.

'We need a new plan,' she said, 'and we have until dawn to come up with it.'

CHAPTER 6
WAY STATION

Great Forest, Northern Yearl, Central Provinces – 25th Day of Minula 108

Saffie dreamed that she was lost in the Great Forest. Something was hunting her, and she was running through the trackless wilderness, but her legs weren't moving properly, and her pursuer was getting closer. She glanced over her shoulder, and her dream changed. In an instant, she had forgotten everything about the forest, and she remembered she was in the Palace of Adriano upon Sanctos – the largest and grandest of the imperial residences. Emperor Antonio and his wife Empress Aurora were staring down at Saffie from their thrones, their features stern and unyielding.

Saffie found that she was carrying a silver tray, and she recalled that she was supposed to be bringing wine to Their Imperial Majesties; only, she had neglected to collect the wine, and she would be punished. Saffie turned away, so they wouldn't see what she was about to do.

Saffie raised her right hand.

'Use the evil within me, blessed spirits,' she said, 'to summon two cups of poison that look and taste like wine.'

Two cups appeared on the tray, both filled with a smoking,

bubbling liquid of dark red. Saffie turned back to the twin thrones, and offered her sovereigns a cup each. The emperor reached out and took one, then the empress did the same.

Saffie watched in silent terror as they gazed into the cups. They would notice. Real wine didn't bubble like that, and Saffie would be executed for being a vile Maker. She longed for them to take a sip; she yearned to watch them suffer and die. She hated them. How dare they betroth her to her cousin Arturo; they hadn't even asked her first if she liked him. They had, instead, announced it casually one day, as though they had expected Saffie to be pleased with their decision.

Antonio lifted his cup and drank, then Aurora did the same. Their faces turned green, and they began screaming in agony. Soldiers hurried into the grand audience chamber, just as the emperor and his wife fell from their thrones.

'There is a Maker in the palace!' Saffie cried. 'Kill her!'

Saffie's eyes shot open, the words *Kill her* reverberating around her head. She sat up in the back of the moving wagon, panting and trembling. It was still dark outside, and Agent Marco of the Offices of Purgation was wrapped up in blankets next to her in the back of the covered wagon. Saffie watched his chest rise and fall for a moment, then she turned to the driver's bench. Captain Zola was sitting there, along with a soldier from the imperial army. They were guiding the wagon along an unpaved, overgrown track that ran to the left of the river, deep within the Great Forest. Saffie rubbed her eyes, trying to dispel the fear the dream had inspired. Once again, she had dreamed of being a Maker, and, once again, she had murdered the emperor. What did it mean?

She was angry about her betrothal, but that didn't translate into a desire to kill the sovereign ruler of the empire. Saffie was loyal. She would fight and die for the empire; she would cut down its enemies, and she would do her duty. She had never disobeyed an order – the very idea made her feel sick; so why did she keep dreaming about slaying Antonio? And why was she always a Maker in those dreams?

Zola turned. 'Ahh, you're awake, ma'am,' he said. 'If you can't sleep, come up here and join us.'

Saffie stared at him for a moment before she realised that he had really spoken.

Zola frowned. 'Rough night, ma'am?'

'I had a nightmare about being lost in the forest,' she said, 'and I am feeling a little disorientated.'

'Not to worry, ma'am,' Zola said, 'the Great Forest can have that effect.'

She pulled the blanket from her shoulders and folded it up next to the sleeping agent. Zola and the soldier moved along the driver's bench to create some room for her, and she climbed out of the back of the wagon and sat down next to them. She narrowed her eyes at the condition of the track they were on.

'Yesterday evening,' she said, 'we were on a wide, paved road, and now I can barely see any sign of one at all.'

'It is in a bad state of repair,' said Zola, 'and it gets worse the further north we go. A few miles from here, it stops altogether, and we shall have to continue on foot.'

'Are we that close to the border of Jallin?'

'We are, ma'am,' said Zola. 'We shall rest for a day and a night at the frontier post, and then carry on tomorrow morning.'

Saffie glanced up at the sky to their right. It was brightening over the treetops, and a wind was blowing the clouds to the west. She turned her head, and looked back at the route they had taken. The other wagons were stretched out in a line behind them, and each one was filled with soldiers, weapons and supplies. The trees on the left-hand side of the wagons were encroaching on to the track; their long branches reaching out to cover the wagons, as though they were fingers trying to pluck them from the road. Saffie turned again, and looked down at the river. Its surface was glistening in the reflected light of the full Silver Moon, which lay over the horizon ahead of them. The current of the river looked strong, and any branches that had fallen from the trees were being carried swiftly downstream.

'What are our tactics?' she said.

Zola eyed her. 'Regarding what, ma'am?'

'Well, say we find this Whalebone King, and say we discover proof that he is, in fact, a Master – how do we intend to take care of the situation?'

Zola smiled. 'A crossbow bolt to the back of the head should suffice, ma'am,' he said.

'That's not exactly what I meant,' she said. 'If he can kill with a gesture, how do we get close enough to loose a bolt?'

Zola said nothing for a moment, then he gazed down at the rough track. 'Have you read the Doctrine of the Offices of Purgation in its entirety, ma'am?'

'No, not in its entirety,' she said. 'It is several hundred pages long.'

'There is a small section near the end of the Doctrine that discusses the question you raised,' Zola went on. 'It provides guidelines on how to act when faced with a suspected Master or Maker who might have the potential to kill. The Doctrine states that it is better to strike without warning, even if we occasionally target the wrong person. In other words, ma'am, we will not be wasting any time trying to gather evidence. We already have the eyewitness account of that Jallian bargeman. If we see the Whalebone King, we are permitted to kill him on sight. If it turns out that he was a Master, then we shall be rewarded. If it turns out that the bargeman was lying, and we have killed an innocent man, then the Doctrine will defend us from prosecution. We need only have a reasonable suspicion in order to act decisively.'

Saffie frowned. 'How many innocent people have the Offices of Purgation killed?'

'Altogether? That would be hard to say. Personally, I have witnessed or been involved in three cases of mistaken identity. The worst one concerned an old woman in Campsie, whose village neighbours had sworn was a Maker. They provided signed testimony, so we sent a squad to arrest her. She resisted arrest, and the old woman was slain by our forces. It was only afterwards that one of the neighbours confessed to the deception. It turned out that the woman's neighbours had been holding a grudge against her for years, and they used the Offices of Purgation to eliminate her. Five of the neighbours were hanged for that. It was a distressing case, and one that the Offices of Purgation need to learn from. However, in the grand scheme of things, such a case should not distract us from the noble work we do. If we execute one innocent for every ten Masters and Makers we successfully eliminate, then any mistakes, however tragic, are justified by the Doctrine.'

Saffie said nothing.

'Do you agree with my conclusion, ma'am?' said Zola.

'Yes,' she said, without knowing if it was true or not. 'My exalted grandfather approved the Doctrine, so it cannot be wrong.'

Zola nodded. 'To return to your original question – our tactics are simple. As soon as we reach the silver mine, we hunt down and slay the Whalebone King without hesitation. We are also permitted to kill any who try to stop us.'

'He has mercenaries to protect him.'

Zola smiled. 'Soldiers from the imperial army are far superior to any rabble of hired swords, ma'am. Remember that I have questioned many bargemen over the last couple of years. Do you know what they have said about these mercenaries? They were unanimous in their scorn. According to them, the mercenaries are cruel, rapacious, corrupt and lazy. All they do is bully and harass the slaves who work in the mine. They have neglected their training, and are ill-disciplined and out-of-shape. If they try to oppose us, we shall cut them down. Does that satisfy you?'

Saffie nodded.

'Our biggest concern is an economic one,' Zola went on.

'How so?'

'The silver mine supplies bullion for the mints of both Elestia and Jalburg,' he said. 'The Whalebone King has a well-earned reputation for paying his taxes on time. Of course, if he is indeed a Master, then it is in his interests to do so. This has prevented us from taking action against him in the past, as neither the Yearlian nor the Jallian governments wished to disrupt the steady flow of silver. Now that Yearl is a province of the empire, the Offices of Purgation have overruled such qualms; but we would do well to leave the silver mine as a functioning enterprise.'

'How will we do that if we kill Hemming and the mercenaries?'

'If all goes well, we shall send a message to Elestia, requesting a permanent garrison to guard the mine.'

'But the mine is in Jallin, and Jallin is not yet a part of the empire.'

'We shall say that we have taken the mine under our protection, as the Jallians have proved unable to do so. The government in Jalburg will protest, but what can they do about it? We shall mollify them by ensuring that the silver continues to flow into their coffers.' He eyed her. 'Of course, there is another, more cynical approach to this. If, say, the silver mine was put out of action, then the treasury of Jallin would begin to suffer from a shortage of coin. This would put immense pressure on their government, pressure that could be alleviated if Jallin decided to formally join the empire.'

'Are you in favour of such an approach?' said Saffie.

Zola smiled. 'Did I say that, ma'am? It is merely one of many possibilities. Our priority is to destroy the Whalebone King – the political consequences can be dealt with afterwards.'

'We are approaching the way station, sir,' said the soldier holding the reins.

Zola and Saffie peered through the dim light. Ahead of them, a tall, wooden structure was emerging from the pre-dawn gloom. It was sitting next to the overgrown path, nestled on the banks of the river. A few short piers were protruding out from a wooden wharf, where two long barges were tied up. More details came into focus as the lead wagon got closer. The building was four storeys high, and the top two floors had wide balconies overhanging the river. The structure was also old and rickety, as though it had not been maintained in a long time.

'The Yearlians built this two decades ago,' Zola said, 'to replace a ruined border station from the time of the Elestian Empire. Its purpose is to monitor any cross-border traffic coming down the river, and to provide supplies and shelter to travellers. It houses a small garrison of Yearlian militia, and a few border officials. Beyond lies Jallin.'

'Does the road end here?'

'It does,' he said. 'The Jallians have never felt the need to build any roads in this part of the Great Forest. If we seize the silver mine, we shall have to correct that mistake.'

The lead wagon began to grind to a halt on the track. There was a large space to the left of the building that seemed designed to provide space for several wagons to park, but it was overgrown, and the forest was starting to encroach upon it. Behind the lead wagon, the others also came to a halt, and a few soldiers jumped down to the ground to see what was happening. In the back of the lead wagon, Agent Marco was beginning to stir, and Zola eyed him.

'Wake up, Marco,' he said. 'We are at the border.'

Zola climbed down to the track, then he extended a hand for Saffie. She didn't need it, but took it out of politeness, and she stepped down next to the captain.

A door in the building opened, and two dishevelled militiamen stepped outside, looking as though they had just awoken.

'Who's there?' cried one, then they saw the Sanctian uniforms, and their eyes widened.

One of the men darted back inside the building, as the other stood frozen to the track.

'Good morning,' said Zola, as he walked forwards.

Saffie kept pace with him, and several soldiers from the other wagons joined them as they walked up to the building.

'A message was sent ahead of us,' Zola went on. 'Was it not received? Were you not aware that we were coming?'

The dishevelled man stared at them, then Saffie noticed that he stank of alcohol.

'Well?' said Zola. 'Answer me.'

'I, uh... we...' muttered the man.

Zola frowned and shook his head. 'Are you on duty this morning?'

he said. 'Have you been drinking? Why is your uniform filthy? Where is your superior officer? Come to attention when you speak to me.'

The man tried to straighten his back, and he raised a weak salute.

'You are a disgrace,' said Zola. 'To which unit do you belong?'

'I am in the Twelfth Battalion of Foot, sir,' said the man.

'Yearlian militia?' said Saffie.

'Yes, ma'am.'

'Amateurs,' said Zola.

Another man emerged from the building. He was still fastening the buttons on his shirt, but his shoulders held the insignia of a lieutenant in the militia of Yearl.

'Are you in charge of this way station?' said Zola.

The lieutenant blinked, and gazed around at the wagons and soldiers.

'You're early,' he muttered. 'I mean, sir. We weren't expecting you for another couple of days.'

'Are you in charge?' Zola repeated.

'Yes, sir. My name is Lieutenant Werven of the Twelfth Battalion of...'

'Yes, we know which unit is stationed here,' said Zola. 'Well, well, so this is the situation on the border, eh? What a mess. Is it normal practice to allow those on duty to get drunk, Lieutenant, or are you a particularly incompetent officer?'

'We... we didn't think you were coming today, sir. You have caught us a little off guard.'

'So I see, but you didn't answer my question.' He gestured to the other soldier. 'This man is clearly intoxicated, and yet he seems to have been on duty. How do you explain this?'

'I can only apologise, sir,' said Werven.

'Summon the entire garrison,' said Zola. 'I want them all lined up outside within the next five minutes. Get to it.'

'Yes, sir.'

The lieutenant hurried back into the building, leaving the drunken soldier staring at the ground.

Zola gestured to one of his sergeants. 'Give this man a damn good beating,' he said. 'He has shamed his uniform. Make an example of him.'

The sergeant saluted. 'Yes, sir.'

He pointed at a few other Sanctian soldiers, and they approached the drunken guard from all sides.

'Wait,' cried the Yearlian, then the fists began to fly. One of the soldiers produced a baton, and he brought it down on the back of the militiaman's head, knocking him to the ground. The soldiers switched to using their boots, and they stamped and kicked him until he lay still. Saffie watched, saying nothing. Part of her felt sorry for the Yearlian militiaman, but if he was drunk while on duty, then he deserved what he got. The Sanctians pulled back at a signal from the sergeant, and they left the militiaman unconscious and bleeding on the ground.

The main entrance of the building opened wide, and a double column of bleary-eyed militia soldiers began to troop out into the growing light of dawn. They saw the body of their comrade lying next to the track and, while none spoke, they all stared. The lieutenant joined them, and he also stared at the fallen militiaman. By the lead wagon, Agent Marco of the Offices of Purgation stepped down to the ground, his eyes bleary. He yawned, and took his place by the side of Zola and Saffie.

'Is this the full garrison, Lieutenant Werven?' said Zola.

'Yes, sir,' he said, 'apart from two in the sick bay, sir. There are also four customs officials in the building. Shall we summon them also?'

Zola frowned as he eyed the two dozen Yearlian militiamen assembled in front of the building. Several looked ill, and Saffie wondered if they were suffering from hangovers or something worse. At that moment, the sun began to rise, and the sky brightened up overhead. Forest birds called out in the morning light, a loud chorus to greet the dawn.

'Sir?' said Werven.

Zola shook his head. 'The civilians can continue to rest,' he said. 'I must say, Lieutenant, that I am extremely disappointed by the slovenly manner in which your garrison is arrayed. Mismatched uniforms, a lack of equipment... some of these men are missing their boots. Is this how you have been conducting your duties?'

'We were stationed here eight months ago, sir,' said Werven, 'and, apart from a few postal deliveries, you are the first visitors we have had coming up from the south. Normally, we see no one for many long days at a time; no one apart from the monthly convoy of barges that come downstream from the silver mine. There is nothing to do here, sir, and I'm afraid that discipline can be hard to maintain in such conditions.'

'If no one has been here from the south,' said Zola, 'then from where do you obtain alcohol?'

'The barges deliver it, sir.'

'The barges from the silver mine?'

'Yes, sir.'

'I see. Apart from the alcohol, do you accept other bribes from the bargemen?'

'Bribes, sir?'

'Do you think I am naïve? There have been several cases recently when the barges from the silver mine have turned up in Elestia loaded with contraband goods – goods that this border post is supposed to confiscate. Now, at last, I understand the reason for this lapse.'

'But, sir...'

'Silence, Lieutenant. Have your rabble unload the wagons. Feed and water the horses, and find them shelter. Prepare food for my soldiers, and accommodation for the coming night.'

'Yes, sir,' said Werven. He turned to the militiamen. 'Unload the wagons and bring everything inside. Now!'

The Sanctians soldiers stood by as the militiamen made their way towards the wagons. A few militiamen hurried in the direction of their beaten comrade, but Sanctions blocked their path.

'Leave him where he fucking lies,' growled a sergeant, 'you useless Yearlian gobshites.'

The militiamen backed away.

'How many soldiers have you brought, sir?' said Werven.

'A hundred and twenty,' said Zola, 'along with three agents from the Offices of Purgation, including myself. We shall require our own rooms.'

Werven's gaze went to Saffie. 'Yes, sir,' he said. 'Shall I show you, the lady, and the other agent to your quarters?'

A lieutenant from the Sanctian army had been appointed to lead the detachment of one hundred and twenty soldiers, and Zola gestured for him to approach.

'I'm leaving you in charge, Aldo,' Zola said. 'Make sure my orders are carried out while Lieutenant Werven takes us inside.'

Aldo saluted. 'Yes, sir.'

Werven gestured towards the entrance, then he hesitated 'Do I have permission to take the injured man to the sick bay, sir?'

'No,' said Zola. 'Let him lie here as a warning to the others.'

'But his wounds look severe, sir. He may die if left untreated.'

'He may. Proceed.'

Werven bowed his head as though he wished to hide his growing anger, then he gestured towards the building again. 'Come with me, if you please.'

The three Sanctians followed Werven into the dark interior of the building. Many of the wooden beams and planks were warped, and some were starting to rot. They went up a creaky staircase, and passed empty barrack rooms lined with bunk beds, then they ascended to a higher level, where the air seemed a little cleaner.

'This is where the customs officials and I sleep, sir,' Werven said. 'The guest accommodation is on the floor above, but there are only six rooms. Your soldiers will have to share the barracks we passed. The dining facilities are also on this floor, and we shall prepare a suitable breakfast for you and your detachment.'

Saffie gazed at the mess. 'I assume you would have cleaned this place had we arrived when you expected us to, Lieutenant?'

'Of course, my lady,' said Werven. 'I apologise unreservedly for the current state of the building.'

'It has been a long journey from Elestia,' Saffie went on, 'and I would very much like to avail myself of your bathroom facilities. Where may I find them?'

'There, uh, there are no bathroom facilities, my lady,' Werven said.

'Then where do your men wash?'

'In the river, my lady. Only, you must wash upstream of the piers.'

'Why?'

'Because, my lady, downstream is where… is where the men relieve themselves.'

Zola's eyes glimmered with rage. 'This is unacceptable,' he cried. 'Her ladyship cannot be expected to perform her business out in the open like an animal.'

'I'll manage,' said Saffie. 'After all, it's what we've been doing on the way here. I did not accompany you on this expedition because of the comfortable facilities. We have a job to do, and I am prepared to be inconvenienced.'

'About that,' said Werven. 'Might I be told the purpose of your expedition? The note we received did not specify anything.'

Zola narrowed his eyes. 'Surely you can guess. Why do you think the Offices of Purgation are here?'

'Then you intend to enter Jallin, sir?' said Werven. 'I, too, have heard the rumours about the Whalebone King. However, there is no evidence that he is a Master. As far as I can tell, it remains nothing but idle bargemen gossip. Furthermore, by entering Jallin, you would be in breach of the empire's treaty with that nation, and I shall have to report this to the relevant authorities.'

Zola laughed out loud, and Werven took a step back.

'Did you hear that?' Zola cried. 'He is going to report us! Maybe I should also report you, Werven. You have been taking bribes from the silver mine; you have allowed your men to get drunk while on duty; need I go on? Let's take it to a court martial. I am a captain in the Offices of Purgation – who do you think the court will believe? Regardless, by the time we have reached our destination, the Jallians will only just be learning of our incursion into their territory. If they wish to evict us from the silver mine, they are most welcome to try.'

Werven said nothing for a while, then he lowered his gaze. 'Follow me.'

He led them into a dining room set out with a few long tables. It had open windows that faced east, and the morning sunshine was dispelling the gloom.

'Please sit,' said Werven. 'Food will be here shortly. I shall have your luggage taken up to your rooms.'

The three Sanctians sat down as Lieutenant Werven left the room.

'Can you believe the gall of that man?' said Zola. 'Imagine threatening agents from the Offices of Purgation.'

Marco shrugged his broad shoulders. 'He's Yearlian, sir; and if he's been here for eight months, then Yearl was not part of the empire when he first arrived at this forsaken place.'

'Good point, Marco,' said Zola. 'He probably discovered that he had become a citizen of the empire by post. Still, that does not excuse the manner in which he has been leading this garrison. When we return to Elestia, we shall have to ensure that a decent company of Sanctians are sent here to take over this border station.'

'I heard, sir,' said Marco, 'that there is a Sanctian official based in the silver mine. Is that true?'

Zola frowned. 'When did you learn that?'

Marco looked away. 'I cannot recall, sir. Is it just a rumour?'

'Truth be told,' said Zola, 'we do not know for sure. It is a fact that a certain Lord Matteo was dispatched to the silver mine some twenty years ago. His job was to ensure that the silver continued to flow out of the forest. For the first ten years, he submitted regular reports on the status of the mine, assuring us that all was well, and then he went silent. He might be dead. In truth, I hope he is dead.'

'Why, sir?' said Marco.

'Because if he isn't, then he has aligned himself with the Whalebone King.'

'Have none of the bargemen seen him in that time?' said Saffie.

'The bargemen are not allowed into many areas of Steppen, ma'am. They see only what they are permitted to see, which is why we were very fortunate that our witness managed to get himself lost within the temple compound. If he had been caught, then I believe he would have been killed.'

'To which family does Lord Matteo belong?'

'He is a scion of the duchy of Trinitas, ma'am,' Zola said.

'Is he a relative of Princess Eleanor?'

'A distant cousin, I think, ma'am. If he has disgraced the family name, then he will no doubt be formally ostracised. Again, I hope that he died a loyal subject of the empire. The alternative is too appalling to contemplate.'

'I cannot believe that an aristocratic Sanctian would ever side with a disgusting Master,' said Saffie. 'He might be confined to a prison cell.'

'I doubt the Whalebone King would have kept him locked up for ten years, ma'am; I fear his rule is far more brutal than that.' Zola lowered his voice. 'If our worst fears are realised, and we do happen to find that Lord Matteo has succumbed to a life of corruption and disloyalty, we shall have to ensure two things – first, that we end his life; and second, that no word of this reaches his family on Sanctos. Let them believe that he died in service of the empire. We shall each swear to keep the sordid truth to ourselves.'

Two militiamen walked into the room bearing baskets of food. They set them down onto the table without a word. One of them took a flagon from a basket, and arranged cups in front of the three Sanctians.

'What's in the flagon?' said Marco.

'Water, sir,' said the militiaman; 'from the river.'

Saffie narrowed her eyes at the low quality of the food on offer. There was some tired-looking salted ham, a few blocks of sweating cheese, a dozen brown apples, and a loaf of bread that looked tough enough to break teeth.

'I'm not eating this muck,' said Zola, 'nor will I be drinking any river water that I haven't seen being collected with my own eyes. Take it all away, and have some of the food from the wagons brought up to us; at once. Ensure that you include a decent bottle of wine from my personal supply.'

'Yes, sir.'

They picked up the flagon and the baskets and walked from the room.

Zola smiled. 'It appears that we Sanctians have annexed Yearl just in time. Any longer, and they would have drifted into barbarity.'

CHAPTER 7
RUNT OF THE LITTER

Steppen, Great Forest, Jallin, Central Provinces – 25th Day of Minula 108

Magnus lifted his head as a scream arose from somewhere outside the Temple of Steppen. He got up from his bed, walked to one of his windows, and opened the badly-fitting wooden shutters. He glanced down past the intricately carved exterior of the temple, and saw three mercenaries beating a slave with sticks. The slave was lying on a path with his arms over his head, and he was crying out as the soldiers brought their clubs down. Blood leaked out from several wounds, pooling on the neat path that led to the shanty settlement. The cries faded, then the slave fell silent. The soldiers leaned over, then they dragged the man towards a low bridge that went over one of the many channels formed by the waterfalls. They crouched over the unconscious slave, blocking Magnus's view, then one drew a sword. The heavy blade was brought down a few times, then the slave's severed head was lifted by the hair. The body was kicked into the channel, where the current began to carry it downstream, then the head was impaled onto one of the spikes that ran along the side of the bridge. The head was turned so that it faced the shanty settlement where the slaves lived, then the three soldiers walked off as though nothing had happened.

Magnus kept his gaze on the bridge for a moment. A large crow from the forest swooped down to investigate. It alighted onto the head, then began to peck leisurely at the slave's eyes, as blood dripped down onto the bridge.

Magnus tried to imagine what offence the slave had committed. It couldn't have been too serious, as the soldiers hadn't tortured or mutilated him first; in fact, as deaths in Steppen went, his had been mercifully quick. Male slaves who had broken into the female slaves' quarters were routinely castrated before death, so that could also be ruled out. Perhaps he had taken more food than he was due, or maybe he had spoken back to one of the mercenaries. Magnus walked to his bed and sat down. He was supposed to be practising his Master powers, but he had found it impossible to transform anything that day, and he wondered what he was doing wrong. Twelve days had passed since he had managed to prove his abilities to Ragnvald, and in that time Magnus's list of successful transformations was pitifully short. He had managed to change some wood into metal again, twice, but both attempts had only partly worked. He had also been able to turn some water a tiny bit salty, but the difference was so slight as to be almost unnoticeable.

The front door of his quarters opened without anyone knocking, and Erling walked in.

'Get up, you lazy bastard,' Erling said.

'You're supposed to knock before coming in,' said Magnus. 'These are my private quarters.'

Erling unleashed a slap, and the back of his hand cracked against Magnus's face, knocking him off the bed. Magnus fell onto the floor, and Erling kicked him in the ribs.

'What was that, you little wanker?' Erling said. 'Did you say something?'

Magnus groaned in pain.

'The boss wants you,' Erling went on.

Magnus didn't respond.

Erling opened his mouth, and spat down onto his younger half-brother. 'Did you hear me?'

'Fuck off.'

Erling raised a boot, and pushed it down onto Magnus's chest, pinning him to the floor.

'Do you think Einar and I give a shit that you might be a Master?' Erling said. 'Well, do you? It makes no fucking difference to me; you're still a weak little runt. Get up, or I might pay your mother a visit.'

Erling removed his foot, and Magnus pulled himself upright, his ribs burning with pain.

'That's better,' said Erling. 'The boss is up on the roof, in his usual place. He's expecting you.'

Erling turned and walked from the chamber, leaving the door wide open. A couple of mercenaries were on duty in the corridor outside, and they smirked at the pain Magnus was in. All three of Magnus's half brothers were tall and well-built; compared to them, Magnus looked like a mere boy. He wiped the spittle from the front of his clothes, smothered the pain, and walked out of his quarters. He closed the door, and made his way towards the nearest stairwell.

He would kill Erling one day; and Einar, too. Not for anything they had ever done to him, though they had done much, but for the times they had beaten his mother for no reason other than the fact that Magnus was her son. They knew he loved her; it was his weak point, the gap in his armour that they liked to exploit. In many ways, life would be easier for Magnus if he hated his mother; then, his half brothers wouldn't be able to keep him so tightly under their control. If he was ever too defiant, then all they had to do was threaten his mother, and he would fall back into line. If Magnus was truly ruthless, he wouldn't care what they did to her, but he wasn't built that way.

He found the stairs and ascended a few floors of the temple, until he reached the open air of the multi-layered roof. He walked between two rows of carved pinnacles, and climbed more steps to a higher level. The Whalebone King was sitting in his favourite spot. A Westlander slave was wafting air into his face with a large fan, while another was bathing his feet in a pewter basin. Lord Matteo was sunning himself on a reclining chair next to the king with a glass of wine in his hand, and a few soldiers were dotted around, keeping watch over the roof.

Magnus approached his father and bowed low.

'You took your time,' said Hemming. 'I dispatched Erling to summon you almost an hour ago.'

'Sorry, sir.'

Hemming gestured to an empty chair. 'Sit.'

Magnus sat on the chair. He caught the gaze of one of the slaves for a moment, and recognised her from the women's quarters within the palace. They quickly looked away from each other.

'I wanted to talk to you, son,' Hemming went on. 'It strikes me that I hardly know you. Were you aware that I had originally planned for your mother to provide me with more children, but I could barely stand to be in her company? I would like a few more sons, but not from her. When the new Westlander slaves arrive, I will be sure to select the one I think will give me the strongest boys.'

Magnus said nothing.

'Do you plan to father a few of your own when you get your Westlander slave?'

'I don't know, sir.'

'I don't want you having any girls, is that clear? Drown them at birth. Sons only. Right; where shall we start? Tell me about your ambitions, Magnus.'

'I'm not sure I understand the question, sir.'

'I won't be alive forever,' said the Whalebone King. 'When I finally go, you will have to act quickly if you wish to survive. Let's face it – you shall never be king. You are far too weak, and your half brothers are strong. Ragnvald will likely win any struggle, so here is my advice – stay close to your eldest brother. Try to be useful to him, so that he might keep you alive when he becomes king. You need to be thinking about these things.'

'You have many years left to live, sir.'

'Maybe. You know, before I discovered that you were a Master, I hadn't given your future a single thought. But now I see that I will have to guide you into adulthood. What can you do? Can you fight?'

Magnus shook his head.

'Have you been practising your abilities?'

'Yes, sir. Every day, just like you said. I turned water salty.'

'Good lad. Enough to kill a man?'

'I'm not sure, sir.'

'Don't be shy about experimenting on a few slaves, son. Pick the ones who are old or injured, though; there's no point in culling the able-bodied. That will give you an idea if you are progressing.'

'I am finding it difficult to concentrate, sir,' he said. 'What should I think about when I am trying to transform a substance?'

'You should be thinking of nothing; has no one ever told you that? Clear your head of thoughts, and your abilities will work better. It can take time to get it right, but you are still only... only... Damn it – how old are you?'

'Seventeen, sir.'

'Still young. You have plenty of time. I will protect you for as long I remain alive, and then you will be on your own. That's why I am advising you to make an alliance with Ragnvald. So, what kind of things do you like to do in your spare time?'

Magnus suppressed a look of astonishment that almost crept over his face. His father had never shown any interest in him, and yet there he was, asking him questions about his life. Should he be pleased? Perhaps, but Magnus would have preferred to have remained anonymous.

'I like to read, sir, and...'

'Read? *Read?* Read what?'

'Books, sir. There are a few books in the women's quarters, and I sometimes borrow them.'

'And who taught you to read? Wait – let me guess. It was your damnable mother, wasn't it? Tell me, lad – what is the point of reading? If you want to hear a story, ask one of my old crewmates to tell you one. They know more about the world than any damn book. If you want news, ask me or Ragnvald. There is no need to read anything; it's a complete waste of time. At one point, I was in charge of eight vessels plying the ocean, and I've never read a book in my entire life. Can you write, too?'

'Yes, sir; I can.'

The king groaned.

Matteo laughed from his reclining chair. 'At least you have one studious child, Your Majesty. Young Magnus has picked up some useful skills.'

'Shut up, you Sanctian wanker,' said Hemming. 'Your ability to read and write is the only reason I haven't killed you, Matteo; but now I know that Magnus could sign and check the silver receipts, I might decide that you are expendable.' He turned back to his son. 'All right, Magnus; here are some more suitable ways to pass the time – sword practice, swimming, hunting in the forest with spears and bows, climbing, running, boxing, wrestling. You need to bulk up, lad, like my other sons. The Westlander slaves look at you and think how easy it would be to overpower you. You're too thin, and you need more muscle on you. Stop reading, and start doing all the things I just mentioned, and that's an order.'

'Yes, sir.'

'I'll speak to Ragnvald, and get him to take you out into the forest on a hunting trip. Use the time to ingratiate yourself with your brother.'

'Mightn't Ragnvald see me as a rival Master, sir?'

'You are far too pathetic for Ragnvald to consider you a rival in any field, lad. But it's not too late. Start the training regime, and you'll fill out in no time. If you show promise, then Ragnvald might begin to see you as an ally against your other brothers.'

'Wouldn't it be easier, sir, if you were to appoint a successor?'

'The next king after me needs to be the strongest of my litter, and I want Einar and Erling to think they have a chance to rule. If I was to proclaim Ragnvald as my successor, then I would have to kill the other two lads to stop them rebelling, and that would be a shame.' He glanced down at the slave washing his feet. 'That's quite enough of that. Dry them off, and then rub some oil into them.'

'Yes, my lord,' she said.

Magnus watched in silence as the woman lifted the king's feet out of the basin and set them down onto a thick towel. She moved the basin to the side, and began to dry Hemming's feet. The old man smiled, then he picked up a glass of wine and drained it.

'I think we've made a good start, lad,' he said. 'I know a bit more about you, and we've agreed a training plan to get you fit and strong. The next thing I want to know about is your loyalty.'

'I am loyal to you, sir.'

Hemming waved him away. 'Mere words. Anyone can claim to be loyal – it's actions that count. Now, what could I ask you to do to prove your loyalty?' He gestured towards Lord Matteo. 'If, for example, I asked you to kill that worthless piece of Sanctian trash, would you do it?'

Magnus blinked. 'Yes, sir.'

Hemming gestured to the slave drying his feet. 'What about her? Would you kill her?'

'Yes, sir.'

'Then do it. Strangle her.'

The slave glanced up, her eyes widening.

Magnus frowned. 'Now, sir?'

'Yes. Now. What are you waiting for?'

Magnus's face paled, then Hemming started to laugh.

'So, lad, you ain't that loyal,' the king said. 'I'm disappointed, but not surprised. I'll let you off with it this time, because you're new to this, but the next time I tell you to do something, you jump to it, no questions asked.'

'Yes, sir. Sorry, sir.'

'I don't ask for much,' Hemming went on, 'but I do expect my orders to be obeyed. Without that, this place would be anarchy.'

Several soldiers ascended the roof and bowed low before the king. In their midst was a man who looked like he had stepped off a Jallian barge.

Hemming narrowed his eyes. 'The next convoy isn't due for a couple of days.'

'They arrived early, boss,' said a soldier.

The bargeman edged forward. 'We made all possible speed, sir.'

'Why?' said the king.

'Because, sir, as well as the usual supplies, we have brought you some... cargo that I think you will be very interested in, sir.'

'What kind of cargo?'

'The human kind, sir.'

Hemming's frown deepened. 'Explain.'

'We picked up four youngsters from Jallin, sir. Two boys, two girls.'

'Westlanders?'

'No, sir.'

Hemming put a hand to his face. 'What are you trying to do to me? If the Jallian authorities hear about this, they'll send soldiers into the forest. What if their families are looking for them? We stopped raiding the countryside for slaves years ago. It's too much damn trouble. I'm going to have to slip the rulers of Jallin a fortune in silver to buy them off this time.'

'Please, sir,' said the bargeman; 'let me tell you a little more. The four youngsters were itinerant travellers – they were only passing through. None of them are locals, and none of them have any family in Jallin. I also know for a fact that the people they were with will not be reporting their disappearance to the authorities, because they are all on the run from the Sanctians. We had to snatch them quickly, which is another reason we're early this month.'

'Ages?'

'They are all fourteen years old, sir. You can have them for three thousand silver shillings each, or ten for all four.'

'Do you consider me a fool, Jallian? I'm not paying that price. I'll take the girls for five hundred apiece, and you can do what you like with the boys.'

'There is one more detail, sir – a detail that justifies the price I am setting.'

'Go on.'

The bargeman beamed. 'The boys are Masters, and the girls are Makers.'

Hemming's mouth fell open, and he sat upright on his chair.

'I can see why they are on the run from the Sanctians,' said Matteo. 'Where did you find them?'

'In a village along the route from Jalburg,' said the bargeman. 'We stop there to pick up the last of the supplies before entering the Great Forest. One of the girls has a loud mouth, and we overheard her bragging about being a Maker. They fled from Klef Mordain.'

'Where are they?' said Hemming.

'We are guarding them on the floor below us, sir,' said a soldier. 'The barges are currently being lowered to the bottom of the cliffs, but we thought it best to transport the captives directly here.'

'Bring them to me,' said the king. 'Wait. How good are they?'

The bargeman shrugged. 'We survived the entire journey here, sir, so none of them can be that good. The girls tried to summon things a few times, but nothing came out right. The boys are also pretty hopeless, but they're only fourteen.'

Hemming nodded, then he gestured to the soldiers. Two of them walked back to the stairs and disappeared from sight.

'Do we have a deal, sir?' said the bargeman. 'All four are healthy, and none of them were touched on the way here.'

Matteo frowned. 'Did you say that they were in the company of others?'

'I did.'

'Were those others also Masters and Makers?'

'I don't know. It's possible.'

'Possible?' said Matteo. 'And might they decide to come here to search for their missing fellows?'

The bargeman hesitated.

'Is that another reason you came as quickly as you could,' Matteo went on; 'so that you could avoid them catching up with you?'

'We didn't see any sign of pursuit.'

'Of course you didn't,' said Matteo, 'not at the speed you were going.' He turned to the king. 'We should be very careful, Your Majesty. The last thing we need is for a group of *possible* Masters and Makers to turn up at our door, demanding the return of their missing companions.'

Hemming rubbed his chin for a few moments, then whatever response he had planned was interrupted by the return of the soldiers, who were leading two boys and two girls across the roof. Each child had their wrists tied behind their backs, but none looked as though they had been beaten. Magnus sat forward on his chair, his eyes on the four children.

'Welcome to Steppen,' said the king. 'What are your names?'

None spoke.

'You will not be harmed if you answer my questions,' the king went on. He pointed at one of the girls. 'What is your name, red-haired lass?'

'Nyli,' she whispered.

'You are a very pretty girl, Nyli,' said the king. He looked at the other girl. 'What about you?'

'Piss off, you old pervert,' said the girl with black hair.

'See what I mean?' said the bargeman. 'That one has a mouth on her. I had to restrain a couple of my lads from slapping her about the face on the way here.'

'You are going to die for what you've done to us,' the dark-haired girl said to the bargeman.

'Why do you say that?' said Magnus.

The girl shrugged.

'Are your companions likely to come looking for you?' said Matteo.

'Yes,' said one of the boys, 'and they will kill you all. One of them is...'

'Tell them nothing,' said the other boy.

Hemming gazed at all four captives, then he stared at the last boy to speak. 'You will tell me your name, or your friends will suffer.'

'That is all I will tell you,' said the boy. 'My name is Ignatius.'

'And you?' he said to the other boy.

'Salus.'

'And, once again, I ask you, raven-haired girl. What is your name? You don't want Nyli to be hurt, do you? Your name; that's all.'

'It's Reath, you piece of shit.'

'Stop it,' said Nyli to the other girl. 'Stop provoking them.'

'I'm not cooperating,' said Reath. 'You three can do what you like, but I will never be a slave.'

Hemming laughed. 'Who said anything about being a slave? You are my guests.' He pushed away the woman drying his feet and stood. 'Guests require hospitality. Food, and somewhere nice and safe to sleep. I know just the place.' He glanced at Matteo. 'Find my other sons and tell them to meet us by the entrance to the women's quarters. Magnus, stand over here by me.'

Magnus got to his feet, as Lord Matteo hurried away.

'Wait,' said the bargeman. 'What about my money? Ten thousand shillings for all four. I went to a lot of trouble to snatch them, and I expect to be recompensed.'

'Just a moment,' said the king. He turned to face Magnus, then he slipped his son a knife from his robes, and leaned in close. 'Are you ready to prove your loyalty to me, son?'

'Yes, sir,' whispered Magnus.

'Kill that wretch, and throw his body from the temple.'

Magnus acted without thinking. He moved quickly, the knife in his right hand. He plunged the blade into the bargeman's stomach, then again into the side of his neck.

'And you said you couldn't fight, lad,' cried Hemming, as the bargeman fell onto the flat surface of the roof. 'Ragnvald couldn't have done a better job.'

Magnus passed his father the knife, then he kicked the bargeman, and rolled him off the edge of the roof. The man fell a hundred feet, then his body hit a gravel path. A few soldiers down on the ground glanced up at the roof, then they began to drag the body away. Magnus watched without feeling anything. The man he had killed had stolen four children from their friends, and had brought them to one of the most terrible places in the Central Provinces; for a man like that, Magnus had no sympathy.

'Was that your first, lad?' said his father, as they watched the bargeman's body being dumped in a river channel.

'No, sir.'

'I see. Perhaps I have been underestimating you a little. Tell me – why do you allow your brothers to bully you so?'

'There are three of them, sir, and only one of me.'

Hemming nodded, then he turned to the others. The four children were staring at Magnus, but Reath was doing so with a gleam in her eyes, as though she approved of the murder of the bargeman. Nyli and Salus looked terrified, while Reath and the other boy had remained calm.

'Shall we take a look at your luxurious new quarters, my guests?' said the king. He clicked his fingers at the soldiers, and they herded the four children towards the stairs. Hemming led the way with Magnus trailing a foot behind, and they made for the guarded women's quarters. Ragnvald and Erling were already there, with Lord Matteo close by.

Ragnvald opened his mouth to speak, then he noticed the presence of the new arrivals, and his eyes widened.

'We have four young guests,' said the king.

'Guests, boss?' said Erling.

'That's right – guests. Be sure to always refer to them by that name. Where is Einar?'

'He's out hunting in the forest, boss,' said Erling.

'That can't be helped, I suppose,' said Hemming. He glanced at Ragnvald. 'Did you know that Magnus is quite skilled with a knife?'

Ragnvald laughed, then he realised that his father was being serious. 'What? That useless little shitstain?'

'He isn't quite as useless as we had believed,' said the king. 'Open the door.'

The soldiers by the entrance to the women's quarters saluted, then they unlocked the door and pushed it open. Hemming walked inside, and the others followed. Five women were sitting in the large chamber immediately behind the door, and others could be heard talking in the neighbouring rooms. Seeing the king, the five women present got to their feet and bowed low.

The king gestured towards the four young Masters and Makers. 'These children shall be staying here with you for a while. You will care for them, and ensure that they are clean and well fed.'

More women appeared by the other entrances to the chamber, and they watched in silence as Nyli, Reath, Salus and Ignatius were herded forward.

'I know that it is unusual for boys to be living within these quarters,' Hemming went on, 'but they are only fourteen, and this is the safest place for them. Magnus, remain here to see that our guests settle in, while I speak to Ragnvald and Erling about the circumstances of their arrival.'

Magnus bowed his head. 'Yes, sir.'

Hemming smiled at the children. 'I do hope you enjoy your stay with us.'

The king turned, then they left the quarters, leaving Magnus with the four children. Magnus heard the door being locked, then he turned, and looked for his mother. Colette walked out from a doorway, her eyes narrow.

'New slaves?' she said.

'The king says they are his *guests*,' said Magnus.

A few of the women rolled their eyes. Some of them approached the new arrivals.

'Are you hungry?' said one. 'If not, we can run a bath for you. We have a nice bathroom up here, and there's hot water in the mornings.'

'What are their names?' said another.

Magnus pointed at each in turn. 'Salus, Reath, Nyli and Ignatius. The bargemen snatched them from a village in Jallin.'

Nyli sat down and started to cry. 'Is this our new prison?' she said.

'It's not exactly a prison,' said Magnus.

'Don't lie to them, son,' said Colette. 'It might be more comfortable than a prison, but the door is locked and the windows barred.' She turned to the children who were still standing. 'Sit, all of you, and we can talk about where you are, and what life is like here.'

Reath pointed at Magnus as they sat. 'I want that bastard out of here first,' she said.

'That *bastard* is my son,' said Colette.

'Your son?' said Reath. 'Why are you locked up if he isn't?'

'That is one of the things we shall explain to you,' said Colette.

'Magnus is the only gentleman among them,' said an older woman. 'Colette raised him well.'

'A gentleman?' said Nyli. 'He killed a bargeman right in front of us.'

Colette narrowed her eyes. 'Is that true, son?'

'It is, Mother,' said Magnus. 'I killed the man who stole them from the village.'

'Then he deserved it,' said Colette.

'I agree,' said Reath, 'but we can't trust him, even if he is your son. He was sitting next to the so-called king up on the roof.'

'Of course he was,' said Colette. 'The so-called king is his father. Magnus is as much a prisoner as the rest of us, except that he is allowed to wander the entire temple, while we are restricted to these rooms.'

'Is the king an evil man?' said Ignatius.

'He is as wicked as they come,' said Colette, 'and his three eldest sons take after him in every respect. I am sorry to have to tell you this, but you have arrived in a truly awful place. We will do all we can to protect you, but I cannot promise that things will turn out for the best.'

'Are you the leader here?' said Reath.

'That would be putting it too strongly,' said Colette. 'I am despised by the king and his older sons, and Magnus is the only reason I am still alive. My son, and the hate I bear towards the Whalebone King are all that sustains me. Now, let's start at the beginning; we have a lot to discuss.'

CHAPTER 8
THE HUNTED

Great Forest, South-Western Jallin, Central Provinces – 25th Day of Minula 108

Walter sat on the deck of the small barge and stared at the empty bottle of brandy.

'No matter how many times you look at it, sir,' said Otto, from where he was crouched by the tiller, 'that bottle will still be empty.'

Walter set the bottle down and rubbed his face. He was in a daze from another night of poor sleep on the riverboat. The constant movement, along with the lack of alcohol, had made him queasy and restless. He glanced towards the front of the barge, and saw Dietar standing with the long pole, waiting for Walter to relieve him.

'I'm coming,' said Walter, as he staggered to his feet.

'No offence, sir,' said Dietar, 'but you're not much of a waterman.'

'I have never claimed to be,' said Walter. 'Give me a horse and an open road; or a mountain track with a good pair of boots, and I'm as happy as the next man. But this?' He waved his hand at the river and the forest on either side. 'This isn't natural.'

'If Jallian peasants can manage it, sir,' said Dietar, 'then it should be no problem for the Mountain Rangers.'

Walter reached the front of the barge, and Dietar handed him the pole.

'Thank you, Lieutenant,' said Walter.

'Try not to fall in, sir,' said Dietar.

'And don't drop the bloody pole,' said Otto.

'Thank you for the advice, boys,' said Walter. 'We had a good run of it with Count Sebastian, but the holiday is well and truly over. Have a good rest, Dietar.'

'Thank you, sir,' said the lieutenant, then he disappeared down the hatch into the barge's only cabin.

Walter placed a boot on the bow to brace himself, then he leaned out with the pole, steering the craft away from a wild tangle of rushes that were spreading out from the bank on the left. They had been caught in the undergrowth several times over the previous six days aboard the barge, and had lost valuable time as a consequence. It would have been quicker and cheaper if they had paid professional bargemen to take them down the river on one of their larger craft, but Walter hadn't trusted any of them. Instead, he had bought their own barge, and the three Mountain Rangers were crewing it themselves.

'I reckon we're over half way, sir,' said Otto.

'I hope so,' said Walter, as he plunged the pole into the muddy depths again. The end of the pole found the bottom of the river, and the pressure applied by Walter kept the nose of the barge pointing in the right direction.

'At least the weather's holding up,' Otto went on. 'Back in Upper Down, the autumn rains will have started, and we would be freezing our arses off. It's quite mild down here.'

'Imagine doing this in the rain,' said Walter. He glanced up at the sky and watched a few white clouds being blown to the west. The barge began to drift to the left again, and Walter pulled his attention back to his job.

'What will we do when we find the princess, sir?' said Otto.

'That depends on a host of possibilities. We might need to help her look for the missing students; or she might have already found them. If she has found them, then I need to talk to her about where she intends to go next. Amery mentioned a place called Geathan, but I'm not familiar with it.'

'Neither am I, sir,' said Otto.

'I guess I should have looked at a few maps before we left Upper Down. Because we were travelling with Count Sebastian, and he knows every road in the Central Provinces, I didn't see any need.'

Otto gazed at the trees on either bank.

'This forest goes on forever,' he said. 'Six days of nothing but trees.'

'I heard it once covered the whole region of the Central Provinces,' said Walter. 'It was the Elestians who started cutting a lot of it down, when they were building their empire. It reached as far as Greater Down and the edge of the mountains.'

'And now the Sanctians will be cutting down more of it to construct their navy,' said Otto. 'One day, there might be none of it left.'

'That day is hundreds of years away,' said Walter. 'And who needs forests, anyway? They're bloody useless – a waste of good land. You can't farm it, and there's no food. I mean, how many damn trees do we need?'

'Watch out for that bend coming up, sir,' said Otto. 'The current looks strong by the right bank.'

Walter caught a glimpse of a few eddies by the undergrowth ahead and to their right, where the course of the river turned west.

'I see it,' he said, as he readied the pole.

The small barge began to speed up as it neared the bend, then, as it drifted towards the right bank, Walter dug the pole into the riverbed and corrected their course. He felt the muscles in his arms strain from the constant exercise. His back was aching a little from having to stoop with the pole, and he wished he was back on dry land. They followed the bend in the river, and cleared a patch of trees on their right. Just beyond, a dozen armed men were sitting or standing by the banks of the river, just a few yards away from the barge.

Walter and Otto stared at them, and the men stared back. One of the men reached for a crossbow, and the others began pointing and shouting at the barge. Walter dived to the deck as a crossbow bolt whistled past his head, and the barge was pulled closer to the armed men by the current. More bolts were loosed at them, then the barge moved past the men, the river carrying it further downstream. Walter gripped the pole, his eyes on the men as they slowly retreated into the distance, then the barge veered off towards the left bank as the river twisted again, and they crashed into and through a thick tangle of undergrowth. The barge was swallowed up amid the rushes and trailing branches, and it slowed to a halt.

'Shit,' muttered Walter. He ran to the rear of the barge, and then he and Otto peered through the undergrowth at the far bank, but the armed men were out of sight.

'Did they see us get caught up in the rushes?' said Walter.

'I don't think so, sir,' said Otto.

'That was my fault, Sergeant,' Walter went on; 'I wasn't guiding us with the pole.'

'We were being shot at, sir,' said Otto. 'I think the spirits will forgive you.'

Dietar poked his head out of the hatch, then he grimaced when he saw that they had stopped amid a wreath of thick undergrowth.

'How did we get caught up in this shit again?' he said.

'We passed a dozen men a few minutes ago,' said Otto, 'and they started loosing their crossbows at us.'

Dietar climbed up onto the deck and crouched by Walter and Otto.

'Armed men?' he whispered. 'Jallian militia?'

'They weren't wearing any standard type of uniform,' said Walter, 'and none of their weapons or armour matched; so, I would guess no would be the answer to that question. Maybe the silver mine sends out patrols.'

'I would guess that we are still a few hundred miles from the mine, sir,' said Dietar. 'That seems too far for a routine patrol.'

'Should we dig ourselves out of the rushes?' said Otto.

'Not yet,' said Walter. 'If they didn't see us going into the undergrowth, then they might walk right past us.' He glanced around the vessel. 'No one should be able to see us while we're stuck in here, but if we try to dislodge the barge, we'll make all kinds of noise. Let's remain quiet and still for a while longer.'

The three Mountain Rangers sat down on the deck, and broke out some food. The barge was stuck fast in the thick rushes, and Walter felt his queasiness fade as he ate.

'Do we still have plenty of supplies?' he said.

'Enough to get us all the way to Elestia, sir,' said Dietar, 'though we're likely to get a little bored of eating the same thing every day.'

'I'd rather boredom than starvation, Lieutenant,' said Walter. 'Perhaps we should load a couple of crossbows.'

'I have my short bow, sir,' said Dietar. 'I'll fetch it from below.'

The lieutenant disappeared down into the hatch, then he returned a few moments later, carrying his bow and a bundle of arrows. He removed the waterproof sheath from the bow, and then he strung it as the others kept watch on the far bank.

'I wonder if they were looking for someone,' said Otto. 'Chasing someone, perhaps. Is it possible that the four children who were abducted have freed themselves?

'It's possible, I suppose,' said Walter.

Dietar stretched the bowstring, and nodded. 'All done, sir. I'll stay up on deck for now, in case anyone approaches.'

The three men settled down, and waited. Walter kept his eyes on the position of the sun, and judged that an hour should suffice. When half of that time had elapsed, Otto tapped him on the shoulder.

'Movement, sir,' whispered the sergeant.

Walter squinted at the far bank, but saw nothing amid the trees.

'Not that way,' Otto said; 'on the near bank.'

Walter turned his head, and stared through the undergrowth at the bank where the barge had become snagged. A few branches were swaying, but there was no wind, then he heard something rustling.

'Get the bow ready, Dietar,' Walter whispered.

Otto pointed. 'There.'

Walter remained silent, his gaze on the trees, then he saw two figures creeping along the near bank. They flitted past a gap in the trees, and Walter got a brief look at them – a man and a woman, dressed in ragged clothing. They were unarmed, apart from a makeshift club being carried by the man; and they were both tall with fair hair.

'They look like Westlanders,' Walter whispered. 'What are Westlanders doing down here?'

'Escaping from those men, by the looks of it, sir,' whispered Otto.

'But they are on opposite sides of the river.'

'Shit,' said Dietar; 'they're coming towards us.'

'Stay low,' said Walter, 'and loose only if they attack.'

The three Rangers kept quiet as the man and the woman on the bank crept closer. The man was peering through the undergrowth, his eyes tight, while the woman kept looking over her shoulder, as though she feared pursuit. They pushed through some thick bushes, and came face to face with Walter and the others, with only a few feet separating them. The man came to an abrupt halt, then he saw Dietar's bow pointing at him.

'Stay where you are,' said Walter. 'We are not the ones hunting you.'

The woman turned, and stared at the barge. Her mouth opened to scream, then she caught herself.

'We are not your enemies,' Walter went on. 'We are looking for the silver mine.'

The man and the woman exchanged a brief glance, then they turned and bolted back through the forest, disappearing from sight.

Dietar lowered his arms and relaxed the bowstring. 'Did you see the state of them, sir? Both looked as though they were badly beaten not too long ago.'

'They ran as soon as I mentioned the mine,' said Walter.

'It strikes me, sir,' said Otto, 'that it's legal to own Westlanders as slaves down in this part of the Central Provinces. Maybe those two escaped from the mine, and the others are trying to drag them back.'

'Maybe,' said Walter. 'But what would a mine want with Abigone's fourteen-year-olds?'

'Small hands? Maybe the mine uses children to access areas the Westlanders can't get to.'

'That seems a stretch,' said Walter. 'It comes down to whether or not the folk who snatched them were aware that they were taking young Masters and Makers. If they knew, then the silver mine might be a distraction. What if they are taking the four children directly to Elestia, so they can hand them over to the Sanctians for a reward? If they don't know, then maybe the mine takes any and all slaves sent its way.'

'Here's a thought, sir,' said Dietar. 'What if we were to capture those two Westlanders and take them to the mine? We would be returning their property, and the owners of the mine might be more inclined to help us.'

Walter narrowed his eyes. 'As much as I loath the Westlanders,' he said, 'we won't be helping any slavers.'

'The Westlanders were more than happy to steal folk from all over the Central Provinces as slaves, sir.'

'I know, but I don't want it said that we're as uncivilised as the damn Westlanders. Come on; let's free up the barge and get back on our way.'

Dietar took up the pole, then Walter and Otto slipped over the side of the vessel into the river. The water came up to Walter's waist, and he could feel the current swirling by his ankles. He took out his knife, and began cutting through the rushes and weeds holding the barge in place, as Otto did the same a few yards to his right. Dietar was leaning on the pole, trying to push them back out into the middle of the river, but it was hard-going, and Walter was tiring as he stumbled around in the deep mud by the bank.

Without warning, a figure jumped over from the bank and landed onto the deck of the barge. Dietar was facing the other way at the time, and the figure kicked him into the river, where he fell with a splash. The figure grabbed the bow and a bag from the deck, then he jumped back on to the bank, and sprinted off into the trees.

'Westlander bastard!' cried Otto. 'Did you see that?'

They helped Dietar back onto the deck, and recovered the bargepole before it could drift away. They searched along the deck, looking for what had been taken.

'One half-eaten bag of food,' said Dietar, his clothes and hair dripping water onto the barge, 'and my damn bow.' He picked up the bundle of arrows. 'They forgot these, though.'

Otto turned to face the forest, and cupped his hands by his mouth. 'You forgot the arrows, you dozy prick!' he shouted.

'That was brave of them; I have to admit it,' said Walter. 'They must be starving out here in the forest. I want our bow back, though.'

Otto nodded. 'You can keep the food,' he called out into the forest, 'but we want our fucking bow!'

A few birds ascended into the air, disturbed by the noise.

'You might want to keep it down, Sergeant,' said Dietar. 'Those slave hunters are out there somewhere.'

'Let's move everything below decks,' said Walter, 'to remove any temptation the Westlanders might feel about trying that little trick again.'

Dietar got to work, and Walter and Otto resumed their cutting of the rushes and branches. It took another hour's labour to free up most of the undergrowth that was keeping the barge held to the bank, and the sun was setting by the time the vessel was ready to go. Walter and Dietar had switched places, and Walter was using the pole to keep them steady, as the last branches were removed from their path.

'We want the rest of your food,' said a voice from the bank – a voice with a strong Westlander accent.

Walter glanced up, and saw the man from before, his female companion standing a couple of yards to his right. The Westlander man was aiming the bow at Otto, who was standing in the river a few yards from him.

'Your food,' the man repeated. 'Hand it over.'

Walter gave the Westlanders a wry smile. 'That won't be happening. Where did you get the arrow?'

'I fucking made it, you piece of shit,' said the male Westlander.

'Have you escaped from the silver mine?' Walter went on, as Otto raised his arms.

The Westlanders said nothing.

'We were attacked by about a dozen men earlier today,' said Walter; 'and we got stuck here getting away from them. They were on the other bank.'

'We swam across the river last night,' said the Westlander.

Walter nodded. 'Put the bow down. Let's talk.'

'Shut your mouth,' said the Westlander. 'Throw your food onto the bank, and I might not loose.'

Walter looked as though he was considering the man's request for a moment, then he dropped the pole onto the deck and leapt across the gap. He landed onto the bank and slammed into the man. The Westlander loosed, but his newly-made arrow spun off into the river, missing Otto by several feet. Walter drew his knife. The woman was closer, so he took her arm and held the blade to her throat.

The Westlander male stared at him, his fists clenching.

'Drop the bow,' said Walter.

The man let go of the bow, and it fell to the mud.

Walter removed the blade from the woman's neck and stepped back, his hands raised.

'Let's talk,' he said. 'We could help each other. Food for information.'

The Westlander woman punched him in the face, then both fled back into the forest. Walter staggered, a hand on his bloody nose, and his eyes smarting.

Otto laughed.

'I'm glad that amused you, Sergeant,' said Walter, as blood trickled down his chin. He leaned over and picked up the bow. He threw it onto the deck, then he placed his knife back into his belt. He turned back to face the forest.

'If you can hear me, Westlanders,' he said, 'listen carefully. Some of our friends have been stolen from us, and we think they are being taken to the silver mine. We intend to rescue them, but we don't know anything about this mine. If you've been there, then we are prepared to give you food if you tell us what you know. Think it over. We'll wait here until it gets dark, then we'll continue on our way downstream.'

'You're fucking lying,' a voice shouted back. 'You're trying to trick us.'

'No tricks,' he said. 'My name is Walter. If you are heading east, then you should know that you have at least another six or seven more days of walking before you get out of the forest. What do you plan to eat in that time? Fresh air?'

The voice didn't respond. Walter turned back to the barge. 'We'll tie the boat to the nearest tree, and wait until the sun goes down.'

Otto nodded, then he went below and retrieved a long coil of rope. He looped it round the trunk of a tree that hung over the river, and tied the other end to the rear of the barge. Dietar dealt with the last of the rushes by the bow, and the barge moved a few feet downstream, before the rope went taut. Walter remained on the bank, his senses alert for any sign of the Westlanders or their pursuers.

Nothing happened for nearly an hour. The daylight slipped away, and the Silver Moon came out in all its glory, sending its rays over the waters of the river, and turning the forest a hue of silvery-green.

'Should we go, sir?' said Dietar. 'We should be able to navigate by the light of the Silver Moon.'

Walter frowned. He stared into the darkening forest. 'Queen Ninia has risen,' he called out. 'Do you see her, Westlanders? She's full tonight; maybe that's a sign.'

'Fuck off,' came a voice. 'What do you know about Queen Ninia, southerner?'

'Hey,' said Walter. 'I take offence at that. We're from Upper Down; we're not southerners.'

'Get rid of the bow. Snap it in half, and then we might be ready to talk.'

'There's no chance of that,' said Dietar. 'We'll need it to hunt when the food runs low.'

'How about we lock it in the cabin?' said Walter. 'Dietar, place the bow into the cabin and close the hatch.'

Dietar narrowed his eyes for a moment, then nodded. 'Yes, sir.' He picked up the cleaned bow, held it above his head for a moment, then he walked over to the hatch. He dropped the bow into the cabin, then he swung the hatch over to close it.

'Were you watching?' said Walter. 'The bow has gone.'

The undergrowth rustled, and the two Westlanders emerged from the gloom. The man was holding a sharpened stick, and he glanced at Walter's belt.

'You still have the knife,' he said.

'Yes,' said Walter. 'You must have one, too; otherwise, how could you make an arrow? And that spear you're carrying didn't sharpen itself.' He glanced at the woman. 'Nice right hook, by the way. That fucking hurt.'

'Good,' she said. 'You had a blade to my throat.'

'Sorry about that, but your boyfriend was pointing a bow at my sergeant.'

'She's my sister,' said the man.

'Ah. You escaped together, did you?'

'You said that four of your friends were taken?'

'That's right. Four children. Two boys and two girls. Some of my other friends set off a few days before us to look for them – we are lagging behind.'

'Don't go to Steppen,' said the woman. 'Forget your friends, and get out of the forest as fast as you can.'

'No, I don't think so,' said Walter. 'Let's sit down, and we'll eat. Dietar, Otto, get over here, and bring a bag of food.'

Walter sat down by the edge of the river, as the two Westlanders continued to stare at him. Otto got a bag of food from below deck, then Dietar lowered the barge's long gangway, which bridged the gap between the vessel and the bank. The two Rangers walked over it, and Otto handed the bag of food to Walter.

'Upper Down, did you say?' said the Westlander man.

'That's right,' said Walter.

'Do you have any whisky?'

Walter rolled his eyes. 'I wish. We have nothing decent to drink, I'm afraid; nothing but damn water.' He opened the bag of food, and spread some out on the ground in front of him. 'Ham, cheese, fruit, bread, olives,' he said. 'Sit down and help yourselves.'

The two Westlanders stared at the food, then they began to talk to each other in their own language.

Walter eyed Otto. 'What are they saying?'

'The woman is saying that she doesn't trust us,' said the sergeant, 'and the man replied by saying that she doesn't trust anyone, and that he's too hungry to worry about us attacking them. She then said...'

'Stop it,' said the Westlander man. 'We will eat with you. Sit with me, sister.'

The woman narrowed her eyes, but sat down when her brother did. They grabbed whatever food they could fit into their hands, and began eating.

'Does anyone in the silver mine speak your language?' said Walter.

The man shook his head.

'Is that how you were able to escape? You could plot and plan without anyone understanding you?'

The man shrugged, and continued to stuff his face.

'You mentioned a place called Steppen,' Walter went on. 'Is that close to the silver mine?'

'What silver mine?' said the man. 'Steppen is the name of a huge temple by the waterfalls.'

'Waterfalls, eh? Didn't you both work in the silver mine?'

'I've never seen a silver mine in my fucking life,' the man said.

'No? Then what were you doing in Steppen?'

'I was dredging water channels every day,' the man said.

'And your sister?'

The man stared at Walter. 'You don't want to know. The mercenaries who run that place are the worst bastards I have ever met.'

'I assume you were captured together?'

The man nodded.

'Where was that?'

'Lesser Down.'

'How long did you stay in the mine?'

'Stop calling it a fucking mine. Neither of us saw any sign of a mine.'

'But that's what we were told.'

'I've heard others call it that, too,' said the man, 'but I don't know why.'

'We were there for about half a year,' said the woman, as she stopped eating. 'It was like living in a nightmare. All of our friends are dead.'

Walter frowned. 'Why?'

'Did you not hear my brother?' she said. 'The soldiers are animals; worse than animals. They forced us to clean and cook and wash their clothes; that was if we were lucky. The younger girls...' She put a hand to her face. 'I feel sick.'

'You ate too much,' said her brother. 'You need to be careful.'

'It's not the food,' she said. 'I would rather die than go back to Steppen.'

'I would like to go back,' said the man, 'but at the head of a fucking army, so I could kill every bastard who lives there, and so I could free the slaves. There are thousands of Westlander slaves in Steppen. They do all the work – the farming, repairs, dredging, operating the cranes, everything, while the soldiers watch them day and night. They kill anyone who looks at them the wrong way. I was beaten so bad that I couldn't walk, and they threw me into a water channel. They thought I was dead, and I let them believe that I was. I floated downstream until I was out of sight of the temple, then I doubled back to get my sister. I crawled through the forest to find her.'

'Praise Aloth that you did, brother,' said his sister.

The two Westlanders fell into silence.

'You know my name,' said Walter. 'What are yours?'

'I'm Duggan,' said the man. 'My sister is called Aisly.'

'What if you were to come with us?' Walter went on. 'You could help us find Steppen, and you could tell us everything you know about it while we travel. Then, when we get there, we could help you take revenge on the bastards who enslaved you. If Steppen has taken our friends, then I intend to disrupt their tranquillity. We could burn the place to the ground.'

'Forget it,' said Duggan. 'The Whalebone King has hundreds of soldiers working for him.'

'The who? The Whalebone what?'

'The Whalebone King,' said Duggan. 'He's the ruler of Steppen. He lives in the temple with his sons, and lords it over the whole place.'

'Then we kill him, too,' said Walter.

'It can't be done. If it was possible, then the thousands of Westlander slaves would have already rebelled.'

'Maybe, but we would be sneaking up on them from the outside,' said Walter. 'We would have the element of surprise, and we could use the forest as a base to attack the soldiers. We could lure them away from the temple one squad at a time, and cut their throats. Listen; I get why you're reluctant to go back. You just got away, so why would you consider returning? But, me and my two friends are going, whether you come with us or not. Do you want a chance to get some revenge? Do you want a chance to free your fellow Westlanders?'

'There will be three of you against hundreds.'

'Do these soldiers ever train? Are they in good condition?'

Aisly shook her head. 'They're lazy and stupid,' she said. 'They spend half their time drinking, and the other half abusing the slaves. I never once saw them train.'

'They're complacent,' said Walter. 'That means they're also lacking discipline.' He gestured to Otto and Dietar. 'My friends and I are Mountain Rangers; the best soldiers in Upper Down. The bastards will have no idea how to deal with us. We'll be like shadows in the forest, never staying in the same place twice. If we can free even a handful of slaves, we can arm them, and they can join our force. That will be a lot easier if you two are with us. They might be more willing to trust other Westlanders.'

He pointed up at the Silver Moon and smiled. 'Queen Ninia is watching over us. Come on board, and we can get underway. We'll share what food we have, and we can take turns on the tiller and the bargepole. At any point along the route, if you change your mind, we can drop you off, and you can make your way east again.'

'I need more before I can trust you,' said Aisly.

Walter nodded, then he pulled his knife from his belt and held it out for her to take. She eyed the blade, then snatched it from Walter's palm.

'You can take the cabin, Aisly,' Walter said. 'The rest of us will sleep on the deck.'

'Excuse me, sir?' said Dietar. 'What if it rains?'

'Then we'll get wet,' said Walter. 'She'll be the only girl on board, and she can have the cabin.'

'I want my brother to sleep by the hatch,' she said.

'All right,' said Walter.

'And you will let us leave the barge at any time, if we ask?' she went on.

'You have my word. The folk in Steppen will never expect you to return.'

'And we kill them all, and free the Westlanders?'

'And my four friends,' said Walter.

Aisly stared at the knife in her hands. 'I do want to kill them. I want them to suffer for what they did to us, and for all of the Westlanders they've killed.'

'We'll still be up against hundreds,' said Duggan.

'We might die, brother,' she said, 'but if we do, it will be in battle, not as slaves. There will be a place for us at Logar's unending feast.'

Duggan stared at the ground, then he nodded. 'All right; we're in.'

CHAPTER 9
A STEP DOWN

Great Forest, South-Western Jallin, Central Provinces – 26th Day of Minula 108

Abigone gazed at the others in the grey light of dawn. It had rained overnight and, despite the shelter provided by the branches under which they had rested, all of them were cold and wet.

'We should try to get a fire going,' Abigone said. 'We need something warm to eat, and we need to dry our clothes.'

'We are too close to Steppen to light a fire,' said Fyenna. 'The smoke would be seen.'

Stanza shivered in her blanket, while Annalise's features were drawn and tired.

'I think those bargemen might have tricked us,' said Raewyn. 'We've been walking for two whole days through the forest. Are we lost?'

'We have been following the path,' said Abigone, 'as we were instructed.'

'But what if the bargemen just wanted rid of us?' said Constans. 'They told us that this was a safe way to get into Steppen – one that avoided the soldiers by the waterfalls; but we haven't seen any sign of a temple, and we haven't seen any cliffs.'

'We have no choice but to go on,' said Abigone. 'If we keep to the path, and it continues to go south, then we will come to the line of cliffs eventually.'

'Can we rest for today?' said Stanza. 'My feet are blistered, and my shoes are wet.'

Fyenna gazed at the students. 'We can only eat what we carry with us. If we stay here to rest, then we will have wasted an entire day's worth of food. I'm sorry, but we need to keep going.'

Raewyn and Constans frowned, while Stanza looked as though she was about to cry.

'We should all get up and move around,' said Denny, getting to his feet. 'We need to warm up before we set off on another day of walking. Come on; up.'

Abigone watched as Denny cajoled the younger students into standing. They folded their damp blankets, while Fyenna started to distribute some food. Abigone got up. She added her folded blanket to the pile, and walked over to where Annalise was sitting. She crouched by the older woman.

'How are you doing this morning?' said Abigone.

'I'm well, ma'am,' said Annalise. 'It's the children I worry about.'

'They will be fine,' said Abigone. 'They are all young and fit.'

'Implying that I'm not, ma'am?'

'That's not what I meant.'

'It's fine, ma'am. You don't need to say anything. It was foolish of me to think that I could walk for twenty miles a day through a damn forest. And I thought sitting in a carriage for hours was tiring. Perhaps I should have left with Mister Amery and Miss Loryn, and gone back to Upper Down. I'm too old for this.'

Abigone said nothing.

Annalise turned her head to watch Fyenna, who was passing out small bundles of food to the students.

'Or maybe it's not just my age,' Annalise went on. 'Lady Fyenna is only a couple of years younger than me, and she looks as though she could run for a mile if you asked her to. I tried to pick up her pack yesterday – it's twice as heavy as mine. I think I am becoming a burden.'

'Your value is not related to how fit and strong you are,' said Abigone. 'Can you imagine Mister Amery trying to trek through the forest? I daresay that you have done a better job than he would have managed, but that doesn't make him any less valuable.'

'But he is a lawyer, ma'am; what am I?'

'You are loyal, kind and a fount of common sense,' said Abigone; 'and you are a friend. I trust you more than I trust Mister Amery.'

The branches to their left moved, and Lothar walked into the small forest clearing where the others were gathered.

Fyenna handed him a water skin, and he took a long drink.

'What did you find?' said Mor Galthide.

'I have good news and bad news,' said Lothar. 'The good news is that the edge of the cliff is only a few minutes' walk from here; and I could see the start of the path that runs down to the bottom.'

'Praise the spirits,' said Fyenna. 'A few minutes – did you hear that, children? We are almost at the cliff's edge.'

'Do you want the bad news?' said Lothar.

'Not particularly,' said Abigone. 'Are we being hunted?'

'It's nothing like that, ma'am,' said Lothar. 'I saw no sign of anyone else while I was out scouting the area. I'm fairly certain that our presence here has gone unnoticed so far. The problem is with the path. Without ropes and equipment, the way down will be perilous. We will need to take it very slowly. I suggest that we go down in pairs. Each pair should consist of a stronger climber and a weaker climber.'

Mor Galthide snorted. 'Who will have the painful job of telling half of our number that they are weak?'

'I'll do it,' said Lothar. 'All that matters is that we make it down in one piece. Our pride shouldn't come into it.'

'That's easy for you to say,' said Fyenna. 'You are the fittest among us, Lothar.'

'There are twelve of us,' Lothar went on. 'I'll call out the names of the six I deem to be the most capable of making the journey down unassisted. Each of those will then choose one of the others to pair up with. Shall I start?'

The others said nothing.

'Fine,' said Fyenna. 'Please proceed, Lothar.'

'All right. There's me, Princess Abigone, Denny, Mor Galthide, Eshia and Marlow. Each of us should now select a companion.' He turned to Annalise. 'I would be more than happy to assist you down the path, Annalise, if you'll accept my help.'

The woman nodded. 'Thank you, Lothar.'

'Why were Eshia and Marlow chosen over me?' said Constans.

'You're a tall lad,' said Lothar, 'but you're all skin and bone. Marlow is built like a stocky little bull. Have you ever shaken his hand? He has impressive grip strength for a fifteen-year-old. And Eshia's experience of working in a blacksmith's has toughened her up. She has decent upper body strength from all that hammering. Should I go on?'

Constans stared at the ground.

'This seems like a rather divisive way to go about things,' said Fyenna.

'Maybe so,' said Lothar, 'but I'd rather offend a few people than see them fall to their deaths.'

'I agree,' said Abigone. 'We should accept that some people are better at certain things than others, and that includes climbing down a cliff. It doesn't mean that any of us are useless. In truth, I am a little surprised that I have been chosen as part of the stronger group.'

'It was a toss up between you and Fyenna, ma'am,' said Lothar. 'Age won out.'

Fyenna frowned.

'You are the weakest of the strong group, Abigone,' Lothar went on, 'so perhaps you should pair with Fyenna, who is the strongest of the weak group.'

'Enough,' said Fyenna. 'We get the message, Lothar. Everyone, get ready to leave. We shall walk to the edge of the cliff and observe this path for ourselves.'

The group began to clear away the blankets and leftover food. They packed their bags in silence, as Lothar ate some breakfast. Abigone walked over to him.

'You aren't making yourself very popular,' she said to him.

'My job is to keep everyone alive, ma'am,' he said. 'I couldn't give a shit about popularity.' He glanced at the others. 'Let's go.'

Lothar led them along the track for almost an hour, as the forest woke up for the new day. Rain was dripping down from the countless leaves, and steam was rising from the forest as the sun grew warmer. The group had quietly organised themselves into pairs as they had walked, and Abigone was by Fyenna's side as they trekked among the trees. They came to a rise, and Lothar led them up it. He stopped at the top, and the others lined up next to him.

Abigone's mouth opened at the view. They were standing on the top of a line of cliffs that stretched off to the left and right as far as the eye could see; while, below them, the forest continued on – a vast ocean of green that began at the bottom of the cliffs. It carried on until it met the horizon in the south, unbroken and featureless.

Fyenna raised an eyebrow at Lothar. 'You told us that the cliff was a few minutes away; that wasn't a few minutes.'

Lothar smiled, then he pointed to the right. 'Do you see that faint line meandering through the forest? That's the River Ario, which flows all the way down to Elestia.'

'I thought we had been following the Antiago,' said Abigone.

'We have been,' said Lothar. 'That river merges with three others at the base of the cliffs, and the new river is called the Ario. The temple is situated where the three rivers combine.'

'How do you know all this?' said Raewyn.

'Because I asked the bargemen before we disembarked,' said Lothar. 'At the moment, we are only a few miles from the temple, but we can't see it because the Menjano Step curves; it doesn't run in a straight line.'

'The what?' said Constans.

'The Menjano Step,' said Lothar. 'This thing that we are standing upon right now – that's its name. The entire land steps down, as it were, from one level to another. Now, I want you all to be very silent, and then I want you to listen.'

The group hushed, and Abigone strained her ears. For a few moments, she heard nothing but the chorus of birds in the forest, then she noticed a faint roaring sound in the distance.

'What is it?' said Stanza. 'What can we hear?'

'The waterfalls,' said Lothar. 'That slight noise is the sound of thousands of gallons of water falling over the cliffs every minute. That is how we know the bargemen weren't lying to us. We're close.'

'And the path?' said Fyenna.

Lothar gestured to his left. 'This way. Follow me.'

Lothar led them to a track that ran along the top of the cliff, in the direction of the rising sun.

'Why is he in charge?' whispered Constans. 'Mor Galthide is the better fighter.'

'I am glad you think so,' said Mor Galthide.

Constans jumped.

'You knew not that I was right behind you, did you, lad?' Mor Galthide went on. 'If our business concerned boats or battlefields, then I would be proud to lead this little group; but Lothar is a Mountain Ranger. His expertise lies in this area, and I am happy to follow his lead. You know, lad, you should ponder Lothar's words to you. If you trained, you could become as fit and strong as any boy your age, and then you would not be humiliated in front of your peers.'

Lothar came to a halt, and the others gathered round him. He pointed down, and Abigone saw the steep path that led down the side of the cliff. The way down seemed worse than perilous, it looked almost impossible. Part of the path had been washed away in places, and much of the rest seemed to consist of narrow steps cut into the rock. One slip, and anyone climbing down would fall over two hundred feet to their deaths.

'Oh my,' said Annalise.

'You and I shall lead the way,' said Lothar.

Annalise's face paled.

Lothar smiled. 'Come on, Annalise; let's show them how it is done.'

The descent of the cliff took all morning. The sun was high in the sky by the time the last pair consisting of Denny and Constans reached the bottom of the track, where it levelled out next to the start of the lower forest. Annalise and a few others were still lying on a grassy bank, exhaustion etched into their faces, and Constans slumped down next to them, his hands shaking.

Fyenna began handing out food and water, her spirits seemingly undimmed. Abigone had been her partner on the way down, and the older woman had been determined not to be outshone by a princess who had lived a life of luxury in a palace for most of her nineteen years. In turn, Abigone had been equally determined not to show any fear, despite the fact that parts of the descent had left her terrified and almost unable to move. Abigone glanced at Lothar, who was sitting on his own with a half-smile on his lips.

'I think he knew exactly what he was doing,' said Denny, walking over to her. 'He gave everyone a reason to prove themselves.'

'I'm glad we have him with us,' said Abigone.

'Are all Mountain Rangers from Upper Down as professional as him?'

'They have always been the best of our small armed forces, but there are only a few hundred of them, and they seem to spend most of their time training in the mountains. How was Constans?'

'He didn't like being paired with me,' said Denny. 'He kept insisting that he didn't need my help. To his credit, he managed it on his own, but I don't think we'll be getting much out of him for the rest of the day.'

'You could say that about quite a few of us. Look at Annalise – she's utterly exhausted, and Raewyn and Stanza aren't much better.'

'You seem fine.'

'I am just relieved that it is over,' she said. 'My knees, hands and back are aching.'

'You look as though you could do it again.'

'Do I? It must be the years of practice I've had at hiding my true feelings.' She gazed at him. 'It's been so long since we were alone together that I'm starting to forget what it feels like.'

'I know what you mean,' he said. He glanced at the others. 'Maybe we could slip away for a moment or two while the others rest? We won't be leaving any time soon.'

'We should tell someone first.'

Denny nodded. He walked up to Lothar, and crouched by him. He whispered something to the Mountain Ranger, who nodded and whispered something back. Denny stood, and walked back to Abigone.

'What did he say?' she said.

'He told us to stay close, and to be back soon. He said he will hoot like an owl if he needs us to return.'

Abigone laughed. 'He will hoot like an owl?'

'That's what he said.'

'I have no idea what an owl sounds like.'

'Well, I guess it depends upon the species.'

He took her hand, and they walked away from the group and the side of the cliff.

'It seems warmer down here,' she said. 'It felt like autumn when we were at the top of the Step, and now it feels as though it could be summer again.'

'If you think this feels like summer, then Geathan might be too warm for you,' he said.

They walked until they were out of sight of the group. They stopped by a thick stand of ash trees, then they reached out for each other and kissed. Abigone closed her eyes, her hands round Denny's neck, as his hands held her waist.

Something tapped the back of Abigone's head, and she turned to see a crossbow being aimed into her face. Another bow was pointed at Denny's back.

'Don't move,' growled a broad soldier with a sword in his hand.

Abigone kept still. She and Denny were surrounded by over a dozen men, all armed.

'You should have been paying attention to what was around you,' said the soldier with the sword, 'instead of sticking your tongues down each other's throats.' He glanced at one of his men. 'Fetch the commander. Tell him we've found them.'

One of the men ran off.

The swordsman turned back to Denny and Abigone. 'Where are the others? We saw more than a dozen of you climb down the cliffs – where are they?'

Neither Denny nor Abigone spoke.

The man jabbed his sword at Abigone, hard enough that she felt it, but not hard enough to break the skin.

'How about you talk to me, lad, or I hurt your girl?' the man said.

Denny narrowed his eyes, then a low hooting sound came from the edge of the cliff, followed by shouts and a few cries of alarm.

'Never mind,' said the man, lowering his sword. 'Looks like we've found them. This way.'

The armed men escorted Denny and Abigone back towards the cliffs. The soldiers kept their bows aimed at their backs for the length of the short journey, then they appeared in the clearing. Another two dozen armed men were surrounding the group who had climbed down the cliffs. Lothar and Mor Galthide were kneeling on the ground with their hands clasped by their heads, while someone was tying Fyenna's wrists behind her back.

'We found the other two,' said the man with the sword, as Abigone and Denny were pushed into the midst of the group. 'You'll never guess what they were doing.' He glanced down at Lothar and Mor Galthide. 'These must be the two soldiers we heard about.'

Abigone remained quiet as she observed the armed men. They were wearing no recognisable uniforms, and their equipment didn't match. Some had crossbows, which were being aimed at the group, while others had swords or long spears. They also looked older than the usual soldiers Abigone had known. All of them seemed to be at least ten years older than Lothar, and a few looked older than Mor Galthide.

'Has anyone sent for the commander?' said one.

'I did,' said the swordsman. 'He should be along any moment.' He leered at the group. 'The boss is going to give us all raises for this, lads.'

A broad-shouldered man walked into the clearing, wearing a battered old breastplate. His eyes widened when he saw the group, then he smiled.

'We found them, sir,' said one of the soldiers; 'exactly where you said they would be.'

The man gazed at each of the prisoners in turn. 'Who is in charge of this group?'

Lothar tilted his head. 'That would be me.'

The man eyed him. 'Why have you come to Steppen?'

Lothar said nothing.

'It is in your interests to cooperate,' said the man. 'If you are who we think you are, then you have nothing to fear from us.'

'We are looking for four children' said Fyenna. 'They were taken from us by the edge of the Great Forest.'

'Prove it,' said the man. 'What are their names?'

'Reath, Nyli, Ignatius and Salus.'

The man nodded. 'Lower your weapons, lads,' he said to the soldiers. 'These people are friends.'

The soldiers relaxed. Lothar and Mor Galthide got to their feet, while a soldier freed Fyenna's wrists.

'My name is Ragnvald,' said the man; 'the eldest son of the Whalebone King. Your young companions are safe and well. We have been feeding them and caring for them since they arrived here a few days ago. Would you like to see them?'

'We would,' said Fyenna.

Ragnvald gave her an ingratiating smile. 'Then follow me, if you please.'

They set off along the base of the cliff, then they took a path that veered away from the solid wall of rock. They passed through dense woodlands, then, after twenty minutes, they emerged onto the banks of a narrow stream. The first thing Abigone noticed was the five waterfalls. The two on either side were further away from the three clustered in the centre, but all five were roaring, their water white as it fell down the cliff. Where the three central waterfalls met lay an enormous building that looked like an ancient palace, its stone the same colour as the cliffs. Dozens of small water channels intermingled with pools around the temple, crossed by slender bridges of stone. All of the channels merged into the largest, which flowed along from where the waterfall on the right fell. At the top of the cliff, four large cranes were sitting motionless next to the flank of the right-most waterfall. The only thing to blot the view was the existence of a sprawling shanty town set back from the temple – a collection of shacks and huts, from where several thin tendrils of smoke were rising.

'Welcome to the Temple of Steppen,' said Ragnvald.

'How did you know where we would be?' said Lothar. 'Or is that a stupid question?'

Ragnvald eyed him. 'Never trust a Jallian bargeman, soldier,' he said. 'They would sell their children for a couple of shillings.'

'Where is the silver mine?' said Fyenna.

Ragnvald pointed at the three waterfalls. 'There are caves that extend for hundreds of feet into those cliffs. The king is awaiting us in the temple; let's not be late.'

They carried on, traversing a bridge over the stream. Abigone frowned as she walked. From what the bargemen had told her, she had been expecting Steppen to be a violent, sordid place; instead, it was beautiful. The waterfalls, the trees, the pools, and the temple – it all seemed idyllic. She wondered where all the people were. There was no one outside that she could see apart from the soldiers who were accompanying them towards the temple. Where were the slaves she had heard about?

They crossed a long bridge over the widest watercourse, and Abigone guessed that they were looking at the River Ario. If she was right, then it was the river that went all the way to Elestia and, as such, it was the only way out of Steppen that she was aware of. They neared the temple, and the group paused for a moment as the newcomers stared up at the face of the building. Every inch had been intricately carved with engravings of animals, birds and plants, and Abigone could see no joins in the stonework.

'It's been carved out of solid rock,' said Denny, as he gazed up.

'That's right,' said Ragnvald. 'Hundreds of years ago, or so I'm told. Here's a piece of advice that I want you all to listen to – when we get inside, do not wander off. The interior of the temple is like a fucking warren, with passageways that lead nowhere, and others that are sure to get you lost. If you do get lost, stay where you are, and someone will find you. Probably.'

He walked up to a tall entrance, and passed inside. The soldiers ushered the group along, and they followed Ragnvald into the darkness of the temple. Ragnvald led them on a bewildering route of twisting passageways and narrow stairs, until Abigone had no idea which way she was facing, let alone her position within the temple. None of the passageways had any windows that looked onto the outside, and there were few oil lamps to light the way. They climbed another flight of stairs, and came to a doorway, where two soldiers were on duty. They saluted Ragnvald, then one opened the door.

Inside was a comfortable-looking chamber, with a large open window that was letting in fresh air and light. Four children were sitting alone by a table, and Fyenna rushed forward. The four children got to their feet, and Fyenna embraced them.

'Thank the spirits,' Fyenna said, her voice breaking.

'Do you see?' said Ragnvald. 'All four are in fine fettle. I'll leave you to talk for a few moments while I fetch the king.'

Ragnvald retreated from the chamber, and the door was closed. The students gathered round their found comrades.

'Have you been well treated?' said Mor Galthide.

'I guess we can't complain too much,' said Reath. 'The bargemen were worse than the folk here have been.'

'Did the bargemen attempt to sell you to the Whalebone King?' said Fyenna.

'The guy in charge of the bargemen did,' said Reath.

'What happened?' said Abigone.

'The king's son killed him. Then the king said that we were his guests, not his slaves.'

'Is this where you have been staying?' said Lothar.

Ignatius shook his head. 'We were moved here this morning,' he said. 'Before that, we were living with a group of women.'

'Slaves,' said Reath. 'The king put us in with slave women. Some of them were Westlanders, but there were a few from Jallin as well.'

The door to the chamber opened, and Ragnvald walked back in, accompanied by two other men. One of them was older, and was dressed in rich robes, with a strange, yellowed crown sitting on his brow.

'That's him,' muttered Reath. 'That's the Whalebone King.'

'Greetings!' cried the king, as he approached. 'Well, well, what a delightful sight to cure any heartache – the children are reunited with their friends. You would have arrived here yesterday, if you hadn't left your boat and decided to travel overland, but that can't be helped. At least you made it down the cliff without any mishaps.' He paused as his gaze settled on Raewyn. His eyes tightened a little, then he seemed to regain his composure. 'Now,' he went on, 'who is responsible for the children?'

'I am,' said Fyenna.

The king smiled. 'I do not wish this to sound harsh, but perhaps you should have kept a closer eye on the little ones, eh? It was negligent of you to have allowed a few Jallian bargemen to make off with them. But, your troubles are at an end. You are very fortunate that your friends were brought to me.'

'Why were they brought here?' said Lothar. 'Why did the bargemen believe that you would be a willing buyer of children?'

'Who can say?' said the Whalebone King. 'It is an open secret that I am always prepared to buy new slaves; but I always do it legally.

Perhaps the bargemen wrongly suspected that I was as amoral as they seem to be, eh? Let's do some introductions. I am the king of Steppen, ruler of these parts, and I think you have already met my son Ragnvald.' He gestured to the other man. 'This is another of my sons – Erling.' He stared at Fyenna. 'Who are you?'

'My name is Fyenna,' she said.

'Hmm.' He glanced at Reath. 'See? That wasn't difficult, was it? This one here, Fyenna, was quite impertinent when she first arrived. She has a very suspicious nature. Now, are any of you hungry? Or perhaps you need to rest first? This chamber opens out onto a large suite of rooms; big enough to fit you all. We have running water, and inside toilets – all the luxuries you can imagine. You are my guests, and I want you to feel at home.'

'Thank you for your hospitality,' said Fyenna.

'It's the very least I can do, my lady,' said the king; 'especially as you will be staying with us for quite some time.'

'Why?' said Lothar. 'We were planning on leaving in the morning. Will you try to stop us?'

'Of course not,' said the king. 'You are free to come and go as you please; well, not exactly. I would ask that you stay out of any private rooms. I wouldn't want you walking in on me while I'm having a bath, eh? But what I mean is this – you are not my prisoners; none of you are. You are guests.'

'Then why will we be staying?' said Abigone.

'Are you aware of the local terrain, young lady?' said the king. 'We are deep within the Great Forest; a wild, trackless place that extends for hundreds of miles in every direction. The only safe way to leave Steppen is by barge, and no barges are due to pass through this place for another month.'

'But haven't the barges recently arrived?' said Abigone.

'They have been and gone,' said the Whalebone King. 'They have a tight schedule to keep, and Elestia needs the silver delivered on time.'

Lothar walked up to the open window and gazed out. 'We could follow the River Ario all the way to Yearl.'

'You could certainly try,' said the king. 'I strongly advise against it, but I will not stop you if you are determined to kill yourselves. Actually, you might be robust enough to make the journey. To my eyes, you look like you might have seen some active service. Am I right?'

'You are.'

'Now tell me, soldier – how many of your friends would be capable of trekking through four hundred miles of unmapped and pathless forest? It would take at least a month and, by that time, the next convoy of barges will have arrived here from Jallin.' He smiled again. 'This is your choice – a month of dangerous toil that could easily prove to be fatal, or a month of relaxing here while you enjoy our hospitality.'

'It sits ill with me that you have slaves here,' said Fyenna.

'It is a perfectly legal business enterprise, my lady.'

'Then you have no slaves from any of the Central Provinces?'

'Oh, we have a few; but all of them come from the time before the Sanctians reintroduced the old Elestian laws on slavery. Why don't you report me to the authorities when you reach Elestia? The magistrates there will assure you that I am working within the law.' He smiled again. 'Are there any more questions?'

No one spoke.

'Marvellous,' said the king. 'We shall leave you to get settled in. Food shall be brought up soon, and some wine, to help you relax. I shall be posting guards outside your suite of rooms, in order to prevent the inquisitive from bothering you. If you need anything, let them know.'

'When shall we see you again?' said Abigone.

'Don't worry about that, little lady,' the king said. 'I'm sure we will be seeing lots of each other over the coming days. We seldom entertain guests, and I want to find out everything there is to know about you.'

The king's gaze found Raewyn again, then he turned and walked for the door. His two sons eyed the group for a little longer, then they followed their father out of the chamber, and the door was closed behind them.

'I don't trust him,' said Reath.

'I think that goes for all of us,' said Fyenna. 'I particularly did not care for the way he was looking at Raewyn.'

'Should we break out, slay the Whale-arsed king and his sons, and escape, my lady?' said Mor Galthide.

'We could, but then what?' said Fyenna. 'Four hundred miles of forest. You all saw what two days of trekking through the forest did to us – how could we possibly do that for a month?'

'We would be lucky if half of us survived the trip,' said Lothar.

'Let me guess,' said the Fyenna; 'the strongest half?'

'Couldn't we summon barges?' said Abigone.

Fyenna narrowed her eyes. 'Have any of us Makers ever studied river-going vessels? I fear that any such attempted summoning would result in failure.'

'I'm not going anywhere,' said Annalise, as she lowered herself into a seat with a grimace. 'I don't see why we can't stay here for a month, and then take the next barge that comes.'

'There's something else you need to know,' said Reath; 'something that the slave women told us.'

'What?' said Abigone.

Reath gazed at the faces looking at her. 'The Whalebone King and two of his sons are Masters.'

CHAPTER 10
UPRIVER

Great Forest, South-Western Jallin, Central Provinces – 1st Day of Quoma 108

Saffie leaned against a gnarled old tree trunk as the squads of soldiers rotated their positions. Fresh soldiers who had been near the back of the column were moving forward, to relieve those who had been hacking and cutting their way through the undergrowth at the front. The River Ario lay a few yards to their right, its dark waters being borne downstream by the strong current. Small groups of soldiers were filling their water skins by the bank, while other squads were taking their chance to rest for a few moments. Those who had been carrying the sick placed the stretchers onto the rough ground. Over three dozen men had succumbed to severe illness during the nine days they had been forcing their way north through the forest, and, out of that number, seventeen had died from dysentery. The others were groaning and mumbling from their stretchers, or had slipped into unconsciousness.

No one knew the cause of the illness, but the main suspects were the hordes of flies that swarmed over the waters and banks of the river. Clouds of them would hover amid the soldiers as they marched, leaving a multitude of red bite marks over any exposed skin. To counter them, the soldiers had wrapped cloth round their hands, necks and faces, but it seemed that the flies were always able to get through. Saffie had several bites of her own. Each one itched and swelled for three or four days before starting to calm, but she had yet to experience any of the symptoms exhibited by those who had fallen ill.

'The squads have been rotated, sir,' said Lieutenant Aldo.

Captain Zola glanced at the long column of soldiers, a scarf obscuring everything on his face except for his eyes.

'We have several more miles to cover today,' Zola said. 'Get the column moving, Lieutenant.'

'Yes, sir.' The lieutenant turned. 'Get moving!' he cried. 'Let's go.'

The soldiers moved back into line. The stretchers were picked up, along with any packs that had been set down, and the new soldiers at the front of the line began cutting a path through the thick undergrowth. Water skins were passed around, then the column got underway. Saffie kept pace next to Captain Zola and Agent Marco.

'Damn this forest,' muttered Zola, as they walked.

Saffie glanced at him. In Elestia, Zola had been urbane and sophisticated, but his composure was being steadily whittled away by the long days of sweat, sickness, flies and toil of the journey. Saffie had disliked being stuck in a carriage, but the nine days of trekking had made that seem almost enjoyable in comparison.

'Halt the line!' cried Aldo, from a few yards behind them.

'What the blazes is it now?' said Zola, as he turned to face the army lieutenant. 'There had better be a good reason for this delay.'

Lieutenant Aldo was standing next to one of the stretchers. He gestured down. 'This man is dead, sir.'

Zola said nothing as the column came to a halt. Already, soldiers were setting down their packs again. Each knew that it took around twenty minutes to dig a grave, and they began to rest among the trees.

'You two,' Aldo said to the dead soldier's stretcher bearers; 'get your trenching tools and dig a grave. It has to be at least four feet deep. Afterwards, you can move to the rear of the column.'

The two men placed the stretcher onto the ground. Saffie walked over to it and crouched by the latest fatality, as the two soldiers unpacked their short spades from their packs and started to dig. The dead soldier's eyes were still open, and he was staring up at the patches of blue sky scattered amid the thick tree cover. The smell coming from the corpse was rank, and Saffie held her breath as she examined the body.

'Should you be getting that close, ma'am?' said Zola, as he watched from a few yards away. 'Whatever is causing this might be contagious.'

'If it's contagious,' said Saffie, 'then it's already too late. We have been living in each other's shadows ever since we entered Jallin.' She glanced at the men digging the grave. 'Symptoms?'

'Same as the others, ma'am,' said one. 'Vomiting, fever, dysentery, headaches, delirium. He was calling out for his mother this morning, and we should have noticed something was wrong when he fell silent.'

'It's an epidemic,' said Aldo, as he watched Saffie look over the corpse.

'But what is causing it?' said Saffie.

'The flies, ma'am?'

'I don't think it's the flies. I have seen cases of malaria on Sanctos, and these men are not suffering from that.'

'Perhaps the air itself is tainted,' said Aldo.

Saffie got to her feet, and walked over to the banks of the river to wash her hands. She knelt down, and lowered her hands into the flowing water, rinsing them of the cold sweat that had covered the skin of the dead soldier. She cupped her hands to drink from the river, then she paused. Could it be the water that was causing the spate of illness? But Saffie and the others had all been drinking it, just as they had all been breathing the same air. She stood without taking a drink, and walked back to the column. A soldier ten yards down the line was on his knees, his hands clutching his stomach, then he vomited over the ground.

'Don't put that stretcher away,' said a sergeant. 'We've got another one.'

Aldo walked up to Captain Zola. 'Sir, perhaps we should consider returning to Yearl. A quarter of our men have either died or are experiencing at least one of the symptoms. We might not be in any condition to fight once we reach Steppen.'

'We are too close to turn back,' said Zola.

'But the sickness is getting worse the further north we go, sir,' said Aldo. 'Perhaps this place is cursed by the spirits. Perhaps they are warning us to turn back.'

Saffie rolled her eyes at the army lieutenant's primitive theology. That wasn't how it worked. The spirits wouldn't make a few dozen soldiers sick in order to send a cryptic message to the others. It was absurd. From the look in Zola's eyes, it was clear that he felt the same as Saffie.

'We will carry on,' the captain said, 'the spirits are with us.'

'If the Whalebone King is a Master, sir,' Aldo persisted, 'then he might have made the air or the water turn bad.'

'Nonsense. Go to the front of the column, Aldo, and watch the route ahead from there. The men don't need to hear your foolish gossip.'

Aldo saluted, then he walked off to the head of the column, as the rest of the soldiers watched in silence. Saffie turned to the grave diggers, then she saw the latest casualty being lowered onto the empty stretcher. The afflicted man was groaning aloud, his eyes closed in pain, then his bowels could no longer be constrained, and a rank smell drifted up from the path. A few other soldiers nearby looked queasy, and several moved back a few steps.

The two diggers climbed out of the grave. They rolled the corpse into the pit, and began the task of filling it again. Zola gestured to the column as soon as they had finished.

'Proceed,' he called out, and the column got underway.

They covered six miles over the following two hours, making brisk time whenever the undergrowth thinned.

Agent Marco from the Offices of Purgation had slipped into place to Saffie's right as they walked through the dark forest, as Zola had been overseeing the front of the column. It was clear that Marco had wanted to strike up a conversation with Saffie, but she had remained tight-lipped. She had developed a keen sense for whenever people were trying to ingratiate themselves with her because of who her grandfather happened to be, and Marco seemed to fit the description of an aspiring sycophant.

'You are bearing up very well, ma'am, under the circumstances,' Marco said.

Saffie kept her eyes on the route ahead.

'Despite the illness and privations,' Marco went on, 'you have never once complained; and your steps have not faltered. Others your age would have despaired by now, but you have shown the mettle and quality of a true princess of Sanctos.'

'Thank you,' she said.

A commotion broke out ahead, and the column came to a halt.

'Is it time for a break?' said Marco, his face glistening with sweat. He swatted a fly away. 'A break would be most welcome.'

'I shall see what is causing the delay,' said Saffie.

She left his side and walked along the flank of the column, passing a few stretcher bearers as she reached the front. Soldiers were standing by the bank of the river, at a spot where the Ario turned to the north-west, and some were crouching and pointing. Zola and Aldo were among them, and the army lieutenant looked angry.

'What is happening?' said Saffie. 'What have you seen?'

The officers turned, then Zola pointed upstream.

Saffie squinted into the dim shadows. Zola was pointing at a thick tangle of undergrowth and rushes that were trailing into the river. Caught among the branches were several dozen rotting corpses, all tangled up in the undergrowth. Most of the bodies were missing their heads, while other severed body parts had also been caught up in the eddies by the bank.

'Now we know the cause of the sickness,' Saffie said. 'We have been drinking downstream of this for days.'

Saffie joined Zola and the others as they walked along the bank to take a closer look.

'Every one of these men and women has been murdered,' said Zola, 'and then their bodies were dumped in the river.' He pointed. 'That one has whip marks over her back. I think we are looking at slaves from the silver mine.'

'We must issue an order to throw away the contents of every water skin, sir,' said Aldo.

'See to it at once,' said Zola. 'No one must drink from the river, not until we are sure it is clean.'

Saffie crouched by the bank, her gaze on the tangled heap of bodies in the water. It was clear that some had been there for a long time. Their discoloured flesh was covered in flies, and fish and birds had been eating their way into them. She saw the severed head of a young man, and then one that had belonged to an old woman.

'Savages,' she muttered.

'What was that, ma'am?' said Zola.

'The Whalebone King is an ignorant savage,' she said. 'He cares naught for the damage he is doing by throwing these bodies into the Ario; when he should be burying or burning them. The bend in the river is gathering the bodies here, but there might be more bends upstream, and there might be more corpses. And why are there so many? Why would any mine kill their workforce in such numbers?'

'Perhaps the slaves staged a rebellion, ma'am.'

Saffie pointed at the head of the old woman. 'Does she look like a dangerous rebel? We should press on with all speed, before the soldiers grow too thirsty.'

'I agree, ma'am,' said Zola. He turned to the others. 'Get the column moving again. At once.'

They retreated from the river bank, and the soldiers resumed their journey.

'Is it true, ma'am?' said Marco, when Saffie reached him. 'Were there bodies in the river? I heard Aldo tell everyone to empty their water skins.'

'It's true,' said Saffie.

'Truly, this place is cursed. What are we supposed to drink now?'

'We can lay out sheets at night to gather the dew,' she said; 'and we can collect water whenever it rains. It won't be much, but it should suffice to stave off severe dehydration.'

'Once again, ma'am, your wisdom gives me sustenance. How do you know so much about these matters?'

'You know who I am, Marco. You know what the most exalted emperor put me and my cousins through. Do you think this is my first trek through the wilderness?'

'I have heard many rumours about the training you underwent, ma'am,' said Marco, his eyes lighting up at Saffie's response. It was the most she had said to him in several days, and he seemed determined to make the best of it. 'Were you ever abandoned in a forest and told to make your way home?'

Saffie nodded.

'And how old were you, ma'am?'

'Twelve.'

'Were you truly alone?'

'Not quite. I learned many years later that Count Sebastian had been told to keep an eye on us, from a distance. He was ordered not to intervene unless we were in imminent risk of death, but none of us knew this at the time – we believed we were utterly alone. We all made it back to the Palace of Adriano alive, so Count Sebastian's help was never required. I walked for days without food, sprained my ankle, got bitten by a snake, and caught pneumonia from the constant rain, but I received no assistance from Count Sebastian. Much later, when I got the truth out of him, he told me that he had wanted to help me, but that his orders were clear.'

'Had it been me, ma'am, I would have rushed to your assistance.'

'Then I'm glad it wasn't you. The other cousins would have mocked me relentlessly had I been the only one who had needed to be rescued. I earned an approving smile from the most exalted emperor when he visited me in the infirmary after my return. All the suffering I endured was worth it for that one moment.'

'A smile from the most exalted emperor is a truly blessed gift, ma'am,' Marco said.

The column came to a halt again, and Saffie heard Zola curse. The stretcher bearers set their burdens down, and the soldiers slumped to the ground. Aldo came hurrying down from the front of the line, then he and Zola talked for a few moments. Aldo saluted, then he walked down the column, picking out soldiers from the line.

'Battle gear; get ready – you, you, you,' Aldo said, as more of the fittest-looking soldiers were selected from the column.

'Battle gear?' said Saffie. She walked up to Zola. 'Are we about to fight?'

'A ruined tower has been seen ahead of us, ma'am,' said the captain, 'and smoke is rising from it. I think we are approaching the frontier of the Whalebone's King's little realm.'

Within a few moments, twenty soldiers had been pulled out of the line, and were strapping on their breastplates and loading their crossbows. Packs were opened, and bundles of bolts were passed out, along with a few spare helmets.

A scout appeared on the path, and he ran up to Captain Zola.

'Sir,' said the scout, as he bowed his head; 'I approached the tower along the banks of the river, and remained unseen. The structure is three storeys high, but the upper levels look too unsafe to occupy. I got as far as being able to peer in through a ground floor window, and I saw the bodies of two women lying dead on the floor. I saw no one alive, sir, but I could hear voices coming from a neighbouring chamber.'

'What were they saying?' said Zola.

'They were mostly grumbling, sir,' said the scout. 'They sounded like bored soldiers, fed up with their lot in life.'

Zola turned to the twenty soldiers who were getting ready for battle.

'I want prisoners,' he said, 'but the priority is that no one is able to flee bearing news of our advance. Surround the tower before moving in. Lieutenant Aldo will lead.'

'I shall go with them,' said Saffie.

Zola eyed her, but he knew better than to try to overrule her in front of the others.

'You will need armour, ma'am,' said Aldo.

'I would prefer to remain unburdened,' she said, 'and I have my own sword.'

'Perhaps you should let the soldiers do their jobs, ma'am,' said Marco.

'I will not interfere with their work,' said Saffie. 'I will remain at the rear, and help ensure that no one escapes.'

'Keep her safe, Aldo,' said Captain Zola.

Aldo saluted. 'Yes, sir.'

The army lieutenant gestured to the twenty soldiers, and they set off. They passed the lead units of the column, who were crouching amid the undergrowth, then the scout led them along the river bank. They halted when the ruins of a stone tower came into view. It was sitting a few yards from the river, its foundations built upon a low, flat rise. The upper floors were falling to pieces, and the structure had lost its roof, but smoke was coming from a hole in the floor of the second storey.

The scout pointed. 'I looked in through that window, sir,' he whispered to Aldo, 'but the main entrance is to the left.'

Aldo nodded. He gestured for half of the detachment to go left, and the other half to go right, and they set off again, creeping through the forest. Saffie saw another body sprawled out by the muddy bank of the river, just feet from the ancient tower. The man's head was still on his shoulders, but his body showed numerous signs of torture. She followed Aldo down by the right-hand side of the tower, until they were on its northern flank, where a well-tended path set off in the direction of the silver mine. Aldo glanced around, ensuring that his men were in position, then he blew a low note on a whistle. The Sanctian soldiers rushed the building. Some piled in through the main entrance, while others clambered over the ruins and descended into the chambers on the ground floor via the holes in the roof.

Saffie crouched by the path and waited, her right hand resting on the hilt of her sheathed sword. Cries broke out from within the tower, along with the thrum of crossbows and the clash of steel. A man climbed out of a narrow window, and the Sanctians shot him in both legs as he dropped to the ground.

'Keep him quiet,' hissed Aldo.

A soldier ran forward and clamped a hand over the man's mouth, cutting off his cries before they could echo up through the trees. A gag was slipped over his face, then his wrists were bound behind his back. A sergeant emerged from the main entrance and signalled to Aldo. The lieutenant got to his feet, and Saffie joined him. They walked to the entrance of the ruined tower.

'Two prisoners,' said the sergeant, 'and three dead. No casualties on our side, sir.'

'One came out of a window,' said Aldo, 'but we got him.'

'We also found two bodies that were already dead, sir,' said the sergeant.

'I believe the scout mentioned them,' said Aldo. 'Is there enough room for us all to shelter inside?'

'There's just about enough room for everyone, sir.'

Aldo nodded. 'Go back to Captain Zola and tell him the news. Tell him that I suggest we stay here, and use this tower as a base. Our sick can recover, while we plan our next move.'

The sergeant saluted. 'Yes, sir.'

Saffie watched the sergeant hurry back through the undergrowth, then she walked into the ruins of the tower. The first thing that hit her was the smell of blood, sweat and excrement. She passed a few Sanctian soldiers, who were guarding a deep alcove where two of the three prisoners were sitting. One of the prisoners looked as ill as the men in the column, while the other was staring at the floor, a large bruise forming on his left cheek. Saffie pressed on into the interior of the ground floor. There were several large and empty chambers, then she came to one with the two bodies. Both were women, and neither looked as though they had been dead for long.

Saffie nodded to a group of soldiers. 'Make sure these two are buried. We will not be throwing them into the river.'

A few of the soldiers gagged at the sight when they entered the chamber, then they lifted the bloody and tortured bodies up, and carried them outside.

Aldo appeared by her side. 'A terrible business, ma'am,' he said.

'We are fighting barbarians,' she said. 'There shall be no clemency for the mercenaries when we reach Steppen. I want them exterminated.'

'Is that an order, ma'am?' said Aldo. 'Should we check with Captain Zola first?'

Saffie eyed the army officer, but said nothing. She walked out of the chamber. The third prisoner had been placed with the others, then Saffie saw Captain Zola enter the tower.

'Good job, Lieutenant,' he said to Aldo. 'Where can the sick be placed?'

Aldo gestured to an empty chamber. 'In there would be suitable, sir.'

Zola nodded at a sergeant. 'See to it. Bring everyone indoors, apart from the men who are currently watching the road north.'

'Yes, sir,' said the sergeant.

Zola turned to the three prisoners. The one who had been shot in both legs had lapsed into unconsciousness, while the one who was ill was sweating, and shaking uncontrollably. Zola crouched next to the man with the bruise on his cheek, and drew a knife from his belt.

'Your choice is simple,' said Zola. 'Talk, or be tortured to death.'

'Fuck off, Sanctian,' said the man.

'Hold his arm out,' said Zola.

Two soldiers gripped the prisoner, and a third extended the man's right arm out in front of Captain Zola.

'You may wish to look away, ma'am,' Zola said to Saffie.

'Carve him into small pieces for all I care,' said Saffie. 'I have no objections to watching him suffer.'

'Very well, ma'am.' Zola took hold of the man's hand, and moved the knife closer. 'You will describe for us the defences of the silver mine, down to the last detail. I want to know if the path outside this tower leads to the temple, and I want to know the locations of the barracks where the mercenaries live. Lastly, I wish to know everything about the Whalebone King – where he lives, where he eats; everything. If you do this for me, you will be allowed to live. If you refuse, then I will start cutting your fingers off.'

'I know nothing,' said the man. 'Why do you think I was posted to this shithole? We were left down here to rot.'

'Tell me; why were you posted here?' said Zola.

The man shrugged. 'Bad discipline. An inability to obey orders to the king's satisfaction, or so I was told. Fuck the Whalebone King, and fuck his sons.'

'Why were there two dead women in the next chamber along?' said Saffie.

The man shrugged. 'Whores. Erling said we could do whatever we liked to them.'

'Cut his thumb off, Captain,' said Saffie.

'He might need his thumb to draw us a map of the mine's layout, ma'am,' said Zola.

'Then cut his left thumb off.'

'Very well, ma'am. Soldiers, switch arms.'

The Sanctians pulled the man's right arm back to his side, and extended his left. Zola reached out, grasped the man's left hand, and began slicing through his thumb. One of the soldiers put his hand over the man's mouth to suppress his screams. Zola had to place the man's hand against the stone floor to cut through the bone, then the thumb came free, along with a stream of blood. Zola pressed a cloth against the open wound, as the man spasmed and writhed in the soldiers' grip.

Next to them, the sick prisoner stared at the severed thumb lying on the floor.

'I'll tell you everything,' he gasped. 'I can draw you a map; whatever you want. Please don't cut my thumbs off.'

Zola smiled, then he raised his eyes to a sergeant. 'Fetch this man a pencil and some paper.'

'Yes, sir.'

Zola wiped the blood from his knife onto a prisoner's coat, and got to his feet. He and Saffie walked to the entrance of the tower, where Lieutenant Aldo was ushering in the last soldiers from the column.

'All personnel have now entered the tower, sir,' Aldo said, 'apart from the men I have sent to scout the road ahead.'

'Very good,' said Zola. 'Let's see what the sick prisoner has to tell us, and then we can formulate a plan to strike at the silver mine.'

'Yes, sir. The princess suggested that we show no mercy to the mercenaries, sir; that they should be exterminated. Should we adopt this strategy?'

Zola said nothing for a while, then he nodded. 'I agree,' he said. 'We shall kill them all.'

CHAPTER 11
THE UNKNOWN

Steppen, Great Forest, Jallin, Central Provinces – 1st Day of Quoma 108

Magnus walked along the shadow-shrouded passageways of the Temple of Steppen. He ascended a spiral staircase that had a few narrow slits open to the outside world, and he saw that the sun had set over the forest. Lamps had been lit down by the shanty town. The lights weren't for the comfort and convenience of the slaves; instead, they were positioned by the roads and bridges that bordered the squalid settlement, so that the mercenaries could prevent any from escaping.

All slaves had been forbidden from going round to the western flank of the temple, on pain of death, ever since the large group of outsiders had arrived a few days before. The king wished to provide the illusion that no slaves were being mistreated, and so he had decided that none should be visible from the windows of their guests' quarters. Magnus wondered if the ruse had been working. He had no way to know, as he had been told not to go anywhere near the new arrivals.

He came to a guarded door, and a soldier opened it for him. Magnus crossed the threshold and entered a small, dark chamber, where five men were sitting round a candlelit table. They had been eating dinner, and several plates were lying in front of them, along with a few empty bottles of wine.

'What is the runt doing here?' said Erling. 'I thought this meeting was for grown ups.'

'The runt is a Master,' said the Whalebone King. 'I have decided to include him in some of our more private discussions. Take a seat, Magnus. Ragnvald, move your chair up a bit for your half-brother.'

Ragnvald muttered something under his breath, but did as he was told. Magnus picked up a spare chair from the side of the room and placed it down between Ragnvald and Lord Matteo, who was sipping from a glass of red wine.

'Right,' said the king, as Magnus sat; 'we're all here, so let's start. I assume you ate something before coming here, Magnus?'

Magnus hadn't, but he nodded anyway.

'Good,' said the king. 'Pour yourself a glass of wine. In fact, fetch a couple more bottles from the cupboard for us; there's a good lad.'

Magnus got back out of his chair. He went to the row of wooden cupboards, opened one, and extracted two bottles. He set them down on the table and retook his seat. Lord Matteo reached out and took one of the bottles. He pulled out the cork with his teeth, then filled six glasses.

'We're here to decide what, if anything, we should do about our... guests,' said the king. 'The simplest answer is sweet fuck all. We leave them be, and then they get on the barges and bugger off out of Steppen for good. So far, we've done a decent job of keeping them confined to their quarters, and they haven't seen anything they shouldn't have seen. Can we keep it up? Maybe; maybe not. However, if we decide to act, then we'll need to be careful.'

'We ain't never getting this opportunity again, boss,' said Einar. 'We have to act. We kill the old ones, and enslave the young ones.'

'What if a few of the older ones are Masters or Makers?' said Ragnvald. 'Our guests might possess the potential to slaughter everyone in this fucking place. It's too risky. We should let them leave.'

'That's not what you were saying to me and Erling this morning,' snapped Einar. 'You were telling us that you wanted to get your hands on Eshia.'

'Which one is that?' said Lord Matteo.

'I did tell you that, Einar,' said Ragnvald, ignoring the Sanctian, 'but you asked me which one I liked, and I gave you an answer. I didn't say that I thought it was a good idea to do anything about it. We have been living like royalty here for years, and I don't want that to end. If we try to strike at them, we could all die. What if they massacre the mercenaries or the slaves?'

'Who gives a fuck about them?' said Erling. 'We can always get more.'

The king frowned. 'We know that the youngest four are Masters and Makers, but we have no proof about the others, beyond a few suspicions. Do you think our guests are aware of our suspicions?'

'That's the question, boss,' said Ragnvald. 'If we knew the answer to that, then I might be persuaded to act. But, if they know we know, then we should leave them alone.'

'Why?' said Erling.

'Use your fucking brain for once,' said Ragnvald. 'If they think we're ignorant, they might get complacent. They will believe they are untouchable, and if that's the case, we might have a chance at taking them by surprise.'

'What if we can't find out what they know?' said Einar.

'Then I recommend we play it safe,' said Ragnvald.

'You fucking coward,' said Erling.

Ragnvald picked up a full bottle of wine and gripped his brother's throat.

'Settle down, boys,' said the king. 'Ragnvald, unhand your brother; Erling, don't ever call Ragnvald a coward again in my hearing. Do you understand?'

Ragnvald released his brother, and Erling muttered an apology.

'My second question,' the king went on, 'is this – do they know that me, Ragnvald and Magnus are Masters?'

'That runt is barely a Master, boss,' said Einar.

'That doesn't matter,' said the king. 'Do they know?'

Ragnvald shrugged. 'Maybe.'

'I don't like *mights* and *maybes*,' said the king. 'We need to know for certain.'

'My advice for this question is the same as for the other one,' said Ragnvald. 'If they know, we do nothing. If they don't know, we might be able to surprise them.'

Erling looked confused. 'But... why?'

'You dozy dipshit,' said Ragnvald. 'If they know we have Masters, then they will be on their guard. Fucksake, why do I have to explain things to you as if you were a child, Erling? The only way I can be persuaded to act is if our guests don't know anything of any use. We remain trustworthy and keep them supplied with fresh food, booze, hot water – all the comforts, then we wait until the barges are almost here. They'll be too excited by the prospect of leaving to suspect anything; then we hit them hard.'

'Why would we do that?' said Magnus. 'Anyone we enslave who happens to be a Master or a Maker will be able to escape.'

'We could kill the Masters and Makers among them,' Ragnvald went on, 'and keep the rest.'

'There is too much we don't know,' said the king. 'However, I don't see why we have to kill every Maker. Could we not subdue the spirits of the younger girls, and bend them to our will? After a few years of conditioning, Reath and Nyli might have learned to behave themselves, and they would make good bed-companions for Einar and Erling.'

The four sons stared at their father.

'It makes sense if you think about it,' said the king. 'Neither Einar nor Erling are Masters, but, if they couple with Makers, then their children might turn out to have abilities. I'm thinking of the future, lads. I want to build a dynasty that endures.'

'The two soldiers will have to go,' said Ragnvald; 'along with any who are Masters.'

'There is no doubt about that,' said the king. 'The worst case is that they are all Masters and Makers. If that is true, then we will have to kill most of them. But what if a few aren't?' He glanced at Ragnvald. 'What if Eshia isn't a Maker? Then she could be yours. Personally, I have my eye on Raewyn. She looks as though she could bear me a few strong sons.'

Ragnvald rubbed his chin. 'We have to be careful that our desire for these girls doesn't lead to our destruction.'

'I want Raewyn,' said Hemming, 'and I am used to getting what I want; otherwise, what's the point of being a fucking king?'

Magnus suppressed a frown, wishing that he hadn't been invited to his father's table. He had been curious and a little excited when the summons had arrived, thinking that he might benefit from being brought into the king's inner circle, but his worst fears had been realised. All his father and half-brothers could think about was how to get their hands on the young women who had arrived with the others. Only fear was keeping them from acting, fear that their prey might turn out to be predators.

'I agree with Ragnvald,' Magnus said. 'If our guests know too much, then the risk is too high. They will be prepared for any tricks we might try to play on them, and they will be staying vigilant. After all, they travelled hundreds of miles through the forest to find their four missing children, so we already know that they are prepared to go to great lengths to defend each other.'

Ragnvald looked at him, but said nothing, as Einar and Erling rolled their eyes.

The king lifted his glass. 'So, my two Master sons are over-cautious, and my two other sons are over-reckless. Can anyone here come up with a plan?'

'A plan to do what exactly, Your Majesty?' said Lord Matteo.

'A plan that will end up with Raewyn in my bed, you Sanctian imbecile,' said the king.

'The only plan I can suggest is a simple one, Your Majesty,' Matteo went on. 'We lack information; therefore, we need to get hold of some.'

'Yes, but how?'

Matteo smiled. 'We send Magnus into their midst, Your Majesty.

Your youngest son is easily the least threatening of your offspring, and he has an open, trusting demeanour. Ragnvald would terrify them, and I do not think your guests would wish to befriend Einar or Erling. Magnus is more sympathetic. He could gently inquire into the extent of the guests' knowledge, and discover what they know, and what they don't know.'

Einar started to laugh, but the king glared at him.

'Cease cackling, Einar,' Hemming said; 'for once, our Sanctian lodger might have come up with a good idea. How about it, Magnus – do you reckon you could find out what we need to know, without making it obvious that we are fishing for information?'

'Yes, sir,' said Magnus.

'You can't trust that little prick with a job like this, boss,' said Einar.

'I disagree,' said Ragnvald. 'Magnus can do it. He can be a sneaky little bastard when he wants to be. Look at the way he hid the fact that he could use a knife. If he's careful, then it might work.'

Magnus suppressed a smile. Had Ragnvald just told the others that he had faith in him? Magnus couldn't remember a single instance from his past in which his eldest half-brother had taken his side. Einar and Erling were glancing at Ragnvald with narrow eyes, as though they couldn't believe it, either, but his father was nodding in approval.

'It's decided,' said the king. 'Magnus will make an approach towards our guests, and he will see what he can discover.'

'I might not be able to get everything we need from one visit, sir,' said Magnus. 'It may take time before they trust me enough to reveal their secrets.'

The king waved his hand. 'That is understandable. It also means that you should start as soon as possible. Now, in fact. Ragnvald, escort Magnus to the apartment of our guests, and tell the guards on duty there that my youngest son has permission to come and go as he pleases.'

Ragnvald grunted, then he drained his glass and got to his feet. Magnus copied him, feeling at last that he might be of some use to his father.

'Don't make a mess of this, runt,' said Erling. 'If you do, then I might have to pay your mother a little visit.'

Magnus waited for his father to say something, but the king laughed along with Einar at the remark, and Magnus felt his anger return. For the briefest of moments, he had felt like his father's son, and had been keen to please the old king, but that naïve feeling had evaporated amid the laughter. At least Ragnvald hadn't laughed, he thought.

Magnus followed his expressionless older brother out of the dining room, and they set off along the dark passageways of the temple.

'You'll have to be subtle,' Ragnvald said, as they descended a flight of stairs. 'Don't ask them direct questions. Feel your way around, and hope that they volunteer the information.'

'I understand,' said Magnus.

'Do you? If they realise what we're planning, then the situation could get messy fast. If in doubt, say nothing. If they ask you lots of questions, feign ignorance. As far as you know, this place is a fucking paradise, inhabited by happy slaves, professional soldiers, and benevolent overlords. Tell them that we were outraged by the bargeman's suggestion that we might purchase child slaves; that we would never do such a thing. The most important part of your job is sussing out who among them are Masters and Makers. That's the priority.'

'How long should I spend in their quarters this evening?'

'You'll have to judge that for yourself. If you think you are irritating or inconveniencing them, cut the visit short, but stay if things are going well. I'll be in my rooms. Come and find me when you get out, and we can go over what you've discovered.'

Magnus bit his tongue before he could ask his brother why he should report to him and not their father. Was it to keep Erling and Einar in the dark? Despite everything, Magnus had never felt closer to his eldest brother, and the sensation made him queasy and proud at the same time.

They reached the entrance of the guests' apartment, and Ragnvald greeted the two soldiers on duty.

'Magnus has the king's permission to visit the guests whenever he wishes,' Ragnvald said. 'You will let him enter and leave at his request.'

'Sure thing, boss,' said one of the men.

Ragnvald turned to Magnus. 'Good luck in there, and remember everything I've told you.' He gave his youngest brother a ragged smile. 'This is your chance, dickhead. Don't fuck it up.'

Magnus nodded, then he glanced at the soldiers. 'Knock, then let me in.'

One of the soldiers rapped his knuckles on the door a few times, then he turned the key and opened the door. Magnus stepped into the large living area of the apartment, and the door was closed and locked behind him. Three faces peered up at him from a low wicker couch, then a huge man got to his feet.

'We seem to have a visitor,' he said, his voice booming out. 'A little fellow with, I suspect, his father's eyes.'

The other two got to their feet. One was a woman who looked the same age as the huge man, and the other was a burly soldier-type, his eyes suspicious as he looked Magnus up and down.

'I am here to say hello,' he said. 'My name is Magnus.'

The woman and the soldier glanced at each other.

'We have heard the name,' said the soldier. 'You are one of the king's sons, yes?'

'Yes,' said Magnus. 'May I come in? I mean, I know that I am already inside your apartment, but would it be all right if I sat down and talked to you? I want to see how you are getting on, and if you need anything.'

'Did your father send you?' said the woman.

'It was my idea,' said Magnus, 'but I needed my father's permission.'

'It's a little late in the evening for a visit,' said the woman, 'but I suppose it would be fine if you joined us for a short while. Lothar, could you please see if any of the older children are still up? Bring them here if they are.'

'Yes, ma'am,' said the soldier. He eyed Magnus for a moment, then he walked out through another doorway.

Magnus approached the couch and sat down opposite it. The

woman and the huge man retook their seats, their eyes never leaving Magnus.

'Have the food and quarters been to your satisfaction?' Magnus said.

'They have been more than adequate,' said the woman. 'My name is Fyenna, and the man sitting next to me is Mor Galthide.'

'It's nice to meet you both.'

'Why has it taken you several days before coming to visit us?' said Fyenna.

'As I said, I needed my father's permission, and he wanted you to settle in first, before anyone bothered you.'

The side door opened, and Lothar returned to the room, leading three people who looked the same age as Magnus. Two of them were young women, and the other was a young but well-built man.

'These are the only ones who were awake and willing, ma'am,' said Lothar, as they approached. 'Annalise and Eshia are sleeping, and Constans refused to leave his room.'

'This is Magnus,' Fyenna said to the three new arrivals; 'the one Reath mentioned. Magnus, this is Denny, Abigone and Raewyn.'

Raewyn smiled as she sat down on another couch, and Magnus had to pull his glance away before his gaze turned into a stare. She was beautiful. He remembered that the king wished to claim her for himself, and he began to feel nauseous at the thought of Raewyn in his father's arms.

'It is nice to see you all,' he said, not meeting their eyes.

Abigone and Denny were looking at him with bemused expressions.

'We have been in here for a few days,' said Denny, 'but you are our first visitor. Why can't we go outside? The waterfalls and pools are stunning, and I would like the opportunity to investigate them.'

'My father doesn't want anyone to wander off and get lost in the forest,' said Magnus.

Denny looked less than convinced, but he sat down next to Abigone and Raewyn. Lothar also retook his seat.

'When are the next barges due?' said the soldier.

'In twenty days or so,' said Magnus. 'It's difficult to be precise.'

'And what happens, exactly?' Lothar went on. 'Are the boats lowered by the cranes while they are still loaded? How long do they stay for, before they set off for Elestia?'

'I'm not entirely sure,' said Magnus. 'I have never dealt with that aspect of the... business. I am deemed too young to be given much responsibility. My three brothers all have jobs, but I don't have much to do.'

'Your mother lives here, I believe?' said Abigone.

'That's right.'

'In a place called the *women's quarters*?'

'Yes.'

'Slaves?'

Magnus's cheeks flushed. 'Yes. The king's most valuable female slaves live in the temple with us.'

'Reath told us that...' Abigone went on, then she paused. 'Do you know to whom I am referring when I say *Reath*?'

'Of course,' said Magnus. 'I met all four of the stolen children. I remember Reath.'

'She told us that she had held several long conversations with your mother.'

'I was there for some of them,' said Magnus.

'Your mother had some strong words to say about Steppen,' Abigone went on.

'I know that. My mother bears a great deal of ill will towards my father; that isn't a secret. My father has equally strong opinions about her. It sometimes puts me into a difficult position.'

'She isn't the mother of your brothers, though, is she?' said Raewyn.

Magnus had been avoiding looking directly at Raewyn, the memory of his father's words regarding the young woman present in his mind, but he turned his gaze in her direction.

'That's right,' he said. 'My half-brothers shared the same mother.'

'What happened to her?' said Raewyn.

'She died giving birth to Erling,' he said. 'That was before I was born, so I never knew her.'

'Tell me,' said Abigone. 'What were the circumstances that led to your mother's enslavement?'

Magnus remained silent, aware that he was the one being bombarded with questions, rather than the other way around.

Mor Galthide chuckled. 'I think you women are starting to embarrass the lad,' he said. 'Young Magnus isn't responsible for the capture of his dear old mother.'

'Let's change the subject,' said Lothar. 'Tell us about the silver mine, Magnus. We assume that you have teams of Westlander slaves working there, but where is it, and where are all the slaves? I gaze out of our window every day, but I never see anyone.'

'I, uh... I have never seen the silver mine,' he said. 'I think it lies deep within the caves behind the three central waterfalls.'

'Right next to the temple, in other words?' said Lothar.

'I guess so.'

'And you have never seen it?'

'Never. Ragnvald takes care of the mine. He's my eldest brother.'

'Do you ever leave the temple?' said Denny.

'Of course I do.'

Denny raised his palms. 'I didn't mean to cause any offence. It's just that you haven't seen the cranes or the silver mine.'

'I have seen the cranes,' said Magnus, 'but I have never worked there. That's Einar's job.'

'How old are you?' said Raewyn.

'Seventeen,' he said. 'You?'

'I am also seventeen,' Raewyn said. 'Have you ever seen the world beyond the Great Forest?'

'No. I have trekked far into the forest, in every direction, but I have never seen any land that wasn't covered in trees, nor have I ever seen the ocean.' He smiled. 'Does it really exist?'

Mor Galthide laughed.

'You have different accents,' Magnus went on, sensing an opportunity to ask a few questions of his own. 'Do you all come from different places?'

'Raewyn and I hail from the same place,' said Fyenna.

'Oh yes,' he said. 'I can hear that now. And I think that Lothar and Abigone also share the same accent, but it is not the same as yours, Fyenna.'

'You have good ears,' said Abigone.

'And Denny's accent reminds me of...' Magnus frowned. 'Are you from Sanctos, Denny?'

Denny raised an eyebrow, then he smiled. 'Yes.'

'A Sanctian agent lives here,' Magnus went on; 'that's how I guessed.'

The others fell silent.

'Did you say that a *Sanctian agent* dwells here in Steppen?' said Lothar. 'Where?'

'He lives in the temple.'

'Is he aware that we have arrived?'

'Yes. Is that a problem?'

'It's no problem,' said Fyenna. 'It just seems a little strange, that's all. Why would a Sanctian agent be living in the midst of the Great Forest?'

'He was sent here by the Sanctians to report on the silver exports,' Magnus said. 'As far as I know, the Sanctians want the flow of silver to continue without interruption. I think it has a considerable effect on the local economies of Yearl and Jallin. They use the silver to mint coins, I believe.'

'Has he lived here for a while?' said Abigone.

'Years and years,' said Magnus. He leaned forward on his chair. 'This is between us, but he isn't particularly... diligent in his duties. If I'm being honest, I think he prefers a life of comfort. He certainly doesn't appear to do much work.'

There was a slightly awkward silence, and Magnus got the impression that his news about the Sanctian agent had caught them off guard. He wondered if he should have kept Matteo's existence a secret.

'It was lovely to meet you all,' he said, as he got to his feet. 'I think I will leave you now, so that you can enjoy the rest of your evening. Would you mind if I visited again? I would like to get to know you all a little better.'

'Why?' said Mor Galthide.

'Because I rarely get to meet strangers,' he said. 'You have travelled to places that I can barely imagine. Twenty days from now, the barges will be taking you away to Elestia, and I don't want to waste an opportunity to learn more about the outside world.'

'You are welcome to visit whenever you like, Magnus,' said Fyenna.

Magnus tilted his head. 'Thank you.'

He turned for the door.

'One last thing,' said Fyenna.

Magnus turned again. 'Yes?'

'Reath told us that it was you who killed the bargeman that stole our friends.'

'That's right,' said Magnus.

'The king asked his seventeen-year-old son to execute a Jallian bargeman?' Fyenna went on. 'Why?'

'My other brothers weren't there,' said Magnus. 'That man tried to sell children to my father. I think his execution was justified. Do you agree?'

'Your actions were commendable, lad,' said Mor Galthide. 'That piece of filth deserved what he got. Good for you.'

Magnus tilted his head again, then he knocked on the door. It was unlocked, and Magnus stepped outside. Ragnvald was still there, standing next to the two soldiers. He motioned with a hand, then Magnus followed his brother along a dark passageway, as the soldiers re-locked the door.

'That was brief,' Ragnvald said.

'It got a little awkward when they asked about Lord Matteo,' said Magnus. 'I think the king was right – they might be on the run from the Sanctians.'

'Did you discover who among them are Masters and Makers?'

Magnus shook his head. 'They wanted to use the meeting to ask me as many questions as possible about Steppen. I decided not to press them too hard. I got them to agree to the most important point – they are happy for me to keep visiting. As for what they know about us, I think they are aware that we have Masters here.'

'Why do you say that?'

'Because my mother talked to the four children when they were in the women's quarters.'

'Damn it,' muttered Ragnvald. 'It was a mistake to have placed them there. Your mother might have blown our chances at surprising them. Silly bitch.'

'I don't like it when you call her that.'

Ragnvald came to a halt, and Magnus braced himself for a beating. Instead, his eldest brother laughed.

'You're a funny little bastard at times,' Ragnvald said. 'Still, I think this was a good start. Go back in there tomorrow, or maybe the day after; we wouldn't want them to think that you are over-keen. Wear them down with your gullible little boy act, and keep at it.'

'All right.'

'Remember to report to me about this,' Ragnvald went on. 'I will inform the king of your progress. If Einar or Erling ask you what's happening, refer them to me.'

'That will probably get me punched in the face.'

'Probably, but it will be worth it in the long run.' He leaned in closer. 'Stick with me, lad, if you know what's good for you. You and I are Masters; we're not like the other two. You would do well to remember that.'

Ragnvald gave him a half-hearted punch on the shoulder, then he turned and walked away.

Magnus remained where he was, both pleased and disgusted with himself. If Ragnvald and the king had their way, most of their guests would be murdered. Only the fourteen-year-old Masters and Makers would be spared, along with the young women. Any who survived would live out the rest of their lives in servitude. If Raewyn was lucky, she would be kept alive to become the king's bed slave, and the thought made Magnus sick.

Magnus turned, and set off towards his own quarters.

He tried to think about his own future. Without Ragnvald's support, he would be isolated within the temple, vulnerable to attack from their other brothers. It would be difficult to survive in those conditions, and it would be even harder to protect his mother. That was his priority – to keep his mother safe. If that meant he had to be complicit in the destruction of their guests, then that was the price he would have to pay.

CHAPTER 12
THE CRANES

Above Steppen, Great Forest, Jallin, Central Provinces – 2nd Day of Quoma 108

Walter gazed through the forest at the four cranes. He and Otto had been lying motionless in the thick undergrowth for hours, their eyes on the guarded compound at the top of the cliffs where the cranes were positioned. None of the cranes had moved since the two Mountain Rangers had arrived at sunset, but Walter understood the gist of the operation. Next to each crane was a massive wooden treadmill, with space inside for around two dozen slaves. Ropes and cables ran from each treadmill up to a series of pulleys, which were connected to the cranes. Presumably, Walter guessed, the slaves would walk one way to lower the crane, and the other way to raise it. Two of the cranes were on the western bank of the Antiago River, and the other two lay opposite them. The arms of all four could reach down into the river, but they were long enough to extend over the side of the cliff, though Walter couldn't see the mechanism by which they were turned.

A low palisade wall ringed the compound, broken only by the waterfall and by a gap in the river to allow approaching barges to pass through. Three large wooden structures sat on one bank, and there was a rope bridge strung out over the river, to allow access to the cranes on the eastern bank.

Walter glanced up. It was a dark night. The Big Red Moon and the Silver Moon were nowhere to be seen, and the Little Red Moon was setting. Perfect conditions, in other words. The background roar of the waterfall was drowning out any sounds coming from the forest, and that would also help them.

'It'll be tonight,' he whispered.

Otto nodded. 'Yes, sir. Objectives?'

'A quick raid, nothing more,' said Walter. 'Do you see any stairs that lead down the cliffs?'

'No, sir, but I'm guessing that they might be behind the largest building. I can't see where else they could be, if they exist.'

'They must exist,' said Walter. 'They surely don't use cranes to raise and lower the same slaves who operate them. If we can find them, then we could head down the cliffs to the lower level, and enter Steppen that way.'

'The stairs are bound to be guarded, sir; at the top and at the bottom. It's one of the main escape routes any fleeing slaves might take.'

Walter nodded. 'I wish we knew if Princess Abigone and the others made it here safely. For all we know, they could be lying dead in the forest, or they might be prisoners of the Whalebone King.'

'The princess is a Maker, sir. I doubt that she would allow herself to be taken prisoner.'

'The Westlanders captured her in Upper Down; have you forgotten?'

'No, sir, but won't she have learned much by now, if she attended a school for Makers in Klef Mordain? And she has others with her – other Masters and Makers. If they have a Master as good as Hector was, then I imagine that they will be able to look after themselves.'

They fell into silence as they watched the mercenaries in the compound perform a changing of the guard. Those who had been manning the gates and watching the cranes were relieved by a new group who had emerged from one of the wooden buildings. The process seemed informal and a little chaotic, and there were periods of time when no one was guarding the approaches along the river. Some of the mercenaries broke away to chat in small groups, while others passed around bottles of something that they swigged in turn.

'Watching this makes me feel embarrassed for all soldiers, sir,' Otto said. 'If I was their sergeant, I would have each one of them whipped for sheer bloody incompetence.'

'They're lazy and complacent, just as Aisly and Duggan told us. I'd bet none of them have ever imagined an attack coming from this direction. Right; I have a plan. Let's go back and tell the others.'

The two men crawled backwards through the undergrowth until they were out of sight of the compound, then they got to their feet and made their way to where Lieutenant Dietar and the two Westlanders were based. It was a ten minute walk through the forest, and the two Rangers moved like ghosts, keeping silent for the entire journey. Walter made a sound like a tawny owl when they were twenty yards away, and Dietar appeared by a thick stand of brambles, his bow in his hand.

Walter and Otto passed the brambles, then they sat down in a small clearing next to Duggan and Aisly.

'You were gone for a long time,' said Aisly. 'We thought you had been captured.'

'We needed a few hours to give the place a decent look,' said Walter. 'Preparation is key, and we needed to know how the compound operates. I assume that the cranes are rarely used?'

'That's right,' said Duggan. 'They are only operated when barges appear.'

'Does that mean there are no slaves kept up here if there are no barges to lower?'

'Not exactly,' said Duggan. 'The soldiers keep a few slaves at the top of the cliff to work for them, but most are only brought up when they are needed.'

'And they go via a flight of stairs?'

'Yes.'

'We couldn't see where any stairs come out at the top of the cliff,' said Otto.

'That's because the stairs begin inside one of the buildings,' said Duggan. 'To go down, you have to enter the building closest to the cliff's edge. There are iron gates, which are locked when the stairs are not in use.'

'That isn't great news,' said Walter.

'There are also iron gates at the bottom,' Duggan went on, 'to stop slaves from climbing up.'

'Again, not the best news I could have heard,' said Walter, 'but these challenges are there to be overcome.'

'Have you told them about the other stairs?' said Aisly.

'There are other stairs?' said Walter.

'They're a few miles to the east of here,' said Duggan; 'but it's more of a rough path, rather than stairs. That's how Aisly and I got out. We climbed up them. It's not easy, especially in the dark.'

'Would you be able to find them from here?'

'Eventually. We would have to trek along the top of the cliff until we found them. We've only seen them once, and it was dark, and we were being chased. We didn't have time to map out the area.'

'And we never thought we'd be coming back,' said Aisly.

'Then, you know how to access the track from the bottom of the cliffs?'

'Yes,' said Duggan; 'but we would have to be down there first.'

'You mentioned you had a plan, sir?' said Otto.

'That plan has already turned to shit,' said Walter. 'I hadn't imagined that we might have to get past a locked iron gate.' He eyed the Westlanders. 'I don't suppose you know where the keys for this gate are kept?'

Duggan emitted a grim laugh. 'If we'd known that, we might have escaped a lot sooner.'

'Bollocks,' said Walter. 'We are going to have to kill more people than I had originally planned for. I wonder if the mercenaries up here have any way to contact Steppen in an emergency. Well, I guess we'll find out soon enough.'

'Are we going in, sir?' said Dietar, who was standing by the edge of the clearing.

Walter nodded. 'Knives and stealth. Make sure we have nothing shiny on our clothes, and we'll need to coat our blades with river mud. And our faces, too. It'll be hard to communicate within the compound at first without giving our positions away, so we will have to go over every detail of the plan, so that we each know what our jobs will be.'

Otto raised an eyebrow. 'I thought you said your plan had gone to shit, sir.'

'Don't worry,' said Walter; 'I have a new one.'

Six mercenaries were posted by the outer defences of the compound, while a further two were guarding each end of the rope bridge that was suspended over the river. The locations of the soldiers had been poorly chosen, and more than one position was out of sight of the others. On top of that, at least three of the soldiers appeared to be sleeping by their posts. The one opposite the undergrowth where Walter had hidden was still awake, but he was drinking from a bottle, and his gaze was rarely on the forest.

Walter ensured he made no sound while he waited for the others in his small band to get into their positions. The three Rangers had gone over the various calls they would make to denote specific messages – the hoot of a barn owl if it all went to shit and they had to retreat in a hurry; or the clicking call of the hawfinch if anyone required immediate assistance; and Walter could only hope that the Westlanders had been able to take it all in. Using untrained Westlanders alongside Mountain Rangers was always going to be a risk, and he had allocated jobs to Aisly and Duggan that he felt were within their capabilities. Whether they would stick to those orders was anyone's guess.

Walter heard a nasally sound that was Otto's best impersonation of a nightjar. The call meant that everyone was in position, and Walter began to inch towards the palisade wall in front of him. He kept low, and worked his way to the side of the wall that faced away from where the soldier was standing. He reached up, gripped the top of the wooden beams, and pulled himself up until he could look over the narrow parapet. The guard had his back to him, and he was gazing over the compound, the half-empty bottle in his right hand. Walter eased himself up and over the wall, and dropped to the other side without a sound. He drew his knife, and almost felt sorry for the mercenary as he stole forwards. The man turned at the last moment, and Walter drove the knife into his neck, his left hand reaching up at the same time to smother any cries. Walter pushed the man to the ground, and eased the blade deep into his heart, holding his hand over his mouth until he had breathed his last. Walter took the man's basin-shaped helmet and put it onto his own head, then he stood, as though he were the guard on duty. He looked out over the dark forest, then he turned to gaze into the compound. He could see the back of one more soldier by the palisade wall, and, in the distance, he could see the man guarding the near end of the bridge. He noticed the bottle lying on the ground next to his feet, and picked it up. He sniffed, and grimaced; then he found the stopper, pushed it into place, and stashed the bottle into an inside pocket of his coat. He rifled through the man's pockets, but found nothing of any use, then he unbuckled the soldier's sword and attached it to his own belt.

He glanced back up at the wall, but the soldier he had seen with his back to him had gone, and Dietar was crouching in his place with a knife in his hands. The lieutenant turned and raised a hand towards Walter and, at this signal, Walter returned the gesture and stepped down from the wall. He crept along to the left, as Dietar moved to his right. Walter came to the next soldier, who was sitting slumped by the wall, snoring. Walter slit the man's throat, spilling blood down the front of his sweat-stained uniform. Again, he searched through the soldier's pockets, but he had been carrying nothing of any value. Walter carried on, and reached the main gate of the compound. Otto, Duggan and Aisly were already there, sheltering in the shadows by the wall, and the two soldiers who had been on duty were lying dead by their feet.

'This almost feels wrong, sir,' Otto whispered. 'The mercenaries are bloody hopeless.' He eyed Duggan and Aisly. 'It couldn't have been that difficult to escape, not with those fools on duty.'

'They've lowered their guard because every slave in the crane compound is locked up for the night,' Duggan said. 'They aren't usually so fucking useless.'

'This is as good as it'll get,' said Walter. 'After tonight, they will be more vigilant. Have you searched for keys?'

'Yes, sir, but we didn't find any.'

Dietar approached from the other side, and entered the shadows next to the others.

'I've killed my two,' he said. 'The only guards left are those by the bridge, and one of them's asleep.'

'Let's carry on with stage two of the plan,' said Walter.

'Should we keep looking for the keys to the stairs, sir?' said Otto. 'They will be somewhere inside one of those buildings.'

'They won't be in the closest building,' said Duggan. 'That holds the slaves who live up here. The central building is where the soldiers eat, drink and sleep.'

'Forget the keys for now,' said Walter. 'Have the gates been unbarred?'

'Yes, sir,' said Otto.

Walter turned to the two Westlanders. 'Duggan and Aisly, I want you to go to the building where the slaves are being held. Wait for the rest of us to attack the barracks, then break in. Release the slaves, and escort them to the main gates. Gather up every weapon you can find, and then lead them out into the forest. Don't go too far though; we will need to find you when we leave.'

The Westlanders nodded.

Walter turned to Otto and Dietar. 'Are you ready for the hardest part of the evening? We'll need to be quick, silent and ruthless. I want every soldier in the barracks dead within a few minutes.'

'There will be more soldiers in the last building,' said Duggan; 'the one next to the cliff where the stairs begin. There will be at least two by the iron gates, and maybe more.'

'We'll deal with them after we've visited the barracks,' said Walter. He gestured to Otto and Dietar. 'Let's go.'

Walter led the way to the central building, as Otto and Dietar crept along behind him. They reached the front of the squat barracks, and stole up the three steps to the main door. Walter listened for several moments, but heard nothing coming from inside. He eased open the door, and they moved into the building. They passed through an empty hallway, and came to a dark room with a line of bunk beds running down each side. Walter listened again, and heard the sound of gentle snoring coming from a few of the beds. Opposite the room was another door, from under which a faint light was emanating. Walter gestured for Otto and Dietar to carry on into the dormitory, while he turned towards the door.

As soon as Walter heard the muffled cries coming from the bunk beds, he opened the other door and ran inside. A mercenary officer was sitting with his feet up on a bench, smoking from an elaborate water pipe. He stared at Walter, then his right hand reached for a sheathed sword. Walter leapt forward. He punched the man in the face, then he pushed the sword away, and held his knife to the officer's throat.

'Good evening,' said Walter. 'You really should think about improving your security.'

'What do you want?' said the officer.

'Some information would be nice. When did the last barges arrive here?'

'A few days ago, but it was only a single barge; and it had no cargo.'

'What was it doing here?'

'The bargemen said they'd been carrying passengers; passengers who were looking for four missing children. I saw those children – the Whalebone King has them.'

'What happened to the passengers?'

'They went down the eastern steps. Lord Ragnvald apprehended them in the forest.'

'Did you see them?'

'No, but I heard they'd been taken to the temple.'

'Where is the single barge now?'

'They've gone. We lowered them down the cliff, and they set off again. They'll be on their way to Elestia by now.'

'Where are the keys for the stair gates?'

'There is a set in my desk drawer. They open the gates at the top of the cliffs, and at the bottom. Who are you?'

Walter grabbed his hair, pushed his head forward, and stabbed him in the back of the neck. He pulled the blade out, wiped it on the officer's uniform, then he rummaged through the desk. He found a large set of keys, and placed them into a coat pocket, then he kept looking. He had just found the officer's supply of alcohol when Otto and Dietar appeared at the door.

'All mercenaries are accounted for, sir,' said Dietar, as he and Otto watched Walter pick up two bottles of Yearlian brandy. 'Are we having a party, sir?'

'The Westlander slaves will be needing a drink,' said Walter, 'once we're all safely back in the forest. Oh, and I have the keys for the stairs.'

'Are we descending tonight, sir?'

'Not if there are slaves to be freed up here,' said Walter. 'Have Duggan and Aisly made their move?'

'Perhaps we should take a look, sir.'

They left the barracks, and saw Duggan and Aisly trying to break through the entrance of the building housing the slaves. They were making far too much noise, and a door opened in the third building along.

'What's going on over there?' called a voice.

'Bloody Westlanders,' muttered Walter. 'There goes our surprise.'

He glanced back into the hallway of the barracks, and saw a rack of crossbows. He grabbed one, found where the bolts were stored, and began loading it. Otto and Dietar joined in, and the three Rangers got the bows ready as quickly as possible.

'I don't think these things have been used in quite a while, sir,' said Otto.

'Shut up and keep loading,' said Walter. 'When you've finished with that one, start loading two more, while Dietar and I loose.'

Walter cradled his loaded crossbow, then he knelt by the open doorway of the barracks. Dietar knelt down next to him, and they both aimed out into the compound. They could hear more mercenaries coming out of the building on their left, then five entered their line of sight. The mercenaries were drawing their swords and running towards Duggan and Aisly.

'You go for the one on the left; I'll take the one on the right,' said Walter.

Dietar nodded, then both men loosed. Two of the mercenaries fell, the bolts hitting their backs. Walter and Dietar dropped their bows, and Otto passed them two freshly-loaded ones. They raised the bows, aimed, and loosed again, and two more mercenaries fell. One of them was still alive, and he began screaming in pain, waking up the guard who was sleeping by the rope bridge. Aisly ran over to the injured mercenary, holding the knife that Walter had given her, and she drove it into the man's chest, stilling his cries. The fifth mercenary had fled by that time, running back towards the third building. The guard from the rope bridge took one look at the carnage and did the same thing, sprinting across the courtyard towards the safety of the building perched upon the top of the cliff.

Otto handed Walter another loaded bow. Walter tracked left, aimed, and loosed at the guard from the bridge. The bolt hit the soldier in the back of the head, and he fell to the ground.

'Good shot, sir,' said Dietar.

The three Rangers walked out of the barrack building and bounded down the steps. They turned to face the third building along. Faces were peering out at them from a couple of windows on the ground floor, and the door had been closed.

'If I had to guess, sir,' said Otto, 'then, right about now, someone is running down the stairs to warn the others that the cranes are under attack.'

'I think you might be right,' said Walter.

They walked over to the building housing the slaves, where Duggan and Aisly were standing.

'You appear to have woken everyone up,' Walter went on.

'We couldn't get the doors open,' said Duggan.

Walter took out the set of keys and threw them to the Westlander. 'Try one of these,' he said. 'I'm going back to the barracks to gather as many weapons as I can find. Otto, keep an eye on the last building. Shout for me if anyone else is brave enough to come out. Dietar, take a knife and cut through the ropes of the bridge.'

Walter walked back to the barrack building. He found a large sack, and began filling it, throwing in crossbows, bolts, blankets, and the two bottles of brandy. He then filled another sack with the contents of a few crates of food he discovered in the corner of the officer's room. He pulled out another, opened it, and smiled. It was full of jars containing oil for the compound's lamps. He dragged the two sacks outside, then he smashed several of the jars in the different rooms of the building. He found the matches the officer had been using to light his pipe, struck one, and dropped it into a puddle of lamp oil. The flames whooshed up, and began to spread. Walter hurried out of the building. Dietar had cut through the ropes on the western side of the bridge, and it had collapsed into the river, leaving a solitary guard on the other side, who seemed too drunk to understand what was happening. Over by the slave building, Duggan was still trying to find the right key for the lock, so Walter took what remained of the jars to the base of one of the tall, wooden cranes. The beams were thick and strong, and unlikely to burn without a lot of heat and flames, so Walter turned his attentions to the ropes and pulleys. He opened the last jars and poured their contents onto the tall coils of ropes, then he lit another match and stood back to admire the flames.

The sound of a roaring fire was coming from behind him, so he turned and saw the flames that had taken hold of the barrack building.

Smoke was streaming up into the night sky, obscuring the stars. Another noise distracted him – the sound of voices. Walter walked past the burning barracks, and saw slaves staggering out of the front of the first building. Duggan and Aisly were talking to them in their own language, and Walter saw Otto standing close by, listening. Walter reached the two sacks, and dragged them over to the small crowd of filthy and emaciated Westlanders. All of them were men, and several looked ill or injured.

'This is the one in charge,' Duggan said, pointing towards him.

The Westlanders eyed Walter as he pulled the sacks towards them. Dietar rejoined them, and the three Mountain Rangers formed a line, as the suspicious Westlanders stared at them.

'We have food, we have weapons, and we have brandy,' said Walter. 'Anyone who wants to stay is welcome to, but I advise that we get the fuck out of here as quickly as possible, before reinforcements arrive at the top of the stairs.'

'There are thousands of our kinsfolk enslaved at the bottom of the cliffs,' said a tall Westlander, 'including hundreds of our womenfolk. I would be ashamed if we ran away without helping them.'

'One thing at a time,' said Walter. 'This was just our first raid. If you stick with me, there will be many more to come.'

'Why?' said the Westlander. 'Why are you doing this?'

'Several reasons,' said Walter. 'I also have friends who are trapped in Steppen. I want to cause the Whalebone King as much pain as possible, to distract him, so that my friends can do what they need to do. Also, I don't like slavers, and I don't like people who buy and sell children. I think it's time we taught them a painful lesson.'

'Should we follow him?' said another.

'I trust him,' said Duggan. 'He has been true to his word.'

The tall Westlander nodded. 'All right; we shall come with you, but only if you promise us that we shall return to free the others.'

'I promise,' said Walter. 'Otto, open the gate. Let's go.'

. . .

It was dawn before Walter allowed the freed slaves to rest. They had walked for hours through the dark forest, putting miles between them and the cranes at the top of the cliffs, until they found a sheltered spot near a stream that flowed down to the Antiago. They set up a small camp, and Walter unpacked the food, weapons and brandy. He left everything there for the Westlanders to distribute among themselves, and then Walter took Otto and Dietar aside. They climbed up a steep bank by the edge of the clearing and sat down as the sun rose over the great expanse of forest. In the distance ahead of them, a small plume of smoke marked the location of the barracks building, and Walter smiled at the sight.

'A decent night's work,' said Walter.

'I counted twenty dead mercenaries, one damaged crane, one barracks razed to the ground, and one damaged bridge,' said Dietar; 'as well as thirteen freed Westlanders to add to the two we already had with us, sir. Eighteen mouths are a lot to feed. We shall need to think carefully about how to gather enough food.'

'We also have the keys for the stairs,' said Walter, 'but I don't know how much use they'll be. The mercenaries are bound to reinforce the entire area next to the cranes, and they will probably be watching the path over to the east. Princess Abigone and the others took that path when they got here, but they were arrested when they reached the bottom of the cliffs.'

'Did the officer tell you that, sir?' said Otto.

Walter nodded. 'We now know that the four abducted children are here, along with Princess Abigone, Lothar, and whoever else was with them.'

Dietar frowned. 'What is our priority, sir? Are we here to help Princess Abigone, or to free a bunch of Westlander slaves? I was under the impression that the only reason we travelled all the way into the middle of the forest was to assist the princess, but I heard the promise you made to the Westlanders. Are we supposed to do both? Is that even possible?'

Walter said nothing.

'I agree with Lieutenant Dietar, sir,' said Otto. 'I haven't forgotten that the Westlanders were trying to take over Upper Down not so long ago. They killed Alfgang the Pius, and tried to slaughter us all at the Battle of the Gap. You have a good heart, sir, but rescuing thousands of Westlanders is not our responsibility.'

The Rangers fell into silence as Aisly climbed up the bank to join them. She gazed out at the view of the sunrise over the forest, then she turned to face the three men.

'I had my doubts about you,' she said. 'I couldn't believe that anyone from Upper Down would want to help Westlanders, and I didn't trust you. I was wrong. Thank you for saving the men from the crane compound, and thank you for restoring my faith in humanity.'

'You're welcome,' said Walter.

'You are good men,' she went on, 'and Aloth knows we need them right now. Where you lead, we will follow.'

CHAPTER 13
PROPOSITIONED

Steppen, Great Forest, Jallin, Central Provinces – 3rd Day of Quoma 108

'There are many legends and stories about Makers who have been able to summon living animals,' said Fyenna, as Abigone, Raewyn and Stanza listened; 'but the last confirmed case occurred nearly four hundred years ago. It was Empress Regula who performed the summoning, and her act was witnessed by dozens of the imperial court. Regula was possibly the greatest Maker of all time, but this particular summoning might have done more damage to the reputation of Makers than any other episode during the time of the Elestian Empire.'

'What did she summon?' said Abigone.

'A dog,' said Fyenna. 'The empress first had six healthy dogs killed, then she summoned her new dog from the flesh, blood and bone of their remains. The waste shocked everyone who saw it, and that overshadowed what was otherwise an astonishing achievement. Regula's popularity plummeted, for how could anyone justify the deaths of six living beings in order to create one?'

'Did the dog survive, ma'am?' said Stanza.

'The dog outlived the empress,' said Fyenna. 'Regula sank into despair after this highly-public display of her powers, and she died four years later, while the dog went on to live for another two years after that. Some believe that the act of summoning had utterly exhausted the empress. Imagine – for the few seconds in which the summoning took place, Regula had to hold every single piece of information about the physical make up of a dog within her mind. Every detail, and it all had to be accurate. She had studied and practised for years leading up to the summoning; in many ways it was the summit of her life's work. And yet, despite the scale of her achievement, she was vilified afterwards, and had to withdraw from public life.' She glanced at her three students. 'The lesson here is that any attempt to summon a living being is doomed to failure, even if the summoning itself is a success. Summoning life has but one purpose – to destroy life. It is a weapon every bit as terrible as that of a Master changing blood to salt, but if you are ever seen using this power, you will be feared and hated, just as Regula was.'

Raewyn lowered her glance. 'I still feel terrible about what we did to the Sanctian sailors. I understand that they would have killed us, but to murder them in such a fashion…'

'We did an awful thing,' said Fyenna. 'That it was necessary does not alter that fact.'

'I disagree,' said Abigone. 'Which part of it was awful? If anything, we were merciful, as we gave the sailors a quick death. Was it disgusting? Yes. Seeing the blood, bone and muscle trying to form itself into horses was a repellent sight, but I don't think we did anything wrong.'

'The spirits disapprove of Makers trying to summon life,' said Stanza. 'The spirits gave us this power in order to do good; we shouldn't use it to murder people.'

'I don't think the spirits care,' said Abigone. 'If they did, then couldn't they remove our abilities? My brother once refused to use his Master powers when he was ambushed by Westlanders, and they killed him. He could have defended himself, but he thought like you, Stanza.'

'Despite what the priests say, no one knows how the spirits feel about the use of our powers,' said Fyenna. 'Some religious sects believe that the spirits only approve of some of our actions; while the Sanctians believe that Masters and Makers have corrupted the power bestowed upon us by the spirits. No one knows the truth, so be wary of what any individual priest tells you.'

A few shouts rose up from outside the temple, and Abigone and the others turned towards the chamber's large window. Lothar was standing there, gazing out.

'There seems to be a lot of shouting going on this morning,' Fyenna said. 'Can you see anything?'

Lothar shook his head. 'I can't see anyone down on the ground,' he said, 'but I can hear soldiers moving, and I can hear them talking. Something went on last night; something bad, but I don't know what.'

'Perhaps Magnus will visit us today,' said Raewyn. 'He might know what's going on.'

'I don't know if we should trust anything that boy says,' said Fyenna.

'But you said he was welcome to visit us at any time.'

'He is our only contact with the outside world,' said Fyenna.

'Remember what Reath told us,' said Abigone. 'She said that the slave women liked Magnus; they said he was different from his father and his brothers, that he was decent at heart. All the same, it is likely that his father sent him here to learn what he could about us.'

'Do they know that we are Masters and Makers?' said Stanza.

'They know about the youngest four,' said Abigone, 'but I don't think they know about the rest of us.'

'I would like to keep it that way,' said Fyenna. 'If Magnus appears, we must not tell him too much. Let the Whalebone King speculate and guess as to whom among us might have abilities. His lack of certainty will keep us safe.'

'Safe?' said Lothar. 'We could break out of here any time we liked, and yet we are acting like prisoners.'

'My responsibility is to ensure that my students survive,' said Fyenna. 'If we escaped, we would face a terrible month of trekking through the forest; and escaping might not be as easy as you think. The king and at least two of his sons are Masters; they could do us terrible damage.'

'One of those sons is Magnus,' said Lothar; 'I doubt he could do all that much.'

'But the other is Ragnvald,' said Fyenna, 'and he strikes me as a particularly callous young man. The simple option is that we stay here, and wait for the next barges to arrive. I think the king is wary of us. He is probably looking forward to us leaving Steppen, so that he can go back to doing whatever it is that he does here.'

'What about the slaves?' said Abigone. 'If some of them are citizens of the Central Provinces, then shouldn't we do something to help them?'

'We could save Magnus's mother,' said Raewyn.

'My priority is you, not the slaves,' said Fyenna. 'We can report the king's activities to the proper authorities in Elestia, if that will salve your conscience.'

'You would report a Master to the Sanctians?' said Stanza.

'The fact that he is a Master is irrelevant if he is breaking the law,' said Fyenna.

'But we are breaking the law,' said Abigone. 'All Masters and Makers are supposed to hand themselves in to the Sanctians; and yet we haven't.'

Fyenna looked exasperated. 'You might understand compromises a little better when you are older,' she said. 'For now, you will have to trust me. I think I shall see how the other students are doing. I must say, Abigone, that it was a good idea to restart our lessons while we are confined to these quarters.'

Fyenna got to her feet and walked towards another doorway.

'I know that Lady Fyenna is trying to keep us safe,' said Abigone, 'but there is something about this place that unsettles me. The Whalebone King knows that some of us are Masters and Makers; and we know that three of them are Masters, and yet none of us have mentioned it openly in front of each other.'

'Maybe they just want us to leave,' said Stanza.

'Then why didn't the king keep the barge here, to take us away? They knew we were coming, because the bargemen told them. If they wanted to see the back of us, then why didn't the barge wait? Why did it rush off as though it was in a hurry? The king must have known that we would be stuck here for a month if the barge continued onwards. He wants something from us.'

'What?' said Raewyn.

'I don't know.'

Fyenna walked back into the room. 'The others are doing well,' she said. 'Mor Galthide is giving some lessons in self defence, and Denny is assisting him.'

More shouts echoed up from outside, and Abigone joined Lothar by the window. The others got up and walked over. Abigone leaned out of the window, and saw a small group of soldiers running past the left-hand edge of the temple.

'I wonder if some slaves have escaped,' she said.

Abigone turned her head to face the other direction. In the distance, she could see three of the five waterfalls. The one on the left was on its own, some two hundred yards to the west, but the other two were close together. Dark cave entrances littered the side of the cliffs by the central waterfalls, but there was no one in sight.

'If the silver mine is in there,' she said, 'then why do we never see anyone going in or out?'

Someone rapped on their front door, and they turned to see it swing open. Magnus walked in, then the door was closed and locked behind him.

'Hello,' he said. 'How are you all today?'

'We are well,' said Fyenna. 'How is Steppen? There seems to be a considerable amount of activity this morning, especially from the soldiers stationed here.'

Magnus walked over to the window.

'I didn't think you would have heard any of that,' he said.

'What does that mean?' said Abigone. 'Are you trying to keep something from us? Why don't we ever see any slaves when we look out of the window?'

Magnus looked embarrassed for a moment.

'Does your father not wish us to see certain things?' said Abigone.

'Maybe,' he said.

Lothar laughed. 'By trying to hide things from us, you are only making us more suspicious.'

'It's nothing sinister,' said Magnus. 'The king knows that you do not approve of slavery, so he asked that the slaves go by the other side of the temple while you're here.'

'And what about this morning's activity?' said Fyenna.

Magnus lowered his gaze. 'Steppen was attacked last night, by brigands sneaking about in the forest. They assaulted the cranes at the top of the cliff and killed several soldiers.'

'Steppen was assaulted, eh?' said Lothar. 'Were any of these brigands captured?'

'No. They all got away. They burned down a barracks, killed twenty soldiers, and captured a dozen Westlander slaves.'

'These brigands seem quite professional,' said Lothar. 'Did they *capture* the slaves; or did they release them?'

'That depends on your point of view, I suppose,' said Magnus. 'Anyway, the crane compound is being reinforced, and extra soldiers are keeping watch on the stairs that you used when you came down the Step. We are certain that the brigands are still on the upper level, and we want to keep them there.'

'Do brigands regularly attack Steppen?' said Abigone.

'This is the first time I can remember it happening,' said Magnus. 'They sometimes attack the barge convoys, but never Steppen itself. Why would anyone want to attack us? I know that my father used to raid for slaves in Jallin, but that hasn't happened for twenty years. Who would want to do us harm? But, don't worry. You are all safe in here. The temple is guarded by the king's best soldiers.'

'If the mine is at risk,' said Fyenna, 'then shouldn't the Sanctian agent resident here send for help?'

'He, uh... I don't think Lord Matteo wishes to get involved,' said Magnus.

'And why would that be? He is corrupt, isn't he? You can say it, Magnus. Lord Matteo wouldn't be the first corrupt servant of the Sanctian Empire. They like to believe that they are better than everyone else, but they are prey to the same temptations faced by anyone with too much power.'

Magnus said nothing.

'Don't scare him away,' said Raewyn. 'He comes here to see how we are, not to be interrogated.'

Fyenna shot Raewyn a withering glance, and she looked away.

'Let's sit down and chat about something else,' said Abigone.

She led the others to the couches, and they sat down, except for Lothar, who remained by the window.

'Were there other children here when you were growing up?' Raewyn said.

'Just my brothers,' said Magnus. 'Ragnvald is thirteen years older than me. Where did you grow up?'

Raewyn eyed Fyenna, who nodded.

'I am from Klef Mordain,' said Raewyn. 'Have you heard of it?'

'I've heard the name. It's a city, yes? I've never seen a city.'

'It's a big city, and it's also a port. It lies on the coast of the ocean. Every day, there would be dozens of ships in the harbour, and some of those ships used to cross the ocean, to trade with the lands on the other side.'

'Can you see these other lands from Klef Mordain?'

Raewyn laughed. 'No. The other side is thousands of miles away. It takes a ship weeks to get there.'

'I must seem very stupid to you.'

'It's not stupidity; it's ignorance,' said Raewyn; 'and ignorance can be overcome with a little education. I don't mind teaching you about the outside world.'

'Have you seen much of it?'

'I once sailed all the way down the coast to Subnestia,' she said; 'and I've seen Jallin, Campsie, Esttal and Lesser Down.'

'Wow,' said Magnus. 'I haven't even heard of some of those places. And you've been on a ship?'

'Many times,' she said, 'although I confess that I have never learned how to sail properly.'

'Have you ever crossed the ocean?'

'My father has, once. He told me about the mountains he saw there, and the trading posts. And the strange people.'

'Why did you leave Klef Mordain?' said Magnus. 'Why did you travel to Jallin?'

Raewyn hesitated.

'There are certain things we would rather not discuss,' said Fyenna.

'Oh. Sorry,' said Magnus.

'Don't apologise,' said Raewyn. 'You weren't to know. Do you have a school here?'

Magnus shook his head. 'My mother taught me to read and write.'

'I would like to meet her,' said Abigone.

'That... that's not allowed. Sorry. The king doesn't want my mother speaking to any of you. He said that she would fill your heads with lies about him.'

Denny and Constans walked into the room. Constans saw Magnus sitting on the couch next to Raewyn, and he gave the young man a look of contempt.

'Good morning, Magnus,' said Denny.

'Good morning,' said Magnus.

'Can I speak to you for a moment, Raewyn?' said Constans.

'I am in the middle of a conversation,' she said.

'I should probably leave,' said Magnus, getting to his feet.

'You don't need to,' said Raewyn. 'Don't you like speaking to me?'

Magnus gazed down at her for a moment, then he looked away. 'Yes, but... I should go.'

He walked towards the front door of the apartment just as it opened again. In walked the king, Ragnvald and Erling. The king smiled broadly, then he noticed Magnus.

'Here again, eh?' said the king. 'I hope my boy hasn't been pestering you all.'

'Magnus has been a charming and gracious visitor,' said Fyenna.

Erling laughed. 'Charming? That little runt?'

'Close your mouth,' the king said, giving Erling a look that would have melted iron. 'Ignore my rude third son; I beg you. He sometimes speaks before his brain has woken up for the day. Now, my Lady Fyenna, I would be obliged if all of the guests could be summoned, as I wish to speak to you about an important matter.'

'I'll do it,' said Lothar.

'You have my thanks, soldier,' said the king. 'Shall we sit, my sons?'

The king, Ragnvald and Erling sat down on a couch, while Magnus remained standing behind his father with his head bowed.

'Have the barges arrived?' said Constans.

'No, not yet,' said the king.

'Are you here to discuss last night's attack?' said Abigone.

The king blinked, then he and his elder sons turned to look at Magnus.

'I told them what happened, sir,' said Magnus. 'Was I not supposed to?'

Ragnvald rolled his eyes, then they turned back to face the others.

'We are not here to discuss that trivial incident,' said the king. 'A few desperate brigands are the least of my worries. My other son, Einar, is taking care of the matter.'

A side door opened, and the rest of the party filed through. Reath, Nyli, Ignatius and Salus stared at the sight of the Whalebone King sitting on the couch, but no one spoke as they all found seats.

'Is that everyone?' said the king. 'Let me begin by saying that I hope your stay here has been comfortable. You have been in Steppen for ten days, which means you have another twenty before the next convoy arrives. Twenty days, and then you will be on your way; or perhaps not.'

'What do you mean?' said Fyenna.

'I will get to that shortly,' said the king. 'I am an old man, Fyenna, and the older I get, the more I begin to dwell upon the legacy I will leave behind. For over thirty years, I have ruled Steppen, and in that time I have fathered four sons. Is it wrong of me to be concerned for their futures? The only people who live here are soldiers, the workers, my old crewmates, and my sons. I couldn't be prouder of my fine boys, but what will happen to them without wives? There are no young women here; and then you all appear one day.'

Fyenna's eyes tightened. 'You can stop there,' she said. 'When the barges come, we shall all be leaving.'

'But you haven't listened to my proposition, my lady,' said the king.

'I don't need to,' she said. 'None of my students will be staying here as wives for your sons.'

'I can promise them a life of safety and comfort,' said the king. 'A life of riches and security. Why not let the girls decide for themselves? Let them talk to my sons, and we shall see if any sparks are generated.'

'Lady Fyenna has given you her reply,' said Mor Galthide.

'Does she control the lives of everyone in this chamber?' said Ragnvald. 'Eshia, Raewyn and Abigone look old enough to make their own decisions.'

'I am already betrothed,' said Abigone, 'and so I politely decline your kind invitation.'

'I also decline,' said Eshia. 'I have no interest in getting married, thank you.'

Several people glanced at Raewyn, whose features flushed.

'Raewyn also declines,' said Fyenna. 'Isn't that so, Raewyn?'

Raewyn nodded, her gaze downcast.

'Let's not make any definite pronouncements on this matter,' said the king. 'You have twenty days in which to mull it over. If any of you girls wish to speak to my sons in that time, the soldiers on duty outside can fetch us.' He smiled, a crafty look on his face. 'Some of my sons, in their haste, have already picked out their favourites from among you. Ragnvald, for instance, has his heart set on you, Eshia.'

Eshia's eyes widened.

Ragnvald shook his head at his father, then he turned to Eshia. 'I apologise for that. The king thinks Erling has a big mouth, but he is just as bad. I would like to get to know you better, Eshia, but I would respect any decision you came to. Give me a chance, that's all I ask.'

Eshia said nothing.

The king glanced around at the faces of the others. 'We seem to have embarrassed everyone, boys, so perhaps we should take our leave.' He got to his feet, and Erling and Ragnvald did the same. 'Still,' the king went on, 'you can't blame an old man for trying; especially not an old man with four unmarried sons. I hope you take some time to think it over. It's not every day you get the chance to join the ranks of a royal family, eh?'

They walked to the front door, and Ragnvald knocked upon it. For a moment, Magnus looked as though he was going to stay behind, but a curt glance from his father sent him hurrying towards the door. A soldier opened it, and the four men left the chamber.

'What the fuck was all that about?' said Lothar, as soon as the door was closed.

'At least we know the reason for all the awkwardness,' said Abigone. 'The king must have had this in mind since we arrived.'

'But he should have known what our response would be,' said Fyenna.

'Perhaps we should consider it from his point of view,' said Mor Galthide. 'Steppen gets few visitors from the outside world; is it any wonder that he sees an opportunity to marry off a few of his sons?'

'It was creepy and weird,' said Reath. 'That's not how people meet each other.'

'It is in the world of the aristocracy, little one,' said Mor Galthide. 'A duke says to a count – I have a son and you have a daughter; let's marry them off and unite our families. It happens all the time.'

'That's very true,' said Abigone. 'My father chose who his children were to marry; we didn't have much say in it.'

'The same thing happens in the imperial court on Sanctos,' said Denny. 'No one there marries out of love.'

'All right,' said Reath; 'then you're all weird and creepy, too. Us normal folk don't behave like that. And besides, the Whalebone King isn't a real king, just because he wears that horrible yellow thing on his head. We wouldn't be marrying into a proper royal family.'

'The sooner we are out of here, the better,' said Lothar.

'I feel a little more relaxed about our stay now,' said Annalise. 'I had suspected that they wanted to keep us here for nefarious reasons, not because the king is trying to find wives for his sons.'

A few of the others drifted away, going back to the rooms where they had been holding their lessons. Constans remained where he was, his eyes on Raewyn.

'Why didn't you decline?' he said.

Raewyn looked up at him.

'Abigone and Eshia both declined,' Constans went on, 'but you just sat there, saying nothing.'

'I... I was embarrassed.'

'You're lying to me. Admit that you like Magnus.'

'I don't know what you're talking about.'

'Raewyn did decline,' said Fyenna. 'I clearly saw her nod her head.'

'That was only after you spoke up for her,' said Constans.

'You are making something out of nothing, Constans.'

'Am I?' he said. 'When I walked in here earlier, I saw the way she was looking at Magnus. She didn't decline, because she wants to stay here.'

'That's not true,' said Raewyn. 'Are you suggesting that I wish to marry a boy I barely know? How ridiculous you sound, Constans.'

'Do you deny that you like him?'

'I... He... He seems nice, I suppose. That doesn't mean I want to marry him.'

Constans got to his feet. 'That's all I needed to hear. You like him. You like him more than you like me. You haven't been the same since we left Klef Mordain. You know something – I hope you do decide to stay here. I hope you and Magnus will be very happy together.'

He stormed out of the room, slamming the door behind him. Raewyn stared at the floor.

'Do you need a hanky?' said Fyenna.

'No, ma'am,' said Raewyn. 'I am past shedding tears over Constans.'

'Then I shall reprimand him for his words,' Fyenna said, standing. 'I will get an apology out of him; wait here.'

She walked out of the chamber, leaving only Raewyn, Abigone, Denny and Stanza still sitting on the couches.

'I don't want to marry Magnus,' Raewyn said.

'We know that,' said Abigone.

'But,' Raewyn went on, 'Constans was right about something – I do prefer Magnus to him. Maybe, if we could get the chance to talk more, then we might... I don't know. There's something about him. He seems vulnerable, but he killed the bargeman who stole Reath and the others. It's as though he's kind, but also strong when he has to be. Dear spirits, I don't even know what I'm saying any more. Please forget everything I've just said.'

'I like Magnus, too,' said Denny. 'Clearly not in the same way that you like him, Raewyn; but I know what you mean. He seems completely different from his father and brothers; as though he doesn't quite belong here.'

'And he's a Master,' said Abigone, 'though, none of us are supposed to mention that.'

'I wonder what he can do,' said Denny. 'With two older Masters in his family, he might have received a lot of training over the years.'

'What training?' said Abigone. 'Masters hardly require any.'

Denny smiled. 'You say that as if it were our fault.'

'Did you see poor Eshia's face?' said Stanza. 'Imagine a big brute like Ragnvald fancying you. I would have died of embarrassment. I wonder which one that horrible Erling likes. He makes my skin crawl. Magnus is certainly the nicest of them; not that I'm interested in him, Raewyn.'

Raewyn gave Stanza a look, but said nothing.

More shouts came from outside, and Abigone and Denny walked to the open window and looked out. A few soldiers were running past the temple, but they disappeared from view. Abigone turned her attention to the endless forest stretching out into the distance. Her earlier worries had abated a little. The Whalebone King had been hiding something from them, but it was something they didn't need to worry about. The twenty days would pass, and then they would get onto the barges and leave Steppen forever.

The king would have to look elsewhere to find wives for his sons, but that wasn't Abigone's problem.

CHAPTER 14
THE QUIET RAID

South of Steppen, Great Forest, Jallin, Central Provinces – 4th Day of Quoma 108

Saffie and a few soldiers crept up the dark track through the forest. It was a perfect night for moving undetected – of the three moons, only the Big Red Moon was out, and it was a mere sliver in the sky. Without the moons, the stars were shining brighter than usual, and the sky was filled with them.

Saffie and the others reached an abandoned shack by the side of the track, where a dozen more soldiers were waiting. Lieutenant Aldo was standing by the entrance to the shack, and he inclined his head when he saw Saffie approach.

'It's good to see you, ma'am,' said Aldo; 'I was just about to brief the detachment.'

Saffie got into line with the others, and Aldo faced them.

'I have a few points to cover before we raid Steppen this evening,' he said. 'First, this is not a full attack. Our purpose is to snatch an officer of the mercenary units based in the settlement, not to cause panic and alarm, and not to go on a rampage. I know that feelings have been running high over the last few days. I know that many of you would like nothing more than to give those damn savages a bloody nose, but that is not the objective of tonight's raid. Be patient – we shall attack in good time, and when we do, we will wipe the bastards out. Half of you will be staying here, ready to cover our retreat, while the other half will be coming with me. We shall enter the shanty settlement from the south, seize our victim, and withdraw. If we are successful, the mercenaries will not even realise that we have been in the settlement. If we are lucky, they will think that their officer wandered off and got lost in the forest. We will take him back to the ruined tower, where Captain Zola will interrogate him. Any questions?'

A soldier raised his arm. 'I thought we had already interrogated a prisoner, sir?'

'We have,' said Aldo. 'He was useful, to a certain extent, and it is thanks to his testimony that we were able to map the approaches to the settlement. However, he knew nothing about the interior of the Temple of Steppen, and that is where we shall strike when the full attack is ordered. The Whalebone King rarely leaves the temple, and his sons live there. For any attack to succeed, we shall need to know the layout of the building.' He stood back and regarded the lines of soldiers. 'Those in the front line shall be coming with me,' he went on. 'Those in the second line will remain here. Check your equipment, and secure anything that rattles. We shall be setting off as soon as the scouts return.'

The soldiers separated into two groups, and began to examine each other's kit. Saffie checked the armour straps of a young private, then he did the same with her. She glanced at the others as the soldier tightened the buckles at her back, and she saw the anger and hatred in their eyes. It had taken them almost a month to reach the southern outskirts of Steppen, and after the sights they had seen along the way, most of the soldiers were in the mood for a fight. They had left over sixty of their number back at the ruined tower, half of whom were still ill. A small, unpolluted stream had been found a quarter of a mile from the tower, and the Sanctians were getting their supplies of water from there. With that simple change, few had fallen ill since they had arrived at the tower, although another dozen had perished from the sickness they had picked up on the march north, and two or three were still dying every day.

The two scouts emerged from the shadows along the track and found Lieutenant Aldo.

'The way is clear, sir,' said one. 'There are sentries on the track where it meets the shanty town, but we have found a route that will bypass them. We should be able to enter and exit the settlement via the same route.'

'It does involve a certain amount of wading through shallow channels, sir,' said the other.

'Is the route unguarded?' said the lieutenant.

'It appears to be, sir. For some reason, there are more soldiers on duty than normal, but they are based to the north and east of the settlement, not the south.'

Aldo rubbed his chin. 'I wonder why that might be.'

'It might be connected to the smoke we saw coming from the vicinity of the cranes a couple of nights ago, sir.'

'Maybe.'

'Is there a delay, Lieutenant?' said Saffie.

'No, ma'am,' said Aldo; 'just an unexpected change in the settlement's usual procedures. There will be more soldiers than usual, but not in the areas we are targeting.' He gestured to those who were to accompany him. 'Let's go. Keep to a single column, and follow the scouts.'

Saffie found a place in the line of soldiers, and they set off along the track towards Steppen. Like the others, she was looking forward to eradicating the Master who ruled the town, along with every one of his mercenaries. For decades, the Whalebone King had got away with torture, enslavement and murder, but his time was coming to an end, and the righteous swords of the Sanctians would make sure of it. Saffie recalled everything she had learned about Masters while on Sanctos. The Whalebone King seemed to fit the description perfectly – he was cruel, rapacious, and greedy, just as the last rulers of the Elestian Empire had been, and the world would be a better, more civilised place without him. They would carry his head back to Elestia, and put it on display for the citizens of the city, as evidence that yet another vile Master had been eliminated.

Saffie began to see faint lights in the distance, and the column slowed. The scouts led them through the thick undergrowth to the right of the track, and they carried on for another few minutes, moving quietly through the forest, until they reached the banks of the Ario. Several smaller water channels were draining into the main river, and the scouts led them to one, then they halted, crouching by the waterway.

'We are going to follow this water course for a few hundred yards,' one of the scouts whispered. 'It's about three feet deep, and it leads to the southern flank of the shanty town. It passes under two bridges before then, and both will have a few soldiers guarding them, but they will be watching the roads, not the water channels. Stay as quiet as possible.'

The first scout descended into the water channel, then the others followed him in. Saffie edged down the bank, then she felt the cold water wrap itself round her legs. Her boots reached the bottom, which was uneven, as though debris had fallen in. The column set off, keeping to the darkness on the left side of the channel, where bushes were hanging over the edge. The lights in the distance grew nearer, and Saffie got her first view of the enormous Temple of Steppen. It lay on the other side of the sprawling shanty town, but she could see its upper floors, along with its pinnacles and slender towers. She stared at the building, conscious that a living, breathing Master dwelt within its walls, like a spider at the centre of its web. Saffie prayed to the spirits that she would be the one to separate the Master's head from his shoulders. She didn't long for glory or recognition; she would be satisfied if there was one fewer being of pure evil alive on the continent.

They came to the first bridge. As the scout had said, there were three soldiers standing on top of the bridge, but their eyes were on the rear of the fenced-off shanty town, and none were facing south. The column crept along. They gathered under the wooden beams of the bridge, and came to a halt. Saffie frowned, then she saw that several decapitated bodies were jammed together, partly blocking the water channel. Two soldiers inched forward, and began to pull the bodies free of each other, and a rancid smell of decay hit Saffie's nostrils. The first body was freed, and it floated downstream towards the Ario. Saffie had meant to look away, but her eyes were drawn to the body. It was of a young man, whose torso showed many signs of torture. The next body was that of a middle-aged woman who still had her head. Her eyes had been gouged out, and her neck broken. The soldiers said nothing as more bodies were freed from the blockage, but their rage and disgust were almost tangible.

The column set off again as soon as there was enough space to pass through. Saffie squeezed through the gap in the bodies, and came out from under the bridge. She glanced over her shoulder, but the soldiers were out of sight beyond the bridge parapet. They continued along the water channel, passing more bodies that were drifting downstream. One of them had wounds on his back that were still bleeding, as though he had been dead for only a few moments, and then a splash came from just ahead of the scouts. The column halted in the darkness. Saffie heard voices from the opposite bank, then a fresh body floated by, its torso punctured by stab wounds, and its head gone. The column waited until the voices had receded into the distance, then they carried on.

Ahead, Saffie could see the buildings of the shanty town through the timber beams of the fence that surrounded it. Each dwelling had been constructed from wood, and some had thatched roofs, but most were filthy and in danger of collapse. There were no paved streets in the settlement, just tracks of mud, and the odour of raw sewage grew stronger. They came to the second bridge, where eight soldiers were standing, their crossbows pointed into the settlement, and the column came to another halt.

The lieutenant slipped back down the line to where Saffie was standing in the thigh-deep water.

'We have a problem, ma'am,' whispered Aldo. 'If we go under this bridge, there is a good chance that we will be seen by those soldiers when we emerge on the other side. It's not worth the risk, so I am considering ordering a withdrawal.'

'The mercenaries have their backs to us,' Saffie whispered back. 'Could we not eliminate them quietly?'

'Even if we are successful, ma'am, it is likely that the slaves in the closest shacks will see us, and their response is unpredictable. They may think we are here to rescue them.'

'But, as you said, we need to know the layout of the temple's interior if we are to stage an attack. What if we leave two of those soldiers alive, and take them back with us?'

'My highest priority is that we remain undiscovered, ma'am. If we cause a scene here, then the other mercenaries might track us back to the tower. Our current base is not hard to find. All they would need to do is follow the road south. I'm calling off the raid.'

Saffie bit her lip. As a granddaughter of the emperor, she knew that she had the power to overrule a mere lieutenant, but her time in the navy had taught her to respect the chain of command, and Aldo had been placed in charge of that night's operation. The lieutenant began to move back to the front of the column, in order to relay his new orders, when two of the soldiers on the bridge turned.

'Did you hear something?' said one. 'Shine the lamp into the channel; I think someone might be down there.'

The Sanctians below them froze for a moment, then several pulled their crossbows from over their shoulders. A lamp was shone down at them, and the Sanctians loosed. A hail of bolts shot up from the water course, and both mercenaries were hit.

'Retreat!' cried Aldo, then a bolt shot from the bridge struck him in the neck and he plunged into the filthy water.

'Attack!' Saffie called out. 'Get up there and kill them!'

Chaos descended over the water channel. Bolts were flying in both directions, and many of the soldiers were temporarily blinded by the rays of the lamp. Another two Sanctians were hit, then the others pulled themselves out of the water, drew their knives and ran onto the bridge. Saffie climbed up the slippery bank, and sprinted towards the remaining mercenaries. The soldiers on the bridge were trying to reload their bows when the Sanctians slammed into them, their knives cutting them down.

Saffie ran onto the bridge. 'Spare any officers,' she said.

'None are officers, ma'am,' said a sergeant.

'Then kill them all.'

Saffie watched as the last mercenary was stabbed by three Sanctians. 'I am assuming command of the operation,' she said. 'Throw the bodies into the water. I want guards at either end of the bridge to warn us if any more mercenaries approach along the road. Move.'

The Sanctians got to work. They picked up the bodies of the slain mercenaries and dropped them into the channel, then they turned back to Saffie. She looked for the scouts, and beckoned them towards her.

'Where will this road take us?' she said.

'If we go left, ma'am,' said one, 'we will reach the main track that heads south back to the tower. That way will be heavily guarded. We're not entirely sure where the road goes in the other direction, but my guess would be that it encircles the shanty town.'

'Someone's coming from the left,' said the soldier posted by the western end of the bridge. 'At least a dozen more mercenaries.'

Saffie cursed. She glanced into the dark waters of the channel, but she knew if they were caught there again, they could be cut down by the bows of the mercenaries. The way to the right was also dangerous, especially if it took them into the centre of the settlement.

'We're going right,' she said. 'Get off the bridge and follow me.'

Saffie raced down to her right until she had left the bridge behind, keeping the fence that surrounded the slave settlement to her left. The fence had been designed to keep the inhabitants locked up inside at night, but it was equally impassable from the outside. Saffie kept running, the Sanctian soldiers following her. They came to a large pool, which was fed by three narrow channels, each with its own bridge. Lining the pool on one side was a row of large stakes, upon which the bodies of three Westlander slaves had been impaled. Saffie gazed up at the display. Flies were buzzing round the corpses, and their remains were dripping into the waters of the pool.

One of the scouts ran up to her, then he pointed ahead of them. 'That way lies the barracks of the mercenaries, ma'am.'

Saffie nodded, as the sound of boots on the road behind them grew louder.

Saffie set off again. She bounded over the three short bridges, and entered the tight, narrow lanes of the mercenaries' settlement. The Sanctian soldiers followed her, then they took cover amid the piles of refuse that lay next to the rough wooden barrack blocks. Saffie held her breath as she watched the mercenaries reach the bridge where the fight had taken place. They looked down at the splashes of blood, then several leaned over the side of the bridge to gaze into the channel. Several men pointed, and Saffie could hear them talking.

'Reload your bow,' Saffie whispered to the soldier next to her. 'Do it quietly, but first, pass the message down the line.'

The soldier nodded, then he whispered to the next man along. Saffie went back to gazing at the mercenaries. A few of them looked in the direction of the mercenaries' settlement, but Saffie and the soldiers were buried deep in the thick shadows. Saffie sensed movement to her right, then she saw a pair of eyes staring out at her from behind the boarded-up window of a barrack block.

'We've been seen,' Saffie said.

The front door of another block opened, and three drunken mercenaries peered out into the darkness.

'Who's hiding out here, eh?' said one, drawing a sword. 'If one of you bastarding slaves is trying to escape, I'll cut your fucking balls off.'

Saffie raised a hand. 'Kill them.'

The Sanctians charged at the front door, and the three mercenaries went down under a torrent of knife blows. The mercenaries from the bridge appeared at the end of the street, and a whistle was blown.

'Intruders!' someone cried. 'Defend the barracks!'

Within seconds the narrow street was a battlefield. Mercenaries were coming out of the barrack blocks, some drunk, and others unarmed, while the mercenaries from the bridge charged into the Sanctians. A sergeant brought down a mercenary who was staggering out of a barrack block. He clubbed him over the head with the butt of his crossbow, then he dragged him across the street towards Saffie.

'I've got us a captain, ma'am,' he said. 'Now all we need to do is get the fuck out of here.'

'Loose!' cried Saffie.

A hail of bolts left the Sanctians' bows, and seven mercenaries went down, clearing a route out of the settlement.

'Follow me!' Saffie shouted, then she raced along the street.

Behind her, two soldiers were carrying the unconscious captain, while the others protected their flanks. They charged out of the mercenary district, and ran back to the wide water channel. More whistles were sounding all over the settlement, and several slaves were watching from the shanty town, their gazes on the Sanctian soldiers as they retreated from Steppen. Saffie reached the water channel.

'Everybody back in the water,' she said. 'Quickly. Get under the bridge.'

The Sanctians slid and clambered their way down the bank, and got back into the cold water. Saffie joined them, then they crouched under the wooden beams of the bridge, as the entire camp seemed to awaken. Boots thudded over the bridge, and voices rang out.

Saffie found the sergeant. 'Did we leave anyone behind?' she whispered.

The sergeant shook his head.

Saffie waited until the sound of boots had faded into the distance, then she pointed south. She led the way back down the water channel, keeping close to the right-hand side where the shadows were thickest, and resisting the temptation to look over her shoulder. They edged along as quietly as possible, halting whenever they heard anyone approach on either bank. The minutes dragged by, each step south seeming to take an age. They came to the body of Lieutenant Aldo, which was floating gently towards the south. Two soldiers reached out, and dragged it closer, then they pulled it along with them as they went. They collected the bodies of the other two Sanctians who had fallen by the bridge, and guided them along as they retraced their steps from before.

They came to the next bridge, but the three mercenaries who had been there were gone. Saffie led the soldiers under it without pausing, and they passed the cluster of bodies that had held them up on their way north. Saffie increased her speed, and the column hurried along. A scout tapped Saffie on the shoulder, and pointed to their right.

'That's where we entered the channel, ma'am,' he whispered.

'Praise the spirits,' said Saffie. 'Take the lead, if you will.'

'Yes, ma'am.'

Saffie waited in the water as she watched the scout haul himself out of the channel. The rest of the soldiers followed him, dragging the three bodies of their fallen, along with the unconscious body of the mercenary captain. The last soldier to get out of the water turned and extended his hand. Saffie took it, and he pulled her up onto the bank.

Another three hours had elapsed before they reached the ruins of the tower where the rest of the Sanctians were based. They had passed by the abandoned shack where the raiding party had assembled earlier that evening, and Saffie had ordered four of them to stay there, to keep watch on the road. The others had taken over the duties of carrying the bodies, and the soldiers were quiet and subdued when they arrived at the tower.

Captain Zola was sitting outside waiting for them, and he got to his feet as Saffie approached.

'Where is Lieutenant Aldo, ma'am?' he said.

Saffie gestured to one of the bodies. 'We lost three soldiers,' Saffie said, 'including Aldo. Our silent raid turned into a full skirmish, and I estimate that we killed or injured at least twenty mercenaries.'

'Should we relocate, ma'am?' Zola said. 'Are our enemies on their way here?'

'I think we got away successfully,' said Saffie, 'and we left no injured or dead behind. Four men have been posted by the abandoned shack, and they are under orders to run here as fast as they can if they see any signs of pursuit. And, we got ourselves a captain.'

Zola glanced down at the bound and unconscious mercenary, and smiled.

Saffie went off to rest in a quiet room of the tower, exhausted by being up all night. She rolled off her damp leggings, dried her legs with a blanket, then pulled on a fresh pair that she had washed in the river two days before. A few of the soldiers had looked horrified to see an imperial princess doing her own laundry, and several had offered to help, but she had waved them away. She fell asleep as soon as she lay down, then she dreamed of creeping into the emperor's bedchamber. She watched her grandfather's chest rise and fall for a few moments, transfixed. The light from the Silver Moon was coming in through an open window, and it was illuminating the face of the emperor, making him appear almost divine.

Saffie held out her hand.

'Blessed spirits,' she said, 'witness the evil that corrupts my heart, and summon a knife.'

The blade appeared in her hand. She edged closer to the bed, then she grasped the handle of the knife in both hands, and held it over her grandfather's chest.

'Die, you wicked old bastard,' she said, then she rammed the blade down into his heart.

The emperor's eyes opened wide, and he stared at her. 'You,' he said. 'I always knew it would be you.'

Saffie juddered awake, and saw the pale light of dawn seeping into the cold room where she lay. She sat up, feeling worse than she had before she had gone to sleep. She rubbed the side of her face. A sickly sensation arose in the pit of her stomach as she recalled the dream. Once again, she had transformed into a vile Maker and had murdered the emperor. What did it mean? Under normal circumstances, she might have considered consulting a priest or priestess about the meaning of a strange dream, to see if it might have been inspired by the spirits; but such was the subject matter of her dreams that to do so would only invite suspicion.

Was she a traitor at heart? Did she harbour emotions buried so deep that she didn't even know they existed?

Captain Zola appeared at the door, and wiped fresh blood from his hands. He leaned closer to a soldier, and whispered something. The soldier saluted, then he gathered a colleague, and they went into the chamber from where Zola had just emerged.

The captain approached Saffie.

'The interrogation has been completed, ma'am,' Zola said. 'The mercenary has given all he had to give, and I daresay that much of it will be quite useful. Come. I shall gather the other officers and go over what I have learned.'

Saffie stared at him, then she got to her feet. She followed him out of the ruined tower, where Agent Marco of the Offices of Purgation was talking to the detachment's junior lieutenant, the sole army officer remaining after Aldo's demise.

Saffie joined them, and Zola produced a bloodstained scrap of paper from a pocket.

'This is a map of the layout of the temple's interior,' he said. 'It doesn't cover every room and every passageway, but it marks out the location of the Whalebone King's quarters in relation to the main gates, and, for our purposes, it shall suffice.'

The three other officers peered down at the sketch on the paper.

'We shall wait a few days before launching our attack,' Zola went on, 'to allow more soldiers to recover from the illness that plagued us on our way here, as we shall require as many men as possible to guarantee success.'

'Was the mercenary officer cooperative, sir?' said Marco.

'Not exactly,' said Zola. 'Indeed, for a while, he seemed to have us confused with someone else. It appears that we were not the first to attack Steppen in recent days. A raid on the cranes at the top of the cliffs took place two nights ago. One crane was damaged, and twenty mercenaries were killed. From what the mercenary told me, it seems that the attacking force was numerous, organised and professional; and he assumed that we were part of the same force.'

'Another force is attacking Steppen, sir?'

Zola narrowed his eyes. 'That is what I said, Marco.'

'But who, sir?'

'One can only assume that a detachment of Jallian militia has been sent down the Antiago,' said Zola, 'but for what purpose, and why now? Blasted Jallians. I will be most upset if they hinder our work here. They should have notified us of their intentions, and then we could have coordinated our attacks.'

'That explains why our scouts reported reinforcements being deployed to the north and east of the temple,' said Saffie. 'If the Jallians have arrived, then they have already done us a favour. We might not have got out of Steppen with so few casualties, had the usual number of mercenaries been guarding the southern flank of the settlement.'

'At least they are useful for something,' said Marco.

'Who has jurisdiction if we meet the Jallians?' said Saffie. 'We are technically within the frontiers of Jallin.'

'Our mission was approved by the highest levels of the Offices of Purgation,' said Zola. 'If we meet any Jallians, they would be wise to bow to our authority.' He stared out into the forest amid the growing light of dawn. 'We shall need to relocate our camp before we launch our next attack. I suspect that no one pursued Aldo's small force, but the officer I interrogated assured me that patrols would be sent in this direction. I want our men out of here within the hour. Pack everything up, and we shall move deeper into the forest. We shall follow the stream for a few miles, and then,' he said, his eyes tightening, 'then, we shall prepare to end the reign of the Whalebone King.'

CHAPTER 15
CULLING THE USELESS

Steppen, Great Forest, Jallin, Central Provinces – 5th Day of Quoma 108

Magnus could hear his father's anger before he had reached the highest level of the temple's roof. The king was sitting in his usual place, reclining in the shade of a canvas canopy, while one slave fanned him, and another was massaging his feet. Magnus's three half-brothers were standing close by, listening to their father rant, while Lord Matteo seemed unperturbed, and was sitting with a large glass of brandy in his left hand, despite the early hour of the day.

'It's a fucking conspiracy!' the king shouted. 'Soldiers are attacking us from every side, and I want answers. Einar – please tell me you have some good news.'

'I'm afraid not, boss,' said Einar. 'I sent out soldiers to search the area close to the cranes. They found evidence of a few small encampments, but they had been abandoned.' He paused as Magnus approached. 'Why is this little prick getting invited to these meetings?'

'I summoned him,' said the king, 'and I don't need to hear your complaints. Carry on with your report.'

'There's not much else to add, boss,' said Einar. 'We don't know who attacked the cranes.'

'Didn't some of your men say that a few of the attackers were in uniform?'

'That might be true, boss,' said Einar; 'though their reports are contradictory and confused. Some claim to have seen dozens of attackers, while others saw only a small handful. If they were in uniform, then it was no uniform my men have ever seen before.'

'Does that rule out the Jallian militia?' said Erling.

'Not necessarily,' said Ragnvald. 'The Jallians' forces are not very professional, and their militia wear whatever they have to hand.'

'But who else could it be?' said Einar.

Hemming's eyes went to his eldest son. 'What about last night's attack? Were any uniforms seen?'

'Yes, boss,' said Ragnvald; 'but, again, the eye-witness reports are confused. Some claim that the uniforms were Yearlian, others that they were Sanctian, and yet others say it was too dark to see anything of any use.'

Hemming leaned forward, his eyes filled with rage. 'So, we are under attack from the north and the south, squeezed like a grapefruit in the grip of a vice. And fifty mercenaries – dead.'

'It gets worse, boss,' said Ragnvald. 'Some witnesses reported that the attackers were seen making off with one of our men; carrying him as though he was unconscious. When the bodies were all accounted for, we discovered that we are missing Captain Osgood. He was last seen stepping out of the barracks, and then we think the enemy spirited him away.'

Hemming shrugged. 'So, we lost an officer? That hardly seems catastrophic.'

'But, boss,' said Ragnvald, 'Osgood knew every inch of our defences, and he was familiar with the interior of the temple, including how to get to your quarters. If our attackers have forced this information out of him, then we could be in trouble.'

Fury seemed to possess Hemming. His eyes bulged, and he picked up an empty bottle of wine from the little table next to him. His gaze flitted about, looking for something or someone to strike, then he brought the bottle down onto the head of the slave who was rubbing his feet. The woman cried out, raising her hands to the blood streaming from her head, then Hemming got to his feet. He kicked the slave in the chest, then stamped on her midriff. He brought the bottle down again, and again, and she fell silent beneath the bludgeoning, her head splitting open. Hemming brought the bottle down one last time, and it shattered, sending shards of glass over the bloodied corpse by his feet. Hemming staggered back a step, his eyes on his handiwork, then he stared at his sons.

'Look what you made me do,' he said.

None of his sons spoke.

Hemming glanced at Matteo, who was continuing to sip his brandy as though nothing had happened.

'Pass me that towel,' he said.

Matteo reached over and gave the king a folded towel. Hemming wiped his bloody hands on it, then he draped it over the dead slave's head.

'We will need to move a few people into the caves,' the king said. 'Empty the women's quarters, and have them all guarded securely in one of the deepest caverns. Do the same with our guests. If the temple is under threat of attack, then I want that lot to be safe. Magnus, you can deliver the news; they trust you. Tell them that we are concerned for their safety, and that the move is only temporary.'

'Yes, sir,' said Magnus. 'Should I do this now?'

'Not yet. We are expecting others to join us shortly. Carry out my orders when the meeting is over.'

Magnus bowed his head, then he caught the glance of the slave who was continuing to fan the king. Her eyes stared at him for a moment, and he could see how terrified she was. Magnus glanced down at the body. As far as he knew, that slave had been washing and massaging the king's feet for years. He wondered if she had believed that her position had been made safe by her daily proximity to the king, as though she had been favoured over the others in the women's quarters. Twenty seconds of brutal violence had put an end to those illusions, and Magnus's feelings turned against his father again.

'What shall I say, sir,' he said, 'if our guests ask about the last time we all met together?'

Hemming retook his seat. 'Tell them that we await their considered response. Tell them that, of course, we shall respect any decisions they reach. Give them no hint that we are merely lulling them into a false sense of security. They will imagine that they understand our motives, and that will keep them off guard. Tell Eshia that Ragnvald is pining for her...' He broke off to laugh, and Ragnvald rolled his eyes. 'Yes,' Hemming went on, 'be sure to mention that poor Ragnvald is sick with longing for the fair Eshia. Take her a flower, as a token of my son's undying love. That should do the trick.'

'Let's not overplay our hand, boss,' said Ragnvald. 'We did a good job of masking our true intentions when we visited our guests, but we don't want them getting suspicious.'

'What are our true intentions?' said Einar. 'I wasn't there when you went to see them. I didn't see how you acted.'

'We were humble and respectful,' said Hemming. 'I played the role of a worried old man, concerned that his sons might never find wives.'

Einar frowned. 'And they believed that, boss?'

'They certainly appeared to.' A glint appeared in his eyes. 'Raewyn was very bashful when we were there. It was almost as though she could barely glance in my direction. To her mind, I would have appeared like a strong and powerful king, and she was probably giddy with adulation.' He shuddered. 'How I long to break that girl under me. I will...'

His voice trailed away as a small group appeared on the roof. Two of their number were high-ranking officers from the mercenary force, while the other five were old crewmates of the king from their time as pirates.

Magnus smothered a gasp of relief. He had been dreading the moment when his father would decide to bring up Raewyn, and it seemed that the new arrivals had cut short a long rant about what he was intending to do to the young woman. Magnus lowered his gaze. He loathed his father, but could see no way to escape his cloying hold over him.

'Greetings, Your Majesty,' said one of his father's old cronies. 'These are dark days for our community, and the others are starting to get worried.'

Hemming waved a hand at them. 'Everything is under control.'

'Is that right?' said another, his gaze on the body of the dead slave. 'With all due respect, that's not what we've been hearing. Two attacks in two days? This is a coordinated assault on our way of life. What are you going to do about it?'

'We have scouts out searching for the miscreants who dared to assault us,' said Hemming. 'We will hunt down those damn cowards, and I shall have their heads mounted on spikes.'

The crewmates eyed each other.

'We have another problem sir,' said one of the mercenary officers.

'If this is about Osgood, then I already know.'

'It doesn't concern Captain Osgood, sir,' said the officer. 'My fear is that we are spreading ourselves too thinly. We have over a hundred men out searching the riverbanks of the Antiago to the north, and another hundred have been sent south to scout out the main road by the Ario. With fifty casualties sustained in recent nights, we barely have enough men left over to securely guard the temple and the slaves at the same time. Worse, many of the slaves witnessed the events that took place last night. They saw our men being defeated by the enemy. This has made them more truculent than usual. Some of them seem to be under the impression that their liberators are at hand, and that they will soon be released.'

'Can they be contained while the searches are carried out?' said Ragnvald.

'Perhaps, sir,' said the officer, 'but we would be running a grave risk. Already, there have been a few instances of disobedience and reluctance to work this morning. If these feelings spread, then the shanty town might erupt into a full revolt.'

'How many slaves live within the shanty town?' said a crewmate.

'Right now, sir, there are some two thousand, eight hundred slaves in the settlement. That excludes all those held elsewhere, such as inside the temple, or within the private houses and quarters of men like yourselves. We usually like a ratio of five slaves to every soldier but, at the moment, that has slipped to a ratio of ten to one. We might not be able to withstand a serious outbreak of violence.'

'Brutal times call for brutal measures,' said the king. 'If there are too many slaves to guard, then we must reduce the number of slaves. Recall the search teams and concentrate our forces, then have them storm the shanty town. Eliminate around eight hundred of the weakest, the sickest and the oldest. That should bring your precious ratio back to normal. And kill only men.'

'But we need the men to work,' said one of the crewmates. 'As far as I can see, the only use for the women in the shanty town is to keep the beds of the mercenaries warm at night.'

'Exactly,' said Hemming. 'The women are essential to keep up the morale of the soldiers. How easy do you think it is to retain decent staff under these conditions? One must offer a few perks, or we wouldn't be able to attract any soldiers here at all.' He glanced at the officer. 'You may also cull the older women, if there are any left inside the shanty town.'

'Yes, sir,' said the officer.

The king eyed his former crewmates. 'Don't look so fucking miserable. We can always replace dead slaves.'

'From where, Your Majesty?' said one. 'The Westlanders have become the only guaranteed source of slaves in recent years, and their cost is always increasing.'

'Then the mine shall produce more silver,' said Hemming. 'Have a little faith in me, boys. Did I not captain us for decades upon the open seas? Have I not ruled Steppen with a fair hand, allowing my old crewmates to live lives of luxury? The only time I ever see any of you is when you want something from me, or if you are worried about losing your privileges.'

'There is something else that concerns us, Your Majesty,' said one of them.

The king's frown deepened. 'Well? Get on with it.'

'It has come to our attention, Your Majesty,' the crewmate went on, 'that you are harbouring a certain number of Masters and Makers within the temple.'

Hemming's face twisted with fury. 'Who told you that? That was a secret.' He glared at Lord Matteo.

'It certainly wasn't I who informed them, Your Majesty,' said the Sanctian agent.

'It is difficult to keep many secrets from us,' said a crewmate. 'Soldiers talk, and gossip spreads, whether you like it or not, Your Majesty. What are your intentions towards these Masters and Makers?'

'Intentions?' said Hemming. 'We have no intentions. They arrived here looking for some of their comrades, and they missed the barges. That's it. I knew you boys would get over-excited if you found out, so I decided that a little discretion was in order. Our guests will leave as soon as the next convoy reaches us.'

'You can't allow them to leave,' said a crewmate, his eyes wide. 'What if they go straight to the authorities in Elestia?'

'They won't. Did you miss the part about some of their number being Masters and Makers? The last thing they will do when they reach Elestia is decide they want to talk to any Sanctian officials. Besides, I have been very careful. They have seen nothing of Steppen – not a single beating or execution, and I have isolated them from everyone else. Even if they desired to tell the authorities about us, they would have nothing to say.'

'All the same, they present a considerable risk to the community.'

'What do you suggest I do? Attack them, when we have no idea who among them might have the ability to strike us down? There would be carnage, and I am not going to risk the lives of my sons, not when the problem will resolve itself as soon as the barges arrive. Now, fuck off back to your luxurious villas and give me a moment to plan my strategy.'

The crewmates frowned. Some of them bowed their heads towards the king, and then they walked away.

'Perhaps you shouldn't be pissing off the old crewmates, boss,' said Ragnvald. 'We need their support to rule Steppen. If they turn against us, then...'

'Shut up,' muttered Hemming. 'They won't turn against us, because they know their blood would become salt if they tried. Not one of them has ever attempted to overthrow my rule, because, at heart, they are frightened of me. As they should be.' He turned to the two officers. 'You have your orders. Withdraw from the shanty town when you have eradicated eight hundred slaves.'

'What shall we do with the bodies, sir?' said one of the officers.

Hemming shrugged. 'Dump them in the river; I couldn't give a shit.'

The officers bowed. 'Yes, sir.'

Magnus watched them walk from the roof. Eight hundred slaves were soon to die, and the shanty town had no inkling of the cataclysm that was about to envelop it.

'I also think, boss,' Ragnvald went on, 'that it was unwise to have lied to your crewmates.'

'What did you say?' said Hemming. 'What lies did I tell them?'

'You told them that we had no intentions towards our guests, boss. That was a lie.'

'Oh that? Who cares? By the time we act against our guests, the crewmates will be tucked up in their villas, drinking brandy and fucking their slaves.' He eyed Magnus. 'The meeting is over, lad. Haven't you got a job to do?'

Magnus bowed his head. 'When is the move planned for, sir?'

'We shall need to prepare a few of the caves, first,' the king said, 'so let's relocate the women's quarters and our guests tomorrow, at dawn. See to it, Magnus.'

'Yes, sir.'

Magnus turned and made his way down to a lower level of the roof. He passed two soldiers by a stairwell, and descended into the darkness of the temple. The women's quarters were closer than the apartment where their guests were living, so he went there first. The guards by the door unlocked it for him, and he entered.

He saw his mother sitting next to a few other women in the entrance hall, and he smiled.

'There you are, son,' Colette said, getting to her feet. 'You haven't been to see me in quite a while.'

Magnus walked up to her, and she kissed him on the cheek.

'There have been two attacks on Steppen over the past few nights,' he said.

The gazes of the other women turned to him, and they fell into silence.

'Attacks?' said Colette. 'By whom?'

'We don't know. Possibly soldiers in strange uniforms, but that's just a rumour. They killed fifty mercenaries.'

Colette smiled. 'Praise the spirits! We heard last night's disturbances coming from the shanty town but, of course, we couldn't see what was happening.' She gestured towards the windows high up on the wall. 'After all, your father placed us here to keep us in ignorance. Could it be? Could our liberation be coming?'

'Don't say that, Colette,' said another woman. 'The last thing I need is hope.'

'I also have some bad news,' said Magnus. 'The king was so angry, he killed the woman who washed his feet.'

'Elaine?' said Colette.

Magnus glanced away. 'I, uh... I didn't know her name.'

'She worked up on the roof for nearly seven years, washing and rubbing that monster's feet, and you didn't know her name? Shame on you, son.'

'Sorry. She never once spoke to me in that entire time. Father beat her to death.'

Two of the women started to cry, but the others merely shook their heads, as though the news had not surprised them.

Colette sat down, and Magnus took a seat next to her.

'There's more,' he said. 'You are all being relocated.'

'Where?' said his mother.

'Into a cave,' he said. 'The king is worried that the next attack will be on the temple, and so he wants you all kept safe.'

'As safe as Elaine was?' said Colette.

'Safe from the attackers, not from Father,' he said. 'The guests are also being moved, but probably not to the same cave.'

'How are the children among them?' said another woman. 'How is little Nyli? Is she safe and well? And Salus? That boy seemed so lost.'

'They are all fine,' said Magnus. 'My father has been keeping them well fed, and they are being shielded from the... rougher aspects of life in Steppen. I need you all to pack up some clothes; we are moving you tomorrow morning.'

'Will we be returning here afterwards?' said an older woman.

'That's the plan,' said Magnus. 'There might be a battle first.'

'What if...' said Colette. 'What if it's the Sanctians? What if the Sanctians have discovered that Hemming is a Master? Everyone knows that the Sanctians love nothing more than hunting down Masters and Makers. Would they send a force to kill the Whalebone King?'

'I am also a Master, Mother,' he said. 'If it's the Sanctians, then they will kill me, too.'

'Every woman here will deny it, son. None of us would tell the Sanctians anything about you. Perhaps you should slip away into the forest before the attack comes. Do not die for that vile king, Magnus; you are worth so much more than that.'

Magnus said nothing, then he got to his feet.

'Are you leaving already?' said Colette.

'I need to tell the guests the same thing I told you, Mother,' he said, 'and then I need to organise food and blankets for the caves. I have never actually been in the caves before, but I will try to find the most comfortable ones.'

He walked to the door, then he hesitated. 'You might hear screams soon,' he said.

'Screams? From where?' said Colette.

'From the shanty town. We don't have enough soldiers to guard all the slaves, apparently, so father has organised a cull. Eight hundred slaves are to be killed.'

He knocked on the door before any of the women could say anything, and the soldiers allowed him to leave. He walked through the temple, his thoughts darkening. A wild plan appeared in his mind, and he pondered the possibilities of giving the female slaves who lived in the palace an opportunity to flee during the transfer to the caves. Perhaps the network of caves had multiple entrances, and his mother would be able to slip out of one at night, and run into the forest. If Magnus was caught helping them, then his father would be enraged, and a base fear gnawed at his insides. It was too risky. Any punishment would involve a severe beating, at least, or perhaps Magnus would be mutilated. His father might even kill him in a rage of temper, just as he had killed Elaine. His heart fell further into despair. Why had he never learned the name of the woman who had washed his father's feet every day? It occurred to him that he also didn't know the name of the woman who held the fan. She had been doing the same job for years, and Magnus had never spoken to her.

He reached the entrance to the huge apartment where the guests were living. The soldiers eyed him as he approached, then he knocked on the door as one unlocked it. He entered the quarters, and saw Denny, Abigone, Lothar and the enormous warrior known as Mor Galthide sitting on wicker chairs. Raewyn was also there, and Magnus caught her gaze for the briefest of moments.

'Hello, Magnus,' said Denny. 'Another night of shouts and noise has passed. Are you here to tell us what caused it? Was it another attack?'

'Yes,' said Magnus. 'This time, it was from the south.'

Abigone frowned. 'I thought you said that the group who attacked the cranes were still up on the cliffs. How did they descend to the lower level?'

'We think it was a different group,' said Magnus. 'We're not sure.'

'It sounds as though you are in a pickle,' said Mor Galthide. 'Are you here for some military advice?'

Magnus raised an eyebrow. 'Would you offer some if I asked for it?'

'Are we under threat, lad?' said the giant man. 'If so, then it would be in our interests to help you repel any assault.'

'Thank you,' said Magnus, 'but that is not why I am here. I have come to tell you that you are all being temporarily relocated to the caves. The king believes that the temple will be attacked next, and it is our responsibility to keep you all safe if intruders enter the building. After all, you have no way to defend yourselves.'

A few of them glanced at each other, but they said nothing.

'I need you to pack up your things by dawn tomorrow,' Magnus went on. 'I will come to collect you, and we shall move you to the caves. It's probably just for a day or two, until the threat of attack has gone.'

'Thank you for considering our safety,' said Abigone. 'Might I ask you about the last time you were here? The king said some interesting things to us.'

Magnus said nothing.

'Was he being serious?' said Denny.

'As far as I know,' said Magnus. 'Ragnvald, eh... my brother Ragnvald wants to ask after Miss Eshia. Is she well?'

Abigone gave him a strange look, then she nodded. 'She is a little perturbed by your brother's unexpected advances towards her. Did you know what the king was going to say when he entered the room?'

'I confess that I didn't,' he said.

'You did look a little surprised,' Abigone went on. 'Did your father really believe that he would be able to find wives for his sons among us?'

'I think so. We don't... well, we don't see many women here.'

'There are plenty of female slaves, are there not?'

'I meant that we don't see many free women here. I will be honest – this whole subject is embarrassing for me. I had no idea that my father was going to try to set me up with one of you. It's not how I would have done things.'

'No?' said Abigone. She smiled. 'How would you have done things, Magnus?'

'Well,' said Magnus, his gaze on the floor, 'I would have tried to get to know someone first, before declaring my intentions. My father put you all into a difficult position.'

'It wasn't too difficult to decline his offer,' Abigone said.

'Are you really betrothed, Abigone?'

'I am.'

Magnus lifted his gaze. 'To Denny, I assume? You two always look close.'

'We are close,' said Abigone.

'Have any of the other girls said anything about the offer?' said Magnus.

Abigone glanced at Raewyn, then she shook her head. 'Not really.'

'All right. My father wanted me to tell you that he will respect whatever decision you reach.'

'Will he?' said Lothar. 'Can you guarantee that, Magnus?'

Magnus shrugged. 'It's what he said.'

'Then you can't guarantee it?' said Lothar. 'It seems to me, Magnus, that you are not being completely honest with us, but I can't work out which part of what you have said is a lie.'

'I'm not lying,' said Magnus.

'Then we have nothing to worry about?' said Lothar. 'Your father and your brothers aren't planning something?'

'Like what?'

Lothar smiled. 'You tell me.'

'Stop badgering him,' said Raewyn.

'It speaks,' said Lothar. 'I noticed the way your mouth clamped shut as soon as Magnus entered the room. Am I the only one here with a suspicious nature? I don't trust the Whalebone King; I don't trust Ragnvald; and I don't trust you, Magnus. Do you know what might win my trust? Allowing us to leave this fucking apartment might be a good start.'

Magnus eyed the soldier. Was Lothar bluffing, or had he seen through Magnus's veil of lies and half-truths? Part of him wanted to blurt out that they were all in terrible danger; that Lothar was right – the king had other plans for his guests, plans that would destroy their lives. He turned away, unable to look at Raewyn, as his father's words echoed round his mind.

'Be ready at dawn,' he said, then he hurried away.

The guards opened the door, and he almost ran out. He rushed along a passageway, then down a flight of narrow stairs. He remembered that his next job was to inspect the caves, but his mind was spiralling. How could he agree to his father's plans if it meant a life of misery and pain for Raewyn and the others who survived? His mother's life was also in the balance, as she would be punished if Magnus dared to warn the guests of the danger they were facing. He had to harden his heart if he and his mother were to live through the next month; and that meant sacrificing Raewyn and the others.

He leaned against a wall, then the screams started. Magnus hurried along to a south-facing window and looked outside. Down by the shanty town, heavily armed mercenaries had begun the slave cull. They had opened several gates in the outer fence, and were piling through, hacking down any slave within reach. The old, the young, men, women – it didn't seem to matter; dozens of unarmed and starving slaves were falling, their blood spilling over the muddy tracks that wound their way through the settlement.

Magnus turned away, then he sank to the floor, and wept.

CHAPTER 16
A WEAKNESS

Above Steppen, Great Forest, Jallin, Central Provinces – 5th Day of Quoma 108

Walter sat by the river's edge and swigged from the bottle. The rough alcohol burned his throat, then his chest warmed, and his nerves settled down. He had taken the bottle from the body of a mercenary soldier guarding the crane compound, and then, when he had distributed the brandy to the freed Westlanders, he had kept hold of it, keeping it hidden in a deep coat pocket.

A light mist had formed over the flowing river, and the opposite bank was barely visible through the grey haze. The conditions weren't perfect for a crossing, but Walter and the others were starting to run low on food, and there was always the pressing need to keep moving. Soldiers from Steppen had been searching the area close to the cranes, but they had made so much noise that it had been easy to hear them coming.

Walter heard a sound behind him, and he slipped the bottle back into his coat. Dietar emerged from the edge of the forest, and glanced down at Walter. If he had noticed the bottle, he didn't mention it. Instead, he sat down on the river bank next to Walter.

'Some of the Westlanders are questioning the need to cross the Antiago, sir,' he said.

'Are they?' said Walter. 'I can't force them to follow me. Now that I think of it, it might be a good idea to keep a few of them on this side of the river. They could feign an attack on the crane compound, to draw attention away from the rest of us. I'll ask them if they are willing to give it a try.'

'I was more of the opinion that you should assert your authority over them, sir,' said Dietar. 'They are ill-disciplined and disorganised. They all have their own ideas about what we should do next, and several of them have almost come to blows over their differing schemes. They need a strong leader to keep them together.'

'Am I a strong leader, Lieutenant?'

Dietar eyed him for a moment.

Walter smiled. 'Your response is noted.'

'You are an exceptional leader, sir,' Dietar said.

'But? Speak your mind, Lieutenant.'

'Well, it's no secret that you spent several years in Upper Down too drunk to be of any use to the Mountain Rangers. I know what you have achieved since that time, sir – your defence of the Kendril Gap restored your reputation among the townsfolk of Torrent; but those of us who were in the Rangers during the period of continual drunkenness do not remember you as a fine leader.'

'Do you recall what I was like before I became King's Champion?'

Dietar smiled. 'Yes, sir. You were one of the finest young officers the Mountain Rangers had seen for years. When I joined up, I wanted to be just like you. And then... then King Alfgang the Great appointed you as his Champion, and you seemed to disintegrate before our eyes. We never stopped being loyal to you, but... well, it's fair to say that you lost some of our respect.'

'Who do the Rangers blame?'

'Blame, sir? Are you talking about Commander Lothar? We all know that Duke Hector was paying the commander to keep you drunk, but I think that you have to take some measure of responsibility for your actions. Lothar wasn't holding you down and pouring the whisky into your throat, sir.'

Walter said nothing.

'It is fairly clear to me why it happened, sir,' Dietar went on. 'You were making a name for yourself in the Mountain Rangers, but Duke Hector took your promotion to King's Champion badly. Perhaps he viewed you as a potential rival, and he wished to have you discredited. However, his plan wouldn't have worked if you had shown a little will power and resolve. Most Rangers like to have a few drinks now and again, but every night for three years? And it wasn't just a couple of beers; you were drinking yourself into oblivion.'

'I have a weakness.'

'Yes, and your brother the duke exploited it thoroughly, sir. Your marriage to Princess Kilbride saved you, I think, if you don't mind me saying so. You were willing to sober up for Her Highness, and then...'

'And then I went back to my old ways as soon as Sebastian and I left Upper Down?'

'Well, yes, sir. I have no doubt that the count is a decent and honourable man, but he is a bad influence in that regard. What you need, sir, if I might give you some advice, is a loyal aide who will do the opposite of what Commander Lothar did.'

'Someone who will nag me into not drinking?'

'To put it bluntly, sir, yes.'

'Do you have anyone in mind? Are you angling for the job, Dietar?'

'If I were, sir, my first suggestion would be to take the bottle hidden in your coat, and pour it into the river.'

Walter got to his feet. He would give serious consideration to Dietar's words but, at that moment, he had more important things to do.

'Let's get the Westlanders organised,' he said.

Dietar stood, his eyes tight. 'Yes, sir.'

They walked along the bank of the river until they reached a shallow bay where the Westlanders were waiting for them. The small barge that had borne the three Mountain Rangers down the Antiago had been pulled up onto the bank next to them. Eight Westlanders had carried it all the way upstream from where Walter and the others had left it, and it had been loaded with every weapon they had collected from the crane compound, along with what remained of their food.

Walter walked into their midst.

'I'm not swimming across that fucking river,' said one of the Westlanders.

'Fine,' said Walter. 'I have another job for those of you who don't like getting wet.'

'The current's too strong,' said another.

'Is it?' said Walter. 'Duggan and Aisly managed to cross the river a while back. Are you admitting that Aisly has more strength and endurance than you do?'

A few of the Westlander men bristled.

'I'm crossing the river,' Walter went on. 'The mercenaries are searching this side of the Antiago, but they will never imagine that we were bold enough to cross over to the other bank. All the same, I want a small number of volunteers to stay on this side. I need them to carry out a diversionary attack this evening on the crane compound.'

'You're a fucking idiot,' said one of the Westlanders. 'The mercenaries have brought up a shitload of reinforcements. We'd be shot down before we could get inside the compound.'

'I'm not asking anyone to enter the compound,' said Walter; 'hence the name *diversionary attack*. All I need is the appearance of an assault – a lot of shouting and running around, so that the mercenaries believe that a full scale attack is imminent. After that, you can flee into the forest. Then, you can do whatever the fuck you like. Who wants to stay on this side of the river?'

One of the men stared at him. 'Are you cutting us loose?'

'Here's my offer,' Walter said. 'The way I figure it, you owe me something for freeing you from those bastards in Steppen. A one-time favour. You have two choices – stay on this side of the river and take part in the pretend attack on the compound tonight; or cross over with me to the other side. If you stay here to take part in the attack, then you can consider your debt to be paid in full. But, if you come with me, then I will expect you to start obeying my orders as though I were your superior officer. That's the deal. Those of you who cross over with me today will be taking part in more raids on Steppen. I intend to free the other slaves, and generally be a right pain in the arse to the Whalebone King.'

'What kind of raids?' said one. 'What are you going to do?'

Walter smiled. 'I won't be divulging that information for now,' he said. 'Some of you men might decide to stay here, and I don't want the mercenaries knowing what I am going to do if you are captured.'

Aisly frowned. 'Did you forget that I'm sitting here?'

'No,' said Walter. 'Will you and Duggan be crossing over with me today?'

'You promised me revenge,' she said, 'and so far, I've only had the chance to kill one of those mercenary bastards. If you plan on killing more, then I'm coming along.'

'Me, too,' said Duggan, 'but I'm not looking forward to swimming that fucking river again. When Aisly and I did it last time, we were several miles ahead of the soldiers chasing us; but the current swept us back so far downstream, that we ended up level with them.'

'But on the opposite bank,' said Walter.

'Obviously.'

'The current is the reason we transported the barge a few miles upstream,' said Walter. 'We can anticipate that we'll be carried back towards the cliffs, and we might get separated during the crossing. Do you remember where we camped last night? We were next to a bend in the river. That is where we will gather when we get to the other side. Otto and Dietar will steer the barge to that location, and the rest of us will assemble there, before we move on.'

'What's the point of this?' said one. 'Why do we need to cross?'

'Because our enemy won't be expecting it. They've reinforced this side of the river, all the way from the cranes to the stairs that Duggan and Aisly used when they escaped. If we want to hurt them, we have to attack from an unexpected direction.'

'We still need to find a way down the cliffs.'

'Clearly,' said Walter. 'Let's deal with one obstacle at a time. The river first, then the cliffs.'

'How many folk do you want to remain on this side?' said Duggan.

Walter shrugged. 'Five? Those who think I'm a fucking idiot should stay, as well as any who don't feel that they could obey my orders. If you think you would struggle with that, then stay here; you'll be no good to me on the other side.'

'I'm the one who called you a *fucking idiot*,' said a Westlander. 'I'm grateful that you released us, but I won't be taking any orders from a soldier from Upper Down.'

'Will you take part in the diversionary attack?'

The Westlander narrowed his eyes, then nodded. 'I'll do it.'

'Then you can call me whatever the fuck you like. Find four others who agree with you, and the rest of us will cross the river. Otto, get the barge back into the water.'

'Yes, sir,' said the Ranger.

Walter walked down to the edge of the river. He began removing loose items from his clothing, and placing them onto the barge, then he took off his coat, carefully folded it up, and set it down onto the deck. A few of the Westlanders got to their feet and stood next to him on the riverbank, their eyes on the dark waters.

'I can't swim,' said one.

'Then stay here,' said Walter. 'I'd rather you helped with the diversionary attack than drowned.'

Otto and a few of the Westlanders pushed the barge into the river. A rope had been secured to its stern, and Otto took a hold of it, his feet bracing against the mud of the bank. Dietar scrambled on board, then a Westlander took the rope, and Otto joined the other Ranger on the barge. Otto went to the tiller, while Dietar picked up the long bargepole. Otto turned, and nodded to Walter.

'See you on the other side,' said Walter.

The Westlander threw the rope onto the deck, and the barge began to drift with the current. Dietar dug the pole into the depths of the water, and pushed them closer to the centre of the river. Walter turned.

A small group had detached itself from the others, and were sitting under the branches of a tree.

'Attack the crane compound two hours after sunset,' he said to them. 'Make enough noise to awaken the Whalebone King, then get your arses out of there. Good luck.'

The men nodded, but said nothing. Walter glanced at the others. Ten Westlanders had decided to follow him across the river, including both Duggan and Aisly.

'This is going to be cold, isn't it?' he said to Duggan.

'Freezing,' said the Westlander.

'I can't believe I'm doing this again,' said Aisly.

Walter watched the barge drift into a thick bank of mist, then he waded out into the river. He felt the current drag on his legs as the cold water hit him, then he dived in and started to swim. He was a strong swimmer, despite the lack of much practice, but he could feel his body being carried downstream with every stroke he took. Within a few minutes, his arms and shoulders were aching as he battled the current, and the mist was too thick for him to be able to see either bank. He heard the sound of splashing on either side of him, and took a little comfort from that. The patches of mist grew thicker, and he felt as though he was dreaming. He shut out his thoughts and kept going.

When Walter dragged himself out of the cold water, he was exhausted and alone. The mist had petered out the closer he had swum to the opposite bank, but he could see no sign of the barge, the other swimmers, or the bend in the river where they had agreed to meet. He lay still by the water's edge for a few minutes, panting, and resting his arms and legs. The sky above him was a deep blue, and the sun's rays were warm on his skin. He heard a noise from his right, and saw a sodden Westlander staggering through the forest towards him.

'Where are the others?' said the Westlander.

'They'll be scattered up and down this bank,' said Walter, sitting up.

'I reckon we drifted downstream for miles,' he said. 'We passed the bend you were talking about.'

'Did we? I couldn't see for all the mist.'

The Westlander extended a hand, and Walter took it. The man pulled Walter to his feet, and they walked along the riverbank, heading upstream again. They came to the bend in the river, and Otto and Dietar greeted them from the deck of the barge.

'There you are, sir,' said Otto. 'We were about to send out a search party for you.'

Walter smiled, then he noticed the other Westlanders on the riverbank, sitting a few yards behind the barge.

'Is everyone here?' he said.

'We all made it across,' said Duggan. 'Are we supposed to call you *sir* now?'

A few of the Westlanders laughed.

'I don't expect any of you to call me that,' Walter said, 'but I do expect you to obey my orders while we are on an operation. The first operation starts now. We are going to unload the barge and leave it here, then we are heading towards the cliffs. Our objective is to find a way down to Steppen without alerting the mercenaries. Grab your shit from the barge; let's go.'

Two hours later, Walter and the others had reached the next river, where it split into the three channels that formed the central waterfalls next to Steppen. The channels were fordable, so they crossed all three, and carried on until they reached the westernmost of the rivers that plunged down the cliffs. They followed the river to the cliff's edge, where it turned into a great waterfall that spilled down the sheer slope in a roar of noise. Walter crouched by the top of the ridge, from where he could see the whole of Steppen laid out in front of him.

'What are we looking at?' said Walter.

'The big building on the left is the Temple of Steppen,' said Duggan; 'and to the right of that is the settlement where the slaves are corralled every night. Beyond the settlement are the barracks where the mercenaries live, and those big wooden houses are... well, I'm not sure who lives there.'

'The king's old pirate crewmates stay in those houses,' said another Westlander. 'They spread right back into the forest.'

Walter squinted his eyes. 'Are there people on the roof of the temple?'

'I heard that the Whalebone King sits up there every day,' said Aisly, 'but only a few Westlanders are allowed inside the temple, so that might just be a story.'

Otto frowned as he gazed at the forest from the top of the cliffs. 'How are we going to get down there, sir? The rocks are too steep to climb.'

'I'm working on it,' said Walter.

'If we had rope,' said Duggan, 'then I think we could make it down. We could secure one end to the trunk of a tree, and climb down that way.'

'We would need an awful lot of rope,' said Otto. 'The cliff is two hundred feet high at this point. Where are we going to find that amount of rope in the middle of a damn forest?'

Walter smiled. 'I have an idea. Do you think we can get back to the crane compound before the diversionary attack begins?'

Dietar glanced at the setting sun. 'If we hurry, sir.'

One of the Westlanders groaned. 'Another march through the forest?'

Walter laughed. 'That's the spirit. Brace yourselves, Westlanders; it's going to be a long night.'

Walter set the pace as they retraced their steps eastward. They reforded the three channels of the middle river, then they hugged the cliff's edge all the way back to the Antiago. They stopped when they came in sight of the palisade wall protecting the western bank of the crane compound.

'I know you've been walking for hours,' Walter said to the Westlanders, 'but we are going to attack the compound as soon as the diversionary assault begins.'

'What the fuck?' cried one.

'Hush there,' hissed Dietar. 'Do you want those mercenary bastards to hear us?'

'We will need to be quiet,' Walter went on. 'Let the others make all the noise – our raid should be swift and silent. As soon as we're over the wall, we'll split into two groups. The first group shall target the mercenaries on this side of the river, while the second group sets fire to anything that will burn. We had matches on the barge – who has them?'

'Me, sir,' said Otto.

'Then you will lead the fire-raising team,' said Walter. 'Amid all the confusion, the second group will then steal what we need. Then, we pull out the same way we went in, and run like bastards back towards the west.' He glanced up at the sky. 'Your moon gods are smiling down on us; it's going to be another dark night. Get some rest, but be ready to move as soon as the attack on the far bank begins.'

The Westlanders settled down on the ground to rest, while Walter kept his eyes on the palisade wall.

'How many mercenaries will we have to face, do you think, sir?' said Otto.

'With any luck, they will be on the eastern bank,' said Walter. 'We should assume that the rope bridge has been repaired, but they won't be expecting us to be here. We should disable the bridge again if we get the chance. You take that job, Dietar.'

'Yes, sir.'

'I'm going to take a closer look,' said Walter. 'Tawny owl means come as fast as you can.'

The two other Mountain Rangers eyed him as he got to his feet. For a brief moment, Walter wondered what they thought of him, and if they approved of what he was doing, then he shook such notions from his mind and set off through the forest, moving silently towards the defences of the crane compound. There was no walkway or parapet on the wooden palisade, and Walter reached it without being seen. He crept along its outer edge, and found a small gap in the beams. He peered through.

What *was* he doing? Was he trying to rescue Westlanders, or was his priority to find and help Princess Abigone? It was a contradiction he had yet to resolve. One step at a time, he told himself. He waited for his eyes to adjust to the lack of light, and looked through the gap. He saw the two huge cranes, and the giant wheels that sat next to them. The rope bridge had been repaired, but most of the mercenaries were on the opposite bank. There were far more of them than had been the case when he had led the last attack on the compound, but most were concentrated by the main gates. Unlike the previous occasion, none of them seemed drunk.

Walter crouched down and waited. His thoughts wandered to Kilbride. What would she think if she could see what he was doing? Would she have any sympathy for the enslaved Westlanders? Before he had left Torrent, she and Walter had worked hard to expel the last of the Westlanders from every corner of Upper Down; would she understand why he was now helping them? Walter wasn't sure he understood it himself.

The sound of shouts and cries rose up from the forest. Walter turned back to the narrow gap between the beams of the palisade wall and saw over a dozen soldiers running towards the main gates. Several were pointing, and the entire compound seemed to wake up. Walter turned, and made the call he had agreed with the others. Seconds later, Otto appeared, leading a group of Westlanders, then Dietar emerged from the shadows with the others. Walter leaned his back against the wall, and cupped his hands together.

'Up and over,' he whispered, 'while their attention is on the other bank.'

Otto joined Walter by the wall. He braced his knees and cupped his hands, then the first Westlanders climbed the wall, using Walter and Otto to reach the top. One after another, they clambered up, then each one disappeared over the wall. Dietar used Otto's hands to climb up, then he turned at the top, and helped Walter ascend. Walter took his hand and climbed to the top of the wall, then he dropped over the other side and drew his knife. Otto and Dietar landed next to him a moment later, then the three Mountain Rangers watched as the ten Westlanders tore through the few mercenaries on that side of the river. All the pent-up rage the Westlanders had felt about their enslavement came bursting out of them in the form of extreme violence, and they ripped the mercenaries to pieces.

'Make sure the arseholes don't try to cross the bridge, Dietar,' Walter said. 'Otto, come with me.'

Walter ran towards the cranes, with Otto by his side. Two Westlanders were kicking a mercenary to death, and Walter grabbed them both by the arms and pulled them along. They reached the cranes, and the great coils of rope that connected them to the wheels.

'Pick up as much rope as you can carry, then get back over the wall,' Walter said to the Westlanders.

Otto began cutting through the rope where it joined a crane, and the two Westlanders lifted a great coil of it and started running back to the wall.

Dietar sprinted over. 'The bridge is down, sir,' he said, 'and all mercenaries on this side of the river are dead.'

Walter smiled, and straightened his back. The victorious Westlanders were lining the western bank of the river, their hands raised as they taunted the mercenaries on the other side. Several of them were holding the heads they had cut from their victims, and they were yelling insults and curses at the silent mercenaries, who could do nothing but observe from the other side. Walter walked down to join them, and watched the mercenaries for a few moments.

'Tell the Whalebone King we're coming for him!' Walter shouted, and the Westlanders cheered.

A couple of mercenaries loosed their crossbows at them, but the range was too far, and the bolts dropped into the rushing waters of the Antiago.

Walter turned. 'The rope. Let's go.'

A few of the Westlanders had to be dragged away from the riverbank, their fury at the mercenaries unabated, then Walter noticed smoke rising from one of the cranes. Otto was standing back, admiring his fire-raising skills as flames licked the beams of the crane. Next to him, large sections of rope had been detached from the wheels, and were sitting in coiled piles. The Westlanders took hold of them, and the raiding party fled into the night.

Midnight had come and gone by the time Walter and the others had reached the westernmost river again. Despite complaints and grumbling, Walter ordered the ropes to be joined together, until they had two stretches long enough to reach the bottom of the cliffs. The ends were secured to thick tree trunks, and the rest was dropped over the side of the cliff, just a few feet from the waterfall. Its roar was drowning out every other sound, and the spray coming from it had soaked everyone for the second time that day. They had no gloves, so Walter ordered everyone to tear strips of fabric from the blankets they had stolen, to protect their hands during the climb down.

Walter set off first, while Duggan took the rope a yard to his right.

'Watch how I do it,' Walter called out over the roar of the waterfall. 'Make sure your hands are well wrapped-up, and let the rope slide through your grip, a few feet at a time.' He nodded to Duggan. 'Let's go.'

Walter eased himself over the edge, his boots finding plenty of places in the cliff to gain purchase, then he began to lower himself down in stages, the rope burning through his grip. He kicked out each time he lowered himself, and it was a while before he realised that he was descending far quicker than Duggan. He took a few seconds to glance down at the ground. There were no buildings close to the westernmost waterfall, and no mercenaries or civilians were in sight. Walter smiled, almost enjoying himself, then he started to descend again. He came to the tops of the trees, and kept going. The last few yards of the rope were lying on the forest floor, and he let go with two feet to go. He landed on the soft ground, his arms and legs aching. He leaned against a tree trunk, and waited for the others to reach him.

He pulled the half-empty bottle of spirits from his coat, removed the stopper, and took a long swig. It had been a good day. More mercenaries had been killed, they had crossed the river, and none of their own side had been hurt. Best of all, they had reached the bottom of the cliff.

For all that, he thought, he deserved a little drink.

CHAPTER 17
JUDGE OF CHARACTER

Steppen, Great Forest, Jallin, Central Provinces – 6th Day of Quoma 108

'But it makes no sense!' Reath yelled. 'Surely the temple is safer than a cave.'

'The king thinks that this temple will soon be attacked,' said Abigone.

'That asshole is full of shit,' said Reath.

'Language, Reath,' said Fyenna. 'I expect better from you.'

Reath rolled her eyes.

'There is something I don't understand,' said Nyli. 'Why don't we tell the king that there are lots of Masters and Makers in our group? If he's a Master, then he won't tell the Sanctians.'

'It's because we don't trust the king,' said Denny.

'All the more reason to tell him,' said Reath. 'If we told him who we are, he would be too scared to touch us.'

'The little one makes a fair point,' said Mor Galthide. 'The king knows that we have four Masters and Makers with us. Perhaps he would treat us with more respect if he knew about the others.'

Abigone walked over to the window. The sky was lightening a little, and the first rays of the sun were reaching the tops of the trees stretching out ahead of her. The westernmost waterfall was glistening in the morning sunshine, and she could hear its faint roar in the distance.

'Has everyone packed up their things?' said Lothar. 'Magnus should be here any moment.'

'I'm not going,' said Reath. 'I refuse to live in a cave like an animal.'

Abigone turned. 'You have been complaining about having to stay in this apartment for days, Reath,' she said, 'and now you're complaining about having to go somewhere else?'

'I want the freedom to walk about wherever we like,' the girl said. 'Do you remember what the so-called king said to us when he put us in here? He told us that we would be able to move around freely. He lied to us. He might be lying again. Maybe they are taking us away to kill us. Or worse, maybe they are going to force some of us to become their wives.'

'You're paranoid,' said Constans. 'If they were going to do that, then why did they go to the trouble of asking us politely?'

'I am a good judge of character,' said Mor Galthide, 'and I think the king is a decent enough man. I am not overly fond of a couple of his sons, but Magnus is a likeable lad. I cannot believe that Magnus would hide such wicked plans from us.'

Lothar shook his head at the broad warrior. 'You think the king is a decent man? Have you lost your fucking mind?'

'I might take exception to your tone, soldier,' said Mor Galthide, getting to his feet.

'Stop this,' said Fyenna. 'We must present a united front, even if we happen to disagree with each other. Reath – keep your suspicions to yourself for now. Lothar, please refrain from losing your temper; and Mor Galthide, sit down.'

Reath scowled. 'But...'

'Not now, Reath,' said Fyenna. 'We shall all be going to the caves, and that is my final decision. We are almost halfway there, children – we have been here for thirteen days, and we only have around the same again to wait before the barges get here. I know we've had a trying time but, please, be patient.'

The students from the secret schools quietened, though a few still looked disgruntled.

'Peace at last,' said Annalise, who was sitting with her packed bag on her knee. 'Now I can hear myself think again.'

Eshia glanced up from her chair. 'What will we say if they ask us if we have thought about their offer?'

'The truth,' said Fyenna. 'We can tell them how honoured, even flattered we are that they would ask us, but our decision remains the same.'

'That's not the truth,' said Eshia. 'I don't feel honoured or flattered.'

'You know what I mean, Eshia. We decline their offer. I just meant that we don't have to be rude about it.'

'I wonder which ones Einar and Erling fancy,' said Stanza. 'We know that Ragnvald wants Eshia, but what about the others? Do you think they each picked one of us?'

'Whoever it is,' said Reath, 'it won't be you.' She eyed Raewyn. 'But I can guess who Magnus chose.'

Both Raewyn and Constans looked away, frowning, and Reath laughed.

'Don't make jokes about it, Reath,' said Abigone. 'We have to be very careful about how we deal with the king and his sons. Some people take rejection badly, and we don't want them to think that we are mocking them.'

'Why not?' said Reath.

Aplin glanced up. 'Because they could kill us all,' he said. 'This is what no one is talking about. They have Masters who could turn our blood into salt with a few words. We don't have any Masters who can do that.'

'I can do it,' said Constans.

'You've done it once,' said Aplin. 'And, all right, say you manage to kill one of them, what about the others? The Makers can summon all the swords and armour they like, but they can't defend us from Masters.

Even Mor Galthide, Lothar and Denny can't protect us, no matter how well they can fight. If we want to stay alive, then we have to do whatever the king says. We have no choice.'

The large room fell into silence.

'The Makers can also kill,' said Abigone. 'We killed the sailors on the *Bitter Respite*, didn't we? If we need to, we can summon horses again.'

Fear flitted over the faces of some of the younger students, then everyone turned to the front door as it was pushed open. Erling walked in, followed a pace behind by Magnus, who looked aggrieved.

Erling stared at the gathered group in the large chamber.

'The king has told me to supervise today's move to the caves,' he said. He gestured towards Magnus. 'It was too much for the little runt to handle on his own. Move your arses; it's time to go.'

Annalise got to her feet. 'What kinds of facilities can we expect in the caverns?' she said. 'Will there be a bathroom, or a kitchen?'

'It's a fucking cave,' said Erling.

'We have moved mattresses into the caverns,' said Magnus; 'along with tables and chairs, and over a dozen oil lamps. We've tried to make it comfortable.'

'Is there any ventilation?' said Fyenna. 'All those oil lamps will create a lot of smoke.'

Erling rolled his eyes. 'Why are you still standing around? I told you to move your arses. You'll see the cave when you get there.'

'Speak not towards us in that manner,' said Mor Galthide. 'Are we not your guests?'

'You are,' said Magnus. 'We would be much obliged if you would please follow us.'

He gestured towards the door, and the group began to pick up their luggage.

'Are we walking there with the occupants of the women's quarters?' said Abigone, as she walked with the students to the doorway.

'They have already been transferred to the caves,' Magnus said.

'A different cave,' said Erling. 'You won't be mixing with them.'

'Why not?' said Abigone.

'Because you are guests, and they are slaves,' he said.

Erling and Magnus led them out of the apartment, and they were joined by two dozen heavily-armed mercenaries. Together, they descended several flights of stairs, and traversed long stretches of dark, narrow passageways that twisted and turned in a bewildering fashion. Abigone tried to remember the route they were taking, but had to concede defeat after a few minutes.

'This place is like a maze,' said Denny, as he walked by her side.

Abigone glanced over her shoulder, to make sure that no mercenaries were close enough to hear them.

'Are we walking into a trap?' she whispered.

'I don't think so,' he said. 'If they wanted to kill us, then they could do that here, in the temple. They wouldn't need to transfer us first. And we know that Steppen has been attacked more than once.'

'Who do you think is attacking them?'

'It could be runaway slaves,' he said. 'Or maybe it's the same brigands who ambushed our barge on the way here. I doubt it's the Jallian militia. Jallin makes too much money from the silver to care about how it's extracted.'

'What about the Sanctians?' she said. 'The attackers have made no demands, as far as we know; and they seemed to defeat the mercenaries with ease, as though they might be a professional fighting force. The silver wouldn't stop the Sanctians if they knew there were Masters living here.'

They descended another flight of stairs.

'Well?' said Abigone. 'What do you think of my suggestion?'

'I don't know,' he said. 'Jallin isn't part of the empire, but that might not stop the Sanctians if they have any evidence that the Whalebone King is a Master. Is it possible they know that we are here?'

'If they were chasing us, then it would be easier for them to wait until we travelled down the river to Elestia. It would save them from having to enter the forest.'

'Maybe, but they could attack us here, and no one would ever know.'

They came to a long, straight, stretch of passageway with a door at the far end. Erling pushed his way to the front, and spoke to the soldiers guarding the entrance. The door was unlocked and opened, and daylight spilled into the building. Erling led them all outside, and Abigone's mouth fell open. Directly ahead of them were the three central waterfalls, each edged in the vibrant greens of the forest. Dozens of narrow water channels and pools spread away from the base of the waterfalls, and there were little bridges everywhere, each lined with ivy and flower baskets. Birds were calling and singing from the branches of the trees, and the water was sparkling in the sunlight.

'I think this is the most beautiful thing I've ever seen in my life,' said Abigone, as she stepped onto a perfectly-manicured patch of lawn. She glanced at Denny, but his eyes were narrow.

'Think about how much work it takes to ensure that it remains so beautiful,' he said. 'Every inch has been tended, pruned, mown and maintained. All that work, but where are the workers?'

Abigone glanced around, but saw no one apart from the mercenaries who were escorting them.

'They've been hidden from us,' she said. 'Again.'

Magnus and Erling led them along a series of neat gravel paths, and over a few bridges, as they approached the roaring waterfalls. Cave openings came into view. Some were tucked behind the falls, while others pockmarked the surface of the cliffs. They crossed another bridge, and came to a place where a series of steps led up to the entrances of several caves. Magnus turned.

'This whole area was once an island of rock,' he said, 'separated from the rest of the cliffs by the river course. The Temple of Steppen wasn't built – it was carved out of that island of rock.'

'How long ago was this?' said Abigone.

'Uh, I'm not exactly sure,' said Magnus. 'Centuries ago, I think. There was once a large and thriving community of priests and priestesses living here, and we think that pilgrims used to come from all over the Central Provinces. It was a major religious site.'

'What happened to it?' said Denny.

'Again, we are not completely sure,' said Magnus. 'When the king arrived here over thirty years ago, Steppen was abandoned, and the forest was starting to reclaim it.'

'Did your father discover the silver deposits,' said Abigone, 'or was there a functioning mine already here? Is that how the temple was funded?'

'That's enough questions,' said Erling. 'I don't have time to stand here chatting.'

'But this might be the last time we see sunlight for several days,' said Abigone. 'Could we please savour it for a few more moments?'

'That seems fair,' said Magnus, before Erling could open his mouth.

The mercenaries came to a halt, and took up positions surrounding them. Fyenna, Lothar and Eshia sat down on the steps that led up to the caves, while a few of the others sat on the grass. The sun had cleared the tree cover to the east, and the whole area seemed to be basking in its light. Abigone and Denny walked to the edge of a pool. The water was crystal clear, and small silver fish were darting around under the lilies.

'What a place to live,' said Denny. 'It's a paradise.'

'I keep thinking about what you said earlier, about the workers. I doubt many of them think they're living in paradise, not if they have been enslaved.'

'What if they are all Westlanders?'

'What difference would that make?'

'It would be legal, for a start,' Denny said; 'and Upper Down has a history of trouble with Westlanders. Your father allowed them to occupy your realm for twenty years.'

'And then we kicked them out,' said Abigone. 'I have never met a Westlander that I liked, and I don't want them anywhere near Upper Down again, but... I don't know.'

'Many people in the Central Provinces consider them to be savages.'

'*I* consider them to be savages. I also happen to think that only savages enslave other people. I'd rather be better than that.'

Denny said nothing as he gazed at the waterfalls.

'Do you disagree?' said Abigone.

'No,' he said. 'That's one of the things I like about the Sanctian Empire; in fact, it might be the only thing I like about it. My grandfather has almost eradicated slavery from the old Central Provinces. It's only in isolated places, like here, where it still flourishes.'

'That's enough time,' Erling shouted. He gestured to the mercenaries. 'Herd them into the caves.'

The soldiers began to move across the grass, ushering the king's guests up the rock-cut steps towards the central waterfall and the caves that lay behind it. Abigone felt the spray from the waterfall against the skin on her face and arms, and the path under her feet was wet. Erling steered them towards a wide entrance in the side of the cliffs. More soldiers were waiting there, guarding the entrance, and the guests were led in past them. They came into a wide cavern, lit solely by the wavering sunlight coming through the waterfall. The cavern had several exits, and Erling gestured towards one.

'This way,' he said.

They carried on, leaving the cavern behind as they went along a narrow tunnel, deeper into the side of the cliff. The way grew dark, but Abigone could see the flickering light of lamps ahead. They emerged into another cavern, where around two dozen women were sitting.

'What the fuck are they doing here?' Erling cried.

'I don't know,' said Magnus. 'They are supposed to be in a neighbouring cavern.'

One of the women stood. 'Good morning, son,' she said. 'We were told there would be mattresses and chairs. Where are the...' Her voice tailed away as the last of the guests entered the cavern, and her gaze settled on Reath and Nyli. 'Girls,' she went on, 'it's nice to see you again. How have you been?'

'We've been stuck inside our quarters,' said Reath. 'They wouldn't let us outside, well, not until now.'

Abigone approached the group of women. 'Are you Magnus's mother?' she said.

'I am,' said the woman. 'My name is Colette. Have you been mistreated?'

'Of course they haven't, you miserable old bitch,' said Erling.

Magnus's eyes flashed with anger. He clenched his fists and took a step towards his brother.

'Any closer,' said Erling, 'and I will beat the crap out of your dear mother. Is that what you want, you little prick? She loves it when I slap her around.' Erling paused, as if remembering that Abigone and the others were watching.

Colette raised her chin. 'Such noble words, Erling,' she said. 'Now everyone knows what a gentleman you are.'

Erling raised his fists. 'You are nothing; a slave. A filthy whore not fit to wipe the shit from my boots. I know it; you know it. Even Magnus knows it.'

Magnus swung his fist and struck his brother in the face. Erling's head flinched back, then he charged into his younger brother, and they both fell to the cavern floor. Erling punched Magnus's nose, then he began to throttle him, his hands gripping his throat. Colette tried to pull him off, then the mercenaries piled into the cavern, pushing the guests back and separating the two groups. They formed a ring around the two sons of the king, but did nothing to stop Erling from choking Magnus. Erling laughed, then he punched his brother again. The older son got back to his feet. He kicked Magnus in the ribs, then he stamped on his chest. The enslaved women were crying out and shouting for Erling to stop, while most of the guests were staring open-mouthed, the mercenaries preventing them from getting any closer.

Colette managed to reach Erling, and she tried again to restrain him. Erling turned, and drove his fist into her face. Colette fell back to the floor of the cavern, sobbing, her hands on her bloody face, and Erling kicked her in the stomach.

'This is your fault,' Erling shouted at her. 'Do you hear me, slave?'

'You shame yourself, Mister Erling,' cried Mor Galthide. 'If you wish to fight someone, I would be happy to oblige.'

'Kick his ass, Mor Galthide,' shouted Reath.

Erling turned to face the guests. The mercenaries had pushed them up against the wall opposite the slaves from the women's quarters, and were fencing them in with spears and swords.

'We demand to speak to the king,' said Fyenna. 'What we have just witnessed is an utter disgrace.'

'Fuck you,' said Erling; 'fuck you all. Soldiers, get them into their cavern; now.'

The mercenaries moved forward, and shepherded the guests through into another tunnel. They were pushed along until they reached another large cave, which had been lit by oil lamps hanging from chains driven into the cavern walls. Several mattress had been lined up, and, on the other side, a row of tables with chairs had been laid out. As soon as the last of the guests had entered, the mercenaries sealed off the cavern by fixing a stout wooden door over the entrance, blocking it completely.

'Why did he do that?' said Stanza, her eyes red. 'Why did he have to hurt them?'

'He is a beast,' said Annalise; 'a wild animal. If only his father knew how he behaved.'

'I'm sure Erling's father knows exactly what he's like,' said Lothar.

'Should I have intervened?' said Mor Galthide. 'I wanted to, but it would have meant having to fight the mercenaries also, and I wished not to place the little ones at risk.'

Fyenna sat down on a chair, and stared at the cavern floor.

'We need to get out of here,' said Lothar. 'Is it any wonder they've been hiding the slaves from us if that's how they're being treated? We don't have to put up with this shit. We have Makers who could rip that door down in seconds; Makers who could arm us; Makers who could summon fucking horses if they wanted to.'

'And where would we go?' said Fyenna. 'Elestia is hundreds of miles from here.'

'We could trek through the forest,' said Lothar. 'It would be difficult, but it's better than staying here.'

'No,' said Fyenna. 'The forest is a wilderness; half of us would not survive the trek.'

'What about Magnus?' said Raewyn, her voice quavering.

'What about him?' said Lothar.

'He is trapped here too,' Raewyn said. 'Reath told us that, and we saw the truth of it today. How can we help him?'

'I'm sorry, Raewyn, but I don't trust Magnus, either. His brothers might bully and beat him, but that doesn't mean he would betray them.' Lothar's gaze sought out Reath. 'What do you remember being told in the women's quarters? Is Erling a Master?'

'I'm pretty sure he's not,' said Reath. 'Magnus's mother told us it was just the king, Ragnvald and Magnus.'

'Then why would Magnus allow himself to get beaten like that, if he's a Master?'

'Maybe Colette doesn't know about Erling,' said Abigone, 'or maybe Magnus's abilities are under-developed.'

'Like mine,' said Denny. 'I'm a Master, but it's not as though I can snap my fingers and kill people. Let's assume Colette knew the truth, because Magnus wouldn't have lied to her. That gives us three Masters to face, one of whom might be on our side.'

Lothar grimaced and shook his head. 'Weren't you listening to what I said, Denny? Magnus isn't on our side. It doesn't matter if he has endured a life of constant misery here in Steppen, that doesn't mean he'll be willing to turn against his own father. As far as I can see, Magnus has been playing along with his family this entire time. He probably wants to impress his father.'

'All right,' said Denny, 'but we can discount him as a Master. That leaves two. How do we deal with them?'

'We will not be dealing with them,' said Fyenna. 'I feel sorry for Magnus and his mother, but my only priority is to keep everyone alive. We have three choices – to escape into the forest, where we will probably die; to fight against Masters who could kill us in seconds; or to wait for the barges to take us to Elestia. It's simple – we wait it out.'

'That's not good enough,' said Lothar. 'Do lambs sit waiting for the wolf to strike?'

'I am no lamb, soldier,' said Mor Galthide.

'Then you agree with me?' said Lothar.

The Geathian prince narrowed his eyes. 'I will fight if we are attacked; but the king has not once harmed us. Erling is a brute; that is clear, but I see no evidence that the king is at fault.'

Everyone turned as the wooden door was opened. Ragnvald walked into the cavern alone, his eyes lit with fury.

'I want to apologise to you all,' he said, 'and to assure you that Erling will be severely punished for what transpired in the other cavern. His behaviour was unacceptable, both to me and to the king.'

'Is Magnus all right?' said Raewyn.

Ragnvald's gaze settled on her. 'My youngest brother will be fine. He has a broken nose and some bruised ribs, but he'll recover. Again, I apologise for Erling's temper.'

Abigone narrowed her eyes. 'That wasn't the first time Erling has beaten Magnus, was it?'

'That is a private family matter,' said Ragnvald.

'What will happen to Erling?' said Marlow.

'That will be up to the king,' said Ragnvald. 'Erling is on his way to see him as I speak. Rest assured that Erling will have no more contact with you during your stay here. I shall step in for now, until Magnus has fully recovered.' He shook his head, seeming genuinely pained. 'What must you think of us? I will understand if none of the young women here would desire to become Erling's bride. He has shamed the family this day, but we are not all like him. Is there anything I can do to set your minds at ease?'

'You could let us speak to Magnus,' said Abigone.

Ragnvald hesitated for a moment, then he attempted a smile. 'Very well. I shall ask him if he is prepared to see you, but any visit would have to be brief, as his wounds need attention.'

He bowed slightly, then he walked out of the chamber and the door was pushed back into place.

Lothar frowned. 'I don't believe a word that comes out of that bastard's mouth.'

'Come now, Lothar,' said Annalise. 'Ragnvald might be a little rough around the edges, but he has always behaved like a gentleman in our presence.'

Reath snorted. 'That's not what Magnus's mother said about him.'

'I don't like the way he looks at me,' said Eshia.

'That is understandable,' said Annalise; 'as you are the object of his affections. It seems to me that many of you are spending your time looking for the bad in others. Should we not at least wait until we hear what Magnus has to say before we jump to any wild conclusions?'

Lothar shook his head. 'Magnus will say whatever Ragnvald tells him to say.'

'There you go again,' said Annalise.

'In Klef Mordain,' said Lothar, 'we quickly learned not to trust anyone; are you now saying that we should trust these ignorant thugs?'

'Erling might well be an ignorant thug, Lothar,' said Annalise, 'but that doesn't mean the others are.'

The door opened again, and Magnus limped into the cavern. Ragnvald was standing behind him, but he didn't enter the cave. Blood was coating Magnus's nose and chin, and he was clearly trying to suppress the pain he was feeling.

Raewyn put a hand to her face.

'Hello,' said Magnus. 'Did you want to see me?'

'We wanted to see if you were all right,' said Abigone.

Magnus shrugged. 'I'll be fine.'

'What Erling did to you and your mother was terrible.'

'My brother can sometimes have a vicious temper,' Magnus said. 'The king will punish him.'

'How fares your mother, lad?' said Mor Galthide.

Magnus lowered his gaze. 'She... she will also recover. The slaves have been moved to a different cavern, and the other women will look after her.' He took a breath. 'Please don't worry about me. I hope the cavern is comfortable enough for you. I should go now. Someone is going to clean the blood from my face.'

He turned, and limped out of the cavern, then the wooden door was set back in place.

'Somehow,' said Abigone, 'I don't feel very reassured. I think Lothar might be right. Did you see the way that Ragnvald was standing behind him?'

'Then you agree that we need to break out of here, Your Highness?' said Lothar.

'We are not breaking out,' said Fyenna, getting to her feet. 'We shall not be doing anything that might provoke the anger of our hosts. This is not a game, Lothar; the lives of children are at stake, and it is our job to protect them. Nothing else matters – not the way Erling treats Magnus, not the suspicious nature of Ragnvald and the king, and not the manner in which they have been trying to conceal things from us. Do you all understand?'

No one replied.

'When the barges come,' Fyenna went on; 'we shall board them and leave this awful place. As soon as we leave Steppen, we can complain about it all we like but, until then, I need everyone to remain calm. Do not allow yourselves to be provoked. Imagine this as a test – a test of our patience and resolve. And that,' she went on, 'is my final word on the matter.'

CHAPTER 18
A CAUSE FOR JOY

South of Steppen, Great Forest, Jallin, Central Provinces – 7th Day of Quoma 108

Saffie walked along the austere hallways of the Palace of Adriano, which was odd, as she was supposed to be in the Great Forest hunting Masters. She must have returned to Sanctos. She passed the Sanctum Pietas, the most sacred temple on the entire island, and one which was reserved for the imperial family's prayers and devotions to the spirits. She heard chanting coming from within, and her heart swelled. She was home. She walked into a large hall that was used by the imperial cousins for all manner of activities. At that particular moment, Count Sebastian was leading a session on sword training, a topic at which Saffie had never excelled. Prince Francesco was matched with Prince Allessandro, one of Saffie's brothers, and the two young men were moving back and forth, their steel blades held in their right hands. Watching from a side wall were Prince Denny and Prince Arturo.

Denny was there? Saffie frowned. Hadn't Denny been abducted by his father nearly two years before? But it wasn't Denny she was there to see; it was Arturo, her betrothed. He noticed her presence and halted the conversation he had been holding with Denny.

'I will never marry you,' she said. 'I don't love you.'

'The emperor has commanded it, Safina,' Arturo said.

Saffie narrowed her eyes. 'Don't call me that.' She raised her right hand. 'Blessed spirits,' she said, 'use the darkness within me to summon a giant spider to eat my cousin.'

A monstrous shape appeared in the hall, six feet tall, and bristling with black hair. It reared up as Arturo screamed, then the spider began devouring him. It started with Arturo's head, swallowing it up whole, then the rest of her cousin's body disappeared into its hideous maw.

Saffie laughed at the sight. Had she ever been so happy?

Saffie awoke with a jolt, and saw that she was still lying on the ground in the midst of the forest. Sanctian soldiers were resting under the trees close by, and Agent Marco of the Offices of Purgation eyed her.

'Are you all right, ma'am?' he said. 'You look as though you have just learned some particularly bad news.'

Saffie narrowed her eyes at him, then she shook her head.

'I'm fine,' she said. 'I didn't mean to fall asleep.'

'You were sleeping for less than an hour, ma'am,' he said.

Saffie didn't want to know how he knew that. She nodded, then closed her eyes again so that she wouldn't have to speak to him. She shivered, not from the autumnal chill, but from the memory of her dream. At least it hadn't been the most exalted emperor that she had murdered; instead, it had been Arturo, a cousin with whom she had always got along well. Arturo was sweet and kind, traits that had led to him being teased by his older cousins, and Saffie liked him. Not enough to marry him, but he certainly didn't deserve to be eaten by a gigantic spider. Could Makers even summon gigantic spiders? Saffie wasn't sure. Her knowledge regarding the precise powers wielded by Masters and Makers was a little shaky. There were very few books in the palace library that even touched on the subject, and Saffie hadn't read them. Almost all of her learning on Masters and Makers had come from her aunt Princess Isabella, who was the high priestess of the Sanctum Pietas. If there was one thing everyone knew about Isabella, it was that she detested Masters and Makers with all of her being. So far did her loathing go, that she made the most exalted emperor look positively tolerant. Both of them would be very pleased with Saffie if she was able to bring home the head of the Whalebone King. Saffie would also be pleased, but possibly for different reasons. Everything she had witnessed since they had first made contact with Steppen had led her to one conclusion – the Whalebone King was irredeemably evil, and his death would be a cause of great joy.

'Ma'am?' Marco whispered.

Saffie opened her eyes.

'Captain Zola is signalling to us, ma'am,' he said. 'It's time to leave.'

Soldiers were starting to stir around them, and Saffie sat up. She felt groggy from the long night's interrupted and uncomfortable sleep, and she sat motionless for a few moments as though in a stupor. A couple of soldiers went through their pre-battle prayers, asking the spirits to guide their hands and help them overcome the Master in his lair; while others ate a quick breakfast of whatever they had left in their packs.

Saffie pulled herself to her feet, and walked back through the forest to where Captain Zola was standing next to the acting senior lieutenant.

'Good morning, ma'am,' said Zola.

'Is it morning?' she said.

'It will be soon,' he said. 'Are you ready for the final act? This is the day we have been waiting for; the day when we take the head of the Whalebone King.'

The acting lieutenant frowned.

'I'm ready,' said Saffie.

'Stay here while I make sure everyone is awake,' said Zola.

The captain walked off, leaving Saffie with the young lieutenant.

Saffie eyed him. 'You don't seem very enthusiastic about the prospect of today's events, Lieutenant.'

His frown deepened.

'Do you have concerns?' she said.

'The captain told me to keep them to myself, ma'am.'

'And now I am asking you to reveal them to me. What's wrong, Lieutenant?'

'I hadn't realised until this morning that we were intending a full frontal assault on the Temple of Steppen, ma'am. I had assumed that we would be continuing our strategy of raids, in order to wear the enemy down. There are six hundred mercenaries guarding that temple, and we have only fifty fit soldiers available to us. It's madness. The captain is throwing away the lives of Sanctian soldiers for nothing.'

'It's not for nothing,' she said; 'it's to find and kill a dangerous Master. And besides, with the spirits on our side, how can we fail?'

'The captain believes that none of us will be returning to Elestia alive, ma'am.'

Saffie's eyes narrowed. 'Did he say that?'

'He didn't need to, ma'am. He has timed the attack for the very day that our food supplies have run out. Even if by some miracle we succeed, we will have no food to get home.' He glanced away, his eyes burning with fury. 'Damn the Offices of Purgation,' he muttered. 'Their desire to find one man has doomed one hundred and twenty Sanctians.'

'Perhaps it would be best if you said nothing more, Lieutenant,' she said. 'Have you forgotten to whom you are speaking? Not only do I work for the Offices of Purgation, but I am also a granddaughter of His Most Exalted Imperial Majesty the Emperor. Hunting Masters and Makers is a divinely-ordained task. By doing so, we are saving this world from the evil they represent. Hasn't the Whalebone King filled your heart with anger and disgust?'

'He has, ma'am,' said the lieutenant. 'There is no doubt that he deserves death, and I only wish we had the forces with us to obliterate him and his damn mercenaries. There is nothing more I would like than to rip the bastard's head from his shoulders, but with only fifty soldiers available to fight? It's not going to happen. Fifty soldiers cannot overcome six hundred. It's impossible.'

'Nothing is impossible if so decreed by the spirits. Have a little faith, Lieutenant. Is Sanctos not outnumbered twenty-to-one by the population of the Central Provinces? And yet we rule the empire, not them.'

'Apologies, ma'am, but that comparison is worthless. We conquered the Central Provinces one piece at a time; not once have we faced the combined forces of all of the provinces together, and we never shall – they are too divided among themselves. If the same was true here, and we had to confront twenty mercenaries at a time, we would be victorious. Somehow, I don't think today's battle is going to follow that pattern.'

Zola returned to where they were standing. He took one look at the young lieutenant's face, and rolled his eyes.

'Has this man been filling your head with defeatist talk, ma'am?' he said.

Saffie kept her features still. 'He has concerns.'

'And I have addressed them,' said Zola. 'What we do this day is for the greater glory of the Sanctian Empire. The spirits shall sing for joy if we butcher the Master and his family. Every time a Master uses his powers, the spirits are wracked with bitter agonies; yet this coward believes that we have no chance of success.'

The lieutenant stood to attention. 'I am not a coward, sir. Give the order, and I shall obey.'

Zola studied the young officer. 'And will you mention any of your… concerns to the lower ranks?'

'No, sir. Complaints go up, not down. However, sir, I should inform you that Sanctian soldiers are not stupid. Several of them have already realised that their chances of returning home are slim.'

'We may have to give our lives in service of the empire today,' said Zola. 'That prospect does not vex me. Can you think of a better way to die?'

'But, sir; don't we have a duty to preserve the life of the princess?'

'Her Highness understood the risks when we departed Elestia; isn't that so, ma'am?'

'I always knew there was a chance that we might have to give our lives,' she said, 'and I don't see why my life is more important than that of a soldier.'

Zola frowned. 'No, ma'am; your life is worth far more than that. You are a member of the imperial household. If you fall this day fighting a vile Master, your martyrdom will stun the empire. To think that a princess would willingly give her life for the noblest cause imaginable? It will inspire the countless faithful of the empire to even greater deeds. Anger towards Masters and Makers will reach new heights all over the Central Provinces, and your name will be remembered for centuries.' He gazed into the distance, and Saffie began to feel a little queasy. 'Is there anything better than martyrdom?' he went on. 'Anything more honourable and beautiful than to die opposing Masters and Makers? I think not. Come; let us prepare to leave.'

Zola walked away again, and called out to the soldiers to assemble into a column.

'He's fucking insane,' muttered the young lieutenant. 'The forest has driven him mad.'

Saffie pretended not to hear, though perhaps she was more inclined to agree with the officer's sentiments than he realised. Zola's state of mind had deteriorated with every step they had taken into the Great Forest. Did the captain wish to become a martyr? More importantly for Saffie, did he wish for her to become a martyr?

She and the acting lieutenant walked towards the column of soldiers. The officer continued on to the head of the column, then Marco moved in to stand next to Saffie.

'I am looking forward to this, ma'am,' Marco said. 'It's about time we got to grips with the foe, eh? We will smash them into pieces.'

He quietened as Zola raised a hand. 'Soldiers of Sanctos,' he said, 'today is the day when the evil reign of the Whalebone King shall be brought to an end. We have all seen the obscene depravity with which this so-called king has governed the town of Steppen. We have witnessed his callous disregard for life, and his cruelty. I have faced Masters and Makers before, but not one who hides deep within the forest; one who acts like a petty tyrant. Truly I say to you that nothing would give the spirits more happiness than the death of this vile creature; and today, that death will come.'

He paused for a moment and bowed his head, as if in prayer.

'We had hoped,' he went on, 'that we would be able to catch the Whalebone King out in the open. We had hoped that a targeted assassination would be all it took to dethrone this monster, but alas! – that has not been the case. Like a craven animal, he has chosen to seal himself up inside a temple, adding the crime of sacrilege to his many offences. Moreover, he has surrounded himself with hired swords – six hundred hired swords. He imagines himself to be safe, but he has not reckoned with the righteous anger and divine purpose of the Sanctian army. One of us is worth twenty of those damn mercenaries – you know this in your hearts, and the Whalebone King shall, this day, also discover the truth of it. For we have the blessed spirits on our side; they will shield us from harm and guide our blades; they will watch over us as we carry out our sacred duty. If any of us fall this day, there will be no mourning or weeping, for it will be a cause of great joy! Our souls will rise to join the blessed spirits; we shall become part of the celestial firmament, where we shall be honoured for all eternity. Remember that when you face the enemy; remember that we all came from dust and ash. Everything that lives must die; what matters is the manner of our deaths, and there is no greater end than to die for our beloved faith. Steel your hearts, and show no mercy to the servants of the wicked king. Onwards, to glory and eternal life!'

The soldiers cheered, and then Zola turned and led the way through the forest.

'Quite an inspiring speech, ma'am; wasn't it?' Marco said.

Saffie eyed him. 'Are you ready to die today?'

Marco puffed out his chest. 'I am, ma'am.'

'Quiet at the back there,' whispered a sergeant, and Saffie fell into silence.

Was she also ready to die? She had always known that any assignment with the Offices of Purgation brought its own risks. Her year-long service with the Sanctian Navy had also held its moments of danger, but she had never seriously imagined that she was about to die. She glanced down at her feet. They were still moving; still walking towards the six hundred mercenaries in Steppen, but her body seemed disconnected from her emotions. A realisation struck her – she didn't want to die. She wasn't ready. She had plans; plans that assumed that she had several decades ahead of her. She wanted to travel across the entire continent; she wanted to study religious law at the seminary on Sanctos; and, one day, perhaps, she might want a family of her own. Part of her also wanted to flee into the depths of the forest, to escape from the misery and violence of Steppen and the Whalebone King; and yet her feet kept moving, following the rest of the column as it made its way north towards the settlement.

Was that how it happened? Was that how soldiers walked willingly to their deaths?

After an hour, the lieutenant signalled a halt to the march to allow the soldiers to load their crossbows.

'Discard all that you do not need,' said Zola. 'Leave it here and we shall collect it once we have obtained the head of the Master. The same applies to your crossbows. Loose once at the enemy, then drop them and draw your swords. There shall be no retreat. Ignore the slaves and kill every man you see carrying a weapon.' He nodded to the lieutenant.

'We will be approaching the main road from the south,' the lieutenant said, as the soldiers began dumping their packs onto the ground. 'The normal practice of the mercenary forces is to post around a dozen men at this junction, as it sits on the south-western corner of the shanty town. The first eight pairs in the column shall loose at these mercenaries; the others will preserve their bolts for the encounters that will follow. Once you have loosed, move to the rear of the column. We shall then proceed northwards along the road, turning right at the next junction, where the temple lies.'

He glanced at the soldiers, waiting for them to ready their bows. All indications of his previous concerns regarding the operation had been wiped from his features, and he appeared resolute and determined. A few of the sergeants were grim-faced, and Saffie wondered how many of them wanted to give their lives for the Offices of Purgation.

When every soldier had a loaded bow cradled in their arms, the lieutenant raised his right hand.

'Follow me,' he said, then he turned and set off through the forest.

The column hurried along behind him. Zola made his way to the rear, where Saffie and Marco were stationed, and they increased their pace to keep up with the soldiers. Saffie saw a few lamps ahead of them through the dense forest, then the leading ranks of the column burst out from the trees and onto the road that led from the south. The first eight pairs formed two lines, then they raised their bows at the mercenaries standing next to the road junction. The bows thrummed, and seven mercenaries fell. The remaining five took one look at the soldiers emerging from the forest, and fled, sprinting along the road towards the temple.

A cheer rose up from within the shanty town, and Saffie realised that they were being watched. On the other side of the fence, several dozen slaves were staring at the soldiers and the dead mercenaries.

'Kill those bastards!' yelled an emaciated Westlander. 'Kill them all!'

'Let us out!' cried another. 'We can fight.'

'Ignore them,' said Zola. 'Our only priority is the Whalebone King. Move.'

The soldiers got underway again, reforming into their column. Those with loaded bows took over the leading positions, and they raced along by the western edge of the fenced-off shanty town. Whistles sounded in the distance, then a horn blew.

Saffie turned to Zola. 'Perhaps we should reconsider our tactics,' she said. 'If we were to double back, we could swing round by the southern side of the slave settlement and raid for supplies. We have already killed seven mercenaries for no loss – couldn't we continue these raids indefinitely, weakening the Whalebone King until the odds are more in our favour?'

Zola pretended not to hear.

'Captain,' she went on, 'if we are patient, then we could wear the mercenaries down, whittling away at their numbers and their morale. A campaign of attrition could succeed; while a full assault on the temple carries a high risk of failure.'

'Your words shame the great and noble name of your family,' Zola spat. 'The Whalebone King is an abomination, and his rule ends today.'

'But what about the other soldiers who have been staging attacks? Isn't there a chance that we could join forces with them to coordinate our efforts?'

'And allow some other band to claim the credit? The glory of this day shall belong to the Sanctians, and to no other.'

The column reached the north-western corner of the shanty town. More slaves were pressing up against the fence, cheering on the Sanctians, and begging to be allowed to take part in the attack. The road split. To the right, a wide paved thoroughfare ran in front of the tall rock-cut Temple of Steppen. It crossed half a dozen small water channels, and was lined with lush lawns and ornamental gardens. There were smaller tracks that led up to a series of doorways in the flank of the temple, including the grand main entrance, which sat at the top of a dozen stone steps. Above the trees to the east, the sky was brightening, and the birds were calling out in anticipation of the coming dawn. Down on the road, however, groups of mercenaries were forming up. Some were spilling out of the temple, while others were hurrying along the road from the east, where the barracks were situated.

'Those with bows, loose at once!' the young lieutenant cried.

The Sanctians moved into ranks, the first row kneeling, as the mercenaries caught sight of them. The clamour coming from the slaves behind the fence increased, and the mercenaries were shouting out their orders amid more whistles and horns.

The Sanctians loosed, and over a dozen mercenaries fell.

'Swords!' cried the young lieutenant.

Every crossbow was dropped onto the road, and the soldiers drew their blades. A few among the mercenaries had loaded their own bows by that time, and several loosed at the Sanctians as they formed themselves into tight ranks. Two Sanctians fell, then another three, as bolts flew at them.

'Charge!' shouted the lieutenant.

The Sanctians roared and ran along the road. The slaves behind the fence to their right were shouting so loudly that Saffie could barely hear herself think. Another two Sanctians fell from crossbow bolts, then their lines slammed into the disorganised mercenaries. The first few ranks of the hired soldiers buckled and broke under the pressure, but more were appearing with every moment that passed. Some arrived on the road behind the Sanctians, cutting off their chances of retreating, and the road in front of the temple descended into chaos. The slaves cheered the death of every mercenary, but their cries became more subdued as they began to realise how heavily outnumbered the Sanctians were. Saffie pulled the knife from her belt, as mercenaries hit their ranks from behind. Marco was cut down by the swing of a large wood axe, the blade ripping open his stomach; then Zola drove his sword into the chest of the mercenary who had dealt the killing blow.

'To me!' shouted Zola. 'To the temple!'

The Sanctians rallied, and they forced their way over a bridge and onto the path that led to a large entrance in the southern flank of the temple. The young lieutenant was leading from the front, his sword stained red. The mercenaries by the temple doors were retreating into the building, and the lieutenant pursued them. Saffie crossed the bridge, half-bundled over by Sanctian soldiers, and they approached the entrance. The lieutenant was the first to cross the threshold, then he disappeared from sight. The mercenaries then became the pursuers, and the Sanctians were attacked from every direction as they bunched together to get through the entrance of the temple. A mercenary pushed his way towards Saffie, and she lashed out with the knife, slashing the man's hand. He dropped his spear, and a Sanctian rammed the tip of his sword into his face. Saffie was shoved to the side, and she stooped down to pick up the spear. She placed the knife back into her belt, and used the spear to fend off more attacks as they edged closer to the temple. More Sanctians were falling by the bottleneck next to the entrance, then Saffie was pushed over the threshold. She found herself in a dark passageway, which was filled with what remained of the Sanctian soldiers, while Zola was one of the few still outside. The captain was fighting with a demented fury, swinging his sword two-handed as he held off the approaching mercenaries. Saffie tried to reach him, then she almost tripped over the body of a dead soldier. Zola raised his sword again, and he was bundled to the ground by four mercenaries. Zola writhed and struggled, then he was clubbed over the back of the head by a spear butt, and his eyes closed.

'Get that door shut!' shouted a Sanctian sergeant.

Two soldiers heaved the heavy wooden door closed as the mercenaries outside tried to force their way in. A thick bar was dropped into place, and the entrance was secured.

For a moment, the noise of battle faded away, and Saffie glanced around at the Sanctian soldiers resting in the thick shadows of the passageway. They had made it into the temple, but they had lost around half of their number in doing so. The young lieutenant walked down past the lines of Sanctians, his gaze passing over them.

'Where is the captain?' he said, when he reached the barred doorway.

'He fell, sir,' said a soldier.

The lieutenant nodded, then he caught sight of Saffie.

'At least the princess still lives,' he said.

Saffie said nothing.

'You are now in charge of this operation, Your Highness,' he went on. 'What are your orders?'

'Do you have a copy of Captain Zola's map of the temple interior?' said Saffie.

The lieutenant patted a pocket. 'I do, ma'am.'

'Sir,' said a soldier from the far end of the line, 'I can hear the sound of boots approaching.'

The lieutenant's face remained expressionless. 'I ask again, ma'am – what are your orders?'

Saffie moved a little so that the other soldiers could see her, and she straightened her back.

'We are in the Temple of Steppen,' she said; 'the lair of the Whalebone King. There is no going back. We shall finish this operation, and we shall be victorious, or we shall die.' She glanced at the young lieutenant. 'Lead us to the king.'

CHAPTER 19
A PROUD FATHER

Steppen, Great Forest, Jallin, Central Provinces – 7th Day of Quoma 108

Einar laughed so hard that he nearly fell off his chair and onto the roof of the temple.

'And then I kicked her,' Erling went on, 'while the little runt was bleeding all over the cavern floor.'

Magnus remained quiet, his face and chest still aching from the beating.

'The funniest part,' Erling said, 'was when Ragnvald had to go in and tell them it was all some sort of terrible mistake.'

'You're a fucking arsehole,' growled Ragnvald. 'Our *guests* will never trust us again after your little temper tantrum. I could see the way they were looking at me. They hate us.'

'But you told them it was all Erling's fault, didn't you?' said the king, his eyes tight.

'Of course I told them that, boss,' said Ragnvald. 'I also told them that the rest of us were disgusted by his behaviour.'

The king frowned, and eyed Magnus. 'I have two things to say to you, boy – first, stop standing up for your mother. Colette is nothing but a miserable old witch, twisted by bitterness. And second – learn how to fight better. Are you going to allow your brothers to beat you up for the remainder of your life?' He picked up his glass and drained it. 'Where's the rest of the brandy?'

Lord Matteo was gently snoring on the seat along from the king, and Hemming slapped him across the face.

Matteo spluttered awake, his eyes wide.

'Where's the fucking brandy, you Sanctian wanker?'

Matteo rubbed his cheek, then he reached under his chair and produced another full bottle.

'Can I go to bed now?' said Magnus.

'No, you cannot,' said the king, snatching the brandy from Matteo's grasp. 'We are drinking until dawn, just like I told you we would.'

'You should feel honoured, you ungrateful prick,' said Einar. 'This is the first time the king has invited you to one of his all-night drinking sessions, and you want to go to bed? What the fuck is wrong with you?'

'Maybe I hit him too hard,' said Erling.

Einar snorted. 'You barely gave him a proper beating at all. I mean, he still has all of his teeth.' He clenched his fists. 'Do you want me to show you how it's done?'

'Leave him,' said Ragnvald.

Einar and Erling laughed.

'Did you hear that?' said Erling. 'Ragnvald's getting soft in his old age.'

'Fuck you,' said Ragnvald. 'The only way I could calm down Eshia and the others was by letting them talk to Magnus. They like the little runt, and if we want them to cooperate, then we can't keep beating the crap out of him.'

The king poured himself a large measure of brandy. 'You know, lads, I'm starting to have second thoughts about our plan. It's partly Erling's fault. I don't care that he beat up Magnus and his mother, but to do it in front of the guests?' He eyed Erling. 'Ragnvald was right – you are an arsehole.'

Erling frowned. 'But...'

'Shut your fucking mouth when I'm speaking,' said the king.

'Thanks to you, it's likely that our guests will be on their guard from now on. It's going to be a lot harder to take them by surprise.' He stared out over the view of the shanty town. 'Maybe we should kill them all; that's what my old crewmates think. They're too dangerous to keep, and too dangerous to let go.'

'I thought you wanted Raewyn, boss?' said Einar.

'I do,' said the king, 'but what if she turns out to be a Maker? I don't want a fucking Maker in my bed; she'd summon a knife and slit my throat while I slept. Or worse, she'd summon an animal, and my flesh would be ripped apart.'

'How would we go about killing them?' said Ragnvald.

'We could poison their food,' said the king, 'and bury them in the forest. We could do it as soon as we move them back into the temple.'

Einar frowned. 'Are you including Reath and Nyli in this plan, boss? I thought we were going to keep them.'

The king shrugged. 'Out of all of them, those two are the ones we definitely know are Makers.'

'But I wanted to break them in, boss,' said Einar. 'You promised that I could.'

'Only one of them was for you,' said the king; 'the other was for Erling. I don't know any more, lads. What if they try to kill us with their powers when they're older?'

'That would seem unlikely, Your Majesty,' said Matteo. 'I have learned a few things about Masters and Makers over the years. Makers require a great deal of education to become proficient. That means book-learning and many long years of study. If you deny them that, then their abilities will be stunted. The older women among them might have been trained, but the younger ones will be harmless.'

The king raised an eyebrow. 'Is that so? I didn't know that.'

Einar leaned forward in his chair. 'Does that mean we can keep them, boss?'

'You're a sick fuck,' said Ragnvald. 'Reath and Nyli are fourteen.'

'So?' said Einar. 'They'll be slaves, and slaves are property, not people. I can do whatever the fuck I like to my own property.'

'I'm taking Nyli,' said Erling. 'You can have the loud-mouthed one.'

'I'm fine with that,' said Einar. 'I'll beat the cheek out of her. She won't be loud-mouthed for long. Then, who knows – she might give me a Master son.' He glanced at Ragnvald. 'And if the younger women are harmless, as Matteo says, then you might be able to keep Eshia.'

'And I could have Raewyn, after all,' said the king. 'You can be quite useful sometimes, Matteo, for a lazy Sanctian prick.'

'So, are we back to keeping them?' said Erling.

The king nodded. 'Maybe.'

Magnus bowed his head, He could feel his anger and disgust rise with every moment that passed. He had to say something, even if it would result in another beating.

He raised his eyes. 'I think we should let them go when the barges get here.'

His father and half-brothers stared at him.

'Fuck that,' said Einar. 'I'm starting to have my doubts about the little runt's loyalty, boss.'

'We could make him prove his loyalty,' said Erling. 'Order him to stick a knife into his mother, boss; then we'll see whose side he's on.'

The king rubbed his chin, as though pondering the suggestion. Ragnvald rolled his eyes and looked away; then he got to his feet.

'Is something going on down there?' he said.

Ragnvald walked to the edge of the roof and peered into the south. Magnus listened, and heard the sound of raised voices in the distance.

'It's just the Westlander slaves complaining about something,' said Erling. 'They're still griping about the cull.'

'They're cheering,' said Ragnvald. 'What the fuck have they got to cheer about?' His eyes widened. 'Shit.'

The other brothers stood, and walked over to where Ragnvald was standing. Soldiers in strange uniforms were running down the road in the direction of the temple, their front ranks holding out crossbows.

A whistle blasted through the night sky, and more shouts rose up.

'We're under attack!' shouted Einar. He gestured to the mercenaries on the roof, several of whom appeared to be sleeping. 'Wake up, you fuckwits, and rally the defences.'

Hemming joined them by the edge of the roof. His eyes narrowed when he saw the group of soldiers turn along the road in front of the temple. The soldiers formed thick lines, loosed their bows at the mercenaries, and charged into them.

'There aren't very many of them,' the king said, as he watched the battle by the front of the temple. 'Is this another diversionary attack? Einar, get down there at once. Go straight to the barracks and organise the defences.'

'But...'

'Do it!' the king shouted. 'There may be other groups of enemy soldiers within Steppen. They might try to free the slaves or set fire to the cranes again. This little group cannot possibly be the only force attacking us. Go.'

Einar bowed his head, then he summoned the mercenaries on the roof, and they left down a staircase.

'The bastards are breaking in,' said Ragnvald.

'Then I was right to move the women and guests out of the temple,' said the king.

'What will we do, boss?' said Erling.

The king said nothing, and they watched the soldiers storm into the temple through one of its entrances.

'How many got in?' said Ragnvald. 'Two dozen?'

'About that number, I think,' said the king. 'I suppose there's nothing else for it but to kill them ourselves.'

'I think I shall remain up here, Your Majesty,' said Lord Matteo, as he walked over. He peered over the edge of the roof, and his face paled. 'My word,' he said. 'Those slain soldiers down there are wearing the uniform of the Sanctian army.'

'They're Sanctians?' said Ragnvald.

'I believe so. Unless they are wearing stolen uniforms, that would be the logical conclusion.' He turned to the king. 'Do you have any idea what this means, Your Majesty? If Sanctians are here, then they know. They know about you; they know what you are.'

The king frowned. 'How would the authorities in Elestia react if not a single one of their soldiers returned from the depths of the Great Forest?'

'In that case, Your Majesty, I believe that another, larger force would be sent.'

'We need to capture some alive,' said Ragnvald. 'We need to know exactly how many Sanctians made the trip up from Yearl. For all we know, there could be hundreds of them hiding in the forest.' He frowned. 'This might change the minds of some of our guests. All Masters and Makers know that the Sanctians are hunting them. They might even be prepared to help us.'

'Perhaps,' said the king. 'For now, though, we have some Sanctians of our own to kill.'

'And then, Your Majesty,' said Matteo, 'we might need to start considering an evacuation. The Sanctians will not give up. If we kill these ones, others will come. I daresay that it will take a few months before any more are sent, and that gives us some time, but an evacuation might become essential if we are to survive.'

The king stared at Matteo, his eyes tight with fury. 'I ought to push you off the roof for saying that,' he said. 'Evacuate? We shall never evacuate Steppen, no matter how many soldiers the Sanctians send. And tell me, wise one – where would we go? Where would we find a better place than here? The Sanctians rule the provinces, the Westlanders hold the north, and both loathe Masters.'

Matteo fell into silence.

'He has no answer,' said the king.

'We're wasting time, boss,' said Ragnvald. 'The soldiers will be roaming around the temple, looking for us.'

'We shall go to them,' said the king. 'Ragnvald, take Magnus, and descend to the third floor, by the old sanctuary. Erling shall come with me, and we will go down by the women's quarters. Between us, we should be able to catch the Sanctians before they can reach the upper floors.'

Ragnvald inclined his head. 'Yes, boss.'

The Whalebone King led the way towards the stairs, and his three sons followed him. Magnus trailed along at the back, his thoughts occupied by what Lord Matteo had said. For the entire course of his life, he had been told that Steppen was safely isolated from the outside world, and that belief had both reassured and terrified him at the same time. Surrounded by nothing but hundreds of miles of forest, and with the bargemen kept away from seeing too much, his father had always been certain that nothing could harm them. They had heard the news about Yearl joining the Sanctian Empire, but it was a change that did not seem to affect them. If Matteo was right, and the Sanctians had discovered that the Whalebone King was a Master, then to what lengths would they go to destroy him?

They descended into the gloom of the temple, and the noise coming from the road outside faded into nothing. Hemming came to a halt by a long passageway.

'I think I'm still drunk,' said Erling.

The king eyed him. 'Your job is to make sure no one attacks me from behind while I am killing; can you manage that?'

Erling nodded.

'Then keep your opinions to yourself.' He glanced at Ragnvald. 'Show the intruders no mercy, son,' he said. 'I will meet you on the second floor, once we have shown the Sanctians what happens if they invade my realm.'

Ragnvald bowed his head, then he gestured to Magnus, and they set off in a different direction.

'Stay behind me at all times,' Ragnvald said to his youngest brother. 'If you get in front of me, I might accidentally kill you.'

'Should I try out my own Master abilities?'

Ragnvald eyed him as they came to another set of stairs. 'Is there any point? Do you think you could change blood to salt?'

'I've never tried.'

'Now is probably not the best time to start.'

'Is it easy?'

Ragnvald shrugged. 'That depends on how relaxed your mind is. I find it easy, but it took a lot of practice. Have you been practising?'

'Every day.'

Ragnvald nodded. 'Why did you allow Erling to beat the shit out of you?'

Magnus frowned. 'I didn't *allow* him to do it. He's much stronger than me.'

'You punched him first,' Ragnvald said. 'You must have known what was going to happen. You punched him because he insulted your mother. That was stupid. When are you going to fucking learn, Magnus? Erling and Einar both know how to bait you, and you fall for it every time. What will you do if the king orders you to beat your mother? Will you obey?'

'He wouldn't do that, would he?'

Ragnvald snorted. 'You ask the most stupid questions sometimes. Unless you break free from your mother, you will never become your own man. If you want my advice, kill her. You need to remove her from your life, or nothing will change.'

'You think I should kill my own mother?'

'You would be freeing yourself. Cut her throat, and Erling and Einar will lose the hold they have over you. More than that, the king will respect you. You will have proved not only your loyalty, but you will have shown everyone that you have balls of steel. You can make it quick and painless. You could even tell yourself that it was an act of mercy, if that makes you feel any better. You would be saving her from suffering in the future.'

Magnus said nothing.

'You would be wise to take care of it before the king takes the others' advice and orders you to do it,' Ragnvald went on. 'I want to help you, but you have to start helping yourself.'

Ragnvald fell silent as they reached the next level down. The passageways were shrouded in thick shadows, and the two men listened. The low sound of boots hurrying along reached Magnus's ears, then a small group of mercenaries appeared from round a corner.

They saluted when they saw the king's sons.

'Have you seen any Sanctians?' said Ragnvald.

'We were heading to the stairs by the sanctuary to prevent them from reaching the upper floors, my lord,' said one.

'That is exactly where my brother and I are going,' said Ragnvald. 'Follow me. You can pick off any I miss.'

Ragnvald turned, and led them along the passageway. They reached a large set of stairs that led down to the ancient sanctuary at the heart of the temple. Due to a quirk of the architecture, there were only two routes that linked the lower floors to the upper levels, and the staircase by the sanctuary was one of them. The mercenaries gathered by the top of the stairs, with Ragnvald and Magnus in the centre.

'Your job is to protect me while I kill them,' said Ragnvald. 'Load your bows and shoot anyone who tries to get up the stairs.'

The mercenaries took their crossbows from their shoulders and began loading them. Magnus peered down the stairs, then two armed men crept into view from a long hallway, their swords held out in front of them.

Ragnvald smiled, and raised his right hand.

He pointed at the first soldier. 'Bone to water.' He turned to the second. 'Blood to fire.'

The two Sanctians fell, one collapsing into a liquefied heap, the other bursting into flames.

Magnus stared, then he heard his brother laugh.

'I like thinking up new combinations,' Ragnvald said. 'Do you want to try?'

'I thought you said there would be no point?'

'I've changed my mind. This might be a good time to practise. If you fuck it up, the mercenaries will shoot them down. That's if I don't get them first, of course.'

More Sanctians crept in from the hallway. They stared at the two bodies on the floor in front of them, then their gazes went to the stairs.

'They have no bows,' Ragnvald said. 'This is too easy.'

The Sanctians stared up at Ragnvald and Magnus.

'Good morning,' Ragnvald called out to them. 'Yes, I am a Master. Who wants to die first?'

He raised his hand, and some of the Sanctians backed away, the terror in the eyes unmistakeable.

'Water to silver,' Ragnvald said, and the first soldier fell, his flesh withered and discoloured. 'Go on, Magnus; give it a go. Remember that the bastards are trying to kill you.'

Magnus raised his hand and pointed at a soldier. 'Turn that man's water to salt.'

Nothing happened. Ragnvald rolled his eyes, then got back to work.

'Bone to wood; water to gold; blood to acid.'

More Sanctians appeared as the soldiers fell. Among them was a solitary woman with a knife in her hand. She stared at the dead soldiers on the floor.

'I want her kept alive,' Ragnvald said to the mercenaries. 'Do you hear me?'

The woman looked up at him. 'Charge them!' she cried. 'Charge them before they kill us all!'

The Sanctians obeyed. They grouped together and ran up the stairs, the woman in their midst.

'Blood to gold; blood to gold; blood to gold,' Ragnvald shouted above the noise, as the Sanctians piled up the steps.

The mercenaries loosed their bows, and three Sanctians fell back down the stairs, their bodies struck with bolts. Magnus drew a knife from his belt as the first Sanctians reached the top of the stairs. A mercenary fell, his head cleaved open by a sword blow, as Ragnvald dealt out death as quickly as he was able to speak.

'Water to wood; water to wood.'

A Sanctian swung his sword at Ragnvald, and Magnus stabbed him in the neck with his knife. The woman reached the top of the stairs, along with three surviving Sanctians. They cut down two mercenaries who were standing between them and Ragnvald.

'Blood to salt; blood to salt,' Ragnvald cried.

The woman lunged at Ragnvald. Her knife slashed his arm, then he punched her in the face. She staggered back, then her feet went over the top step, and she tumbled down the stairs, falling into a heap by the dead soldiers.

A mercenary killed the last Sanctian, driving the point of his sword through his back, and letting his body fall down the stairs.

Ragnvald glanced at the blood flowing from the long cut down his left forearm.

'That fucking bitch,' he said. 'Magnus, get down there and bind her hands, then bring her to me.'

Magnus ran down the stairs, jumping over the bodies that lay there. He reached the bottom, and crouched by the woman. She had fallen awkwardly, and her left leg was broken below the knee. She had also struck her head on the stone steps, and her hair was matted with blood. Magnus felt for a pulse, and found it, then he leaned in close, and could hear her breathing. He glanced at her face. She was a Sanctian, and she had come all the way from Yearl to find and kill Masters; and yet, looking at her, he felt pity. He knew what Ragnvald would do to her if she became his prisoner, and the thought made him sick. If left untended, she would probably die from her wounds, but she was unconscious; if she died before she awoke, then wouldn't that be preferable than the alternative?

'What the fuck's taking so long?' said Ragnvald, from the top of the stairs.

Magnus looked up at him. 'She's dead.'

'What?' shouted Ragnvald. 'I barely touched her.'

'She hit her head on the way down,' Magnus said. 'Her neck's broken.'

Ragnvald shook his head. 'Shit. I hope the king was able to take a few prisoners.'

Magnus glanced at the other Sanctians. One of them had been struck in the stomach by a crossbow bolt, and Magnus could see his chest rising and falling. He got up and pointed at the soldier.

'This one's alive.'

Ragnvald came down the stairs, the mercenaries following him. They gathered round the wounded Sanctian soldier, and Ragnvald took a closer look.

'He'll do,' Ragnvald said. He gestured to the mercenaries. 'Take him upstairs, and have someone look at his injury. Try to keep the bastard alive. Then start dragging the bodies down to the road.'

The mercenaries bowed their heads, then two of them picked up the soldier with the bolt in his stomach.

'What if more soldiers come?' said Magnus. 'That wasn't all of them.'

'Let's find out where the others are,' said Ragnvald, as he watched the wounded soldier being carried up the stairs. He glanced back at Magnus. 'What happened back there when you tried to use your abilities?'

Magnus lowered his gaze. 'I... I couldn't clear my head; there was too much going on.'

'At least you're handy with a knife. I owe you my thanks for stabbing the bastard who was swinging his sword at me. You did all right.'

Magnus felt his spirits fly at his brother's words, despite only moments before having lied to protect a woman from him. Ragnvald was a sadist who tortured and killed for pleasure, and yet Magnus yearned for his approval.

'Come with me,' Ragnvald said, then he set off along the hallway from where the Sanctians had come.

Magnus hurried to keep up, and they passed an entrance to the sanctuary. Ragnvald looked inside, but it was empty.

'I thought some of them might have been hiding in there,' Ragnvald said; 'begging the spirits to save them.'

'Do the Sanctians believe in the spirits?' said Magnus.

'They're big believers in that sort of thing,' said Ragnvald. 'I think that's why they hate us so much.'

They carried on along the hallway. They found the bodies of two dead mercenaries lying close to a window, then Magnus heard voices.

Ragnvald grinned. They turned a corner and saw the king and Erling standing by the foot of the other staircase. The floor was littered in the corpses of Sanctians, and salt was smearing the walls.

'We got over a dozen of them, boss,' said Ragnvald, 'and we secured a live prisoner.'

The king clapped his hands together and laughed. 'Then you did better than me, son,' he said. 'I found the temptation to kill them all too much to resist.'

'There was a woman with them,' Ragnvald went on; 'a woman in a Sanctian uniform.' He held out his bloody arm. 'She was the only one who got close to me.'

'I trust you killed her for that?' said the king.

Ragnvald nodded. 'I punched the bitch down the stairs. She broke her neck.'

'What now?' said Erling.

'First,' said the king, 'we'll drop the bodies into the river, and then...'

Ragnvald frowned. 'Could we stop doing that, boss? It's polluting the water supply. The odd body now and again is fine, but several dozen at once?'

The king eyed him. 'Then what do you suggest?'

'Dump them in the forest, boss.'

'Whatever makes you happy, son,' said the king. 'We will also send out patrols, in case more Sanctians are lurking near Steppen. We'll organise it when Einar gets back.'

'One more thing, boss,' said Ragnvald. 'Magnus saved my life during the fight.'

Hemming smiled. 'Did he, indeed? Did he use his Master abilities?'

'He used his knife.'

'It still counts,' said the king. He eyed Magnus. 'I'm proud of you, boy.'

Magnus lowered his gaze. 'Thank you, sir.'

A group of mercenaries appeared through an entrance, dragging the body of a Sanctian by the shoulders.

'We found this one outside, boss,' said one. 'He's still alive.'

The king and his sons stared at the Sanctian.

'An officer?' said Hemming.

'Yes, boss. A captain, from the insignia on his uniform.'

The mercenaries hauled him upright, and the Sanctian gasped in pain. Hemming reached out, gripped the man's chin, and lifted it. The Sanctian was conscious, and he stared back at the Whalebone King.

'How does it feel, Captain,' said the king, 'to have been captured by Masters?'

'I'm not scared of you,' the man slurred. 'Do your worst.'

The king laughed. 'Be in no doubt about that, Sanctian; we shall certainly do our worst to you, but not until you have answered my questions. The first thing I want to know is your name.'

'I am Captain Zola of the Offices of Purgation,' the officer said, 'and you will be getting nothing more from me.'

'We shall see about that,' said the king. He nodded at the mercenaries. 'Let's get Captain Zola upstairs and make him comfortable.'

'Can I torture him, boss?' said Erling.

Hemming smiled. 'Of course you can; you can get started right away.' He gazed at his three sons. 'You make me proud, lads; very proud.'

CHAPTER 20
A THANKLESS TASK

West of Steppen, Great Forest, Jallin, Central Provinces – 7th Day of Quoma 108

A hand shook Walter's shoulder, and his first reaction was to grab his knife and hold it up.

'It's me, sir,' said Otto.

Walter eyed him, then put the knife down.

Otto shook his head. 'You nearly stabbed me with that thing, sir. Maybe I should use an extra long stick to wake you each morning.'

Walter stretched his arms and sat up on the forest floor. 'What is it?'

'A battle is underway, sir, in Steppen.'

'Shit. Did our Westlanders start it?'

'No, sir. It wasn't them, though they are eager to join in, and it's been a struggle to restrain them. It was soldiers, by Dietar's reckoning – Sanctian soldiers. He was scouting this morning, and saw a few dozen of them running by the shanty town.'

Duggan barged into the small clearing where Walter had been sleeping.

'We're going to Steppen,' the Westlander said. 'Are you coming?'

'You lot are supposed to obey my orders,' Walter said, as he got to his feet.

'That's the only reason we haven't already left the camp,' said Duggan. 'Otto promised to get you up so we could leave. We need to be quick. Dietar said that the mercenaries are all defending the temple. Think how many slaves we could free if we went in hard.'

Walter swayed, his head groggy. He glanced at his hands, and noticed they were trembling.

'All right,' he said. 'We'll go and take a look. Get everyone ready. Give me a minute alone.'

Duggan hurried off, while Otto eyed Walter.

'Bugger off,' said Walter. 'I need to take a piss.'

Otto shook his head and left the small clearing. As soon as he was gone, Walter knelt down and rummaged under the thick pile of leaves he had been using as a pillow. He dug out the bottle from the crane compound, removed the stopper, and drank. There was very little left in the bottle, and he drained it. He grimaced from the harsh taste, and for a moment he thought he was going to vomit it all back up again. He managed to hold it down, then he looked at his hands. They were steady. He placed the empty bottle back under the leaves, picked up the knife, and got to his feet.

He glanced at the sky as he walked out of the clearing. The sun had risen, but there was still a chill in the air. He walked into a larger open space amid the trees, where the Westlanders were standing ready. Walter walked up to Dietar.

'Sanctians?' he said.

'That's right, sir,' said Dietar. 'Around fifty, give or take. They seemed to be intent on assaulting the temple, and every mercenary in Steppen was running to their location.'

Walter frowned. 'Fifty? Nobody is stupid enough to attack the temple with only fifty soldiers.'

'Perhaps they are only one part of a larger plan, sir,' said Dietar. 'The southern flank of the shanty town was left completely unprotected.'

'Did you hear that?' cried a Westlander. 'What are we waiting for?'

Walter glanced at the ten Westlanders. Some of them were still recovering from their ordeal as slaves, but all seemed keen to fight.

'How are we going to get through the fence?' said Aisly.

'There's a fence?' said Walter.

'A large fence, sir,' said Dietar. 'It's made from wooden beams held together with wire; and it surrounds the entirety of the shanty town.'

'Do we have any bolt cutters?'

'We have one small pair of bolt cutters, sir,' said Otto, patting his belt. 'I picked it up in the crane compound.'

'The job of getting through the fence is yours, Sergeant,' said Walter. 'The rest of us will allow you to work in peace. Dietar, lead us to Steppen.'

'Yes, sir,' said the lieutenant.

Dietar set off through the forest, and the Westlanders hurried after him, while Walter and Otto followed at the rear.

'Good job picking up those bolt cutters,' said Walter.

'It wasn't the only tool I grabbed from the compound, sir. I also have matches, a saw, and a hammer.'

'Try to pick up more today.'

'We'll need more than a few tools, sir. If we're planning on freeing more Westlanders, then we'll need food, blankets, cooking equipment, medicines; ideally, a few tents would be handy. Spare clothes, boots, more weapons, bolts... and we'll also need a new place to set up a camp, somewhere a bit deeper into the forest, so that we can light small fires without being detected.'

'Is that all?' said Walter.

Otto eyed him. 'Give me five minutes, and I'm sure I'll be able to think of a few dozen other items we'll need.'

They walked through the forest for twenty minutes, then they came to a halt next to a small water channel. Walter walked forward, and peered through the undergrowth. If a battle had taken place by the Temple of Steppen, then it was already over. He could see the western side of the shanty town ahead of them, and the huge bulk of the temple rose up on its left. Many of the Westlander slaves beyond the fence were crying out in anger and frustration, and Walter noticed bodies being carried along one of the roads.

'There are still no mercenaries guarding the southern flank of the shanty town, sir,' said Dietar.

'All right,' said Walter; 'here's the plan. We'll run straight over to the south-western corner of the slave settlement, and then Otto will open the fence. By that time, we will have probably been seen, so we'll carry on eastwards; straight through the town and out the other side. Any slaves we free will have to follow us. We'll hit the barracks from the west, and raid for supplies, and then we'll carry on into the forest, but on the eastern side of Steppen. Everyone will have to carry what they can, but we need food and blankets.'

'And a hundred other things,' said Otto.

'Stay quiet until we're seen,' said Walter. 'The longer we are unobserved, the more slaves we'll be able to free.' He eyed the Westlanders. 'Are you arseholes capable of remaining silent?'

'You're lucky you are good at what you do, Walter of Upper Down,' said a huge Westlander. 'I would not normally suffer such disrespect.'

Walter smiled. 'You didn't answer the question, big guy.'

'We can be silent,' said Duggan.

Walter turned, and peered through the undergrowth again. He raised his right hand and moved off, picking his way through the last of the trees towards the open ground where Steppen lay. He reached the edge of the forest, his eyes taking in the positions of the nearest mercenaries, who were all over a hundred yards away to the left, by the road that ran in front of the temple. Walter sped off, keeping low as he left the cover of the trees. He ran through some well-tended ornamental gardens, crossed a bridge over a water course, and reached the south-western corner of the shanty town. Not many slaves were in the vicinity, as most had gone north to watch the battle, and Walter instructed Otto to begin cutting through the wire holding the fence posts in place. Dietar and the Westlanders ran off the road and joined Walter, and they crouched, out of sight of the mercenaries on the other side of the shanty town.

'Did you hear us, Walter?' said the huge Westlander.

'You were like little mice,' said Walter. 'Papa's very proud of you.'

An emaciated old Westlander approached the fence from the other direction. His eyes widened at the sight of Otto cutting through the fence, then he saw the ten Westlanders.

Walter winked at him and placed a finger to his lips.

A few of the Westlanders began to speak to the old man in their own language, then Otto frowned, and added a few comments of his own.

'What are they saying?' said Walter.

'They were telling the old guy to bring everyone to this corner of the settlement, sir,' said Otto. 'I reminded him to be discreet about it.'

The old Westlander limped away into the narrow lanes of the camp, as Otto removed a tall beam from the fence. The Mountain Ranger got to his feet, and began cutting away another section. On the far side of the fence, more Westlanders began to gather, including a couple of women. Aisly went up to the fence and starting talking to them, and the volume of conversations rose.

'Keep quiet,' said Walter, but few of the Westlanders were listening to him.

Otto removed another piece of the fence, then the Westlanders inside the camp began pushing at a large post, bending it over at the weak point until it snapped, bringing down a section of fence two yards long. The slaves began to spill out of the settlement. Cries rose up, cries of relief and jubilation.

'Follow me!' Walter shouted. 'Move.'

He set off for the east, keeping the shanty town on his left. He glanced over his shoulder as he crossed a wide bridge, and saw dozens of Westlanders pouring out of the hole in the fence. Walter came to a large pool, where three Westlanders had been impaled upon stakes, then he reached the area where the mercenaries lived. He came to a halt, and guided the escaping slaves into the streets where the barracks lay.

'Look for a supply depot,' he said to them, as they passed. 'Search for food and weapons.'

Some of the Westlanders took that as an invitation to ransack the barrack blocks, and over a dozen smashed their way into one. A few off-duty mercenaries came out of their barracks to see what was causing the noise, and the slaves were upon them in seconds, ripping their bodies to pieces with their bare hands, and relieving them of their weapons. Whistles sounded.

Walter ushered a few large groups of starving Westlanders through the narrow streets of the mercenary settlement, as more whistles blasted through the air. He saw two Westlanders emerge from a building carrying swords, and then smoke belched out after them.

'Burn the place to the ground!' a Westlander shouted.

'Keep moving,' Walter cried. 'The mercenaries are coming.'

'No,' said a huge, blond Westlander. 'We fight.'

Walter walked up to him. 'If we fight now, every escaped slave will die,' he said. 'Look at the condition of your kinsfolk – some of them can barely walk, never mind fight.'

'Who the fuck are you?' said the blond Westlander.

'I'm the man who just saved your arses,' Walter said. 'Lead everyone into the forest, to the east. Pick up food and supplies on the way.'

'Fuck you. Get out of my way or I'll snap your fucking neck.'

Duggan and a few of the Westlanders from the crane compound ran over, and they pushed the blond Westlander back. Walter returned to leading the others away towards the east. More smoke was rising from several other barrack blocks, and dead mercenaries in their night clothes were lying butchered on the ground on every street. Another barrack block was raided, its doors smashed in, then cries for help rang out. More Westlanders went inside, then they helped over two dozen young slaves to leave the block. Many of them were in a poor way, and some had to be carried out. A few Westlanders broke down at the sight, and waves of anger and grief rolled over the escaped slaves.

'Look what they have done to our children,' cried one.

'We will save them all,' shouted Walter. 'Keep moving.'

They came to the eastern edge of the mercenary settlement, where a large bridge sat. A few large villas lay beyond it, and then the forest restarted. They crossed the bridge that spanned the River Ario, and the Westlanders broke their way into the first villa. An elderly man was dragged outside and beaten to death, then the Westlanders emerged carrying crates of food, and escorting more slaves to freedom.

Walter remained by the bridge as the slaves continued to cross. He tried to count them, but gave up. Most were men, but several dozen women were mixed in among them, along with the two dozen children they had rescued from the barracks. Most stared blankly at Walter as they passed, and he kept pointing to the east.

'Into the forest,' he said, over and over.

'Holy shit, sir,' said Otto; 'what have we done? There are hundreds of the big bastards.'

Dietar crossed the bridge, leading the last of the slaves.

'The mercenaries have sealed off the hole in the fence, sir,' he said; 'and they're coming this way.'

'Can we tear down the bridge?' said Walter.

Otto and Dietar glanced at the sturdy beams of the bridge, then back at Walter.

'Not unless we had a fucking cannon, sir,' said Otto.

'You know, Sergeant,' said Walter. 'I think these Westlanders are a bad influence on you. Your language has deteriorated somewhat since we met them.' He gazed along the road. The first mercenaries were racing along it, heading past the burning barrack blocks towards the bridge. 'I need thirty Westlanders fit and strong enough to fight,' he said. 'Find me some armed volunteers, and tell them to bring furniture from the ransacked villa; then lead the others ten miles to the east.'

'Ten miles, sir?' said Dietar.

'Do you think we should go further?'

'I'm worried that many might not make it that far, sir.'

'Then use your judgement. Keep a lookout closer to Steppen; someone who can guide us to our new camp, assuming, you know, that we don't all get killed.'

Dietar and Otto saluted, then they raced off, leaving Walter alone by the end of the bridge. Walter leaned against a large post, and watched the mercenaries approach.

'Am I doing the right thing, Killie?' he whispered. 'I don't want to die, but what else could I do? I couldn't look away.'

He heard boots behind him, and turned to see over thirty armed Westlanders charging towards him. They were carrying tables and chairs looted from the villa, and two of them were dragging along a massive bedstead. They halted by the bridge, and a few stared at the approaching mercenaries. Walter noticed the huge blond Westlander who had threatened to snap his neck among them.

'Do you lads want a chance to fight?' Walter said.

No one replied, as though the answer was too obvious to warrant a response.

'All we have to do is delay the mercenaries for as long as possible,' Walter went on, 'so that everyone can get away into the forest. We will stand here, and stop anyone crossing the bridge. In other words, not one of you big bastards is to take a single step backwards without my express fucking permission.'

'If you knew how long we have awaited this day, southerner,' said one, 'you would not be wasting your breath.'

'I'm not a southerner,' said Walter.

'He's Upper Down,' said one of the Westlanders rescued from the crane compound. 'He's a good lad.'

'Pile up the furniture onto the bridge,' said Walter. 'The mercenaries will have crossbows. They'll loose once and charge. Keep your heads down until you see them draw their swords.'

The Westlanders laid out the tables, chairs, and the bedstead along the width of the bridge. It wasn't a perfect barricade, but it was better than nothing.

'Here they come,' said one.

'Stay down,' said Walter, and the Westlanders crouched behind the furniture.

The mercenaries ran onto the bridge. The front ranks had loaded bows in their hands and, at a signal from a tall officer, they loosed into Walter and the Westlanders. Most bolts slammed into the furniture, and some skittered off the side of the bridge, but others got through, and three Westlanders were hit.

Walter drew his sword. 'Don't charge,' he said to the others. 'Wait for them to come to us.'

The mercenaries in the front ranks moved back, and others came forward with loaded bows. Another volley was sent into the barricade, and two more Westlanders were hit.

'We should be attacking those bastards!' cried a Westlander.

'The plan is already working,' said Walter. 'We've slowed them to a halt. That's the only reason we're here; remember that.'

'They're dropping their bows and drawing their weapons,' said one.

'About fucking time,' said a Westlander, getting to his feet.

One of the wounded Westlanders had been wielding a pike, so Walter sheathed his sword and picked it up. He aimed it forward, between the legs of the table, and watched as the mercenaries began their charge.

'Come on!' the huge, blond Westlander screamed, then the mercenaries slammed into the barricade. One of them ran onto the end of Walter's pike and impaled himself, then Walter lost any sense of what was going on around him as he concentrated on killing the enemy and staying alive. Some of the mercenaries tried to climb over the barricade, and they were skewered by the spears and swords of the Westlanders. The tall officer advanced, his chest covered in a steel breastplate, and his right hand gripping a longsword.

'I recognise that bastard,' shouted a Westlander. 'It's Einar!'

'Is he important?' said Walter.

'The Whalebone King has four sons,' said the Westlander, 'and that prick's one of them.'

'I'm going after him,' said Walter.

'But you told us to stay here.'

'Fuck that,' said Walter; 'change of plan. We're going to charge them.'

The Westlanders roared out a cheer. They scaled the barricade in seconds and tore into the ranks of the mercenaries. Walter pushed a table out of the way and hurried after them. Faced with the onslaught of the Westlanders, the front rows of the mercenaries broke, and some jumped into the river rather than face an enemy desperate for revenge.

Walter went straight for Einar. He avoided fighting anyone else, dodging and weaving his way through the melee. He ducked under the wild backswing of a Westlander's sword, and gripped the pike in both hands as he neared the son of the Whalebone King. Einar was trying to rally his forces when he saw Walter approach.

'You Sanctian bastard,' Einar cried.

Walter laughed. 'First I'm a southerner, now I'm a Sanctian? Could this day get any worse?'

Einar charged forward, but the reach of the pike kept him back from Walter. Walter feinted high, then he stabbed Einar's left thigh, ripping a wound three inches long down his leg.

'Did you like that?' said Walter.

A horn blasted in the distance.

'Hundreds more mercenaries are coming,' Einar spat, 'and they will...'

Walter jabbed with the pike, and the blade tore through Einar's nose and cheeks. Einar dropped his sword and staggered, his hands on his face, and Walter drove the pike into his groin. Einar tried to scream, but only flecks of blood came from his mouth as he toppled onto the bridge.

At once, the mercenaries broke and ran, fleeing back over the bridge and into the streets of the barrack blocks.

The two dozen surviving Westlanders raised their weapons and cheered, and several slapped Walter on the back, nearly knocking him over. Walter gripped the pike and walked over to the body of Einar. He was still alive, though blood was flowing freely from his three wounds. His hands were by the patch of blood covering his crotch, and Walter could see that he was breathing by the bubbles of blood that appeared on his lips.

Walter turned. The Westlanders were looking through the bodies of the slain mercenaries, rifling through their pockets and killing any who still lived.

'Leave one alive for me,' he said; 'one who isn't going to die from his injuries.'

'This one has a sword wound in his guts,' said a Westlander. 'He'll live for a few days yet.'

Walter knelt by Einar and took his knife out. He gripped the man's hair with his left hand, and cut Einar's head off, as the Westlanders watched. Walter stood, gripping Einar's head by the hair, his hands dripping blood onto the bridge, then he walked over to the injured mercenary. He thrust the head into the mercenary's hands.

'See that his father receives this,' said Walter. 'Tell him it was a gift from the drunken champion. Will you remember that?'

The mercenary grimaced in pain, and nodded.

'Who is it from?' said Walter.

'The drunken champion,' the mercenary gasped.

'That's right. Tell the Whalebone King that nothing is going to save him. Tell him that I will do the same to all of his sons, and then to him.' He glanced up. The mercenaries who had fled from the bridge were watching from the shadows of the barrack blocks. He looked back down at the injured man. 'Stay alive until your comrades are brave enough to set foot onto the bridge, and remember my message.'

Walter stood. He eyed the Westlanders. 'Time to go.'

They clambered over the barricade, collected their wounded, and sprinted towards the forest.

They ran for over an hour, threading their way through the forest. They passed the easternmost waterfall, above which stood the four cranes, and headed deeper into the forest. They slowed to a walk, catching their breath as they walked among the trees.

The huge blond Westlander came up to Walter's side, and walked with him.

'You did well for a southerner,' he said, 'but hundreds of my people are now free. A new leader will arise from among us, and you will have to accept this, Walter of Upper Down. Or should I call you the drunken champion? Why did you not wish that man to know your name?'

'I have friends in the temple,' said Walter.

'You have friends who are guests of the Whalebone King?'

'I don't know under what conditions they are being held, but if I had to guess, I would say that they are prisoners. They will understand my message – it was meant for them.'

'They might not hear it if they are prisoners.'

'It was the best I could do at the time. So, are you angling to be the new leader?'

'I will do it if I can gain enough support. I have led war bands in the past. In fact, I have seen you before, years ago. I had forgotten about you, until I heard someone mention your name.'

Walter narrowed his eyes. 'Were you in Upper Down?'

'I was. Like many of my kin, I went there to see if I could win my fortune. I went on a few raids in Greater Down, but the land had been picked bare by years of pillaging, and so I decided to roam further south. That was my mistake. I was jumped by ten Jallians in a tavern.'

'Who did you work for when you were in Upper Down?'

'Chief Rymont.'

Walter shook his head. 'He was one of Dravid's friends.'

'And you were the King's Champion. You were drunk when I saw you. You killed many of my people, or so I am told.'

'You can only fight the enemy that's in front of you. I killed many more Sanctians that day than Westlanders.'

'Are we enemies, Walter?'

'Only if you insist upon it. I'm not here to fight your people.'

'No, you are here to free them, or so it seems. Do you feel guilt for what you did to my kin in Upper Down?'

'No.'

'Then why are you risking yourself for us?'

'No one deserves to be treated the way the Whalebone King has been treating the slaves in Steppen. I couldn't... I couldn't walk away and do nothing. I don't care if you think that makes me a fool.'

'You are a fool,' said the blond Westlander. 'All the same, you have earned my respect. If I become leader, I will place you under my protection.'

Walter smiled. 'Is there going to be a vote? Or are you going to knock each other senseless, and the last man standing becomes chief?'

'I shall issue a challenge, claiming the leadership, and we shall see if any are brave enough to stand against me.'

'Or,' said Walter, 'I stay in charge, and that will prevent the Westlanders from fighting among themselves. What's your name?'

'Johan of Blackheath.'

'Over the next few days, Johan, I intend to form a coherent fighting force out of every fit and willing Westlander. A battalion of perhaps two hundred. I'm going to teach them how to move in formation, and then we're going to launch a series of raids on Steppen. We're going to grind the mercenaries down, piece by piece. That will involve a large logistical operation, to ensure that we have enough food, tools, weapons and everything else we need. We'll no doubt have dozens of people to care for – the elderly, the sick, the starving, the traumatised; and we'll have to post sentries and work out schedules for them. We will also have to move camp regularly, for two reasons. First, for basic sanitation. We can't stay in the same place for too long if hundreds of people are shitting there; and second, to ensure that we aren't caught out by a mercenary counter-attack. Whoever is in charge of all that will have to work every hour of every day, and every complaint will be directed at them. It's a fucking thankless job, and a bastard of a responsibility.'

'Why are you telling me this?' said Johan.

'If you haven't worked that out, big guy, then you might not be up to the job. Do you really want all that responsibility? Do you want the blame when things go wrong? Do you want to spend hours listening to complaints and trying to sort out grievances?'

Johan frowned and looked away. 'Fuck you.'

Walter laughed. 'I have no doubt that you're a good fighter, Johan. I'll give you command of a hundred warriors.'

Walter heard something, and they came to a halt. Duggan emerged from the trees and approached them. The Westlander did a quick head-count, then he nodded.

'Most of you made it back,' he said.

'How did you know which route we would take?' said Johan.

'The two Mountain Rangers have posted sentries all over this area,' said Duggan. 'We're not just watching out for you lot, we're to run to the new camp if we see any mercenaries.'

'And where is the new camp?' said Walter.

Duggan gestured behind him. 'It's a mile in that direction. Walk for fifteen minutes, then hoot like a tawny owl, and someone will find you.'

'Hoot like a what?' said Johan.

'I can handle that,' said Walter. 'Good job, Duggan.'

'Thank you, sir.'

Johan shook his head and muttered something in his own language. Duggan muttered something back, and the two men eyed each other.

'Let's go,' said Walter. 'We have a lot to do.'

CHAPTER 21
UNBALANCED

Steppen, Great Forest, Jallin, Central Provinces – 10th Day of Quoma 108

'You have to listen to me, ma'am,' said Lothar, his voice low so that no one else could hear. 'Fyenna and Mor Galthide are wrong. If we stay here, the Whalebone King will have us exactly where he wants us.'

Abigone frowned. 'And what do you suggest that we do?'

'We break out. We get that door down, leave the caves, and escape into the forest.'

'What about the younger ones? Salus and Nyli, for example. Fyenna won't allow them to leave with us.'

'The students are Fyenna's responsibility, ma'am; not yours. If she won't listen to common sense, then there's nothing I can do for her.'

'But we're so close to the next convoy of barges,' she said. 'If we break out, we won't be able to board them.'

Lothar smiled. 'Not so, ma'am. If we trekked south, we could keep close to the river. The barges would have to pass us after they left Steppen. One way or another, we would be getting on board.'

There was a noise by the entrance to the large cavern, and Abigone watched as the thick door was moved aside. Magnus walked in, and several people got up to talk to him, including Fyenna, Denny and Raewyn. They gathered round the son of the king, and began to talk.

'Should we go over?' said Abigone.

Lothar shook his head. 'Magnus might seem decent enough, but he does the bidding of his father and brothers. You'd be better off looking at the door, and trying to work out if your Maker powers could destroy it.'

'I could destroy it,' she said. 'I'd summon something large and wooden, and it would disintegrate. It would be easy.'

'Listen, ma'am; I know you are fond of the students, but you need to put yourself first. You are a princess of Upper Down, and you are betrothed to a grandson of the fucking emperor. You two don't belong here.'

Abigone rubbed her face. 'I can't abandon them, Lothar, even if I agree with you; even if I think Fyenna is making a mistake. I promised her that I would help protect the students.'

Lothar lowered his gaze. 'And I promised the regents of Upper Down that I would protect you. I hardly saw you in Klef Mordain, and now that I'm with you, you won't listen to my advice.'

'I know what you are trying to do for me, Lothar,' she said. 'I appreciate it; I do, but what kind of person would I be if I walked out on a group of vulnerable children? I am one of the oldest Makers here. I have a responsibility towards the others.'

'If you were in charge, ma'am, what would you do?'

Abigone thought for a moment. 'I would try to engineer a situation where we are face to face with the Whalebone King and his older sons, and then I would kill them. I'd probably need Eshia's help; Raewyn, too. We would kill them together. And then we would await the barges.'

'It's not a terrible plan, ma'am,' he said, 'but it relies upon the king and his sons agreeing to be in the same place at the same time, and they have been careful not to allow that to happen too often.'

'We only need the Masters to be together at the same time – the king and Ragnvald.'

'And Magnus, ma'am.'

'Do we have to kill him, too? Without the influence of his father and brothers, I don't think Magnus would present much of a threat.'

The door moved again, and Magnus left the cave.

'That was quick,' said Abigone. 'Poor Raewyn will be disappointed.'

Denny walked over to the corner of the cave where Abigone and Lothar were sitting.

'There's news,' he said.

'Good news?' said Abigone.

'I'm not sure. A Sanctian detachment attacked the temple a few days ago, but they were all killed; then, on the same day, another force freed over four hundred slaves, while the mercenaries were busy fighting the Sanctians in the temple.'

'Wait,' said Lothar. 'Sanctians were here? Sanctian soldiers?'

'That's right,' said Denny, sitting. 'Four dozen were slain in or near the temple, and the same number were found in a small camp near the Ario River a couple of days later. Most of them were sick. I guess the Sanctians have discovered that the king is a Master.'

'They must have come up from Elestia,' said Lothar. 'What will the Sanctians do when their soldiers don't return south?'

'They will likely send a force ten times as large,' said Denny. 'They could enter Jallin, float cannon down the river, and bombard Steppen from the cliffs.'

'That would be a terrible shame,' said Lothar. 'I might laugh myself to death if that happens.'

'Have the four hundred slaves been found?' said Abigone.

Denny shook his head. 'They are still on the loose. The king is too distraught to have done anything about them yet. One of his sons was killed in the battle.'

Lothar clenched his fists. 'Yes. At last, something I can thank the Sanctians for.'

'It wasn't the Sanctians who did it,' said Denny. 'Einar was killed when the slaves were freed. He was beheaded by a man claiming to be the *drunken champion*, whatever that means.'

Abigone's eyes narrowed. 'The what?'

'The drunken champion,' said Denny. 'He told a surviving mercenary that he was going to kill the king and all of his sons, and then he escaped into the forest with the freed slaves.'

Lothar got to his feet, his cheeks puffed out, and his eyes wide.

'Is he all right?' said Denny.

Lothar started to laugh, then he turned to Denny. 'I need to speak to the princess alone for a moment.'

Denny frowned, then he got to his feet.

'It's Upper Down business,' said Lothar; 'nothing personal.'

'I'll tell you about it later,' said Abigone.

Denny walked away, and sat down next to Marlow.

'That was a little rude,' said Abigone.

'I couldn't give a shit, ma'am,' said Lothar, crouching next to her. 'Did you hear that? Walter is here. It has to be him. Who else would describe themselves as the *drunken champion*? That name is meaningless to the folk in Steppen, but he knew that we would understand it if we heard it. He was sending us a message.'

'It cannot be Lord Walter,' said Abigone. 'There is no reason whatsoever that he would happen to be in the Great Forest at the same time as we are. It is far too much of a coincidence.'

'Not if he's looking for us. Amery and Loryn were on their way to Upper Down; they could have met Walter on the road.'

'That seems highly implausible.'

'Perhaps Walter was heading south for some reason. Before we left Upper Down, do you recall that there were rumours the emperor would want to renegotiate the treaty we made with the Sanctian Empire? Count Sebastian thought it was likely, and Walter would be the obvious choice to go to Sanctos.'

'All right; say it is him. Say that Lord Walter has come all this way because he heard that we were here. How does that change things? Shouldn't we wait for him to act?'

Lothar scowled with frustration. 'But, ma'am, this plan boils down to the same as Fyenna's one – sit here, and wait to see what happens next. We should act, rather than react. If we escape, we could find Walter.'

'Not if the king's mercenaries are searching for him; they would be likely to find us, instead.' She narrowed her eyes. 'And why has he freed four hundred slaves? If he is here for us, then why hasn't he tried to free us?'

'He won't know anything about the circumstances under which we are being held, ma'am. He might not even know that there are Masters living here. As for the slaves – I don't know. Walter has a good heart; he might have felt sorry for them.'

'It sounds as though he has become distracted.'

'Then we need to send him a message. If he knew we were trapped in this cavern, he would...' Lothar gazed away for a moment. 'I think I know what he's doing, ma'am. He's raising a force large enough to be able to topple the king. That has to be it. If Walter was travelling south on a diplomatic mission, then he probably doesn't have many soldiers with him, so he's building his own army.'

'Yet more speculation.'

'I know, but it's all we have to work with.'

'I should speak to Denny and Fyenna about this.'

'Is that wise?'

'If Walter is planning to attack with hundreds of slaves, then they should be told.'

'But...'

'But what? Spell it out for me, Lothar. Why don't you want me to tell Denny and Fyenna?'

'Because, ma'am, I don't trust them.'

Abigone gave him a cold expression. 'Denny is my betrothed. We are planning on getting married as soon as we are free to do so.'

'Why? So you can be queen of Geathan?'

'That comment was beneath you, Lothar. Denny has no desire to lead a rebellion in Geathan.'

'That's not what his father thinks. You know what Mor Galthide is like, ma'am. He will keep trying to wear Denny down. Going to

Geathan is just the first step. You and Denny might not want to start a rebellion, but that doesn't matter; neither of you will be able to avoid it. Mor Galthide will see to that.'

Abigone fell into silence, her heart torn in different directions. She remembered the bitter arguments that had split the group before the four youngest had been snatched by the bargemen in Jallin. No clear resolution had been reached then, and the same arguments were still simmering under the surface, despite their stay in Steppen. Fyenna had wanted to go to Upper Down, but she had been forced into diverting into the Great Forest, pushing them closer towards Geathan. Was that why Mor Galthide didn't seem too perturbed by the delay? – he knew that the next stage of the journey would take them to Elestia, by which time any thoughts of Upper Down would probably have to be abandoned.

'I trust Denny,' she said, 'but I don't know what he wants; what he really wants.'

'He doesn't know it himself, ma'am,' said Lothar. 'You and Denny are too young for this responsibility, but it's time to grow up and take charge of your own lives.'

'I wish Kilbride were here. She would know what to do.'

'She probably would, ma'am; but she isn't here. You are no longer the spoiled princess living in blissful ignorance within the walls of the Royal Palace in Torrent; you are a notorious Maker, wanted by the Sanctians for the murder of their ambassador in Klef Mordain.'

Abigone got to her feet. 'Stay here,' she said. 'I am going to approach Denny and Fyenna, but I will be circumspect.'

Lothar said nothing, his eyes wary. Abigone's gaze went to Denny. He was sitting next to Marlow on a bench carved out of the wall of the cave, and he noticed her looking at him. She walked over, and Denny got to his feet.

'Let us talk privately for a moment,' she said to him.

Denny nodded, and they walked to a far corner of the cavern.

'I'm guessing that you know the identity of this drunken champion,' he said. 'Why else would Lothar have reacted like that?'

'It's possible,' she said.

'Who is he?'

'If it is him, which I still deem unlikely, then he would be a friend and ally.'

Denny frowned. 'From Upper Down?'

'That's Lothar's guess.'

'Lord Walter?'

Abigone frowned.

'I've heard you mention him before; more than once,' said Denny. 'He was the King's Champion, wasn't he? A cousin of yours? Why is he here?'

'I wish I knew the answers to your questions, Denny,' she said. 'If it is Walter, then I presume he is here because I am here. Lothar believes that Amery might have told him our location.'

'And what does Lothar want to do about it?' he said. 'Let me guess – he wants us to break out of the cavern and flee into the forest?'

'Would that be such a terrible idea?'

Denny eyed her. 'No.'

'Then you are in favour of escaping?'

'It doesn't really matter what I want; Fyenna and my father will never agree. Both of them are starting to mistrust Lothar. They believe that he only cares about you, and that, to him, the other students are expendable. Are they wrong?'

'Not entirely. Denny, how would your father react if he discovered that an ally of mine from Upper Down has freed four hundred slaves?'

'We should ask him.'

'I daren't risk it.'

'That's my father you're talking about. If it weren't for him, we wouldn't have been able to get out of Klef Mordain. He piloted the *Little Ghost* while seriously injured; who else could have done such a thing?'

'I know all that, but his hopes rest upon you and me going to Geathan – nothing else matters to him. Like Lothar, he thinks the others are expendable.'

'That's a little harsh.'

'But is it untrue?'

Denny looked away.

'What if we approach Fyenna about this?' she went on. 'Unlike Lothar and your father, she doesn't regard any of us as expendable.'

They glanced over at where Fyenna was sitting with Stanza and Aplin. The former Head Maker had been keeping a wary eye on Abigone and Denny, and she glanced up. She whispered something to Stanza and Aplin, and got to her feet. She walked over to where Denny and Abigone were standing.

'I wondered if you were going to include me in your secret conversations,' she said. 'What are you planning?'

'Nothing, as yet,' said Abigone.

'But I presume you wish to speak to me. I saw the pointed looks you sent in my direction.'

'Abigone might know the identity of the leader of the force who freed all those slaves,' said Denny.

'I heard the cryptic message delivered by Magnus when he was here,' said Fyenna. 'That man you mention, he killed one of the king's sons – and you know him, Abigone?'

'Possibly,' she said. 'If it is who I think it is, then he is from Upper Down.'

'What is he trying to accomplish?'

'I would love to know that,' Abigone said. 'Lothar has a theory.'

Fyenna's eyes tightened. 'I am sure he does. Unfortunately, Lothar has but one motivation, to take you back to Upper Down. He cares not for the others. How I wish I had only one person to worry about.'

'If we flee into the forest, we could join forces with this man.'

'The man who murdered the son of the king? Don't get me wrong, Abigone; Einar was a loathsome brute, but your friend has threatened to do the same to the king and his other sons. His presence in Steppen isn't making us any safer; if anything, he has greatly imperilled us. What if the king discovers that you are connected to the *drunken champion*?' She sighed. 'All we had to do was wait it out, and now this happens.'

'Waiting it out is leaving us vulnerable to attack.'

Fyenna's eyes darkened. 'Do you honestly believe I am unaware of that? My trust in the Whalebone King has utterly evaporated, and I fear for our safety. But you are forgetting something, Abigone; if we are attacked, we can defend ourselves, and the king will know this. With every day that passes, we are one step closer to the barges arriving. If we stay resolute and remain united, the king will not dare to touch us. However, if we kill a few mercenaries and flee, and if we then link up with the murderer of Einar, we will be open enemies of the king and his remaining sons. A bloodbath will ensue. Can you guarantee that none of the younger students will be harmed in that struggle?'

'No.'

'Then my position remains unchanged. Denny, what say you? Too often have I noticed that you leave the talking to Abigone. Don't you have an opinion of your own?'

'I am tired of waiting to be attacked,' Denny said.

'You lack patience,' Fyenna said. 'That is understandable, as you are still young; you both are. It falls to older heads to keep calm amid the chaos swirling around us. Abigone, what will your friend do next?'

'I imagine he will strike again,' she said. 'He has four hundred Westlanders with him, and many will be hungry for vengeance.'

'Can we call him off? Can you send him a message, ordering him to stand his forces down?'

'Why would we do that?' said Denny. 'Shouldn't we allow him to attack Steppen? He might kill the king, and then our problems would be over.'

'Isn't it far more likely that the king would kill him? Einar was no Master, but what if Abigone's friend had come up against Ragnvald? I fear the outcome would have been very different.' She turned back to Abigone. 'Is your friend aware of the abilities possessed by the king and his eldest son?'

'I don't know.'

'Then perhaps we should let him know. Your friend might be acting from the noblest sentiments, but it seems that he does not understand the complexity of our situation here.' She lowered her voice. 'Perhaps a small break out might indeed be necessary, if only to send word to this friend of yours.'

The wooden door screeched open, and they turned to see Magnus re-enter, along with Ragnvald.

'Gather round,' said Ragnvald.

The occupants of the cavern approached the two men by the entrance. Ragnvald's eyes were dark, but he was trying to present a friendly exterior.

'I am sorry about your brother,' said Annalise.

'Thank you,' said Ragnvald. 'Einar's death was a terrible blow, one that has overshadowed our victory against the Sanctians. I assume Magnus told you that the Sanctians had attacked the temple?'

There were a few muttered replies of agreement.

'Those bastards were here to kill you,' Ragnvald went on. 'They must have discovered that you have Masters and Makers among your number. My father moved you to these caverns for your protection, and he was right to do so. We fought the Sanctians, and we crushed them; for you. We paid a terrible price in doing so, and my father is deep in mourning.'

Abigone frowned. Was Ragnvald attempting to apportion responsibility for Einar's death onto them? Did he and his father still believe that their guests were ignorant about their status as Masters? Was he trying to make them feel guilty? A few of the students were glancing at each other uncomfortably, and Fyenna looked visibly angry, despite her silence.

'We were able to interrogate a few of the Sanctian criminals,' Ragnvald went on; 'and based upon the information they provided, we have captured and executed the remnants of the Sanctian force, skulking deep within the forest. The threat from Sanctos has been eliminated.'

'You have our thanks,' said Mor Galthide.

'Now that the danger has receded,' said Ragnvald, 'my father has ordered that you be returned to your old quarters within the temple.' He forced a smile onto his features. 'You will be back to running water and proper beds within an hour or so. You have been very patient, and you have my gratitude.' His eyes roamed over Eshia, then he caught himself, and lowered his gaze. 'Please pack up your things.'

Magnus, Abigone noticed, could barely look at any of the guests, as though he knew Ragnvald was hiding something. At that moment, she made her decision. She waited for the others to start placing their clothes and other possessions into their luggage, then she sidled over to Fyenna.

'I will have word sent to my friend,' she whispered. 'Be ready. It will happen during the transfer to the temple.'

Fyenna nodded but said nothing.

Abigone walked over to Lothar in the far corner of the cavern.

'I need you to do something for me,' she said, as she shoved a dress into her bag.

'Yes, ma'am?'

'You will not be joining us in the temple,' Abigone said. 'I need you to find Lord Walter.'

'But, ma'am, I cannot abandon you here.'

'You won't be abandoning me,' she said. 'You will be giving Walter the information he needs to plan his next move. Fyenna and Mor Galthide will not cooperate with a mass break out, and things will turn very messy if we attempt to fight Ragnvald while they oppose us. In fact, Fyenna thinks I am sending you away to persuade Walter to cease his attacks.'

Lothar eyed her.

'You will, of course, do no such thing,' Abigone went on. 'If anything, tell Walter to increase his attacks. I want Steppen brought to its knees. And, naturally, inform him of the fact that there are three Masters based here – he needs to know this. I will remain here to guard the students while you do this, and we shall be ready when Walter makes his move.'

Lothar finished packing and tied the cords on his pack.

'Walter might not understand why I left you here, ma'am,' he said.

'He will understand when he learns that I am responsible for the safety of the children in our group.'

'But you are not responsible, ma'am. The students...'

'Stop. You are wrong, Lothar. I will not walk out on Nyli and the others. Now, if you will excuse me, I need to warn Denny.'

'Wait,' said Lothar. 'Am I supposed to run off on my own? What if some of the students try to follow me? There will be mercenaries on the route to the temple, and I won't have time to sit down and calmly explain what I am doing to any of the others who attempt to join me.'

'You will need to think on your feet. Good luck, Lothar.'

She picked up her bag and walked over to Denny, who was waiting for her in the middle of the cavern. She glanced at Ragnvald and Magnus, who were still by the entrance, but they were out of earshot.

'Lothar is going to escape on the way to the temple,' she whispered.

'Is he going to find Walter?' Denny said.

'That's the plan.'

'Does he need a distraction? I could accidentally push one of the students into a pond.'

Abigone smiled. 'Just don't push me in.'

'Is everyone ready?' shouted Ragnvald. 'Follow me, if you please.'

The eldest son of the king led the way out of the cavern. Magnus walked by his side, his gaze not meeting any of the students, and the others followed. They walked along a dark tunnel, then came into the cavern where Erling had beaten Magnus and his mother. It was empty, and there was no sign that anyone had been there. They carried on through another tunnel, and entered the huge cavern that backed onto the waterfall. The morning sunlight was shining through the torrent of water, and several of the students smiled in relief at the sight.

'Daylight, at last!' cried Reath. 'Praise the spirits that we are out of that stinky cavern.'

Ragnvald glanced at her. 'It was for your own protection,' he said. 'I dread to think what might have occurred if you had been in the temple when the Sanctian soldiers raided the building.'

Reath shrugged.

They emerged onto the steps that ran down from the cavern, and Abigone gazed around at the gardens, pools and flowers. Ahead of them, the great bulk of the temple rose up like a solid chunk of carved rock. Mercenaries had been posted to either side, guarding the route.

'I'll be back in a moment,' said Denny, then he walked off to speak to Lothar.

Abigone eyed him, then she noticed Fyenna doing the same. The former Head Maker looked calm, and Abigone wondered if it was an act. After speaking to Lothar for a few minutes, Denny returned to Abigone's side.

He nodded to Abigone, then he smiled. 'What a beautiful place,' he said, then he tripped and fell into a large pool with a great splash.

'Help!' cried Abigone. 'Over here; help!'

Ragnvald and Magnus ran over to the pool, along with most of the students.

Lothar bolted as soon as the mercenaries turned to see what had happened. He pushed a mercenary off a small bridge, and sprinted towards the west. Without warning, Marlow and Eshia raced after him. A mercenary tried to grab Marlow, but the boy was fast, and he ducked under the soldier's arm and leapt over a water channel. Eshia, too, was fast, and she ran as though a hundred soldiers were chasing her.

'They're getting away!' shouted a mercenary.

Ragnvald turned from where he was staring down at Denny in the pool. His eyes went to Eshia, as some of the mercenaries aimed their crossbows at the three fugitives.

'Don't loose!' Ragnvald shouted.

Lothar, Eshia and Marlow reached another bridge. They ran over it, and disappeared into the thick forest.

Ragnvald clenched his fists in rage. He turned to Fyenna. 'Why did they do that? Answer me.'

'I... I don't know,' said Fyenna, pretending to be shocked. 'Lothar was... well, he was disgruntled with my leadership, but I had no inkling that he would try to run away.'

'He is an utter fool,' cried Mor Galthide, his anger genuine. 'An irresponsible scoundrel. Send soldiers after them, Ragnvald. Bring them back.'

Ragnvald said nothing, his eyes on the area of forest where Lothar, Eshia and Marlow had vanished.

'Get everyone into the temple,' said Magnus. He leaned over the pool and extended a hand for Denny.

Denny took it, and Magnus pulled him out of the water.

'Thank you,' said Denny.

Magnus eyed him with suspicion, then he gestured to the mercenaries. 'Didn't you hear me?' he cried. 'Move everyone into the temple; now.'

'Do as my brother commands,' said Ragnvald, his tone subdued.

'But what about Lothar and the others?' said Mor Galthide, as the mercenaries closed ranks and began to herd the students towards the temple.

Ragnvald shrugged. 'They have made their choice. They are no longer my responsibility. Hunger will bring them back. They will return when they discover how little there is to eat in the forest.'

'And what if those brigands find them?'

'Then they will die at the hands of savage Westlanders. It is sad, but what can I do? I cannot protect those who do not wish to be protected. My mourning father will take this news badly. Your friends have disrespected his hospitality.'

Mor Galthide simmered with anger as they approached an entrance in the flank of the temple. He made his way to Denny, whose clothes were dripping water onto the gravel path.

'I hope you had nothing to do with that, son,' Mor Galthide said.

'Me, Father?' said Denny. 'I don't know what you're talking about.'

'No? Your fall was not a planned diversion, then?'

'Of course not. I slipped on the wet grass and lost my balance.'

Mor Galthide shook his head in fury and strode away.

Denny eyed Abigone. 'I don't think he believed me.'

'It doesn't matter, Denny,' she said. 'Well done.'

He nodded, then glanced up at the temple. 'Back in here again,' he said. 'I hope you were right. I hope that man really is Walter. If not...'

'I'd rather not think about that.'

They paused at the threshold, and Abigone cast a last look out into the forest.

It had to be Walter, she told herself. He had come to help her, and she would have to trust that he would know what to do next. And, while they waited for him to act, Abigone would do her job, and protect the others.

She took Denny's hand, exhaled, and they entered the temple.

CHAPTER 22
BEASTS OF THE FOREST

West of Steppen, Great Forest, Jallin, Central Provinces – 10th Day of Quoma 108

Saffie awoke by the banks of a small stream. Her hand had dipped into the water, and the cold flow of the current had stirred her senses. She opened her eyes. It was daytime, and she was surrounded by trees. She tried to recall how many days it had been since she had first awoken amid the heap of Sanctian corpses. Two? More? At first, she had lain there, unable to move due to the weight of the dead bodies pressing down upon her; and then, when she had finally tried to move, her injuries had paralysed her with agony.

It had been thirst that had driven her to crawl out of the pile of the fallen, a terrible thirst that had overwhelmed all other thoughts. She had pulled herself out of the heap with her arms, letting her wounded legs trail along behind her, then she had crawled through the forest, foot by foot, her head pounding, sick and dizzy, until she had reached the stream. She had drunk deep, before passing out again.

She remembered hearing voices and footsteps during the night that had just passed. Had she been dreaming? There had been torches and lanterns, or had she imagined it all? Why would the mercenaries return to where they had dumped the bodies of the Sanctian soldiers? Saffie turned her head. She could see the heap of the fallen some forty yards away – had she only crawled that distance? It had felt like miles. The heap seemed to have grown, and the bodies on top were fresher than those lying under them. She closed her eyes as a realisation struck her. The mercenaries had found the sick and wounded soldiers they had left behind in the forest. They had found them, and slaughtered them; and Saffie was alone.

She was going to die; it was inevitable. She couldn't walk, and she knew that the forest contained very little to eat; but she would die from exposure long before starvation took hold. Autumn had arrived in the forest, and the leaves were tinged with reds, browns and oranges. The air had a chill to it that penetrated her thin clothing, and she had shivered throughout the night. A few hours of cold rain would probably be enough to end her life. Zola had won – Princess Safina would become a martyr, her death fighting wicked Masters would reverberate around the empire, and the Offices of Purgation would step up its activities. Soldiers would be summoned, and an army would destroy Steppen.

She started to cry. Had her life been for nothing? She longed for her family. Her two older brothers had always watched out for her – where were they when she needed them? Her father, the Illustrious Prince Vincenzo, had warned her of the dangers when she had elected to join the Offices of Purgation, but she had ignored his advice. And what would her mother think when she found out that her only daughter had died alone in a forest?

The stern features of the emperor entered her thoughts. Would her grandfather mourn her, or would his anger at her death outweigh his other emotions? Did he have any emotion besides anger? At once, she understood that her grandfather would indeed be angry with her if he could see her – not because she was dying, but because she had given up. She imagined his furious tirade at her despair. Hadn't he tried to prepare his grandchildren for extreme hardship? Had he forced the sixteen cousins to undergo the harshest training, only for one of them to give up when things looked bleak?

Shame rippled through her; shame at disappointing her grandfather. For him, she would try to survive. She opened her eyes again, and gazed around. The pain in the back of her head was making her sight a little blurry, but her arms were still working. She leaned over and cupped some cold water into her mouth. She had her arms, her vision and she had access to water. She needed food, but first, she needed shelter. She did what she had been dreading to do, and looked down at her legs. To her surprise, they appeared to be intact. She had no doubt that she had broken at least one bone in her left leg, but perhaps her right had only been bruised and sprained. She wiggled the toes on her right foot. They hurt, but they responded.

She lay still to gather her strength, and tried to remember what had happened inside the Temple of Steppen. She recalled searching the lower floors of the building, looking for a way up. The Sanctians had split into two groups. Saffie had led one, and the young acting lieutenant had taken the other; and then... then they had come to the stairs where a Master had been waiting for them. He had cut down most of her soldiers, killing them in a variety of cruel and vile ways, and the mercenaries standing next to him had shot down any who had escaped his wicked powers. Saffie had ordered a charge. Had she really done that? The man at the top of the stairs was the first Master she had encountered in her life, and she had not flinched. That was something her grandfather would have appreciated.

What had happened after that? She remembered getting to the top of the stairs. She had lashed out with her knife, and wounded the Master, then she had fallen back down the stairs. She frowned. Why hadn't they checked to see if she was alive or not? Had they been so incompetent as to assume her fate without bothering to examine if it was true? It didn't matter. Their stupidity had led her to the place where she now found herself – alone, but alive.

She heard something, and her heart raced. Voices, footsteps, the undergrowth rustling as people made their way through it in a hurry. Saffie held her breath. If the mercenaries had returned, she would have to play dead. She half-closed her eyes, keeping them open just enough to see what was about to happen.

Three figures bounded through the forest, then they came to a skidding halt in front of the heap of corpses. A man, a woman, and a boy. The woman gasped at the sight of the fallen.

'I guess these must be the Sanctians,' said the man, leaning his hands on his knees as though he was out of breath.

'We should keep running,' said the boy, as he glanced over his shoulder. 'The mercenaries must be right behind us.'

'Stay quiet for a moment, Marlow,' said the man. 'I want to listen.'

The woman noticed the stream, and she walked over to it, stopping by its bank just a few yards from Saffie. She knelt on the ground and drank some of the cool water, then her head turned, and her mouth opened as she caught sight of Saffie.

'Lothar!' she hissed. 'One of them is still alive.'

The man and the boy ran over. Neither were armed, and they stared down at Saffie. The woman and the man got a little closer, and the man crouched down, just out of Saffie's reach. He looked like a soldier, and his eyes were wary.

'Can you hear me?' he said.

'I can hear you,' Saffie gasped.

'Are you wounded?'

Saffie nodded.

'Can you walk?'

'No.'

'We can't stay here,' said the boy.

'I heard nothing coming from the direction of Steppen,' said the man. 'We'll be safe for a few moments.'

'What should we do with her?' said the woman.

The man frowned. 'The three of us need to talk about what happened back in Steppen, about why you both followed me; but it'll have to wait. For now, we'll carry her with us, and head deeper into the forest.'

'We can't,' said Marlow. 'She'll slow us down.'

The man shook his head at the boy. 'I will not leave a wounded woman out here to die.'

'She's a Sanctian,' said Marlow. 'She wants to kill me and Eshia. She hates us, Lothar.'

'You will do what I command,' said Lothar. 'You chose to accompany me, and now you will have to obey my orders. If you don't like it, go back to Steppen.'

The boy glared at Lothar.

'Search the bodies, Marlow,' said Lothar. 'You have two minutes. Find anything of use – weapons, food, money; anything. Go.'

Marlow remained where he was for a moment, then he ran over to the pile of bodies.

'Eshia,' Lothar went on; 'help me sit her up; but before that...' He turned back to Saffie. 'Is your spine injured? Can we move you?'

'It's my legs, not my back,' Saffie said. 'And my head.'

'Will you allow me to examine you?' he said. 'Eshia can do it if you don't want me touching you.'

'It's fine,' she said. 'Are you running away from Steppen? Were you slaves?'

'Something like that,' said Lothar. His hands reached out, and he began to check her for injuries. 'Can you move your fingers for me?' he said, and Saffie did so.

'Now your toes,' he said.

She grimaced in pain as she tried to wiggle the toes on her left foot. Lothar watched, and examined her lower leg. He nodded, then he moved up to her head and felt through her hair. For some reason, despite being in the hands of a strange man, Saffie felt safe. Perhaps it was due to the other woman's presence. Eshia, the man had called her.

'What's wrong with her?' said Eshia.

'Broken tibia and fibula in her left leg,' Lothar said, 'a large abrasion on her right leg, and a possible concussion. There's dried blood matting her hair. Hunger, dehydration. I'm guessing she was part of the team that attacked the temple a few days ago, and that she's been out here ever since.'

'Then she is our enemy,' said Eshia.

'I don't give a fuck,' Lothar spat. 'She's wounded and she needs our help.' He glanced at Saffie. 'We're going to sit you up now, in preparation for helping you stand.'

Saffie nodded, despite the pain gripping her. 'Thank you,' she said, as a tear fell down her cheek.

Lothar gripped one shoulder, then Eshia muttered something and took hold of the other. They lifted Saffie into a sitting position, and her headache pounded. She groaned in pain.

'You're going to be all right,' Lothar said. 'Look at me. Your injuries are painful, but you will survive them. I can set the bones in your leg later, when we're a lot further away from Steppen. That will involve a journey, which will hurt. Do you understand?'

'Yes.'

Marlow returned from the heap of dead, clutching an assortment of tools, knives, water bottles and a couple of small food parcels.

'Good work, Marlow,' Lothar said. 'Pass me one of those knives.'

Marlow handed him a blade, and Lothar slid it into his belt.

'I, uh... listen; we can't take a Sanctian with us,' said Marlow. 'Please, Lothar. Look at the insignia on her sleeve. She's from the Offices of Purgation.'

'And what the fuck's that?' said Lothar.

'They hunt... people like me and Eshia. That's their entire purpose. When I left Subnestia, it was soldiers from the Offices of Purgation who were chasing me. They killed my uncle.'

Saffie digested the boy's words in silence, keeping her features neutral. Had she been rescued by the very monsters she had pledged to hunt down? No. That was nonsense. It was the concussion; it was making her confused.

Lothar eyed her. 'Why were you in Steppen?' he said. 'Answer honestly.'

'To kill the Whalebone King,' she gasped, her head swimming.

Lothar nodded. 'That's good enough for me. Eshia, I need your help again. We're going to place her onto my back, and I'll carry her. Will you help?'

'I don't know, Lothar,' she said. 'I didn't escape just to help the first Sanctian we came across. They destroyed my city.'

'They didn't destroy it,' said Lothar. 'They annexed it, but the last I checked, it was still standing.'

Eshia folded her arms across her chest and looked away.

'Marlow?' said Lothar. 'Will you help me?'

Marlow shook his head.

'Then fuck the pair of you,' said Lothar. He turned his back to Saffie. 'Put your arms round my neck and hold on tight.'

Saffie leaned forward and gripped her hands round his throat. Lothar got to his feet, lifting Saffie clear of the ground. He took hold of her right leg, and pushed her up.

He nodded. 'Good enough,' he said. He turned to the others. 'You have a choice. Come with me, or don't. I couldn't give a flying fuck either way.'

Lothar set off through the forest, and Saffie clung on to his back with all her strength. He picked up his pace, jumped over the stream, and ran. Behind them, Saffie could hear the other two following, though neither uttered a word.

Lothar had been right – the journey was painful, uncomfortable and exhausting. Saffie's head was throbbing, her arms ached, and the fires in her left leg jolted with every step Lothar took. The minutes passed, then it seemed as though he had been running for hours. They passed the westernmost waterfall to their right, and continued on, deeper and deeper into the uncharted woods. A new fear arose within Saffie, a fear that they would become lost within the depths of the Great Forest, swallowed up by its vast expanse.

At length, Lothar slowed to a walk, then he came to a halt. He turned. Marlow and Eshia were red-faced and panting, and Eshia fell to her knees on a patch of grass, and retched. Marlow sat down next to her, but he kept his eyes on Saffie. Lothar lowered her to the ground with her back against a tree, and then he almost collapsed onto the grass next to her. For a while, no one spoke, and Saffie listened as their breathing started to relax and slow.

'This is where we'll make a camp,' said Lothar. 'We passed a stream a short while ago; we'll get our fresh water from there. We need to build a shelter to keep out of the rain, and to keep us warm at night. We're far enough away from Steppen that we can risk a small fire; that will help. Eshia, I want you to fill the water bottles that Marlow found among the bodies. Clean them thoroughly first. Marlow, I need you to gather firewood. I'll get started on the shelter.'

'You have got to be joking,' said Marlow. 'I need more time to rest. We must have covered ten miles.'

'More like eight,' said Lothar. 'All right; we'll talk before we work. Do either of you want to tell me why you ran off like that?'

'We were following you,' said Marlow.

'I didn't ask anyone to follow me.'

'That's just it, isn't it?' said the boy. 'The adults didn't tell us anything about what was going on. I had a split second to react when I saw you start to run. I didn't know if it was pre-planned or spontaneous. I acted on instinct. It was only when we reached the forest that I realised there were only three of us.'

Lothar nodded. 'Eshia?'

'You know why I came with you,' she said.

'I'm afraid you're going to have to tell me in plain words,' said Lothar. 'I was never any good at riddles.'

Eshia lowered her gaze. 'I ran so that Ragnvald wouldn't get me,' she said. 'Did you see the way he looked at me before we left the caverns? That was all I was thinking about when I saw you run. I needed to get away from him.'

'Who is Ragnvald?' said Saffie.

'He's one of the king's sons,' said Lothar. 'An arsehole of the highest order.'

Saffie wanted to ask if Ragnvald was a Master, but felt that opening up that line of conversation might take them to a dark place. She glanced at Eshia. Was she looking at a Maker? But, if so, then why hadn't she simply summoned a giant spider to eat Ragnvald?

'You're safe now, Eshia,' said Lothar.

'Am I?' she said. She pointed at Saffie. 'What about her? My father and my uncle were killed by people like her. The fact that she's an injured young woman is blinding you, Lothar. You feel a need to help her, but some people don't deserve to be helped.'

'The Offices of Purgation executed my uncle in a public square,' said Marlow.

'Did they?' said Lothar. 'Why have I never heard of these Offices?'

'They have never reached as far north as Upper Down,' said Eshia. 'Klef Mordain will be full of them by now. They will be questioning hundreds of people, trying to root out the families of those who attended...' She paused. 'I can't say any more, not in front of her. You're a good man, Lothar, but you're naïve. You have no idea what this woman is capable of.'

Lothar shook his head, then he turned to face Saffie. 'I assume you heard what they said?'

Saffie nodded.

'Well? What is your response?'

'Could I have some water, please?'

'Eshia,' said Lothar; 'the water bottles. Clean and fill them. Marlow – firewood. I want to speak to this woman alone.'

Eshia and Marlow got to their feet. Marlow handed the water bottles to Eshia, and they both walked off into the forest.

'They have some serious allegations,' Lothar said to Saffie. 'Are they true?'

Saffie said nothing.

'What's your name?'

'Saffie,' she said. 'My leg... please; it hurts so much that I can't think straight.'

'I will set the bones for you,' he said. 'It's going to hurt like a bastard, and you might pass out; so, before I do it, I want you to answer me one question.'

'What?'

'Have you ever killed any Masters or Makers?'

'No. There was a Master in the temple, and I managed to wound his arm; that was as close as I got.'

Lothar nodded. 'All right.' He glanced down at her left leg. 'I'm sorry about this. Brace yourself.'

When Saffie next awoke, Lothar was hard at work constructing their shelter. Marlow was preparing a camp fire, and had stacked up armfuls of branches next to a ring of stones. Saffie looked around for Eshia, but saw no sign of her.

Her leg was in agony, but there was something different about the pain. She glanced down. Her lower left leg was bare, the fabric ripped from it, and a splint had been fixed to the side of her shin, wrapped in strips of cloth. She felt the back of her head. Her hair had been washed, and the dried blood had been scrubbed out. Her fingers went over the large bump behind her right ear. It was sore to touch, but her headache had faded a little.

She looked up at Lothar. 'Are you a doctor?'

He laughed. 'Perhaps I should be,' he said. 'I've plenty of practice of fixing up various wounds and suchlike. I don't suppose you have ever heard of the Mountain Rangers of Upper Down?'

'Is that where you come from?'

He finished securing a woven roof of branches to the top of the shelter, then he eyed her. 'Yes. Upper Down. Technically, we're allies.'

'Then why do the others hate me so much?'

'I'm sure you can guess, Saffie,' he said. 'Your occupation might have something to do with it.'

'Are you a friend of the Whalebone King?'

'Don't be ridiculous. That's who we fled from.'

'Then we share the same enemy, Lothar. The Whalebone King is a tyrannical, sadistic Master. Have you seen the things he does to the slaves? He's a monster.'

Lothar picked up another bundle of foliage. 'I'm not going to argue with that.'

Saffie lowered her voice. 'They are all monsters.'

'I used to know a guy with ginger hair,' Lothar said.

Saffie frowned.

'He was an arsehole,' Lothar went on; 'so, I have decided to annihilate every bastard with red hair. It makes sense, doesn't it? I mean, if one of them is a prick, then they all are.'

Lothar got back to work, and Saffie rolled her eyes at the man's ignorance. Of course he would think that way – he was from Upper Down, one of the last realms on the continent where Masters and Makers remained in charge.

'Is Princess Kilbride a Maker?' she said.

'No.'

'But the king was? Alfgang, who called himself *the Great*.'

'Yes, he was one; and yes, he was also an arsehole. A powerful king, but he nearly brought Upper Down to ruin. His son was also a Master, but a more gentle man you would struggle to find. Too gentle, in fact; far too gentle to be king. The Westlanders knew that, so they killed him. They guessed that he wouldn't fight back, and they were right.'

'He didn't fight back?'

'He refused to use his powers to harm another living being,' said Lothar. 'He believed that being a Master meant that he had been blessed by the spirits, and, therefore, he...'

'Stop,' said Saffie. 'Please. Your blasphemy hurts more than the injuries do. The spirits loathe Masters and Makers; you must know this?'

'I don't pay much attention to religion, to be honest,' he said. 'I'm not even sure I actually believe in the spirits. Has anyone ever seen one?'

'Then to whom do you pray?'

Lothar laughed. 'I prefer to be self-reliant, Saffie. I don't pray to anyone.'

Eshia approached with more firewood, and she placed it down next to Marlow, who had almost finished getting the fire ready. She glanced over at Lothar and Saffie, and walked towards them.

Saffie eyed her.

Eshia eyed her back, then she raised a hand. 'I could kill you, if I wanted to,' she said. 'I should kill you, for all the hurt you have caused me and my family. Do you think I chose to be a Maker? Do you think I want to be one? If I was normal, then I would still be living in Klef Mordain, and I wouldn't be here in this awful place. My father and uncle were tortured to death, because the Sanctians were looking for me. Say something, you Sanctian bitch.'

'That's enough,' said Lothar.

Eshia lowered her hand and sat down on the grass next to the ring of stones, her eyes dark.

Lothar turned to Saffie. 'Eshia made some good points, and I would like to hear you answer them.'

'There is nothing I can say, is there?' said Saffie. 'You three have me at your mercy. Did you bring me out here into the middle of the forest to kill me? Then do it.'

'She's a fanatic,' said Marlow. 'They all are.'

'Don't make the same mistake that she's made,' said Lothar. 'Not all Sanctians are the same.'

'I didn't mean all Sanctians,' said Marlow; 'I was talking about the ones who join the Offices of Purgation – they're the fanatics who want to murder Eshia and me; and everyone else like us.'

'She hasn't murdered a single Master or Maker,' said Lothar.

'But she wants to,' cried Eshia. 'Why are you protecting her?'

'Is that true, Saffie?' said Lothar. 'Do you want to wipe out every Master and Maker; even the children, and those who have never harmed anyone in their lives?'

Saffie closed her eyes. They were going to kill her; she knew it. Everything that had happened since they had found her by the stream had been a trick to lure her away so they could murder her. How would they do it? Would the boy turn her blood into fire; or would the woman summon a savage beast to devour her?

Her hands trembled. 'Yes,' she whispered. 'They are evil; they should all die.'

She braced herself for death, but nothing happened. She waited, her heart pounding, and still nothing happened. She opened her eyes a crack. Lothar, Eshia and Marlow were standing a few dozen feet away from her, arguing in low voices. Lothar seemed to be trying to appeal to them, but Marlow and Eshia were gesticulating furiously.

Lothar had saved her, she realised. He had saved her from a Master and a Maker. Why? Wasn't he in league with them? Hadn't he served the villainous Master King Alfgang, who had raided the Central Provinces with hordes of savage Westlanders?

She watched as Eshia and Marlow walked away. Lothar stared at them for a while, then he bowed his head. He turned, and walked back to Saffie. He sat down next to her.

'Why the fuck did you have to say that?' he said. 'Couldn't you have lied? Would you really kill a little girl, just because she was a Maker; or a little boy, because he was a Master? You're fucked up, Saffie, and now the other two are refusing to sleep anywhere near you. They don't feel safe in your presence, and I can hardly blame them.'

'Why didn't they kill me?'

'Not everyone thinks like you,' he said. 'Marlow is a good lad, and Eshia is one of the nicest people I've met; and both have been through more than you can imagine.' He lowered his gaze. 'I'm starting to wish we hadn't found you by the stream.'

'Then leave me,' she said.

'You will die if I leave you.'

'Maybe not. I am also self-reliant. I can look after myself.'

'And what are you going to eat? How long will it take you to crawl to the river and back for water? What if wild animals come during the night? Are you going to be able to gather enough firewood to stay warm when the temperature drops? You're tough; I get it, but if I leave you here on your own, you'll be dead within a few days.'

'Why do you care?'

'Because I'm a soft-hearted bastard who can't stand the thought of deserting anyone in need. I will help you until your leg heals, and then we can go our separate ways. I will also be out and about in the forest for long stretches of time. I'll need to lay some traps, hunt, gather wood and water; among a few other things I need to do. But I will be back, every time, until you are able to walk on your own.'

'Your friends are angry with you.'

'They'll get over it. Maybe.'

'Where are they going to sleep tonight?'

'Marlow says he's going to build another shelter, and Eshia will take care of the fire. They'll be on the far side of the stream.' He leaned forward. 'I should probably help them, but I'll get our fire lit first.'

'I can do that,' she said. 'You should help your friends.'

'Even though you think my friends are vile monsters who deserve to die?'

Saffie said nothing.

Lothar nodded. 'Do you know how to light a fire?'

'I do. I have been trained on how to survive in the wild, Lothar. I am not as helpless as you think.'

'That's good to know.' He got to his feet. 'Keep the fire low. I'll be back soon.'

Saffie watched as Lothar walked away into the fading light; then she glanced at the ring of stones. It had been a while since she had started a fire on her own without matches, but she had done it a hundred times during her years of training.

A dozen thoughts went through her mind as she got started. She had come face to face with a Master and a Maker, and survived. She had faced her own mortality; once by the stream when she had fallen into despair; and again when she had confessed her beliefs to Eshia and Marlow. And yet, she was still alive.

She sent up a prayer to the spirits, thanking them for their help that day, and asking them for guidance. She would need to work hard to bring Lothar to the truth, to prove to him that Masters and Makers were the enemies of all mankind, but it would take many days for her leg to heal, and she had plenty of time.

She smiled as sparks took hold of a small branch. She fed in more wood, a little at a time, feeling a desire to impress Lothar when he returned. She would show him that she was quite capable of looking after herself. She could cook, she could keep a fire going, and, if it hadn't been for her broken leg, she would have built a shelter every inch as well as Lothar had done. She warmed her hands next to the flames and, for the first time since she had left Elestia, she felt a calm content settle over her, despite the fact that a Master and a Maker were sitting by their own camp fire a few hundred yards away.

She forgot about the Whalebone King and the horrors of Steppen. She was alive, and that was all that mattered.

CHAPTER 23
TOGETHER

Steppen, Great Forest, Jallin, Central Provinces – 14th Day of Quoma 108

The two mercenaries on duty outside the king's small dining chamber looked exhausted, and the smirks and knowing glances that they had previously aimed at Magnus were gone. One of them opened the door for the king's youngest son, and he entered the dark, smoky room. The king was smoking from a small water pipe, and his bleary eyes gazed up at Magnus as the door was closed behind him.

'Sit, boy,' Hemming said.

Magnus pulled out a chair and sat down next to Ragnvald and Erling at the table.

'My three remaining sons,' the king went on. 'The proud, the stupid and the naïve.' He puffed from the pipe. 'Where is Einar?' he cried, then he began to sob thick tears. 'Where is my boy?'

The three brothers said nothing.

The king wiped his face with the corner of the table cloth. 'Ragnvald,' he said, 'have you caught the bastard who killed Einar?'

Ragnvald lowered his gaze. 'No, boss.'

'Why not? Send more soldiers out to hunt him down! Search every inch of the forest, and don't stop until you find him. I want to watch him suffer; I want to hear him scream in agony. I want...'

Magnus watched as his father broke down again. Hemming clenched his fists and let out a howl of grief.

'Answer me!' he bellowed at Ragnvald. 'Why haven't you brought me the bastard's head?'

'We've been over this, boss,' said Ragnvald. 'We have patrols in the forest, but we can't send out too many men, or we risk a slave uprising. We've lost nearly two hundred mercenaries in the past month, and the others are stretched keeping Steppen secure. We'd be better off waiting for the drunken champion to come to us – which he will; I have no doubt about that – and then we set a trap for him.'

'Fucking excuses – that's all I hear,' said the king. 'You're happy that Einar is dead, aren't you? One fewer brother to compete for the throne after I'm gone. You hated him; admit it.'

Ragnvald narrowed his eyes.

Hemming turned to Erling. 'You need to watch your back, lest an *accident* befalls you. You can't trust anyone, least of all your brothers.'

'Not this again, boss,' said Ragnvald. 'I'm a Master. If I wanted to kill Erling, he'd be dead. Did I like Einar? No – I hated the prick; but Steppen was easier to run with Einar alive.'

Erling staggered up from his chair, swaying from the alcohol he had been consuming over the seven days since Einar's death.

'Take that back!' he shouted. 'My brother is dead, and you call him a *prick*?'

Ragnvald raised an eyebrow. 'He was my brother, too,' he said. 'Sit down, and stop behaving like a child. Even Magnus is holding it together better than you. If this... meeting is over, then I have other things I need to be doing. Every slave that maintained the water boilers has either died or escaped, and I have no intention of freezing my balls off this coming winter.'

Ragnvald started to get to his feet, and the king pointed a finger at him.

'You will stay where you are,' Hemming hissed. 'It was you who allowed the three guests to run away, was it not? I heard you told the soldiers not to loose at them.'

Ragnvald shook his head. 'It was me who told you that, boss. I ordered the mercenaries not to shoot, because every fucking guest was watching.'

'And if Eshia hadn't been one of them?' said the king. 'She's the reason you ordered the men not to shoot. You've gone soft on me, son, and you've broken the only rule I ever set you – never fall for a woman.'

'You're talking out of your arse, boss,' said Ragnvald. 'You keep changing your mind about what we should do with the guests. Keep them alive, kill them all, let them go... We never know from one day to the next what we're supposed to do. Magnus – back me up.'

'He's right, sir,' said Magnus. 'The other guests would have seen everything. There was nothing we could do.'

Hemming stared at him. 'Are you and Ragnvald conspiring to take my crown? I should give it to Erling. He might be as stupid as a day-old goat, but at least he's loyal.'

'You're delusional, boss,' said Ragnvald. 'Not about Erling, though – you're right about him. As for the three escapees, they're probably starving in the depths of the forest. They'll be back.'

'Kill them if they return,' said Hemming. 'Impale the ungrateful bastards. Haven't we cared for them, fed them? We even moved them to safety when the Sanctians attacked, and this is how they repay us?' He inhaled from the pipe again. 'Kill them all – do you hear me?'

The three brothers glanced at each other.

'Was that an order, boss?' said Erling.

The king looked up. 'What?' His eyes narrowed as though he was confused. 'Where is Einar? Where is my boy? Ragnvald, bring me the body of the man who killed my son, and take Magnus with you.'

Ragnvald and Magnus stood. The king leaned over and whispered something to Erling, who looked too drunk to understand. Ragnvald left the dark room, and Magnus walked out after him. They followed a passageway until they were out of sight of the guards by the door, then Ragnvald came to a halt.

'The old bastard is losing his mind,' said Ragnvald.

'He's smoking too much,' said Magnus.

'Me and you need to stick together, lad,' Ragnvald said. 'There's no telling what the king will do in this state. He's paranoid and liable to lash out at anyone, including us. Tell me if he orders you to do anything crazy. Now, make yourself fucking useful, and take over some of the duties that Einar used to carry out. The barges will be here in ten days or so, and I need to know if the cranes are operational again after the attacks.'

'Do you really think Eshia and the others will be back?'

'Fuck knows. The soldier-boy among them might know a bit about surviving in the wilds; but it's not them I'm worried about – it's the damn drunken champion. We thought the Sanctians were the threat, but this bastard is far more dangerous. He has four hundred slaves with him in the forest, and they'll be getting hungry about now. If he attacks the cranes again, we're fucked.' He edged closer to Magnus. 'I need to know, lad – are you with me? Can I depend on you?'

Magnus nodded. 'Yes.'

'Good lad. Now, get to work.'

Ragnvald walked away, leaving Magnus alone in the temple passageway. Magnus gazed out of a window at the shanty town. The hole in the fence had been repaired, and the camp was quiet, with most of the remaining slaves out working. He walked to the stairs and descended to the ground floor of the temple, then he stepped out into the chill sunshine. A few mercenaries eyed him as he walked along the road that ran in front of the temple, and Magnus noticed the fear on their faces. For years, the mercenaries had kept order within Steppen. They had governed the slaves with a mixture of brutality and cruelty, and the knowledge that four hundred of those they had persecuted were loose in the forest had destroyed their morale. Each mercenary knew what would happen to them if they were captured by the escaped slaves, and many were refusing to enter the forest. Magnus had loathed the mercenaries for his entire life, but their recent defeat had made him realise that they were the only thing preventing the barbaric Westlanders from burning Steppen to the ground.

Magnus decided to walk round by the western flank of the temple. He glanced up at the high window that opened out from the apartment where their guests were residing. Raewyn was there, along with two others, and Magnus stopped on the gravel track to gaze up at her. With only ten days until the barges were due to arrive, one way or another, things were going to change.

Raewyn glanced down and saw Magnus staring up at her. He averted his gaze, his face reddening, then he hurried away until he reached the north-western corner of the temple, close to where the three guests had fled into the forest. He remembered the look on Eshia's face as she had bolted across the little bridge. She had been prepared to take her chances in the forest rather than stay in Steppen, and part of him understood how she must have felt. Magnus turned, and began walking in the direction of the stairs that led up to the cranes. He had to stay close to Ragnvald – it was his best chance of surviving, and that meant he would have to obey any command his eldest brother gave him. He wondered what kind of king Ragnvald would make, then he imagined a future where he was second in command to his oldest brother. He would be safe, as long as he was obedient.

He crossed over a bridge, and left the three central waterfalls behind. The cranes sat atop the cliffs next to the banks of the River Antiago, and the falls created by that water course were the highest and widest of the five. A large basin with piers and wharves had been constructed next to the base of the waterfall, and it was there that all barges were lowered when they arrived by the cranes. Their supplies would then be unloaded, and their holds filled with chests of silver coins, before they were allowed to carry onwards down the Ario towards Elestia in the south. Magnus reached the wooden wharf by the side of the basin, then he followed the path that led to the stairs. A few caves extended back into the side of the cliff, where some of the supplies were stored, but Magnus knew they would be empty with the next convoy due so soon. The bottom of the stairs was being guarded by two soldiers, and Magnus was about to hail them when he saw the reflection of a lamp coming from within the caves. He frowned. Should he investigate? Einar had been responsible for every aspect of the barges, including the areas where the supplies were stored; was that now Magnus's job?

He hesitated, then he turned back towards the caves. He crossed another bridge, and entered the deep shadows of the caverns. The walls and floor were slick with water from the falls, and a narrow section of the basin reached far into the cave. Magnus slowed and came to a halt. Three men were lurking in the shadows. Two mercenaries were lifting a small barge out of another cave and attempting to lower it into the water, while the third man was holding the lamp.

'Careful with that,' said the man with the lamp.

Magnus frowned. It was Lord Matteo. What was the Sanctian doing out of the temple? As far as Magnus knew, Matteo never left the temple.

There was a soft splash as the barge struck the water of the narrow channel. One of the mercenaries secured a rope from the rear of the barge to an iron hoop embedded into the cavern wall, then the other began to place crates onto the deck of the vessel. Magnus stayed hidden in the thick shadows as he watched the two men work.

'Don't put all the silver in the front,' said Matteo. 'Balance the weight across the entire length of the barge.'

'Yes, sir,' said one of the mercenaries.

'What time are we leaving, sir?' said the other.

'As soon as it gets dark,' said Matteo. 'And yes, you will both be handsomely rewarded when we reach Elestia.'

'Is there space for a fourth man? I have a mate in my barracks who is as desperate to get out of this shithole as we are.'

'I will not risk word of this getting out,' said Matteo. 'I took an enormous gamble asking you two; I will not include another in our little secret. Your friend will have to remain here.'

The two mercenaries kept working, loading more crates into the hold of the barge. Magnus thought about running back to the temple to tell Ragnvald what he had seen, but anger at Matteo's betrayal was surging through him.

He stepped out of the shadows. 'You filthy Sanctian traitor,' he said.

Matteo and the two mercenaries turned to stare at him.

'Whatever do you mean, my dear boy?' said Matteo. 'Traitor? Me? You are deeply mistaken. We are here on the express orders of His Majesty the king, your formidable father. Come and see.'

Magnus narrowed his eyes.

Matteo sighed as though he was being confronted by a petulant child. 'If you come over here, Magnus, you will see that what we are doing is perfectly legitimate.'

Magnus walked forwards until he was level with the barge. He peered down into the hold.

'What am I supposed to be looking at?' he said.

Matteo walked up behind him and clubbed him over the head with a wooden bat. Magnus cried out, and fell to his knees, then he was struck in the face by one of the mercenaries, and he toppled onto the cold stone floor of the cavern.

'Should we kill him?' said one of the mercenaries.

'Certainly not,' said Matteo. 'This boy's untimely visit might be the best thing that could have happened to us. I had been expecting a rough reception from the Sanctians in Elestia, but if we hand over a Master when we arrive, then I would imagine that my previous transgressions will be immediately forgiven. Bind his wrists and gag him.'

Magnus was rolled onto his front. His hands were gripped and pulled behind his back, then a rag was tied round his mouth. Cord was looped round his wrists and pulled tight, then a knee was placed onto his back, pinning him to the ground.

Matteo crouched down next to him. 'We may have to cut out his tongue,' he said, 'as we don't want him saying too much to the Sanctians in Elestia about what's been happening here. We could say that we were frightened of his Master abilities.'

'Should we be frightened of him?' said a mercenary.

'His powers are feeble,' said Matteo. 'We will be safe when he is tied up in the hold. So, Magnus, would you like to see the great former capital of the Elestian Empire? You will have a great view of it when the Offices of Purgation burn you alive. If only your dear father had listened to my advice about evacuating, but I fear that you will have to pay the price for his intransigence.'

'What if his father is looking for him?'

'The king is lost in a cloud of smoke. He's probably forgotten who his sons are. It's Ragnvald we need to worry about. We'll have to keep Magnus hidden until we are ready to leave tonight. Take him below deck.'

The two mercenaries picked Magnus up and carried him onto the barge. Magnus started to struggle in their grasp, and one of the soldiers punched him in the stomach. He was taken into the darkness of the hold, and set down next to a pile of crates, then his ankles were bound with the same cord that was keeping his wrists together. Magnus writhed and struggled against the gag and the cords, but the mercenaries were old hands at subduing people, and they carried out their task with ease.

'It's no wonder they call him the little runt,' said one.

The other glanced over his shoulder to make sure that Matteo wasn't listening. 'I don't know about this plan, mate,' he said. 'Ragnvald will have our balls if he finds out we've taken his brother.' He stared at Magnus. 'Does Ragnvald know where you are, boy? Will he come looking for you?'

Magnus tried to speak, but nothing came out but a muffled cry.

'Hold your knife to his throat,' said one, 'and I'll loosen his gag.'

'Are you sure about this?' said the other.

'You heard his lordship; the little runt's harmless.'

One of the mercenaries drew a knife, and pressed it to Magnus's neck, and the other moved his hand up to the gag. Magnus tried to clear his thoughts. As ordered, he had been practising his skills, but with little success.

The gag was loosened, and it came away from Magnus's mouth.

'Well?' said one of the mercenaries. 'Will Ragnvald be looking for you? Does he know you're down here? Answer me, or we'll make the journey to Elestia a particularly unpleasant one.'

'He asked me to check these caverns,' said Magnus.

The mercenaries glanced at each other, and Magnus focussed on emptying his mind of thoughts. The roar of the waterfall was helping, and he concentrated on nothing but the sound. He could do it, he told himself. He was a Master.

'Water to salt; water to salt,' he hissed.

The two men choked, their voices cut off as their skin paled. The knife fell to the deck of the hold, as the mercenaries gripped their throats, then they collapsed next to Magnus, their lifeless eyes coated with a film of salt. Magnus tried to roll over, then he felt the knife jabbing against his shoulder. Magnus wriggled over the deck, cutting his arm as he tried to position his wrists by the sharp edge of the blade. He moved his hands closer to the knife but only succeeded in pushing it further away. He tried again, and the blade sliced across the back of his hand. The knife lodged itself against the body of one of the dead mercenaries, and Magnus managed to back into it, the blade cutting through the cords. He gripped the handle in his bloody grasp, and cut the cords by his ankles. Blood was streaming from his hands, but Magnus suppressed the pain as he struggled to his feet. He climbed a step and peered out of the hatch. Lord Matteo was inspecting a few crates that were sitting on the wharf to the right of the barge.

Magnus concentrated on the sound of the waterfall, then he pointed a finger at him. 'Matteo,' he called out.

The Sanctian turned, his eyes widening.

'Bone to wood.'

Matteo screamed, his cry filling the narrow cavern. He staggered, then slipped on the slick surface and fell to the ground. Magnus pulled himself up and out of the hatch. He stepped onto the wharf, the knife in his right hand, as Matteo thrashed around, foam coming from his lips.

'I couldn't have done that right,' said Magnus, as he gazed down at Matteo. 'You should be dead by now.'

Matteo clutched his chest, his face distorted by agony. Magnus wondered if the Sanctian's bones had little flecks of wood running through them. Would that be enough to kill him, or could someone survive it? It was unlikely that he had managed to convert all of the water in the two mercenaries to salt, but whatever he had done had sufficed to end their lives. Matteo stared up at him, terror and pain darkening his eyes.

'Are you suffering?' said Magnus. 'Shall I put you out of your misery?'

Matteo nodded. 'Please,' he gasped.

'No,' said Magnus. 'You were going to hand me over to the Sanctians to be burned alive. You deserve this pain. You brought it on yourself.'

Magnus turned, and walked out of the cavern. He saw the soldiers standing guard by the base of the stairs, and beckoned one over.

The mercenary bounded over the bridge. 'Yes, sir?' he said.

'Get a couple of your colleagues and carry Lord Matteo out of the cavern,' Magnus said. 'We're taking him to my brother.'

Half an hour later, Magnus walked back into the temple. Four mercenaries were following him, each holding onto one of Matteo's limbs. They ascended the stairs, and Magnus led them to Ragnvald's quarters. He knocked on the door and opened it. Ragnvald was sitting by a table next to the senior officers of the mercenaries, and they looked up as Magnus entered.

'I'm busy,' said Ragnvald, then his gaze went to the cuts on his brother's hands. 'What the fuck happened to you?'

Magnus gestured to the soldiers behind him. They entered the room and dropped Matteo onto the floor. The Sanctian was whimpering and gasping in agony, and Ragnvald got to his feet.

'He was trying to flee,' Magnus said. 'He had a barge loaded with silver and supplies, and he thought I would make a good hostage to give to the Sanctians in Elestia.' He raised his hands. 'These wounds are from when I cut the bonds around my wrists.'

Ragnvald stared at him.

'He had two mercenaries helping him,' Magnus went on. 'I killed them both.'

'Everyone out,' said Ragnvald. 'Everyone but Magnus.'

The officers got to their feet, then they left the room with the other soldiers. Ragnvald closed the door, and looked down at Magnus's hands.

'Those will need bandages,' he said. 'Did you really kill two soldiers?'

Magnus nodded.

Ragnvald gazed down at Matteo. 'What did you do to him?'

'I tried to turn his bone to wood, but it couldn't have worked properly.'

Ragnvald smiled. 'You tried bone to wood? Well done, lad; that's a tricky one to master.'

Matteo reached out and clutched Ragnvald's foot.

'Get your hands off me,' Ragnvald spat. He kicked Matteo in the ribs. He turned back to Magnus. 'You did the right thing coming to me about this. Did you leave the barge as it was?'

'Yes. It's in the cavern next to the harbour basin.'

'Good lad. Try bone to silver.'

'What, now?' said Magnus.

'Yes, now. I want to see you hurt this treacherous bastard. I want to see him beg for death.'

'He's already done that.'

'And you denied him any mercy?' said Ragnvald. 'This could be a big day for you, Magnus; you're becoming a man. Go on, try bone to silver.'

Magnus pointed down at Matteo. 'Bone to silver.'

Matteo screamed again, and the two brothers took a step back as the Sanctian thrashed about on the floor. Ragnvald laughed, and Magnus felt a surge of pride, as though he was finally being accepted by his eldest brother. They watched as Matteo's body stilled, his features betraying the excruciating pain he was experiencing.

'That looks sore, Matteo,' said Ragnvald. 'What a terrible shame.'

'Kill me,' the Sanctian gasped.

'Not yet,' said Ragnvald; 'we're just getting started.' He glanced at Magnus. 'Use that knife of yours to cut off one of his fingers. I want to see how much wood and silver's in his bones.' He slapped his brother on the back. 'And then we'll fuck him up good and proper.'

Magnus drew the knife from his belt, and stared at the blade.

'You're not going to back out now, are you?' said Ragnvald. 'Come on, Magnus; I want to see what you're made of. If you do this, I'll never call you a little runt again.'

Magnus nodded, then he crouched down next to Matteo. He was starting to feel sorry for the Sanctian, but his brother was watching. He took hold of one of Matteo's hands, held it flat against the floor, and reached out with the knife.

It took Matteo over an hour to die. Ragnvald knew all kinds of ways to prolong his suffering, and Magnus felt sick long before they had finished. They stared at the broken and mutilated body for a few moments, then Ragnvald gripped his brother's shoulder.

'You're one of us now,' he said. 'I'm proud of you, Magnus.'

Magnus nodded, as he concentrated on not throwing up.

'Not a word of this to Erling or the king,' Ragnvald went on. 'We'll tell them that I killed Lord Matteo; agreed? I don't want anyone knowing that you can kill from a distance. That will be our secret. I might give you a hard time in front of the others; you know – the usual abuse and insults – but don't take it personally. The king's health isn't getting any better and, at some point, we'll have to deal with Erling. You and me are in this together. Say it.'

'We're in this together; you and me.'

'When I'm king, you and I will rule this place. Until then, we'll have to stop our father from fucking it up.'

'Will we keep the mine running?' said Magnus. 'We'll have to, won't we? We need the supplies.'

Ragnvald shook his head. 'You can be almost as stupid as Erling sometimes, lad,' he said. 'What fucking mine? The king and I have been transforming rock into silver all this time. There is no mine, Magnus. When I'm king, you will have to step up and do your share of producing silver. In fact, we might have to move the *silver mine* to another location, if you catch my meaning. There's one thing that Matteo got right – the Sanctians will be back, and in force.' He wiped his hands on his tunic. 'I'd better get some slaves in here to clean up the mess. Good work, today, lad. I'll see you later on; there's something else we need to discuss.'

'What?'

'I'll tell you about it soon, but it concerns our *guests*,' said Ragnvald. 'Our father's indecision has gone on for long enough; it's time we took matters into our own hands.'

Magnus nodded, then he left the chamber and went back out into the temple passageway. He kept his head down as he walked to his own quarters. He thought about visiting his mother, to tell her that the existence of the silver mine was nothing but a hoax designed to hide the fact that Masters ruled Steppen; but he was too ashamed of what he had done to Matteo. His mother would hate him if she found out. Why had he done it? Why had he allowed his brother to cajole him into torturing someone to death? He knew the answer. Above all else, he craved Ragnvald's support and approval. Alone, Magnus wasn't strong enough to survive in a place like Steppen; he needed his brother.

He entered his apartment, ran to the toilet, and threw up.

CHAPTER 24
THE VISITATION

East of Steppen, Great Forest, Jallin, Central Provinces – 17th Day of Quoma 108

Walter led the twenty Westlanders through the dark forest. Despite the heavy bags carried by each, they were moving quickly and silently. The sun was due to rise, but the Big Red Moon had been full that night, and its light had bathed the trees in a crimson glow. The Westlanders had been happy to take part in the raid, believing that King Aloth was watching over them, and Walter wondered if their confidence had contributed to their success. The villas of three of the Whalebone King's old crewmates had been attacked, and the raiding party had emptied them of every item of food, along with anything else of use. They had left the murdered bodies of the crewmates inside their homes, there to be discovered by the mercenaries of Steppen once the sun had arisen.

Walter slowed to a walk as they neared the place in the forest where a Westlander sentry had been posted. Johan caught up with him, a grin splitting his features.

'We had a good night,' he said to Walter. 'Aloth blessed us, and our people will be able to eat today.'

'That's the good news,' said Walter. 'What we stole will only last us one day – that's the bad. Why do you Westlanders eat so much, eh?'

'So we can be big and strong,' said Johan. 'Why are the men of Upper Down so short?'

'We're the same damn size as everyone else; well, not everyone else, obviously. It's the Westlanders who are unusually huge; we're the normal ones.'

'Then thank fuck I'm not normal.'

'You know, in Upper Down, I'm considered to be quite tall.'

Johan laughed.

A Westlander armed with a spear and crossbow stepped out from behind a tree.

'There's the sentry,' said Johan.

'Well spotted,' said Walter. He dug into the bag over his shoulder, and threw the sentry an apple. 'Any sign of intruders?'

'Yes, boss,' said the sentry.

Walter blinked. 'That wasn't the answer I was expecting,' he said. 'Were we attacked? I haven't seen any signs of pursuit, and no scouting activity. I was under the impression that the mercenaries were too scared to venture this far into the forest.'

'We weren't attacked, boss,' said the sentry, 'but we picked up three strangers claiming to have escaped from Steppen. One of them says he's a friend of yours.'

'And where is this... friend of mine?'

The sentry thumbed over his shoulder. 'We took him back to the camp, along with the other two. They got here not long after midnight, when King Aloth was high in the sky.'

'Praise Aloth!' cried another Westlander.

'Anyway,' said Walter, 'as I was saying, there's been no signs of pursuit, so I think we got away from Steppen unseen. All the same, keep your eyes open; you'll be relieved in an hour or so.'

The sentry stepped aside. 'Yes, boss.'

Walter led the raiding party along the path. It ran by a small stream, from where the escaped Westlanders drew their drinking water. Walter had quickly discovered that finding water was easy in the region below the Step. Countless small streams flowed down from the higher ground, and most of them found their way to the Ario River to the south of Steppen. It was food that was the difficulty. There were berries, nuts and some edible fungus, along with birds and a few wild animals, but not nearly enough to support four hundred people. Every day at dawn, foragers would set out. They would spend the entire day gathering whatever they could, with the result that every food source in the vicinity had been stripped clean.

'That time is fast approaching again,' he said to Johan; 'we shall need to move camp soon.'

'Again?' muttered the Westlander. 'If you'd listen to me, I could solve all of our food problems.'

'Then please enlighten me.'

'We attack Steppen and kill all the soldiers, then we eat their food. Simple.'

'We're not attacking in force until we can be certain of success.'

'You are too cautious, Walter. Oh, and I found a jug of brandy for you in the second villa we ransacked. I almost forgot to tell you.'

Johan opened his bag and began rooting around inside it. He took out a ceramic jug and gave it to Walter.

'Thanks,' said Walter. He pulled out the stopper and sniffed the contents. 'Not bad. It actually smells like brandy, unlike the usual shite we find. Good job.'

He took a small swig, as Johan eyed him.

'You love that more than you love us, I think,' said the Westlander.

'I don't love you at all, so that wouldn't be hard.'

'You are a bad liar,' said Johan. 'I know that you love us. You think you are the father of all, and love us as though we were your little children. Do not deny it. I saw you weep when that old lady died of illness three days ago. You tried to hide it, but I stood witness.'

'Every death feels like a failure.'

'Her time had come. She died free and content, and surrounded by friends, because of you. That was the greatest gift you could have given her.'

Walter glanced up at the sky. It was brightening to the east, and the birds were singing and calling to each other from the branches of the trees. He wondered how much work he would have to do before he could find some time to sleep, then he remembered the words of the sentry. Had Princess Abigone escaped from Steppen? If so, then Walter's ostensible reason for being in Jallin would evaporate, and his priority would be to escort his royal sister-in-law to safety. He wasn't sure how he felt about that. Of course, he wanted Abigone to be safe – that was paramount in his mind – but part of him would forever regret not being able to topple the Whalebone King and free the rest of the slaves. He thought of the old woman who had died. She had slipped away after seven days of freedom, as though her will to resist the mercenaries was all that had been sustaining her. The other deaths had been harder to take. Some of the Westlanders had been so badly treated by their captors that they had expired from their injuries, dying in pain while the others had watched helplessly. It made Walter angry, and he was channelling his rage in the only way he knew how – through hard work and the application of his military training. Aside from the years spent drunk, Walter had always loved being a Mountain Ranger, but he had seldom had the opportunity to use his skills to do something good; something that made a difference to the lives of those who were suffering.

They left the banks of the stream and entered a dell at the edge of the camp. Several Westlanders were sleeping under the branches of the trees, though a few were already up, and kettles were being heated over small fires.

'We have food!' cried Johan. 'We stole it from under the noses of the bastards in Steppen, and we all came back alive.'

More Westlanders appeared, and they gathered round the raiding party.

'Distribute the food fairly,' said Walter. 'I'm going to find out if the strangers who arrived are really my friends.'

'I am always fair,' said Johan.

'That's why I trust you to distribute it,' said Walter. He nodded to the raiding party. 'Good work, everyone. I'll see you all later.'

Walter continued through the trees, brushing past people heading towards the raiding party and the food they had brought. The camp was spread out along the northern flank of the stream, and Walter made for its centre, where he, Otto and Dietar were based. Otto was preparing a small fire, and he glanced up as Walter approached. Walter set down his bag next to the sergeant.

'Fresh fruit and vegetables,' he said; 'and some fish.'

'Excellent, sir,' said Otto, wiping his hands and getting to his feet. 'You have visitors.'

'So I heard. Where are they?'

'Lieutenant Dietar is talking to them,' he said. He smiled. 'I think you might be happy to see one of them in particular, sir. In fact, I'm coming along, so I can see your face.'

Otto led Walter through the trees, and they came to a small clearing. Dietar was sitting on the ground, speaking to a teenage boy and a young woman, neither of whom Walter recognised. The third new arrival stood, and Walter stared at him.

'Lothar? What the fuck?'

Lothar grinned. 'I got your message, sir,' he said. 'The *drunken champion*, eh? As subtle as a brick in the face.'

Walter threw his arms around his old friend, then he laughed.

'I was hoping you were with the princess,' he said. 'Where is she? Is she all right?'

Lothar's grin faded. 'She was the last time I saw her, sir. But, she's still in the lair of that bastard and his sons. Well, one fewer son now, thanks to you.' He gestured to the boy and the woman. 'This is Eshia and Marlow. They are from the same place where Princess Abigone went. And this,' he went on, 'is Lord Walter of Upper Down.'

'It's Duke Walter now,' said Dietar.

Lothar shook his head. 'They made him a damn duke?'

'Only because I married Princess Kilbride,' said Walter. 'She couldn't wed a mere *lord*, could she?'

'You got married?' said Lothar.

'We did.'

Lothar smiled. 'Congratulations.'

'And Killie's pregnant.'

'Then what the fuck are you doing down here?'

'I've been summoned to Sanctos.'

'Did you run into Amery, by any chance?'

'In Jalburg. Did you find the missing children?'

'We found them. They're locked up in the same place as Abigone.'

'*Princess* Abigone.'

'Of course,' said Lothar. 'I've been in her company so long I sometimes forget she's royalty. Anyway, we came down from Klef Mordain in a group, and Eshia and Marlow were part of it. The princess asked me to escape, so I could make contact with you.'

Walter frowned. 'If you could escape, then why is she still a prisoner?'

'She... she feels responsible for the safety of the others, especially the younger ones. I tried to persuade her to come with me; for days and days I tried, but she refused.' He glanced at the boy and the young woman. 'I was supposed to break out on my own, but we didn't have time to tell everyone the plan, and these two came with me.'

Walter looked down at them, then he sat on the ground, and Lothar did the same.

'Eshia, was it?' said Walter.

'Yes,' said the woman.

'And Marlow?'

The boy nodded.

'Are you both...?'

'They are,' said Lothar.

'That's supposed to be a secret,' said Eshia.

Lothar smiled. 'This is Duke Walter we're talking to. There's no one I trust more.'

'This camp could use a good Maker,' said Walter. 'Can you summon tools, Eshia?'

'Tools? Metal tools?'

Walter nodded.

'I could do that,' said Eshia. 'I've been practising with wood, but I'm better at metal.'

'She's an expert on summoning metal,' said Marlow. 'I saw her summon an entire suit of armour for Mor Galthide.'

'For who?' said Walter.

'He's Denny's father,' said Marlow, 'and Denny is betrothed to Abigone.'

Walter narrowed his eyes. 'Why don't you start at the beginning? I want to know everything.'

Walter listened as Lothar told him all about Klef Mordain. Eshia and Marlow filled in pieces from their memories of the secret schools, then all three related how they had escaped from the Sanctian annexation of the city.

'Horses?' said Walter. 'They summoned horses?'

Eshia nodded. 'I didn't see it. I was lying injured on the deck of the boat.'

'I saw it,' said Marlow. 'They killed dozens of sailors. It rained blood.'

'Then why don't they do the same to the Whalebone King?' said Walter.

'Because he's a Master,' said Lothar. 'So are two of his sons.'

'The one I killed wasn't a Master.'

'The king had four sons,' said Lothar; 'two Masters, and two who aren't Masters. You killed one of the non-Masters. If it had been Ragnvald you'd met, instead of Einar, the result wouldn't have been the same.' He gestured towards Eshia. 'Ragnvald might be the reason Eshia escaped when I did. The Whalebone King said he wanted brides for his sons, and Ragnvald chose Eshia.'

Walter frowned. 'So, we're up against three Masters? And the Masters want to marry the students from the secret schools? Has the king done anything to harm you?'

'No,' said Lothar. 'They tried to be polite in front of us, but it was an act. The king is a savage, and so are his sons.'

'You don't need to tell me that,' said Walter. 'I've seen what he's been doing to the Westlander slaves.'

'About that,' said Lothar. 'Are you building an army of Westlanders? Do you not remember what happened the last time folk from Upper Down got mixed up with Westlanders?'

'What was I supposed to do? Close my eyes and pretend that I wasn't witnessing what was happening in front of me? We attacked the crane compound a couple of times, then we scaled the cliffs and set ourselves up down here. We've freed four hundred slaves, but it's not enough.'

'Not enough for what?' said Lothar.

'Not enough to build a force capable of seizing Steppen; and not enough to satisfy my conscience.'

'The duke wants to free every slave,' said Dietar.

'My priority remains the safety of Princess Abigone,' said Walter. 'I was trying to calculate how many armed fighters I'd need to storm the temple, but that was before I knew there were three Masters inside.'

'The Sanctians have already tried storming the temple,' said Lothar.

'Sanctians?' said Walter. 'They're here, too? That explains a lot. I was aware that there was another force operating in the area. Perhaps we should join with them.'

'They're dead,' said Lothar. 'They were wiped out. The Masters slaughtered them all.'

Eshia glared at him. 'Not quite all, Lothar.'

'All right. No, not quite all. There was one survivor. A woman.'

'Is the Sanctian army employing women in their ranks these days?' said Walter.

'She's from the Offices of Purgation,' said Marlow. 'Their entire job is to hunt down and kill Masters and Makers.'

'Ah,' said Walter.

'I didn't know that when we saved her,' said Lothar; 'and, now that we have saved her, what else can I do but look after her? I don't have to agree with her politics, but I can hardly let her die.'

'She thinks Eshia and I should be executed,' said Marlow. 'She wants to kill every single Master and Maker; she thinks we're evil.'

Walter shrugged. 'That's Sanctians for you. Well, some of them. I know one who happens to disagree.'

'We know two,' said Marlow. 'Denny and Mor Galthide.'

'Denny's a Sanctian?' said Walter. 'You left that bit out.'

'There's a lot to tell you,' said Lothar.

'I assume this Denny is a Master?'

'Not a very good one,' said Lothar.

'He has potential,' said Eshia. 'If he learns how to control his thoughts, he could develop into a proficient Master.'

'He has other skills,' said Lothar. 'He reminds me of a young officer-type. Capable, resourceful, a good leader, a decent fighter.'

'And he's a prince,' said Eshia.

Lothar smiled. 'And there's that.'

'You're kidding me,' said Walter. 'A prince of...'

'Sanctos,' said Lothar. 'He's Hygilt's cousin.'

Walter sat up, his back straightening. 'Princess Abigone is betrothed to a grandson of the emperor?'

Lothar nodded.

Walter started to laugh. 'I always knew that girl would do well for herself. He's not in the direct line of the throne, is he?'

'No, he's a little way off that,' said Lothar.

'He's twelfth in line,' said Marlow.

'So,' said Walter, 'we only need to dispose of eleven members of the imperial family, and Abigone has a shot at becoming empress?'

Marlow smiled. 'Is that the plan? If so, I'd like to help.'

Walter eyed him. 'Where's that accent from?'

'Subnestia,' said the boy.

'I think I'm due to go there.'

'If you're getting a ship to Sanctos,' Marlow went on, 'then you'll probably be sailing from one of the Subnestian ports. But why are you going to Sanctos? They want to kill your princess.'

'We negotiated a treaty with Sanctos last year,' said Walter. 'Well, Prince Valentino negotiated it with us, and the emperor wants to revise its terms. They would have sent another army had I refused the summons. Think of my trip as a delaying operation. I'm not going to agree to anything that undermines Upper Down, or anything that endangers Masters and Makers. Our new king might be one; after all, his father and grandfather were Masters.'

'For the sake of argument,' said Lothar, 'how would Princess Kilbride have reacted if we had turned up in Upper Down?'

'With a school-load of young Masters and Makers?'

Lothar nodded. 'What would she have done?'

Walter sat back, his shoulders leaning against the trunk of a tree. 'I'm not sure. The empire would have had a hairy fit, but Upper Down is an independent realm. If I had to guess, I would say that we would have set up a new school somewhere in the mountains. Killie would want deniability, but she would also see the benefits of keeping a dozen Masters and Makers inside the kingdom. Denny would be a problem, though, if the empire found out that he was a Master. Do they already know?'

'Good question,' said Lothar. 'We're not certain. Princess Abigone and Denny assassinated the Sanctian ambassador in Klef Mordain; so they might have put two and two together.'

'Amery told me that you'd disagreed about your next destination,' said Walter. 'You wanted to return to Upper Down, right? And others wanted to go to... what was it again?'

'Geathan,' said Eshia. 'Mor Galthide wants us to go to Geathan, so Denny can reclaim his ancestral throne.'

Walter rolled his eyes. 'Fucksake.'

'Exactly,' said Lothar. 'It's naught but a stupid dream. Even Denny was reluctant. He has no interest in Geathan.'

A huge Westlander appeared through the trees.

'Boss,' he said, 'a fight's broken out over the food supplies.'

Walter got to his feet. 'Find me ten fighters,' he said to the Westlander. 'We're going in.'

Lothar stood. 'I'll tag along,' he said. 'I like the idea of Westlanders kicking the shit out of each other.'

Walter led Lothar through the camp, following the Westlander who had told them about the fight. They picked up a dozen other Westlanders on the way, all men and women that Walter had grown to trust, and they reached a part of the forest where supplies were strewn over the ground. Eight Westlanders were fighting over a few crates, stealing them from a group of older escapees, who were protesting loudly. Walter sent his reinforcements in, and the dozen men and women he had gathered charged the others, breaking up the fight with wooden clubs.

'Does this happen often?' said Lothar, as they watched from the sidelines.

'Around once a day,' said Walter. 'Trying to feed four hundred people has become an obsession of mine. It's a nightmare; I'm not going to lie to you. We raid, we forage; but it's never enough to feel secure.'

Lothar glanced at the Westlanders with contempt. 'They're savages.'

Walter said nothing. They watched as the crates were recovered and handed back to the older group. The assailants were dispersed, and a small crowd began to comb the ground for fallen morsels of food.

'Come with me, Lothar,' Walter said; 'I want to show you something.'

He led his fellow Mountain Ranger through the trees to another part of the camp, which had a few Westlanders guarding it. They passed the sentries and came into a large clearing. Lothar's expression changed as he gazed around. The clearing was full of Westlander children and young women, most of whom looked sick or injured. Some were staring into space, while others glanced up at the arrival of the two men with fear in their eyes. A few older women were also there, tending to the wounded, and trying to comfort those who had fallen into despair.

'These children are not savages,' Walter said, 'but savages did this to them.'

Lothar remained silent.

'What's the point of becoming a soldier,' Walter said, 'if we can't protect the weak from people who want to hurt them? I know I should try to stay dispassionate, but I look at these children, and I want to rip the Whalebone King's fucking head off.'

'Then let's do it,' said Lothar. 'Let's kill the bastard, and his sons.'

'And the mercenaries,' said Walter. 'All of them.'

Lothar accompanied Walter for the rest of the day, as he made his rounds throughout the camp. Lothar observed the interactions in silence, watching as Walter sorted out a dozen petty squabbles and organised the running of the makeshift settlement. They met with Otto, Dietar and a few of the self-appointed leaders of the Westlanders about the imminent transfer of the camp to a new location, and oversaw the digging of a new toilet ditch downstream of where they collected their drinking water.

When the sun began to set, Walter was tired. Another night and day of toil had resulted in nothing more than staving off the collapse of the camp; and he knew he would have to do it all over again. They returned to the little clearing where Walter slept when he wasn't out raiding, and found Eshia and Marlow still there, along with two Westlanders.

'This is Duggan and Aisly,' Walter said to Lothar, as they sat on the ground. 'We met these two a few miles up the Antiago. They had escaped, and we persuaded them to help us.'

'For revenge,' said Aisly.

'Have you found any?' said Lothar.

Aisly nodded. 'Some. Not enough. I wish I had seen Einar die. I will be satisfied when the rest of the Westlanders are freed, and when every one of our enemies is lying dead on the ground.'

Lothar narrowed his eyes. 'And is Walter the man to do this?'

'Yes,' said Duggan. 'He hasn't let us down. He has done exactly what he said he would do.'

'And you're all happy to follow him?'

'Not all,' said Duggan. 'There are a few who refuse to recognise his authority, but most of us would follow Walter anywhere.'

'He's a good man,' said Aisly.

'He is,' said Lothar. 'Well, he's a better man than I am.'

'I wouldn't say that,' said Walter, as he rummaged around in a sack.

'No?' said Lothar. 'My sole priority is to protect Princess Abigone. If that meant leaving the enslaved Westlanders where they are, then so be it. I hate the Whalebone King, but this is not our problem. Princess Abigone being held by that bastard? – that's our problem. I'm sorry, but that's how it is.'

'You feel no sympathy for the slaves?' said Aisly.

'I feel as much sympathy for them as I felt for everyone the Westlanders enslaved while they were based in Upper Down. Are you aware of how your people acted when they were terrorising my homeland? They had no qualms about murdering farmers and taking captives when they were raiding the Central Provinces.'

Duggan and Aisly glared at him.

'But,' Lothar went on, 'Walter is my commanding officer, and I will obey whatever commands he gives me.'

Walter withdrew a jar of brandy from the sack. 'My first order is to drink some of this,' he said, passing it to Lothar.

Lothar pulled out the cork and took a swig. 'Not bad.'

'My next order is to appoint you as my deputy,' Walter said. 'You can join a raiding party tomorrow night, and then you can start leading them. You can also take some duties from Otto and Dietar; I might have been overworking them in recent days.'

Lothar passed him the jug. 'Do I have permission to visit the woman I am caring for, sir? I've hidden her to the east of Steppen.'

'Why don't you bring her here?' said Walter.

'No,' said Eshia. 'Did you forget the part about her wanting to kill me and Marlow?'

'Who is she,' said Duggan, 'and why would she want to kill you?'

Eshia raised her hand. A branch crackled above them, and a set of four small wooden brandy cups appeared on the grass in front of her. The two Westlanders jumped in surprise, their eyes wide.

'That's why,' she said. 'The woman Lothar is helping is a Sanctian fanatic. She believes that I am evil, because I am a Maker.'

Walter picked up one of the cups. It was engraved on the outside, with carvings of vines.

'Can you make spear heads?' he said.

'Of course,' Eshia said; 'if there is any spare metal to use as a source.'

Walter glanced at Marlow. 'We're a little short of metal,' he said. 'Can you convert wood or rock to iron?'

'I can try,' said Marlow. 'I have done it before, but only once or twice.'

'If there's metal,' said Eshia, 'then I could summon a lot more than just spear heads. I would be very useful to you, Walter; far more useful than a fanatic with a broken leg to match her broken mind. If she comes here, I'm leaving, and I'm taking Marlow with me.'

Walter glanced at Lothar. 'Why did you have to save a religious fanatic?'

'Why do you feel you have to save the Westlanders, sir?' said Lothar. 'Why does Abigone feel responsible for the young students from the schools? All three of us have become... distracted from our primary duty; but I will not abandon Saffie.'

'How often do you need to visit her?'

'Once a day. I was there yesterday evening, sir. She has enough food and water to last until tomorrow morning. I... I think there is hope for her. Despite her beliefs, she isn't a cruel or evil person. She's mistaken, yes, very mistaken, but is that her fault? Look at the way the Sanctians are brought up.'

'Hygilt wasn't a fanatic,' said Walter, 'neither is Sebastian. Is Denny?'

'Denny is different, sir; he's a Master. Who knows what he believed before he discovered that about himself?'

'Move her closer to the camp,' said Walter. 'Shorten the distance and travel time to reach her, and we can work out a compromise that doesn't involve Eshia and Marlow having to come in contact with her.'

A faint smile touched Lothar's face. 'Thank you, sir.'

Walter poured some brandy into one of the summoned cups. 'These are quite beautiful, Eshia.'

'Are you flattering me because you're allowing Lothar to care for a woman who wants to kill me?' she said.

'Am I that transparent?' he said. 'Your skills would be a great help to us, and I don't want you to leave; but, I also don't want to order Lothar to abandon an injured woman to die alone in the forest, no matter who she is or what she might have done.'

'She has never killed a Master or a Maker,' said Lothar.

'I suspect that might be through lack of opportunity,' said Walter.

Lothar shrugged. 'Perhaps.'

'Now for the most important question,' Walter said, his eyes roving over Lothar, Eshia and Marlow. 'Is Princess Abigone in imminent danger? Do we need to strike immediately, or do we have a little more time to build up our strength?'

'The next convoy of barges is due to arrive in around ten days or so, sir' said Lothar. 'That's the critical point. The Whalebone King knows that some of the princess's group are Masters and Makers, but he isn't sure who or how many. That's made them hesitant to act. Of course, I could be wrong.'

'I'm looking for a best guess,' said Walter. 'Ideally, we have a few more days to train our fighters, fashion weapons, and build up our supplies. Then we hit Steppen again. If we can open the fence around the Westlanders in a few separate locations, the mercenaries will be too busy to stop us reaching the temple.'

'But how do we get inside, sir? The Sanctians were slaughtered when they tried to reach the Whalebone King.'

'I haven't worked that part out, yet,' said Walter. 'Do we have a few days?'

Lothar lowered his gaze. 'May the spirits forgive me if I'm wrong, but yes; I think so.'

'Then I'm calling it,' said Walter. 'Five days from now – we strike. We'll hit them with everything we've got, and see how far we get. That will give us time to prepare, and it'll give me time to think about how we can get close enough to the king and his sons to kill them.'

'But we are going to kill them?' said Aisly.

Walter raised his cup. 'Let's drink to it.'

CHAPTER 25
KEPT ASIDE

Steppen, Great Forest, Jallin, Central Provinces – 19th Day of Quoma 108

Abigone stared out of the window at the endless sweep of forest.

'Where is he?' she said. 'It's been nine days.'

'I wish I knew the answer,' said Denny. 'Lothar seems trustworthy, so I can't believe that he has simply fled.'

'He would never do that,' said Abigone. 'He's a Mountain Ranger.'

'I wonder if he has found Walter,' said Denny, 'if it was actually Walter who sent you that cryptic message.'

'It must be him. Walter was the King's Champion, and he had a terrible reputation for always drinking too much. Everyone in Upper Down knew about it.'

'Forgive me, but he doesn't exactly sound reliable.'

'He's reliable, when he needs to be. It's funny – I used to loathe him. I thought he was utterly useless; a disgrace to the royal family. But dig a little beneath the surface, and there's no one I'd rather have on my side in a crisis.' She smiled at Denny. 'And, of course, my sister adores him. They squabbled for years, but they were completely in love with each other. With any luck, my sister has cured him of his drunkenness.'

'I'm not sure it's that easy,' said Denny.

'You haven't met my sister.'

'The famous Princess Kilbride? Everyone who's talked to me about her seems to think that she's a master of cunning.'

'She's clever,' said Abigone; 'but she's not *that* clever. All the same, if anyone can sober up Walter, it's her.'

'What will he do with four hundred slaves?' said Denny. 'Or should I say – four hundred angry and free Westlanders? They could probably match the mercenaries, but that won't get them into the temple.'

'Lothar will have told him that the king and two of his sons are Masters,' said Abigone. 'Perhaps that explains the delay.'

'Eshia is the key,' said Denny. 'She could bring down the temple from the outside.'

Abigone raised an eyebrow. 'Not while we're in it, I hope. I could destroy the temple, but it wouldn't bring us any closer to freedom.' She lowered her voice. 'There's only one thing we can realistically do. We wait for the king, Ragnvald and Magnus to approach us, then we summon horses. We have to kill them at the same time, before they can turn our blood into salt.'

'That's exactly what they have been avoiding,' said Denny. 'Even Magnus doesn't visit us any more.'

'Raewyn caught him staring up at her from the road by the side of the temple a few days ago.'

'Did she?'

'Perhaps he's been ordered to stay away. You know, if it was just you and me who had been captured, we would have escaped a long time ago. All we would need to do is repeat what we did in the Sanctian embassy. But how can we do that, and ensure that the others are also safe? I hate feeling responsible for Reath, Nyli and the rest, but I can't help it.'

Denny glanced in the other direction, his gaze taking in everyone sitting around the large room.

'I think we could do it,' he said. 'The problem isn't our abilities; it's the opposition of Fyenna and my father to any plan that involves us trying to escape. We're going to look silly if the Whalebone King lets us leave on the barges.'

'Do you care about that?'

'No.'

'Do you believe that he will let us go peacefully?'

'Also no.'

'Have you been practising your own abilities? Do you think you could kill from a distance?'

'Possibly. Out of all the Masters here, only Constans has been able to use his skills to kill anyone. I can try, and I will try, but do you remember what happened in the embassy? I turned their food salty.'

'I remember. Are you able to clear your mind?'

Denny frowned. 'Not very well. It's been a struggle ever since we left Klef Mordain. I don't think my mind is suited to being a Master; it's always full of thoughts. It's never quiet when I want it to be. I think I need somewhere peaceful to practise, but I won't find that here.'

Abigone's cheeks flushed a little. 'You used to... think about me. Does that not work any more?'

'It's still the best way to calm my thoughts,' he said, 'but I can't seem to do it in an emergency. The training I received on Sanctos takes over at times like that, but my Master skills seem untameable.' He eyed her. 'Maybe if we got the opportunity for some privacy, and we could be intimate together, that might work.'

She laughed. 'Any excuse to get me into bed.'

'I'm not going to apologise for the way I feel about you,' he said. 'I love you, and I want us to be together.'

'I want that, too,' she said.

Reath walked over to the window.

'Will you two stop looking at each other like that?' she said. 'It's making me feel queasy.'

'I don't recall asking you to look in our direction,' said Abigone.

'Are you missing Marlow?' said Denny.

'What – that stupid oaf?' said Reath. 'A bit. Do you think he's all right?'

'Lothar will look after him,' said Abigone.

'I wish I'd run off, too,' said Reath, 'but it was all over before I knew what was happening. I was too busy laughing at Denny falling into the pool.' She narrowed her eyes. 'You knew, didn't you? You knew what Lothar was going to do.'

'I don't know what you're talking about,' said Denny. 'I can't help being clumsy.'

'Clumsy? You are many things, Denny, but you aren't clumsy.'

'Don't spread this little rumour around,' whispered Abigone. 'Mor Galthide is already suspicious.'

Reath shrugged. 'What does that old bastard know? Oops. Sorry, Denny.'

They turned as a key sounded in the lock. The door to their large apartment opened, and Ragnvald walked in, followed by Magnus, who was keeping his gaze lowered.

'Good morning,' Ragnvald called out. 'My little brother and I thought we would come and see how you were all doing.'

'We are doing well,' said Fyenna, who was sitting on a low couch. 'How many days is it now?'

'Until the barges arrive?' said Ragnvald. 'They are never exactly on time, but I would estimate that you have another five or six days, perhaps? I also came to tell you that we have seen no sign of the three runaways.'

The two brothers moved into the centre of the room. Ragnvald was wearing a cheerful but false expression, while Magnus's gaze was darting about, as though he was checking the positions of the others in the room.

'If I was a betting man,' Ragnvald went on, 'then one of the following two things has happened to Eshia and her companions – they have either fled south, towards Yearl, or they are slowly starving to death in the forest. Of course, both of those might be true at the same time, eh? I hope their fate serves as a warning to the rest of you. The only safe place is here, inside the temple.'

Mor Galthide walked in, and both brothers eyed him.

'Is there news regarding the brigands befouling the area?' Mor Galthide said.

'They have continued to attack isolated targets in the forest,' Ragnvald said, 'but they haven't returned to Steppen.'

'What manner of targets?' said Mor Galthide.

'The villas of the king's old crewmates,' said Ragnvald. 'Some of them are quite far from Steppen, and they are vulnerable.'

'The king should order his fellows to retreat into Steppen in that case,' said the Geathan prince. 'Cut off the brigands' supply of food and weapons, and then the villains will be forced to launch an attack before they are ready.'

'Wise advice,' said Ragnvald. He glanced at his brother, and gave him a slight nod. Magnus looked frightened, but he returned the gesture. Abigone frowned, and readied her powers. There was no one standing between her and the two sons of the king, and she prepared to summon horses.

The front door burst open again, and the Whalebone King hurried into the room.

'Stop,' he shouted at Ragnvald and Magnus.

The two brothers stared at him.

The king rushed over to where Nyli, Salus and Ignatius were sitting, and crouched down next to them, placing their bodies between him and the others in the room.

'You two are hopeless,' the king said to his sons. 'You haven't the slightest idea how to act in these circumstances. Come over here at once.'

Ragnvald and Magnus frowned, then they walked over to where the king was crouching next to the children.

The king smiled. 'Now we can proceed.'

'Excuse me,' said Fyenna; 'but what is happening?'

The king raised a finger at her. 'Water to salt.'

Fyenna toppled off the couch, her hands grasping her throat as salt spilled from her eyes and mouth. She tried to raise her head, then she lay still on the wooden floor. Stanza screamed.

The king pointed at Mor Galthide. 'Bone to wood.'

Pandemonium erupted as Mor Galthide fell onto the floor, convulsing. Stanza raced over to Fyenna's body, crouched by it, and burst into tears. Denny ran to his father, who was still alive. The Geathan prince could no longer move, and his face was contorted with agony.

'Father,' said Denny, taking his hand.

Mor Galthide opened his mouth, then he gasped out his last breath.

Abigone kept her hands by her side. The king and his sons were behind three of the youngest students, and there was no way to harm them without also harming the others.

'Do you see, my stupid sons?' said the king. 'No Makers can touch us, not if we keep the children between us and them. Any flesh-summoning would tear their friends to pieces. Grab a child each.'

The king reached out and pulled Nyli towards him as he stood. Ragnvald did the same with Salus, and Magnus took hold of Ignatius.

Abigone glanced at Raewyn, whose right hand was raised.

'What do we do?' cried Raewyn.

The king laughed.

'There is nothing you can do,' said Ragnvald. 'It's over.' He raised his own hand.

The king wagged a finger in his eldest son's face. 'Don't be ridiculous, Ragnvald. We have eliminated the only two among them who were any threat to us. We shall be keeping the rest.'

Ragnvald gestured towards Raewyn. 'She's a Maker, boss; she has to be. Look at the way she lifted her hand.'

'We will find out the truth in due course,' said the king. 'I have a plan, Ragnvald, a far better plan than the one devised by you and Magnus.'

'And who told you where we were?' Ragnvald went on, his eyes filled with rage. He turned to Magnus. 'Was it you?'

The king shook his head. 'Magnus, to my great disappointment, said nothing about your foolish little plan to kill everyone in this room, Ragnvald.'

'You were going to kill us all?' cried Stanza.

'They were,' said the king. 'Fortunately for you, I am more merciful.' He turned to the door. 'Erling, bring the soldiers in.' He faced the others again. 'Do I need to warn you that Nyli will die if any of my soldiers are harmed? Behave yourselves, and everyone in this room will remain alive.'

'Who told you?' shouted Ragnvald. 'Answer me.'

The king waved him away. 'Calm yourself, boy. It was one of your mercenaries who informed me; it's as simple as that. You and your brother weren't as discreet as you should have been, and the soldiers owe their loyalty to me, not to you. Praise all that is holy that I got here in time. If I hadn't, then you and Magnus would be little more than heaps of bones and flesh by now.'

Erling entered the room, leading over twenty soldiers with him. The mercenaries took up positions around the chamber, their loaded bows pointing at the guests. Abigone edged over to Denny, who was still crouching next to his slain father.

'I don't understand,' said Ragnvald.

'There is little you do understand,' said the king.

'If you think there are Makers hiding among them, then we have to kill them all.'

'Nonsense. We shall isolate them into groups, and exercise great caution. Erling – take hold of Reath.'

Erling walked forwards and grabbed hold of Reath's arm.

'Get your sweaty hands off me,' the girl cried, as she was hauled up from the couch.

'From now on,' the king said, 'each of us will keep our own hostage close at all times. I shall hold on to Nyli, Ragnvald shall take Salus, Magnus will have Ignatius, and Erling will have the joy of looking after Reath. This way, we shall be doubly protected – no Maker will be able to summon flesh without also killing their friend, and we shall be able to use them to guarantee the good behaviour of the others.'

Ragnvald frowned. 'I'm guessing you have stopped your use of the pipe, boss.'

'Ten days of befuddlement and grief was enough,' said the king.

'Right; let us ask the guests for honesty and see what they say. Who among you is a Master or a Maker? We know about the four youngest, but what about the rest of you?'

'None of us possess those abilities,' said Abigone. She gestured at the body of Fyenna. 'She was a Maker. She was the teacher of the four youngest. We fled Klef Mordain in their company before we knew that she was leading four young Master and Makers.'

The king frowned.

'She's lying,' said Ragnvald.

'She isn't lying,' said Denny, glancing up from the body of Mor Galthide. 'You killed my father for nothing; he wasn't a Master.'

'Then why did Raewyn raise her hand?' said Ragnvald.

'I... I was frightened,' said Raewyn. 'I'm still frightened. Please let us go. We haven't done anything to harm you.'

'We are not going to hurt or kill anyone else,' said the king. 'The old Maker and the old warrior were enough.'

'This is madness,' said Ragnvald. 'Your desire for these girls has overwhelmed your common sense. We can't let them go.'

The king smiled. 'Who said anything about letting them go?' He sat down on the couch, keeping Nyli held close to him. 'Let me make one thing perfectly clear. No one will be leaving Steppen. Now, who among you is the oldest?' His eyes settled on Annalise, who was sitting on a chair, her features frozen with terror. 'It's you, obviously,' the king went on. 'You shall be moved to the women's quarters as a slave, I think. You look as though you can cook and clean. Yes, you will do well there.'

'I am not a slave!' cried Annalise. 'I am a free citizen of Upper Down.'

'Be quiet, or I shall allow Ragnvald to kill you,' said the king. 'You are all now my slaves. I have the power to alter your status, because I am the king of Steppen. I own you; you are my possessions. Work hard, and be obedient, and you will survive. Who is the next eldest?'

'Me,' said Denny.

'You seem like a fit and strong lad; you will be going to the slave encampment,' said the king. 'Next?'

'I am the next oldest,' said Abigone; 'but I tell you this – you are no *king*; you are a fraud and a liar, a host who abuses his guests. I, too, hail from Upper Down, and my realm will seek justice for this crime.'

The king laughed. 'You shall be kept aside, young lady,' he said. 'Next?'

'Wait; what does that mean?' said Abigone.

'You will see. Next?'

Constans raised his gaze. 'Me.'

'Slave encampment,' said the king.

Constans clenched his fists. 'How dare you? My father will kill you for this! He will...'

Ragnvald raised a finger. 'Bone to silver.'

Constans screamed, then his body seemed to pull in on itself, and he collapsed onto the floor, his dead eyes staring at the ceiling.

Abigone's left hand twitched, but she did nothing, her mind torn. If she struck, she might be able to kill the king and Ragnvald, but she would also kill Nyli and Salus, and then the soldiers would loose.

The king turned to stare at Ragnvald. 'Was that necessary?'

'He was raising his hands, boss,' said Ragnvald. 'I was protecting you.'

The king rolled his eyes. 'I do not require your protection,' he said. 'No more killing; is that understood?'

Ragnvald simmered in fury, but said nothing.

'Where were we?' said the king, his gaze going back to the corpse of Constans on the floor. 'Ah, yes. Next oldest?'

'Me,' said Raewyn.

The king leered at her. 'Kept aside. Next?'

Aplin raised a hand.

'Slave encampment. Next?'

'Leave us alone,' sobbed Stanza.

'Kept aside,' said the king. 'Is that everyone? Count them for me, Erling, in case I got confused.'

Erling stared at everyone in the room. 'That's them all, boss,' he said. 'One for the women's quarters, two for the shanty town, three kept aside, and we keep the four youngest with us.'

'We are making a terrible mistake,' said Ragnvald.

'So you say,' said the king. 'What do my other sons think? Erling?'

'We keep them alive, boss,' said Erling. 'I don't believe any of them are Masters or Makers, apart from the four little ones.'

The king nodded. 'Magnus?'

The youngest of the king's sons raised his glance, and Abigone could see the fear and bewilderment in his eyes.

'I... I, uh...' he stammered.

'Out with it, boy,' said the king. 'It's only a fucking opinion. I assume you have one?'

'Ragnvald is right in some ways,' Magnus said. 'We don't know if any are Masters or Makers, so maybe we should be careful.'

'We are being careful,' said the king. 'Do you believe that we should execute them all now?'

Magnus's eyes went back to the floor. 'I don't know.'

'How could you, Magnus?' said Raewyn. 'I thought you were our friend.'

'Lothar was right about him,' said Abigone. 'He does whatever he's told.'

'As any good son should, young lady,' said the king. 'Magnus, escort the old woman to her new quarters, but do not linger there. And remember to take Ignatius with you. Where you go, he goes.'

'Yes, sir,' said Magnus. He gestured to Annalise, who glanced at Abigone.

'Do as they say,' said Abigone. 'This is not the end, Annalise. Trust me.'

The king frowned at Abigone, then he turned back to Magnus. 'Get on with it.'

Annalise got to her feet. Magnus gestured towards the front door of the apartment, and Annalise walked towards it. Magnus gripped on to Ignatius's arm, and they went out after her.

'I now have a task for you, Ragnvald,' said the king. 'Take the two lads down to the slave settlement.'

Denny got to his feet, and took Abigone's hand.

'We have no choice but to obey,' she said.

'I know, but this is too much to take. My father... I won't lose you, too.'

'Escape,' she whispered in his ear. 'Escape, and find Walter.'

Ragnvald grabbed Denny's arm and pulled him back from Abigone. Denny pushed his hand away and the two men faced each other.

'I am not afraid of you,' Denny said, keeping his hands by his side. 'You're a coward. Fight me. No Master powers, just me and you; or are you too scared?'

Ragnvald laughed. 'I would eat you for breakfast, you little prick.'

'Then prove it,' said Denny. 'Come on.'

'Ignore him,' said the king. 'Take him and the other boy to the shanty town and throw them inside.'

Two soldiers assisted Ragnvald, and they escorted Denny and Aplin from the room. Ragnvald went after them, pulling Salus along.

'Help!' cried Salus. 'Please help me!'

Abigone lowered her gaze, and Salus was dragged out of the apartment.

The king smiled. 'Who does that leave?' Ah yes – the *kept aside* – Abigone, Raewyn and Stanza. This apartment is now yours, but it comes with a new set of rules. And need I remind you that there shall be penalties for breaking these rules? I can withhold food and water. I also hold the power of life and death over my slaves, and any offence committed by you will mean the slow execution of one of the others. The rules are simple – you shall not leave the apartment; you shall not attempt to contact any of the other slaves, and you shall do exactly as I command. One more rule – if any of you exhibit even the tiniest amount of Maker powers, your deaths will swiftly follow. Do you understand?'

'We do,' said Abigone.

The king gestured to a few soldiers. 'Get the three dead bodies out of here. Dump them in the river.'

Soldiers moved forward, and picked up the bodies of Fyenna, Mor Galthide and Constans. Abigone said nothing as she watched them being carried from the room, her mind concentrating on survival.

The king got to his feet, gripping on to Nyli's arm. The girl was sobbing, and she gazed at Abigone, her eyes pleading.

'I will kill you if you hurt my sister,' Reath shouted.

Erling slapped Reath across the face. 'Shut your mouth,' he said.

'Let us depart, Erling,' the king said. 'I recommend starving Reath for a few days. Hunger usually has a fine effect on a slave's behaviour.' He turned to the three who were being left in the apartment. 'Ponder your new circumstances, girls. The sooner you accept them, the better it will be for you.'

The soldiers surrounded Erling and the king, and they backed out of the chamber. The door was closed and locked, and the apartment fell into silence.

Raewyn sat down, her head in her hands, and Stanza started to cry.

'We did nothing,' said Raewyn. 'Why didn't we fight back?'

'We would be dead if we had fought back,' said Abigone.

'We're as good as dead,' cried Stanza.

'And Magnus betrayed us,' said Raewyn. 'I thought he...'

'You thought he liked you?' said Abigone.

'Was I wrong to think that?' she said. 'You all saw the way he looked at me. I thought he was a sweet boy, but he's just as bad as the others.'

'He didn't kill anyone,' said Stanza.

'Maybe he can't,' said Raewyn.

'Ragnvald was right,' said Abigone. 'They should have killed us. The king has made a mistake.'

'What will we do without Lady Fyenna?' sobbed Stanza. 'All of our teachers are dead, and even Eshia ran away. What can we do on our own? They will kill the others if we disobey the king.'

'It's time to tell you something,' Abigone said. 'I know who is leading the attacks on Steppen – the attacks that freed four hundred slaves; the attacks that killed Einar.'

Raewyn glanced up at her. 'The *drunken champion*? You know him?'

'He is a soldier from Upper Down,' she said; 'a very good soldier. I sent Lothar away to make contact with him.'

Stanza stared at her. 'You sent Lothar away?'

'We couldn't all escape, so I did the next best thing. My friend will now be aware of our situation, if Lothar managed to find him in the forest. He will come for us.'

'Lothar will have told him what happened to the Sanctians when they attacked the temple,' said Raewyn. 'Did you see how good the king and Ragnvald are? They are both experienced Masters, who can kill on command.'

'You and I can also kill on command,' said Abigone.

'But the king knows what Makers can do. You saw the way he ran over to Nyli and the others when he first came in. He knows we can't summon horses without killing others who get in the way.'

'But he doesn't think we're Makers,' said Stanza.

'I'm not so sure about that,' said Abigone. 'Regardless, he intends to treat us as though we might be Makers.'

'Is your plan that we sit here and wait for your friend to arrive?' said Raewyn.

'No,' said Abigone. 'You were right before – the temple is almost impossible to attack when it has two Masters defending it. We are going to have to escape on our own. We need to make weapons.'

'And do what with them?' said Raewyn. 'I don't know how to fight. None of us do.'

'What about the rules?' said Stanza. 'The king might cut off our water if we summon weapons. Or he might kill Denny or one of the others.'

'Forget the weapons,' said Abigone. 'We could bring the temple down and bury the king in a thousand tons of rubble.'

'But then we would kill Reath and the other young ones,' said Stanza.

Abigone's eyes narrowed. 'I'm not giving up. The only mistake the king has made is leaving us alive. We have to use that, and soon. The barges will be here in a few days, and I don't intend to be stuck in this apartment when they get here.'

'But Denny...'

'Denny and Aplin are safer than we are,' said Abigone. 'When my friend next attacks, he might target the shanty town again. Denny will know what to do if that happens.'

Raewyn stared at the patch of floor where Constans had been killed. 'Abigone is right, Stanza. If we stay here, then.... I don't want to think about what might happen to us. We have to escape.'

'Why has the king kept us aside?' Stanza said.

'There are three of us,' said Abigone, 'and the king has three surviving sons.'

Stanza shuddered. 'All right. We escape; but how?'

'We'll find a way,' said Abigone, 'or die in the attempt. I will not be a bride of Steppen.'

CHAPTER 26
THE RAIN

South-East of Steppen, Great Forest, Jallin, Central Provinces – 19th Day of Quoma 108

The rain was pouring down from the overcast sky. The sun had yet to set, but Saffie couldn't see it through the dark clouds. She pulled a blanket over her shoulders to keep out the chill. She was dry under the shelter that Lothar had built for her, but it was starting to get cold. Her stomach rumbled. The man from Upper Down had left her plenty of fresh water, but she had run out of food earlier that day. She could put up with no food for a while, but she wasn't looking forward to the darkness that would descend upon the forest once night fell.

She shifted her weight a little. Her left leg was sorer than usual, and she wondered if the dampness caused by the incessant rain that day was making it worse. Twelve days had passed since the battle for the temple, and her leg was beginning to heal. Lothar had said that he would make her a crutch. He had then joked that he would ask Eshia to summon one for him, to save him the time it would take to construct it, but Saffie hadn't found the remark funny. She glanced to the north. The four hundred freed Westlanders were based less than a mile from Saffie's new hiding place in the forest. Eshia and Marlow were living there, and the thought made Saffie feel slightly ill. Why couldn't Lothar see that they were evil? Lothar didn't seem like a stupid man. He didn't know much about politics, art or literature, but he was highly competent at surviving in the wild, and that was the quality she most needed from him. Without him, she would be dead. She gazed up, hearing the rain pattering off the roof of the shelter. It had taken Lothar almost an entire day to build it, and she was impressed at how no rain was able to penetrate the thick mat of woven branches. Saffie had watched him work. He wasn't what she would have called conventionally handsome, and if she had seen him in one of the palaces of Sanctos, then she might not have given him a second glance. And yet, within the darkness of the forest, she had been unable to take her eyes off him. It was foolish, and she knew it. She was drawn to him because he had saved her life, because she was temporarily dependent upon his kindness for her survival. There was nothing more to it than that.

The darkness around her closed in, and she shivered despite the blanket over her shoulders. She hated the dark. No, that wasn't right. She had never been scared of the dark before, but she felt isolated and vulnerable within the depths of the forest, and the nights were far worse than the days, when she could at least make out her surroundings. When it was dark, every noise around her was a potential threat, and she had nothing but her bare hands with which to defend herself. Were there wolves in the forest? Snakes? Or worse, were mercenaries out scouting? Saffie's greatest fear was that Eshia would decide to hunt her down and kill her. She could summon the giant spider of Saffie's nightmares to eat her. She thought back to the long series of dreams she had been experiencing. For some reason, they had stopped after the attack on the temple, and she hadn't dreamt about being a Maker for twelve days. She wondered why. There was a school of thought among some of the priests and priestesses of Sanctos that all dreams were inspired by the spirits. Others thought such claims to be nonsense and borderline heresy, but Saffie wasn't sure. Why would the spirits make her dream about being a Maker, and why did she always end up killing members of her family in those dreams? The spirits wouldn't play tricks on her; they were far above that level of petty behaviour, and that led her to think that perhaps the dreams had a more natural cause. It was her mind that was faulty, not the spirits.

'Blessed spirits,' she whispered, 'please let Lothar come soon, before it gets too dark. And thank you for another day of life. I promise I will try to do better. Help me show Lothar the correct path; help me to open his eyes to the truth.'

She closed her eyes and listened, but she could hear nothing but the rain. She opened her eyes again, and saw Lothar walking through the forest towards the shelter. Saffie smiled. How could anyone doubt the existence of the spirits when the evidence of their good works was all around? She watched Lothar get closer. He was walking as though it wasn't raining, his head up as his face streamed with water. He ducked low to enter the shelter, then he stood back for a few moments, his hair and clothes dripping rainwater over the soft ground.

'It's wild out there tonight,' he said, dropping a large bag onto the grass. 'How's the leg?'

'It's a bit sore today,' she said.

He nodded. 'That'll be the weather.'

'That's what I thought.'

'Are you hungry, or is that the stupidest question you've ever heard in your life?'

'It's up there,' she said.

He sat down with his back to the shelter's small entrance, and opened the bag. He threw her an apple, and she caught it.

'Eat that while I prepare dinner,' he said. 'Walter's camp had a good selection of food brought in last night, some of which was stolen by myself in the raid. We have some fish, and plenty of vegetables, so I'll make a small fire and start warming a pot of water.'

'Are you going to cook for me?' she said.

'I thought I'd give it a try. It's getting colder, and you could do with some warm food inside you.'

'You were on last night's raid, were you?' she said. 'Where did you go?'

'We hit the last of the villas,' he said, as he took a stack of dry wood from the back of the shelter. 'The old guys living in them had fled, but they'd left behind most of their supplies, so the camp gets to eat for another day. That's all I seem to do at the moment – find food to feed four hundred hungry Westlanders.'

'You do more than that,' she said.

He glanced up at her as he arranged the firewood, but said nothing.

'How is Walter?' she said.

'He's fine. He keeps his face calm, but I can see the strain he's under. There are only three days until we attack Steppen in force, and there's a lot to do.'

'I'm not surprised he's feeling that way if he has an attack to plan.'

'That's the thing, Saffie – he's not worried about the attack. I think he enjoys planning it; it takes his mind off trying to look after four hundred freed slaves. I saw him break up three fights today, and then I saw him trying to cajole an angry crowd into shitting in the correct place; they were in danger of fouling the water supply. It never ends. I'm glad it's not me in charge.'

He took out a box of matches and lit the kindling. He crouched close to the small flames, and coaxed them into life. Saffie smiled as firelight filled the small shelter. She finished the apple and watched Lothar empty a water skin into a metal pot. He added wood to the fire, and hung the pot from a chain fastened to the ceiling of the shelter.

'That'll take a while to heat up,' he said.

'It'll be worth the wait if there's hot food,' she said. 'Can I help with anything?'

'You can chop up the vegetables,' he said.

'I will need a knife for that, and you have neglected to give me one.'

'Can I trust you with a knife?'

'Do you think I'm going to stab the man who brings me food?'

'I don't know what you'd do. I don't really know anything about you, apart from a few of your more objectionable ideas. Eshia has been a great help to us in the camp, you should know that. Walter is very impressed with her. Even Marlow has been useful. He's been converting rock into iron, and then Eshia has been turning the iron into spear heads and cooking pots.' He gestured at the pot warming over the fire. 'This, for instance.'

Saffie narrowed her eyes. 'She summoned a pot?'

'She has summoned dozens of pots. Pots, cups, cutlery; it hasn't just been weapons she's been making for us.'

'Why are you telling me this?'

'You should know that Walter has placed both of them under his protection. Eshia and Marlow are not to be harmed in any way.'

Saffie forced her mouth to remain closed. She was desperate to point out that Eshia was clearly tricking Walter into becoming dependant upon her evil abilities, but she decided to hold her tongue. There was plenty of time.

'Are you staying for dinner?' she said.

He laughed. 'Do you think I would come all this way in the rain to cook a meal that I wasn't going to help eat? Yes, I'll be eating here tonight, if it's all right with you.'

'Of course it's all right. Do I get a knife or not?'

Lothar took out a small pouch and dropped some salt into the heating water.

'Where did you find salt?' she said. 'Wait; I don't want to know. It was Marlow, wasn't it?'

'It was. It took him a dozen attempts until he managed it.'

Saffie nose crinkled. 'I don't know if I can eat that. What if he's poisoned us?'

Lothar dabbed a finger in the salt and tasted it. 'See? It's fine. People in the camp have been using Marlow's salt for the last two days, and no one's been ill. I hesitated before bringing it, because I suspected you might not take it well, but I don't want to eat boiled vegetables without any salt. It's already bland enough.'

He delved into the bag and laid out a selection of vegetables, then he passed Saffie a knife.

'Start chopping,' he said.

Saffie nodded. She gazed at the steel blade for a moment, then sliced through a carrot.

'Thank you,' she said.

'I shouldn't trust you with a knife, but I do,' he said. 'Walter thinks I'm too trusting.'

'And what do you think?' she said.

'I'd rather be too trusting than too suspicious. I trust people until they give me a reason not to, and then I never trust them again.'

'Tell me more about the planned attack,' she said, as she worked on the vegetables.

'There are going to be four separate attacks,' he said. 'I'll be leading one that targets the fence around the shanty town. My objective is to free and arm as many Westlander slaves as possible. Another force will hit the opposite side of the shanty town, and the third will strike the mercenary barracks. The last force will be led by Walter, and it'll go straight for the temple.'

'Then Walter will die,' she said. 'Did you tell him everything I told you about our attack on the temple? There are only two staircases connecting the lower floors with the upper floors. Two Masters will be able to defend them indefinitely.'

'I told him what you'd said. He asked me to thank you for the information.'

'But he still intends to attack?'

'There's someone inside that we need to rescue.'

'Who?'

Lothar smiled. 'I can't tell you that. Walter made me promise.'

'It must be someone important.'

'She is very important.'

'She? It's a woman? Who?'

Lothar shrugged, then he unwrapped the fish from a paper parcel. 'The water's heating up nicely,' he said. 'Do you like fish?'

'Look, Lothar; I want Walter to be successful – you know that. No one will cheer louder than I if Walter manages to kill the Whalebone King and his sons. Every night, I pray to the spirits that they help him win victory in Steppen; but he is going about this the wrong way. Only a surprise attack will work against Masters. You need to lure them out of the temple one at a time, and ambush them before they have a chance to use their powers.'

'Is that what you were taught in the Offices of Purgation?'

'It's what I learned on Sanctos. I had just joined the Offices of Purgation when the raid on Steppen was launched.'

'Is that right? What were you doing before that?'

'I served as a lieutenant in the Sanctian Navy.'

'Tell me something else about your life,' he said. 'Do you have family in Sanctos?'

'Yes. I have two brothers, and my parents.'

'What do they do?'

Saffie hesitated. If Lothar could keep secrets from her regarding the identity of the woman they wanted to rescue from Steppen, then she could do the same about her family heritage. How would he react if he knew she was an imperial princess? She didn't think Lothar would respond negatively, but what would Walter do?

'Who is Walter?' she said. 'You told me that he was a soldier from Upper Down, like you, but why is he in charge?'

'He was... is my commanding officer.'

'And why is he in the Great Forest?'

'He is looking for the woman I mentioned. She is a captive of the Whalebone King.'

'Oh. Then I pity her.'

Lothar smiled, as though he found something amusing. 'The water's hot enough,' he said. 'Let's get those vegetables in before I expire from hunger.'

Dinner was as bland as Lothar had said it would be, but Saffie still ranked it as one of the best meals she had ever eaten, and the feeling of warm food in her stomach felt blissful. Lothar's clothes had dried, and he was sitting with his back to the tree with his legs stretched out, as he used a spoon to scoop out the last of the food from the pot.

Saffie put her fork down, and relaxed.

'Thank you for dinner,' she said.

'You helped make it,' he said, placing the pot back into his bag. He reached in and took something else out.

Saffie eyed the ceramic jug. 'Is that alcohol?'

Lothar laughed. 'It certainly is.'

'Are you trying to get me drunk?'

'No. I intend to have a few of these to fortify myself for the walk back to the camp. You are free to join me, or not. It's up to you.'

'What is it?'

'Brandy. It's pretty good, considering. I found it in the villa we raided last night, and snatched it before one of the Westlanders could take it back for Walter.'

Saffie frowned. 'And why would they take it back for Walter?'

'Walter... likes a drink. The Westlanders know this, and they try to find booze for him; as a favour, you know?'

'Walter is a drunk?'

'Some might call him that, I suppose. It doesn't affect his job; well, it hasn't so far. I'll keep an eye on him. Part of the reason I took the brandy was so Walter couldn't have it. Once he starts, he finds it difficult to stop.'

He placed two small wooden cups onto the grass, and filled one. He glanced at Saffie, as he hovered the jug over the other cup.

'I'll have one,' she said; 'to save you drinking it all.'

'I'm not going to drink it all,' he said, pouring brandy into the second cup. 'I can ration myself.'

Saffie picked up her cup. She gazed at the intricate carvings of vines on the exterior, and wondered if she was holding another item summoned by Eshia. She had eaten the food without any more complaints about the salt – her hunger overriding any qualms she had about its source, and now she was about to drink brandy out of a summoned cup. She raised it to her lips and took a sip.

'Subnestian,' she said.

'What?' said Lothar.

'The brandy comes from Subnestia,' she said. 'I recognise the honey flavours running through it. This is expensive stuff.'

'Then your family is rich?' he said.

'They might be.'

Lothar took a large swig. 'Nice.'

'It's supposed to be savoured, not glugged down.'

'It's supposed to be drunk.'

They finished their first cups of brandy, and Saffie allowed Lothar to pour her another measure. She knew she was potentially taking a grave risk by drinking brandy, but the alcohol was making her feel confident, and she felt safe in Lothar's company. She had been helpless when first injured, and he had been nothing but a gentleman towards her, when he could have easily taken advantage. Her chest began to warm up from the brandy, and she felt her head swim pleasantly.

'Is now a good time to bring up the spirits?' she said.

'I assume you aren't referring to the one we're drinking?'

She smiled, then she felt sad. 'I want to help you, Lothar. I feel sorry that you have doubts about the existence of the spirits. If only I could show you how much praying to the spirits could help you. Do you want to pray together?'

'I'd rather scratch my eyes out.'

'Please don't mock my faith,' she said.

'Look, Saffie; no offence, but I'm not interested. Your beliefs have led you to think that children should be executed.'

'But Masters and Makers aren't fully human,' she said. 'They are possessed by evil spirits; you can't think of them as real people.'

'And that's how you can justify murdering the innocent,' he said. 'As soon as you see others as less than human, then you can do whatever you like to them. But consider this, just for a moment – what if you're wrong? What if Masters and Makers are like everyone else – some good, some middling, and some who are utter arseholes?'

'I can't accept that.'

'You don't want to accept it, because it'll mean that you have devoted your life to a cause that is cruel and murderous.'

Saffie fell silent.

'Let's talk about something else,' he said. 'You mentioned that you had only just joined the Offices of Purgation before the Sanctians sent their forces to Steppen.'

She nodded.

'How did the Sanctians find out about the Whalebone King?'

'He made a mistake, and killed some slaves in front of a bargeman who had got lost inside the temple.'

'Is that all it took?' he said. 'What if the bargeman had been lying?'

'There have been rumours in Elestia about the Whalebone King for a while; that wasn't the first piece of evidence.'

'How many did you bring north?'

'A hundred and twenty soldiers, and three officers from the Offices of Purgation.' She shook her head. 'We thought it would be more than enough. The bargemen we questioned had underestimated how many mercenaries were here, and they didn't know anything about the king's sons. More will be coming, Lothar.'

'A hundred and twenty – and you are the sole survivor?'

'I don't know how it happened. I was pushed down a set of stairs, but they couldn't have checked to see if I was alive or not. So many deaths. I feel guilty that I survived. Those poor soldiers were doing the best they could, but the captain in charge... he... I think the forest had an effect upon his mind, and he ordered the attack on the temple. We tried to tell him that it would fail, but he didn't listen. And now Walter might be about to make the same mistake.' A tear came from her eye, and she gazed down at the ground. The rain was torrential outside the shelter, and its background roar filled her ears.

'Was it a rough journey to get here?' said Lothar.

'It was terrible,' she said. 'Half of our men were struck down by sickness, because the mercenaries had been dumping bodies into the river. We found slaves who had been beaten to death; old women beheaded, young women tortured. I thought I could cope with most things, but what I saw will never leave me. Why do people do these things to each other?'

'Perhaps the mercenaries don't see the slaves as being fully human, Saffie.'

She stared at him.

Lothar refilled his cup. 'I shouldn't have said that. It was a cheap shot. Sorry. I like talking to you, but some of your views are hard to take.'

She held out her cup.

'Are you sure?' he said.

She nodded, and he refilled it with brandy.

'How old are you?' she said.

'Twenty-four.'

'Is that all? I thought you were older.'

'I've been a Mountain Ranger since I was sixteen,' he said. 'Eight years of service.'

'I'm twenty,' she said. 'Almost twenty-one.'

'I had guessed you were around that,' he said.

'Are you married?'

He smiled. 'Why – are you interested?'

Her face flushed.

'Another one of my stupid jokes,' he said. 'No, I'm not married. I haven't been in Upper Down for well over a year, not that I had a steady girlfriend back there. I was Walter's aide for a while; I saw more of him than anyone else. We were a good team before I fucked it up.'

'What did you do?'

Lothar pursed his lips. 'This might change your opinion of me; I warn you.'

'Tell me anyway,' she said, as she started her third cup of brandy.

'Walter's brother hated him,' said Lothar, 'and I was short of money. So, I agreed to take gold from the brother to keep Walter drunk. I was good at it, and Walter was barely sober for three years. His reputation crumbled, and it was my fault. There. Do you hate me now?'

'But I thought you liked Walter?'

'I adore him, in a manly way, of course; I don't fancy the bastard.'

'Then how could you do that to him?'

'Once I started, I found it impossible to stop. Eventually, I confessed everything to Walter, and I lost my job as his aide.' Lothar lowered his gaze. 'I was lucky. Walter is a good man, and he has forgiven me. I don't think many people would be able to do that. I don't deserve him as a friend.'

'You seem regretful.'

'I regret it more than anything else I've done. I wish I could go back and change what happened; but Walter acts as though it's all in the past. He's moved on, while I still feel guilty every time I look at him.'

She reached out and touched his arm. 'We all make mistakes. At least you have taken responsibility for yours. I can see why Walter would forgive you.'

Their eyes met, then both looked away, and Saffie withdrew her hand. She drank more brandy to get through the awkward moment, and realised that she was drunker than she had been in months.

'Tell me something about yourself,' he said.

'Like what?'

'A secret,' he said. 'Something personal.'

Saffie thought for a moment. There was one obvious answer, but she had already decided not to talk about the identity of her family.

'I know,' she said. 'I have dreams about being a Maker.'

He eyed her.

'They're nightmares, if I'm being honest,' she went on. 'I've had them for over a year. I always make something that kills members of my family, which doesn't make any sense, as I love my family. I summon giant spiders that eat people.'

Lothar raised an eyebrow. 'You do know that real Makers can't summon giant spiders, yes?'

'Can't they?' she said.

Lothar laughed. 'No, which is a good thing. No Maker can summon living creatures; they're too complicated.'

'That's actually a relief to know,' she said, her voice slurring a little.

'You believe in the spirits,' he went on. 'Could they be trying to send you a message?'

'What kind of message?'

He leaned forward. 'Maybe you are a Maker.'

Saffie snorted. 'No chance. I would know.'

'How? Have you ever tried to summon anything?'

'Of course not!'

'Then how the fuck would you know?'

Saffie frowned. 'You swear a lot.'

'Don't change the subject. Makers don't automatically realise that they're Makers; many don't find out until they're in their teens, and some never find out.'

'Nonsense.'

'It's true,' he said, smiling. 'How could you know if you never tried? Think about it.'

'But they must know.'

'Why?'

'Because how could you not know that an evil spirit is possessing you?'

'Then you should have no problem trying. Go on; attempt to summon something. Wait – be careful. Don't summon anything metal, and for fuck's sake don't try to summon an animal. Something small and wooden will do. Try to make a cup.'

'I absolutely refuse.'

He laughed. 'Then you'll never know the truth.'

'You're an arsehole.'

'Thank you.'

He laughed again, and she realised that he was also getting drunk.

'Imagine,' he went on, 'someone in the Offices of Purgation is secretly a Maker. That would be pretty funny.'

'I am not a Maker.'

'Prove it. Summon something, and when it doesn't work you will know for certain. What have you got to lose?'

'What if the spirits take offence?'

'What if the spirits are sending you these dreams?'

'You don't believe in the spirits.'

'No, but you do.'

'Fine,' she said, getting angry. 'I will prove to you that I am not a Maker, if that will make you happy. A cup?'

'A small wooden cup. Concentrate on the type of wood and shit like that; how it was made and so on. I think that stuff's important.'

'Shut up.'

Lothar raised his palms and fell silent, his gaze never leaving her.

Saffie held out her hand. 'What do I say?'

'Ask the spirits for permission, then tell them what you want to summon.'

'All right. Blessed spirits,' she said, 'I apologise for what I am about to do, but I am quite drunk, and this idiot won't shut up until I try it. Could I please have your permission to summon something? I want to summon a small wooden cup. Please.'

A branch crackled somewhere above them, and a misshapen lump of wood appeared in the air a foot above the ground.

'Holy fuck!' Lothar shouted. He whipped out his hand and caught the lump of wood as it fell, then Saffie burst into tears.

'No,' she cried, her hands clutching the sides of her head. 'Please, no; please.' She broke down, sobbing uncontrollably. She leaned forward, almost falling, as tears spilled down her cheeks.

She felt a hand on her shoulder.

'I... I didn't think that was going to work, Saffie; I'm sorry.'

'I am a monster!' she shouted.

'You're not,' he said; 'you're the same person you were a few moments ago.'

She began to shake. How could it be true? She would be better off dead than being a cursed Maker. An evil spirit had taken up residence within her body; how had she not known?

'I want to die,' she sobbed.

'Don't say that,' said Lothar. He put his arms round her shoulders and held her. 'Please don't say that. You are still you; you are still Saffie. Look at me. You are going to be all right. Nothing bad is going to happen to you.'

She lifted her head to see Lothar gazing down at her.

'Something bad *has* happened to me,' she whispered. 'I am one of them.'

He wiped her tears away with his fingers. She waited for him to say something, but he remained silent.

'Please tell no one,' she said, her voice faint.

'I won't; I promise.'

'Don't leave me here by myself tonight,' she said; 'I couldn't bear it.'

Lothar said nothing, his gaze held on her, as the rainstorm battered down outside the shelter. She moved her head a little closer to his, pulling herself into his embrace. Lothar didn't back away, and she moved even closer. What was she doing? She wasn't sure, but the combination of Lothar, the brandy, and the most devastating revelation that could have happened was telling her one thing – she didn't want to be alone.

She closed her eyes and kissed him, half expecting him to push her away in disgust. She was a vile Maker, who deserved nothing more; but he returned the kiss, his hands reaching behind her head. Her hands went to his clothes, and he pushed her down to the soft ground of the shelter. She felt his weight on her as he kissed her neck, and she abandoned herself to his embrace.

CHAPTER 27
THE COWARD

Steppen, Great Forest, Jallin, Central Provinces – 19th Day of Quoma 108

'Do you see this pin here?' said Ragnvald, as he gestured towards the shackles. 'You must remember to use it to fix the end of the chain to the iron hoop in the wall. Every night, Magnus; otherwise the little bastard will slit your throat while you sleep. He's fourteen, not four; and he's a Master. He's hardly a helpless child.'

Magnus nodded.

Ragnvald frowned. 'I hate this plan as much as you do,' he said, 'but the king is the king, and while he lives, we have to obey his orders.'

'I understand,' said Magnus.

Ragnvald handed the end of the chain to Magnus. 'I recommend starving him for a couple of days,' he went on. 'Allow him water three times a day, but no food. He'll be more compliant if he's fearful of where his next meal is coming from. And beat him severely at the first sign of insubordination; don't take any shit from him. He's got to learn that you are the boss. If he was a few years younger, it would be easy, but he's at a tricky age where disobedience comes naturally, so be strict. Now, I want to see you fix the chain to the wall; go on.'

Magnus walked to the iron hoop freshly embedded into the wall of his quarters. He lifted the end of the chain, looped it through the hoop, then he placed the metal pin into its slot and twisted it.

Ragnvald nodded, then held out his hand. Laid out on his palm was another metal pin, with grooves cut into it, as though it resembled a key. 'You'll need this to release the pin each morning. Keep it out of the slave's reach while you sleep, and carry it with you when you're moving around. There are iron hoops all over the temple, and you might need to temporarily secure him somewhere; if you have to take a shit, for example.'

Magnus took the pin.

'Right,' said Ragnvald; 'I think you're ready, and it's only taken us half the fucking day to set all this up. Any questions?'

'I don't think so.'

Ragnvald nodded. 'One last piece of advice,' he said; 'whatever you do, don't try to make friends with him. He's not a friend – he's a possession; a hostage. The king might change his mind about this arrangement when he realises how fucking impractical it is, and then he might order us to kill our hostages.'

'Do you think that's likely?' said Magnus.

'He's only doing this because he wants to get his hands on Raewyn,' said Ragnvald. 'The old bastard is risking everything for a piece of ass. As soon as he discovers that Raewyn is a Maker, then this little... experiment will be brought to a swift conclusion.' He glanced out of an open window at the torrential rain. 'It must be close to midnight, and I still have to fix my hostage to the wall of my own quarters. What a fucking ball-ache. I'll see you in the morning.'

He walked over to the two soldiers standing by the front door of Magnus's quarters. One of them handed the end of another chain to Ragnvald, then they left the chamber, dragging Salus out with them.

Magnus gazed at the wooden floorboards, unable to look upon his own hostage. Ignatius had said nothing for hours; he had just sat on the small wooden pallet that had been brought in for him, and stared into space. An iron collar had been attached to his neck, and it was connected to the chain that Magnus had fixed to the wall.

Ragnvald, Einar and Erling had been keeping personal slaves in their quarters for years, but Ignatius was the first for Magnus, and his presence made him uncomfortable.

'Do you need any water before going to sleep?' Magnus said.

Ignatius remained silent.

'If you need to piss, there's a bucket by the pallet,' Magnus went on.

Silence.

Magnus raised his gaze, and looked at his hostage. Ignatius was sitting motionless, his eyes dark.

'Did you hear me?' said Magnus. 'Answer me.'

'Or what?' said Ignatius.

'Or... you don't get any food tomorrow.'

'I heard you,' Ignatius said, 'you dirty coward.'

Magnus took a step back. Was he supposed to beat Ignatius for saying that? Ragnvald would have already been thrashing the slave if he had uttered a comment like that in front of him, but Magnus was alone.

'I don't want to hit you,' Magnus said, 'but I will if you are disobedient.'

'I thought you were our friend!' Ignatius cried, as though his pent-up anger had been released. 'You pretended to be our friend, and then you stabbed us in the back. You were going to kill us all! For what? Constans, Fyenna, Mor Galthide – what did they ever do to you? We trusted you.'

'I... I didn't kill anyone.'

'No, but you were going to. The king stopped you; I saw it – we all saw it. You and Ragnvald were going to slaughter us.'

'I was the one who wanted to let you leave on the barges,' Magnus shouted back at the boy; 'but the others didn't agree.'

'You have no honour,' said Ignatius. 'You're Ragnvald's loyal little dog. I hate you more than I hate the others, because you know this is wrong.'

'I'm just trying to stay alive.'

'What's the king going to do to Raewyn?'

'I don't want to think about that.'

'She likes you; did you know that? Well, she liked you, but that was before you betrayed us. She'll hate you now.'

Magnus sat down on a stool and put his head in his hands.

'We all hate you,' Ignatius went on. 'Even your brothers despise you; it's obvious. I watched Erling kick the crap out of you when you stood up for your mother. You were beaten up, but at least you tried. I actually felt sorry for you.'

'Shut up,' said Magnus.

'I will not,' said Ignatius. 'If you want my silence then you'll have to force my mouth closed. Do you think I'm frightened of you? You're only a couple of years older than me, and I reckon I would win a fair fight.'

'You have to do what you're told,' said Magnus; 'you are my slave.'

'I am a citizen of Klef Mordain. I might be a prisoner, but I will never be a slave.'

Magnus shook his head. He would have to beat Ignatius; he had no choice. If he didn't, then the boy would continue to disrespect his authority, and he would become impossible to manage. Magnus had witnessed many unruly slaves being broken over the years, and he knew what he was supposed to do. Einar and Erling had particularly enjoyed breaking in any Westlanders who showed signs of disobedience; they would beat and torture them until their spirits had been crushed. Images of Lord Matteo's body appeared in his mind. Magnus had tortured the Sanctian to death while Ragnvald had watched, and the memories made him feel sick.

'I can't do it,' he whispered.

Ignatius laughed.

'Stop that!' cried Magnus.

Ignatius laughed again. 'Or what?'

'Why aren't you frightened?'

Ignatius fell quiet. 'I was frightened when the Sanctians invaded Klef Mordain,' he said. 'I was frightened when their supporters murdered our teachers, and we had to flee the city. You don't frighten me.'

'I am always frightened,' said Magnus.

'I know; I can see it in your eyes. The king and your brothers terrify you; they scare you so much that you are prepared to do anything to please them.'

'Is Raewyn really a Maker?'

Ignatius shrugged. 'I'm telling you nothing. Ragnvald is probably beating up Salus right now; why don't you ask him?'

Magnus's gaze went to the stocky wooden bat that Ragnvald had left for him. It had a few dark stains at one end, showing that it had been used to subdue slaves before.

Ignatius clenched his fists. 'I'm ready. Try it, you bastard.'

Magnus reached over and took hold of the bat. He got to his feet, and looked down at Ignatius.

'I will die before I submit,' the boy said, 'and I will fight to the end.'

'I have killed people before,' Magnus said. 'Do you think I would have survived in this place if I couldn't kill? You don't know me.'

'It's a pity you couldn't kill your brothers. If you did that, you would be free. It's not too late to save yourself.'

Magnus dropped the bat. He withdrew the key-pin from a pocket and walked over to the iron hoop.

'What are you doing?' said Ignatius, as he watched Magnus disconnect the chain from the wall.

'I want to speak to my mother,' he said; 'and you'll have to come with me.' Magnus gripped the end of the chain. 'Get up.'

'We're going to visit your mother?' Ignatius said, his eyes narrowing.

'Yes.'

Ignatius stood, his gaze never leaving Magnus.

'It's not a trick,' said Magnus. 'If I wanted Ragnvald to kill you, I would wait until he comes round in the morning.'

He led Ignatius by the chain to the front door of his apartment, and they entered a dark passageway. They passed a few open windows, and Magnus glanced out at the heavy autumnal rains. Bad weather usually had a calming effect on the slaves down in the shanty town, and the fenced-off camp seemed quiet. Magnus and Ignatius went up a flight of stairs, then they came to the two soldiers standing guard outside the women's quarters.

'It's a little late for a visit, is it not, sir?' said one. 'We have been told to be extra cautious.'

'I don't give a shit,' said Magnus. 'Let me pass.'

'The women's quarters are not supposed to be opened between midnight and sunrise,' the mercenary went on. 'We shall have to report this to the king.'

'You do that,' said Magnus. 'Unlock the door.'

The two mercenaries glanced at each other, then one took a key out of a pocket. He turned it in the lock, and pushed the door open.

'Knock when you wish to leave,' said the mercenary.

Magnus led Ignatius inside. The main chamber was in darkness, and Magnus spent a moment lighting a couple of lamps. He took one from the wall, and led Ignatius along a hallway to his mother's small room. He knocked on the door, and waited.

It opened, and his mother peered out. She still had bruises on her face from when Erling had struck her, but her eyes lit up at the sight of her son; then her smile vanished when she saw Ignatius being led by a chain.

'Might we speak, Mother?' said Magnus.

'Why have you brought this boy with you?'

'He has been assigned to me,' said Magnus. 'I have to take him everywhere.'

'Is Annalise here, ma'am?' said Ignatius. 'Is she all right?'

Colette opened the door wider, and Magnus saw Annalise sitting by a table inside the lamplit room.

The woman glanced up. 'Ignatius!' she cried. 'It is good to see you.'

'Come in,' said Colette.

Magnus led Ignatius into the small room, and his mother closed the door. Annalise got up and embraced Ignatius, and Magnus felt embarrassed as he held on to the other end of the chain.

'Sit down, son,' said Colette; 'and let go of that stupid chain. It makes you look as foolish as Erling.'

Magnus sat in a chair next to the table, but he kept hold of the chain. Annalise and Ignatius sat on the low bed, and Colette took the last remaining chair.

'Well, son?' said Colette. 'What do you wish to speak about?'

Magnus glanced at the three faces staring at him. 'I... I don't know what to do, Mother.'

'Are you here for my advice?'

'I already know what your advice would be.'

Colette raised an eyebrow. 'Do you, indeed? Let's hear it, then.'

'You want me to turn on my father and brothers,' he said. 'You want me to set you free.'

'I want more than that,' said Colette; 'a lot more. I want you to free every slave being held in the temple, including all of those who only yesterday were guests of the so-called king. What he has done to them is outrageous – a criminal disgrace. Annalise is a free citizen, as I was. She has told me everything that went on. Is it true that you and Ragnvald arrived in their quarters in order to kill them? I could barely believe what Annalise was telling me. You are better than that, or at least I thought you were.'

'He always seemed like a nice young man,' said Annalise.

'He's a coward,' said Ignatius.

Colette shot him a look. 'Hush, please. Let us see if my son can still be saved.'

'It's too late,' said Magnus. 'I've done... things that are unforgiveable.'

Colette frowned. 'What things?'

Magnus stared at the floor. 'I can't tell you. You'd hate me.'

Colette put a hand to her face. 'Please don't tell me that you have hurt one of the young guests, Magnus; my heart would break.'

'It wasn't a guest,' said Magnus.

'Did you kill one of the slaves?'

Magnus shook his head.

'Then what? Tell me.'

'Do you remember Lord Matteo?' he whispered.

'*Remember* him? Is he...? Did you...?'

'I killed him.'

Colette's expression altered to one of relief. 'You killed that vile, corrupt fool? I can't say that I am too disturbed by this knowledge. His greed led him to betray his duty. I daresay he deserved it.'

'He was trying to escape on a barge loaded with silver,' Magnus went on.

'Then what is all the fuss about?' said Colette. 'Did you feel this guilty when you killed the bargeman who brought Ignatius and the others here?'

'You don't understand, Mother. Ragnvald was there. He made me torture Matteo to death.'

'Ah.'

'You tortured him?' said Annalise.

'I did terrible things to him, but Ragnvald wouldn't let me put him out of his misery. I did *bone to wood* and *bone to silver*, but it wasn't enough for Ragnvald. He kept urging me to do worse things to him, and... and I... I did what he told me to do. Do you see, Mother? I'm like them now. That's what Ragnvald said. I'm one of them. So then, when Ragnvald ordered me to help him murder the guests, I told him that I would. We were about to start when the king arrived.'

'Oh, Magnus,' said Annalise, shaking her head. 'Lothar was right about you, it seems. You are too scared of your brothers to stand up to them.'

'Wait,' said Colette, her eyes tight. 'Son, did you say that you used your Master abilities on Lord Matteo? Is that what you said?'

Magnus nodded.

A grim smile came over his mother's face. 'You can kill from a distance?'

Magnus nodded again.

'This changes everything,' said Colette. 'Does the king know?'

'Only Ragnvald knows.'

'Then you are more than capable of redeeming yourself, my son. You have the power to kill the king and your brothers. You could raise your hand and kill the two soldiers standing outside these quarters.' She leaned forward and took his hand. 'Do it. Do it tonight, before the others discover what you are able to do. The king and Erling will be on their guard when they find out. Kill them!'

'I can't.'

'Yes, you can,' hissed his mother.

'He's weak,' said Ignatius. 'If I had his abilities, we would already be free.'

Colette eyed him. 'You are also a Master, yes? What can you do?'

'Very little,' he said. 'I had one year at the secret school in Klef Mordain, and I was learning how to meditate and clear my mind. I did manage to make water a tiny bit salty once, after about an hour of meditation; and I can make wood crumble when I try to turn it into iron.'

'You went to a school?' said Magnus. 'A school for Masters?'

Ignatius nodded. 'They also taught me how to read and write.'

'All of the students were there,' said Annalise; 'well, the girls attended the school for Makers, of course.'

Magnus's eyes widened, and Ignatius glared at the older woman.

'Was I not supposed to say that?' said Annalise.

'Are they *all* Masters and Makers?' said Magnus.

Annalise looked away. 'Uh... I didn't mean that. No. They, um...'

'But the king will kill them all,' said Magnus. 'The king will kill them if he finds out.'

'Then you'd better not tell him,' said Ignatius.

'Raewyn...' said Magnus, before he could stop himself.

'What about her?' said Colette.

'Nothing.'

'You like her, don't you?' said Annalise. She glanced at Colette. 'They were always talking together whenever Magnus came to visit us.'

'Is that right?' said Colette. 'Let me see if I have this straight. Raewyn is a Maker, and the king will kill her when he discovers this. And you like her, son? Then why are we still sitting here? Your choices are clear. We must act, at once, if Raewyn and the others are to be saved.'

'I will help,' said Ignatius.

'Ragnvald was right,' Magnus said. 'He warned the king that the others were likely to be Masters and Makers. That's why he wanted my help to kill them.'

'And you went along with it,' said Colette, 'even though you have feelings for Raewyn? Would you have stood by and watched your brother kill her? This shocks me profoundly. I tried my best to raise you to be better than that, and I have failed.'

'I did it to protect you, Mother,' he said. 'I was trying to help Ragnvald so that you would be safe.'

'That disgusts me, son. Do you think I would want to live to see you turn into another Ragnvald? I would rather die. Go. Get out of my sight if you aren't going to help us; and never come back. If you wish to be like your brothers, then I want nothing more to do with you.'

'But...'

Colette turned her face away from him, her eyes cold.

'Wait,' said Annalise. 'We still might be able to persuade him to help us.'

'I fear Ignatius hit upon the truth earlier,' Colette said. 'My son is a coward. He was prepared to sacrifice the lives of the guests to curry favour with Ragnvald. He will not help us. He came here to assuage his guilt, but I will not cooperate. I hope he feels guilty; I hope he is ashamed of himself.'

Magnus got to his feet, his right hand still gripping the chain. He stared at his mother, then he turned for the door. Ignatius got up, and followed him out of the room.

'You're an idiot,' said Ignatius. 'You have the power to set things right, but you are too cowardly to use it.'

'Shut your mouth,' said Magnus.

'Or what?'

Magnus turned, his eyes flashing with rage. 'Or I'll beat the shit out of you. I'll beat you so badly that you'll never be able to walk again.'

Ignatius laughed in his face. 'I'd like to see you try.'

Magnus turned for the main entrance, pulling the chain along after him. He knocked on the door, and a mercenary opened it.

'Can I ask what was discussed in there, sir?' said the other mercenary on duty. 'The king will want to know.'

'Mind your own fucking business!' Magnus shouted.

The soldiers glared at him. One of them moved to close the door, but Ignatius was in the way. The mercenary shoved the boy aside, and Ignatius punched him in the face.

'You little shit,' cried the mercenary. He battered a fist into Ignatius's stomach, while the other soldier grabbed the slave's arms and held them back.

Magnus stood back, his eyes wide, as the two soldiers beat Ignatius, doing what he had been unable to do only moments before. He raised his hand.

'Water to salt; water to salt.'

The soldiers grunted, then they collapsed to the floor of the hallway. They convulsed as their eyes bled salt, then they lay still. Ignatius staggered, his nose bloody, then he stared at Magnus.

Magnus let go of the chain. 'Fetch my mother and Annalise.'

'What?'

'Do it now,' said Magnus, 'before I have a chance to change my mind.'

Ignatius picked up the trailing end of the chain and staggered back into the women's quarters. The hallway fell into silence, the only noise coming from the torrential rain outside. Magnus tried to blank his mind. If he thought too deeply about what he had done, and what he might be about to do, then he knew that his fears and anxiety would return in force. His heart pounded in his chest, and he turned away from the sight of the two bodies.

Ignatius hurried back out of the women's quarters, Colette and Annalise following closely behind him. Colette stared down at the bodies, then at her son.

'Why?' she said. 'Why now?'

Magnus said nothing.

'Does it matter?' said Annalise. 'Your son did it, Colette.' She glanced at Magnus. 'What now?'

'Raewyn,' he said.

'Do we know where she is being kept?' said Colette.

'She's still in the guest quarters, with Abigone and Stanza,' said Magnus.

He set off without another word, as his fears began to close in. What was he doing? Was he insane? Ragnvald and his father would tear him to pieces when they found out. He heard the footsteps of the others behind him as they traversed the temple. There were no soldiers around at that time of the night, but some would be stationed outside the guest quarters. They ascended a flight of stairs, and Magnus slowed. He gazed at the floor, then he looked up at his mother.

'Stay here,' he said. 'I'll need the chain for this.'

He extended a hand. Ignatius narrowed his eyes, then he handed the loose end of the chain to Magnus. Magnus turned, and led Ignatius along the passageway. He saw the two soldiers standing outside the entrance to the guest apartment, and they glanced up at his approach.

'These quarters are currently out of bounds, lad,' said one. 'King's orders.'

Magnus lifted a hand. 'Water to salt; water to salt.'

The two soldiers fell, their faces contorting with agony.

'How are you doing that?' said Ignatius. 'Why aren't you saying the proper blessing, and how can you keep your mind clear?'

Magnus let go of the chain, then he crouched by the two bodies and rifled through their pockets. He found a key, stood, and unlocked the door. He pushed it open, and saw the light from a solitary lamp shining within. He stepped over the threshold. To his left, Raewyn was standing next to another doorway, and her eyes hardened. She lifted her hand and pointed at Magnus.

'Wait!' cried Ignatius, running into the room. 'He's on our side now, I think. He's killed four mercenaries, and he's set Annalise and his mother free.'

Abigone and Stanza appeared behind Raewyn. Abigone stepped forward, and pushed Raewyn's hand down.

'That bastard was here to kill us yesterday,' Raewyn said.

'I know,' said Abigone. 'But not here; not now.' She turned to Magnus. 'Get us out of the temple.'

'What about Nyli and Reath?' said Stanza. 'And Salus, too?'

'The king will not kill them if we happen to escape,' said Abigone. 'He needs them for leverage. Besides, to find them, we would have to find Ragnvald, Erling and the king, and they will be well defended. We might be able to rescue one, but not all three.'

'You are cold, Abigone,' said Raewyn.

'Someone needs to be,' she said. 'Each of you, pack a bag. Fill it with food from the kitchen. Ignatius, you too. Quickly.'

Ignatius ran off to another room, and Stanza followed him. Raewyn stared at Magnus, her eyes glimmering with fury.

'I'm sorry,' he said. 'I wanted to please my brother. I was wrong.'

'Food,' Abigone repeated. 'We'll need a lot if we are to survive for even a few days in the forest.'

She led Raewyn and Magnus into the kitchen, where Ignatius and Stanza were already stuffing bread and other food into bags. The others helped, until they had each filled a bag of their own, then they left the apartment. Abigone glanced down at the two bodies.

'Magnus did that,' said Ignatius, 'and he didn't say the proper words.'

Colette and Annalise peered out from the top of the stairs. Annalise smiled, and hurried up to Abigone, Raewyn and Stanza.

'Well done,' said Colette. 'Perhaps there is hope for you after all, son.'

'We still have to get out of here,' said Magnus.

'Aren't we going for the others?' said Annalise.

'Abigone doesn't think it's a good idea,' said Raewyn.

'But poor Nyli is with the king,' said Annalise; 'and Erling has Reath. And what about little Salus? We can't leave them here.'

'One thing at a time,' said Abigone. 'This is our only chance to get out of the temple alive. We could spend hours trying to locate the other children, and every moment in here increases the risk.'

'But the king might kill them if we escape,' said Annalise.

'He won't,' said Abigone.

'I'm sorry, Your Highness, but you don't know that.'

'Abigone is right,' said Magnus. 'The three children should be safe. My father will keep them alive, as hostages. And Ragnvald will still be awake; he needs to set up Salus's shackles. He would kill us as soon as he saw us.'

'But we can't give up on them,' said Annalise.

'We are not giving up on them,' said Abigone. 'We will rescue them, but from a position of strength. We shall also rescue Denny and Aplin from the shanty town, but not tonight. Tonight, we flee into the forest. I am now Head Maker. Trust me.'

'Why did Annalise call you *Your Highness*?' said Colette.

'Because I am a princess of Upper Down,' said Abigone. 'My young nephew is the king.'

'You're royalty?' said Magnus.

'I am. Lead us out of the temple, Magnus.'

Magnus glanced at his mother.

'Best do as she says, son.'

Magnus hurried along the passageway, and the others followed him. He took them down by the old sanctuary, then he led them to a small side door on the ground floor of the temple.

'There will be soldiers beyond that door,' he said.

'How many?' said Abigone.

'Three or four,' said Magnus; 'and there will be a patrol based somewhere along the road. They will see us. I can kill, but not quickly.'

'Open the door,' said Abigone.

Magnus removed the thick bar, and swung the door open.

Three soldiers turned from the side of the road, their eyes widening.

Magnus raised his hand, and Raewyn pushed him aside. She lifted her own hand.

'Summon three horses,' she said, her voice calm and still.

The three soldiers exploded, their flesh ripped from their bodies. The mass of gore reformed into three separate heaps on the grass in front of the temple, and Raewyn stepped over them and into the torrential rain. Another dozen mercenaries were patrolling the northern edge of the shanty town, and they started pulling their bows from their shoulders.

Raewyn raised her hand again, as the rain pelted her.

'Summon a dozen horses,' she cried.

Magnus looked away as the mercenaries were torn to pieces by the power of the Maker. Blood sprayed out in all directions, and the front of Raewyn's dress was speckled red. Abigone led the others into the rain.

Colette was staring at the carnage with her mouth open. Magnus took her hand as Abigone began to shepherd them towards the west.

'Raewyn,' Abigone called out. 'It's time.'

Raewyn turned, her eyes dark, then she ran after the others as they fled into the forest.

CHAPTER 28
ATTRITION

East of Steppen, Great Forest, Jallin, Central Provinces – 22nd Day of Quoma 108

Walter eyed his old friend as they walked through the forest.

'It sounds suspiciously like you took advantage of her,' he said.

Lothar frowned. 'I know how it sounds, but it didn't happen that way; I swear it. We were both drunk, and then she got upset, and one thing led to another.'

'Relax,' said Walter. 'I was joking. You seem a little flustered.'

'I'm not flustered,' he said. 'I'm fine; perfectly fine.'

'I hope you were careful with her broken leg,' said Walter. 'You know, I've seen you with many girls over the years – not all of whom you paid for – but I've never seen you like this. I need your mind clear today; will you be able to stop thinking about her, at least until the operation is over?'

Lothar scowled. 'I'm a professional, sir. I will keep my mind on the job. I would ask, though, that you don't mention too many of the things that we got up to in Upper Down to her. There was a time when we were never out of the brothels of Torrent, and I'd rather she didn't know.'

'I'll be sure to bear that in mind if I ever meet her. Are you thinking that this might actually go somewhere? I thought she was a religious fanatic.'

'I have a few issues with her faith,' Lothar said, 'and I've told her as much. But... I guess I quite like her, you know, for a crazy Sanctian. It'll be over soon, though. I want to come with you, sir, wherever you go next; and she... well, I suppose she might go back to the Offices of Purgation.'

'She *might* go back?' said Walter. 'Have you managed to plant a few seeds of doubt in her mind?'

Lothar glanced away. 'I think she might have done that on her own.'

'And what's this about you wanting to come with me? I assigned you to protect Princess Abigone.'

'I don't think she needs my protection any more, and I'd rather not travel down to Geathan.'

'One thing at a time,' said Walter. 'Let's make sure the princess is free, safe and well before we decide our future arrangements.'

They slowed as they reached a large clearing in the forest. Dozens of armed Westlanders were waiting for them, and they fell into silence as Walter and Lothar walked into their midst.

Walter jumped up onto a boulder and surveyed his little army. Each Westlander was equipped with a long spear, their iron heads fashioned by Eshia from metal made by Marlow. A few also had crossbows that had been taken from the mercenaries, and there was a sprinkling of swords and war axes. Spare spears were lying on the ground in piles next to the hundred and fifty warriors Walter had selected. Among them were nineteen women, who were armed in the same manner as the men. Walter would have baulked at including females soldiers in his force if he had been in Upper Down, but the Westlander women were a tough bunch, and he had no doubt that they would fight well.

'Good morning,' said Walter. 'Today is going to be a little different from usual. Instead of raiding for supplies, we are going to hit the mercenaries with our entire fighting force.'

The Westlanders raised their spears and cheered.

'We will also be freeing more of your country folk,' Walter went on. 'Two teams of thirty Westlanders each will open up breaches in the fence – one on the eastern side, the other from the west – while Johan will lead the assault on the mercenary encampment with fifty warriors. You might be wondering where I will be. While you're off fighting, I'll be sitting here getting drunk.'

A few Westlanders laughed.

'Only kidding,' said Walter. 'I will be leading the crossbow force, and we will be taking up positions close to the temple. Contrary to rumours, I will not be assaulting the temple itself. The Sanctians have already tried that, and they were annihilated. The purpose of the three other attacks is to tempt one of the Masters into leaving the safety of the temple. If and when that happens, my team will emerge from hiding and go straight for his throat. In other words, make a lot of noise, burn shit down, and cause as much terror and confusion as possible. Can you manage that?'

The crowd roared again.

'Let me quash another rumour,' Walter went on. 'Today is not about victory or death. Think of it as a probing attack. The Masters might not leave the temple. All three Masters might emerge at once, and we may have to withdraw. We're wearing the bastards down, and our tactics are working. We'll kill as many mercenaries and free as many Westlanders as possible. If we withdraw, we shall take everything we can carry back with us. I don't like plans like this – I admit it; I prefer an objective that is crystal clear, but we are going to have to be flexible, and able to react to shifting circumstances. Listen to your commanders, as their orders might change during the course of the operation. I am not a glory hound; my priority is to ensure that we don't get slaughtered by the Masters. If you see one approach you, retreat out of their range, and allow the crossbow team to do its job. However, if one has his back to you, and you happen to have a spear in your hand, then by all means kill the bastard. Good luck.'

Walter jumped down from the boulder as the Westlanders began to form up into four separate groups. He nodded to Lothar, who was going to be leading the assault on the western flank of the slave encampment, and the Mountain Ranger tilted his head in reply. Walter walked over to the crossbow team, and took a spare bow from Duggan.

'I wasn't expecting you to be so cautious, sir,' Duggan said. 'I was looking forward to storming the temple.'

'So was I,' said Walter, 'but a new source of intelligence has come to light, and I have information from someone who was part of the failed Sanctian attack. The layout of the temple makes it too easy to defend, and I imagine that the Whalebone King would love to lure us inside. We're not going to take the bait. If they don't come out, then we'll destroy the rest of Steppen, cut off their food and water supplies, and place the temple under siege.' He turned, and eyed the commanders of the other three groups. 'Time to go.'

The Westlanders began to move off through the forest. They held together as one force for the first few miles, then they spilt into their different detachments. Walter followed Lothar's force as they made their way round the southern edge of Steppen towards the west. The Westlanders were travelling quietly, but it didn't matter, as mercenaries no longer ventured far from the settlement. They forded the River Ario, then Lothar brought his force to a halt. Walter led his team past them, and they turned for the north. They circled the town, then closed in on it until they reached the edge of the forest. Walter raised his hand, and his warriors crouched amid the undergrowth. The temple was directly ahead of them, on the other side of the manicured lawns and neat ornamental gardens. A mercenary patrol was standing on the road close to the edge of the shanty town, and Walter could see a few Westlander slaves on the far side of the tall fence.

'Make sure your bows are loaded and ready,' said Walter. 'We'll wait here until we see Lothar's force open up a hole in the side of the encampment, and then we'll move a little closer. If a Master comes out of the temple, don't wait for me to give the order – if he's in range, loose.'

'How quickly can a Master kill?' said one of the Westlanders.

'It depends how good he is,' said Walter. 'The ones inside the temple are fast; they can probably kill one warrior every few seconds. Be under no illusions; if the Masters come out to play, then this team has the most dangerous task.'

'And if they don't, sir?'

'Then we sit here and do fuck all. Our only purpose is to ambush the Masters.'

They settled down to wait, and Walter kept his eyes on the shanty town. Twenty minutes elapsed before anything happened, then Walter saw Lothar leading his force up the western side of the slave encampment. Bolt cutters made by Eshia were used to tear holes in the fence, then the mercenaries noticed what was happening. Whistles blasted, and horns echoed up into the blue sky. Smoke started to rise from the direction of the mercenary barracks, followed by screams, shouts and more whistles.

Walter gripped his crossbow, his gaze switching to the southern flank of the temple. Westlanders were starting to stream out of the hole in the fence, and each was handed a spear by the members of Lothar's force. On the road, a dozen mercenaries loosed their bows at the Westlanders, and three fell. The other Westlanders charged the mercenaries before they could reload, and the soldiers fell back, racing in the direction of the temple. With some effort, Lothar was able to recall the charging warriors, and they returned to the hole in the fence, helping more escape to freedom.

'Follow me,' Walter whispered to his team.

He set off, crouching as he ran, and they followed the edge of the forest to get a better view of the road by the temple. Mercenaries were spilling out from the large building, and officers were ordering them to counter the three separate attacks.

'Come on, you bastards,' Walter muttered.

'What are we looking for, sir?' said Duggan.

'Someone unarmed,' said Walter; 'someone keeping their hands free.'

A tall man emerged from the temple.

'That's Ragnvald!' cried one of the crossbow team. 'He's one of them, sir.'

Walter launched himself forward, and the others raced after him. They leapt over a narrow water channel, and sprinted across the grass towards the road. Ragnvald was talking to a group of mercenary officers, and had yet to notice the new threat running towards him from the west. Walter counted the yards as he ran headlong towards the temple. They were almost in range of Ragnvald when a large group of escaped Westlander slaves appeared from the eastern flank of the shanty town. They swarmed through the mercenaries, their spears cutting down over a dozen soldiers, then Ragnvald raised his hand. Westlanders began to fall in numbers, as each one Ragnvald pointed towards was killed by his Master powers.

Walter skidded to a halt on the road. Ragnvald was lost amid a sea of Westlanders. A ring of mercenaries was surrounding the Master to protect him, and Ragnvald was striking down any Westlander he could see.

Walter cursed. 'Back,' he cried to the crossbow team. 'Duggan, whistle for the retreat.'

Duggan withdrew a wooden whistle from a pocket, and blasted out three sharp notes. He repeated the sounds a moment later, but the escaped Westlanders attacking Ragnvald paid no heed. A large patrol of mercenaries saw the crossbow team, and aimed their own bows at them.

'Loose!' Walter cried, bringing up his own bow.

He loosed, and a mercenary fell, then the others in his team did the same, and the entire patrol was cut down in a blizzard of forty bolts.

'Back into the forest,' Walter cried, as Duggan whistled for the retreat again.

Walter led them back the way they had come, and they came to a halt as soon as they were among the trees again. They turned, and watched Lothar lead his own force and the slaves they had freed back towards the south.

'We failed,' said a Westlander.

'We hit them hard,' said Walter, 'and Lothar's team alone have freed at least another fifty or sixty Westlanders. We'll work out the numbers when we get back to the camp. Let's go.'

Walter suppressed his anger as he led the force south through the forest. He had told his commanders to make sure that none of the freed Westlanders attacked the front of the temple; he had pressed home his point over and over, and yet they had done the opposite of what he had ordered. To get so close to Ragnvald, only for him to be surrounded by Westlanders left a bitter taste in his mouth, and he knew that many would hold him responsible for the failure of the attack.

They reached the River Ario, and met up with Lothar's force, which was sheltering among the trees next to their freed batch of slaves.

'Those fucking idiots!' Lothar cried when he saw Walter. 'Amateurs.'

Walter kept his face calm. 'It's my fault,' he said, in a voice loud enough for everyone to hear. 'I expected too much. One can hardly assume that a newly-freed slave will know how to act like a professional soldier when someone pushes a spear into their hands.' He gazed around at the Westlanders. 'This was not a defeat. We have freed more of your folk, and killed many mercenaries; and we will strike again when we are ready. Remember what I told you this morning – this was a probing attack, to test the enemy's defences. We will use what we have learned when we launch our next assault.'

The Westlanders eyed him, and he wondered if he had retained their loyalty. He had been right to lower expectations during his rallying speech.

He turned to Lothar. 'I have a few ideas for our next attack. We can go over them now while the Westlanders rest for a few minutes.'

'I need to show you something first, sir,' said Lothar.

He gestured towards two freed slaves, who were shorter than the Westlanders.

'This is Denny and Aplin, sir,' said Lothar. 'They arrived with

Princess Abigone and me, and were placed into the shanty town three days ago. The Whalebone King has turned on his guests.'

'Is the princess alive?' said Walter.

'As far as we know,' said the older of the two.

'This one's Denny,' said Lothar; 'Princess Abigone's betrothed.'

Walter lowered his voice. 'The prince of Sanctos?'

'I am,' said Denny, 'though neither I nor Abigone revealed our identities to the Whalebone King.'

'Are you both Masters?'

'We are.'

'Are you as good as Marlow?' Walter said. 'He's back in the camp with Eshia.'

'We are about the same level as Marlow,' said Denny.

'Tell me what happened.'

'All three Masters entered our apartment,' said Denny. 'They killed Lady Fyenna, the Head Maker of the school in Klef Mordain, and... and then they killed my father.'

'I'm sorry to hear that,' said Walter.

'They also killed Constans,' said Aplin, 'who was the only Master among us who could turn water to salt.'

'Did they know he was a Master?'

'They're not sure about any of us,' said Denny, 'but they suspect the truth. They held the younger ones in front of them to prevent any Maker from summoning horses. Then we were separated, and Aplin and I were thrown into the shanty town. The king and his three sons each took one of the younger students as a hostage; and Abigone, Raewyn and Stanza were kept apart from the rest of us.' He turned to Lothar. 'Thank you for freeing us from the slave encampment, but I have to return to the temple to find Abigone.'

'You're staying with us,' said Walter. 'If you walk up to the temple, Ragnvald will kill you.'

'I am not under your command,' said Denny.

'I don't give a shit,' said Walter. 'If you are betrothed to Princess

Abigone, then I will not allow you to throw your life away. I will have Westlanders restrain you if necessary; don't test me.'

Denny's eyes simmered with rage. 'Abigone is helpless in there.'

'And we will rescue her,' said Walter. 'The mercenaries took another pounding today, and we freed a large number of Westlanders. We're wearing them down, piece by piece. What I will not do is order a full scale attack on the temple, not yet. I'm going to have to ask you to be patient.'

'When will you attack again?'

'Tomorrow or the day after,' said Walter, 'depending on casualties and the supply situation. Lothar, order the Westlanders to get moving.'

'Yes, sir,' said Lothar.

'I know you're worried about her,' Walter said to Denny, as they led the Westlanders through the forest, 'but we have to do this carefully. Why do you think Princess Abigone and the other two were isolated from the others?'

'I don't want to think about it,' said Denny.

'Has the princess been harmed in any way?'

'Not that I know of, but it's been three days since we were separated. The Whalebone King is a monster, and his sons are every bit as bad. If they've touched her...'

'We're going to kill them all, Denny; every last one of them. Can you fight?'

Denny nodded.

'Good. I need all the fighters I can muster.'

They walked for an hour, then Lothar caught Walter's attention.

'I intend to visit the other hiding place for a while, if that's all right, sir,' he said.

'Are we close?' said Walter.

'Yes, sir.'

Walter glanced at the Westlanders. 'Keep moving. Return to the camp and rest.' He turned back to Lothar. 'I think it's time I met your...

new friend. I want to thank her for her advice, and ask her for more information.'

Lothar frowned. 'You don't need to go, sir. I can do that for you.'

'I know you could, but I want to see the girl who's managed to get under your skin. I won't tell her anything about your old misbehaviour. Well, I might not.'

Lothar lowered his gaze. 'Fine.'

'Denny, Aplin,' Walter said, 'you might as well come with us. We're going to visit the last surviving member of the Sanctians' assault on the temple. Don't tell her that you're Masters, as I hear she doesn't particularly care for them.'

'She's from Sanctos?' said Denny.

'She works for the Offices of Purgation.'

Denny narrowed his eyes.

'What's that?' said Aplin.

'They hunt Masters and Makers,' said Denny. 'If you had remained in Klef Mordain, they would be hunting you right now.'

'Eshia and Marlow have already met her,' said Lothar. 'She doesn't bite.'

Lothar led the way south through the forest, and they left the moving column of Westlanders behind. They walked for a mile, then Lothar came to a halt.

'Allow me to let her know that you're coming, sir,' he said. 'She won't be expecting visitors.'

Walter nodded, and Lothar disappeared through the trees.

'He seems very protective of this woman,' said Denny.

'I think he might be falling for her,' said Walter.

'She will be a fanatic,' said Denny. 'Only fanatics join the Offices of Purgation.'

'Can I ask you something? What did you think of Masters and Makers before you discovered your abilities?'

'I hated them,' he said. 'I thought they were evil; no better than beasts.'

'Why did you think that?' said Aplin.

'It's what I was taught,' said Denny. 'It's what everyone on Sanctos is taught.'

'I assume you know Count Sebastian?' said Walter.

'Of course. Do you know him?'

'I know him quite well. He isn't a fanatic.'

'My uncle has a reputation for being a little soft on Masters and Makers,' said Denny; 'but he's a fine and gallant knight, and the emperor trusts him.'

Lothar returned. 'She's ready,' he said.

The others followed him through the forest, until they came to a large, well-made shelter.

'This is better than the shelter you built for me in the camp,' said Walter. He crouched by the entrance, and saw a young woman inside. She was sitting with her back to a tree, and had a thick blanket over her shoulders. 'Hello,' he said. 'My name is Walter.'

'How did the attack go?' she said.

'It wasn't a great success, but neither was it a disaster.'

'Did you attack the temple?'

'No. I tried to lure some of the Masters out, so I could ambush them, but a crowd of Westlanders disobeyed orders and charged Ragnvald. We couldn't get close enough.'

'Did you retreat?'

'Yes.'

'Then you did the right thing, Walter. Your mistake was to imagine that you could use Westlanders as real soldiers.'

'I am well aware of my mistake, but one can only work with what one has. At least our casualties were low, and we have a chance to try again. We're wearing the bastards down; we'll get them. I wanted to thank you in person, for the advice. Without it, I might have ordered a full attack on the temple, and then we wouldn't be having this conversation.'

The young woman nodded, then she glanced over Walter's shoulder, and her eyes widened.

'Denny?' she said.

Denny frowned and leaned over so that he could see into the shelter.

'Saffie?'

Walter moved to the side as Denny hurried into the shelter. He and Saffie embraced, and the young woman started to cry.

'I thought you were dead,' she said. 'When your father took you, I thought I'd never see you again.'

'What are you doing here?' he said. 'Did you join the Offices of Purgation?'

She nodded. 'It was possibly the biggest mistake of my life. I was only in Elestia for a few days before we set off for Steppen. But why are you here? Do you know Walter?'

'I know Lothar,' said Denny.

'What is going on here?' said Lothar. 'How do you two know each other? Sanctos isn't a small place.'

Denny smiled. 'You haven't told them who you are, have you, Saffie?'

She shook her head. 'Do they know who you are?'

'I kept it a secret for a long time, but they all know now.' He turned to Walter and Lothar. 'This is Princess Safina of Sanctos, granddaughter of the emperor; my cousin.'

Lothar's mouth dropped open, and Walter laughed.

'Another bloody cousin?' said Walter. 'I've already met Hygilt; how many of them are there? I've forgotten.'

'A lot,' said Saffie. She eyed Lothar. 'I hope this doesn't change things.'

'What things?' said Denny.

'Lothar has been looking after me. I hurt my leg in the attack on the temple, and he's been bringing me food every day.'

'Why don't you come back with us to the main camp?'

'I can't,' she said. 'Eshia... Do you know about Eshia, Denny? She's a Maker, and Marlow is a Master. They... don't feel safe in my company.'

'Did you try to hurt them?'

'Of course not. They helped Lothar save my life. But... you know. It got awkward, quickly. Where did you go after your father stole you away from us? I want to know everything you've been doing.'

Denny turned to Walter. 'Where is the camp? I want to stay here and talk to Saffie. I can find you in a few hours.'

Lothar looked a little put out, but said nothing.

'Walk north-by-north-east for just over a mile,' said Walter. He pointed. 'That way. Once again, Saffie, thank you for your help. I'll leave you two alone just now, but I'll be back before we launch our next attack. I want to know everything you can remember about the interior of the temple. I'll be asking you the same questions, Denny, so make sure you're in the camp by sunset.'

Denny nodded.

'I guess I'll come back here at sunset,' said Lothar.

Saffie nodded. 'I look forward to it, Lothar. Will you cook for me?'

He smiled. 'I might.'

Walter backed out of the shelter and stood. He gestured to Aplin and Lothar, and they began walking towards the camp.

'Dear, oh dear,' Walter said. 'A Sanctian princess, Lothar? Fucksake.'

'Well, I thought to myself, if you can snag a princess, then I should give it a try.'

Walter laughed.

'Clearly, I had no idea,' Lothar went on. 'Oh bollocks. That'll be that, then.'

'Why? Did you not hear her ask if anything would change? That doesn't sound as though she's in a rush to end things. Enjoy it while you can, mate.'

Aplin glared at them. 'Why are you joking about this? She wants to kill Masters and Makers. How do you think she'll react when she finds out Denny is one?'

'I doubt he'll tell her,' said Lothar. 'I haven't mentioned anything to her about the folk I travelled with down here.' He frowned. 'That means we were keeping secrets from each other. I still am.'

'Don't over-think it,' said Walter. 'Everyone's keeping secrets in Steppen.'

Lothar gazed into the distance. 'Never a truer word spoken.'

The Westlanders from the various detachments had returned to the camp when Walter, Lothar and Aplin arrived. Lieutenant Dietar had assembled the commanders and officers, and he approached Walter the moment he saw him.

'Don't hold back,' Walter said. 'How many did we lose?'

'We lost six warriors from the main force, sir,' Dietar said, 'but we estimate that around forty freed Westlanders were killed not long after they had escaped the slave encampment.'

'And the enemy?'

'We don't have a precise figure,' Dietar said, 'but we've spoken to warriors from every detachment, and we think that around sixty to eighty mercenaries were killed or injured. We also stole enough supplies for another two days.'

'My raid was a complete success,' cried Johan. 'We destroyed five barrack blocks, and slaughtered those inside. It was my team who gathered the supplies that will feed us.'

'Good work, Johan,' said Walter. 'How many freed Westlanders made it back to the camp?'

'A hundred and thirty-two, sir,' said Dietar. 'Almost all are men.'

'Any fit enough to fight?'

'Perhaps half that number, sir. The others are willing, but many are sick and exhausted.'

'Then we now have a fighting force of over two hundred?'

'That's about right, sir.'

Walter stood in front of the assembled commanders. 'Don't let today dishearten you,' he said. 'We didn't kill any Masters, but we emerged stronger than ever. The next attack will take place tomorrow night during the hours of darkness, when we will hit Steppen with two hundred warriors. Instruct everyone to use tonight and tomorrow to rest.'

'Will we be following the same plan, sir?' said one.

'No,' said Walter. 'We shall learn from everything we've seen, and adapt ourselves accordingly. I will brief you all tomorrow evening before we set off.'

The commanders and officers dispersed, leaving only Aplin, Lothar and Dietar standing next to Walter.

'I will take Aplin to Eshia and Marlow,' said Walter.

'Do you have a moment, sir?' said Dietar. 'If there is a new plan, then could you please share it with us?'

Walter smiled. 'When I've worked it out, Lieutenant, you'll be the first to know.'

CHAPTER 29
IN CONTROL

North-West of Steppen, Great Forest, Jallin, Central Provinces – 23rd Day of Quoma 108

Abigone sat in the driest part of the cave next to Annalise, her eyes on Magnus, who was pacing up and down. Behind him, the western-most waterfall of Steppen was roaring, as thousands of gallons of water fell across the cave's entrance.

'Well?' said Abigone.

Magnus shook his head. 'It's too dangerous,' he said. 'We should stay here. We have food and water, and we're safe.'

'That is unacceptable,' said Abigone. 'We should leave today.'

'My brother will kill us,' Magnus cried. 'He'll be looking for us, but he never visits these caves, and he has no idea about the old stores of supplies that were being kept here. He'll think we're starving in the forest. Why would we leave a place that offers food and safety?'

Abigone narrowed her eyes. 'Do I need to answer that? There are others we need to rescue. But first, we have to find someone in the forest, and we can't do that if we stay here.'

'You made your decision when we left the temple without trying to rescue Nyli and the others,' said Magnus. 'We can't go back now.'

'Don't twist my words,' she said. 'It was always my intention to rescue the others, once we had managed to escape. If you don't lead us out of here, then I will go on my own.'

'You can't; you'll get lost.'

'He's right, Abigone,' said Colette. 'We arrived here in the middle of the night, during a rainstorm. Only Magnus knows the way back to Steppen.'

'I know roughly where we are,' said Abigone. 'All we have to do is travel east, and we will reach Steppen sooner or later.'

'I'll come with you,' said Raewyn. 'This doesn't feel very different from being trapped in our apartment inside the temple. I don't like being dependant upon Magnus; I don't trust him.'

'That's unfair,' said Colette. 'My son rescued you from the Whalebone King.'

'And now he seems to have reverted to being frightened again,' said Raewyn. 'Even Constans had more courage. I miss him.'

'Then why did you break up with him?' said Stanza.

'I didn't say that I wanted to be his girlfriend, but I still miss his company. He knew me better than anyone else, and now he's dead, thanks to Magnus and his family.'

'Please don't include my son along with the others,' said Colette. 'You know he is not the same as them. He has been terrorised by his father and brothers his whole life, and yet he was brave enough to help us when it really mattered.' She glanced at Magnus. 'And now he has to be brave again. Lead Abigone and Raewyn through the forest, son. The rest of us can stay here, in the caves.'

'But where would we go?' said Magnus.

'We need to find a man called Walter,' said Abigone. 'He is the one who slew Einar. He is based in the forest, but I don't know where. He will be able to help us.'

'You know the leader of the armed force that has been attacking Steppen?'

'I do,' said Abigone. 'He is here because of me. He was the King's Champion of Upper Down, which is why I sent Lothar to meet him.

That's right, Magnus; Lothar didn't escape by accident. He escaped because I asked him to find Walter.'

Magnus stared at her. 'You lied to us?'

'Of course we lied to you,' said Abigone, 'just as you lied to us. We suspected that the so-called king would try to abuse us, and so we kept certain pieces of information from him. Back then, I was under the authority of Lady Fyenna, and so I was restricted in what I was able to achieve; but things have changed, Magnus, and I intend to go on the offensive. The students are under my protection, and I will not rest until I have them all safely in my keeping.'

She got to her feet and walked over to the waterfall. 'You need to come to a decision, Magnus, for I shall not wait for you.'

Raewyn got up and stood next to her.

'Time's up, Magnus,' Abigone said. 'Shall we, Raewyn?'

'Wait!' cried Magnus, as the two young women turned to leave the cave.

'Yes?' said Abigone.

'I will come,' he said. He turned to his mother.

'Don't worry about us, son,' Colette said. 'Annalise and I will look after Stanza and Ignatius. If you do not find this Walter, you can return here.'

Magnus nodded, then he walked to the edge of the waterfall.

'Follow me,' he said, then he walked through the curtain of water.

Abigone and Raewyn followed him, their hair and clothes becoming drenched in the few seconds it took to pass through into the open air. Abigone glanced up at the sky. It was cloudless and blue, and the autumnal sun was shining down upon the forest. She shook the water from her hair and smiled at Raewyn.

'Fresh air again,' said Raewyn; 'at last.'

'How are you feeling?' said Abigone.

'About what?'

'About killing all those mercenaries?'

Raewyn shrugged. 'I don't feel anything. Perhaps I'm becoming as cold as you, Abigone.'

'Am I supposed to take that as an insult?'

'I had thought you would take it as a compliment,' Raewyn said.

'Then I shall.' She glanced at Magnus, who was dripping water onto the grass by the edge of the forest. 'When you were in league with your brothers, did they ever mention where they thought the drunken champion's force might be located?'

'The first attack on Steppen came from the west,' Magnus said. 'That was when Einar was killed, and when over two hundred slaves were freed. The next few attacks – the raids on the villas – they came from the east.'

Abigone nodded. 'Take us round Steppen to the east. If we see any mercenaries out in the forest, kill them on sight. Or no; keep one alive, if possible. Magnus, can you use your Master skills to incapacitate someone while leaving them alive?'

'If I turn their bone to wood, then they will suffer, but not die, at least for a while.'

'That might be useful. Let us begin.'

They entered the forest, and Magnus led them along a series of almost invisible paths and tracks. He would stop every now and again to get his bearings from the sun, then they would carry on, and the line of cliffs began to recede in the distance behind him.

Abigone glanced at Raewyn as they walked, while Magnus was several yards ahead of them.

'Do you still hate him?' she whispered.

'I loathe him,' said Raewyn. 'I can barely believe that I had a crush on him. Don't you hate him, too?'

'I feel sorry for him,' Abigone said. 'He would probably be a decent man if it hadn't been for his upbringing. How many times do you think his brothers beat him up when he was younger? And they used to threaten his mother to keep him in line. Most people would crack under those conditions, but Magnus is trying to do the right thing, even though it might cost him his life.'

'He's a coward.'

'Really? He defied his father and Ragnvald – both powerful Masters

– and he defied an army of mercenaries, just to help us. That doesn't sound very cowardly. Perhaps you should try to speak to him without that tone in your voice.'

Raewyn narrowed her eyes. 'Is that why we're having this conversation? Do you want me to pretend to like him, so that he's more willing to help us?'

'It couldn't hurt.'

'Forget it,' she said. 'I am happy to fight by your side, Abigone, but I take exception to you trying to manipulate me. Is this what you were like in Upper Down?'

'I was quite different in Upper Down,' she said. 'I had a very sheltered upbringing. My father kept me hidden away in the palace, out of sight of the Westlander thugs who used to live there. It is fair to say that my life has not turned out the way I had planned. If I seem ruthless to you, it is because I have recently learned how to be that way in order to survive.' She glanced at Raewyn. 'You have also changed. After everything we have been through, that shouldn't be a surprise. Do you ever think about going home?'

'I no longer have a home,' Raewyn said. 'My parents might have been arrested by the Sanctians, as there is Master and Maker blood running through my family. I wish I had been given the chance to say goodbye to them, but you... you insisted that we go straight to the harbour.'

'Was I wrong to do that?'

'You were heartless about it, but you weren't wrong. I wouldn't have survived if we hadn't escaped Klef Mordain at that moment. But, sometimes, I wonder if it was worth it; I mean, what did I survive for? What am I going to do with my life? Where am I going to live? Steppen has made me realise that I have to look out for myself. I have to be stronger, mentally, and so now I can kill people by making their bodies explode, and it doesn't bother me any more.'

'If we get out of this alive,' Abigone said, 'then I would hope that you might choose to come to Geathan with me and Denny.'

Raewyn smiled and shook her head. 'Why – so you can become a queen? Is being a princess not good enough for you?'

'I was thinking about the school we might set up, rather than any prospect of becoming queen of Geathan. Denny has no interest in seizing the throne and, with Mor Galthide gone, I doubt that he could be persuaded to start a rebellion.'

'But you could?'

'I want to see what it's like there first,' Abigone said. 'Mor Galthide's view of Geathan was coloured by the experience of seeing his father and brother executed by the Sanctians. Imagine how painful it must have been to see his only son brought up on Sanctos.'

'If you and Denny go to Geathan, then I will tag along. Where else am I going to go? I don't know if we'll ever be close friends, Abigone, but you are one of the few people I trust.'

'Thank you,' she said. 'That means a lot to me.'

'Does it? Occasionally, I wonder if you have any feelings.'

'I hide them. My father told me it was better to appear heartless than weak, so I act that way to protect myself.'

Magnus turned his head. 'That sounds like something my father would say.'

'Were you eavesdropping?' said Raewyn.

'Not deliberately,' said Magnus. 'You started off whispering, but then it was as though you had forgotten I was here. That's why I spoke up just now – to remind you not to say anything you might regret me hearing. Are you really going to set up a new secret school for Masters and Makers if you ever get to... what was it? Geathan?'

'I would like to,' said Abigone. 'Do you want to come with us? You are the best young Master I have ever seen, Magnus. How old are you?'

'Seventeen. You?'

'I turned nineteen on the journey here,' Abigone said. 'Raewyn is the same age as you.'

'You can both kill; you are good Makers.'

'It's easy to kill,' said Raewyn. 'It's much harder to summon something complicated. You will have noticed that none of my summoned horses remotely resemble anything like a living, breathing animal. All it requires is the will to destroy another person.'

'I didn't know that,' he said. 'I don't know much about Makers, to be honest. Would you let me join the other students after everything I've done? Wouldn't they object?'

'I'd object,' said Raewyn. 'You came into the temple apartment with Ragnvald to kill us all. That isn't something I'm likely to forgive or forget any time soon. Abigone shouldn't have asked you.'

Magnus surveyed the way ahead. 'I understand. I don't expect you to forgive me, Raewyn. I succumbed to my basest fears when I agreed to go along with Ragnvald that day. My mother was crushed when she found out. She told me to leave the women's quarters and never come back.'

They fell into silence as they walked, and Abigone began to feel sorry for Magnus again.

'We agreed that I have changed,' she said, after a while, 'and I think you have changed, too, Raewyn. Might Magnus be capable of change?'

'Maybe,' she said, 'but I would need to see a lot of evidence of this change before I would be prepared to accept him into our group.'

Abigone smiled. 'Then there's hope.'

'Hope for what?'

'We are currently short of good Masters,' Abigone went on. 'Denny, Marlow and Aplin have potential, but they aren't close to the level Constans had achieved; and Ignatius and Salus are still too young. If we were to consider Magnus, then he might be a very useful addition to our school.'

Raewyn rolled her eyes. 'Did you hear that, Magnus? That's how Abigone measures people, by how useful they can be to her.'

Abigone laughed.

'I would like to be useful,' said Magnus. 'I've been treated as useless my entire life. Ragnvald only became interested in securing my support when he discovered I was a Master. Before that, he looked at me as though I was a piece of shit stuck to the bottom of his boot.'

He came to a halt, and narrowed his eyes. 'Look at that – someone has constructed a shelter out here.'

They walked closer. Abigone gazed at the shelter's construction. Tightly-woven branches formed a solid roof, and poles were holding up the sides.

Magnus crouched by the entrance. 'It's empty, but this was put together recently, by someone who knew what they were doing. I'd guess it's maybe ten days old; fifteen at a push.' He reached inside and picked up a torn piece of fabric. 'This was used to dress an injury.' He frowned. 'It looks like...'

'Like what?' said Abigone.

'I might be wrong, but it looks like it's been ripped from the uniform of a Sanctian soldier. The colour of the material matches what they were wearing. I wonder if some of them survived the attack on the temple.'

'Is the shelter still in use?' said Raewyn. 'Maybe the occupant has gone to collect water.'

Magnus shook his head. 'It's been abandoned for a few days.' He glanced up at them. 'Something happened during the attack on the temple that I have never told anyone about. There was a woman there, among all the Sanctian soldiers. She got very close to Ragnvald with a knife, and slashed his arm; then he pushed her down the stairs. I was asked to see if she was alive, and I told my brother that she was dead. I was lying; her leg was broken, but she wasn't dead.'

'You let her go?' said Raewyn.

'Not exactly. The mercenaries were told to remove the bodies of the Sanctians from the temple and dump them in the forest.'

'Why did you lie to your brother?' said Abigone.

'Because...' He hesitated.

'Tell us,' said Raewyn.

Magnus glanced away, not meeting their eyes. 'Because I knew that Ragnvald would enjoy making her suffer if she had been captured alive. He would have made her life a living nightmare, and I didn't want that to happen to her.'

'Even though she was trying to kill you at the time?' said Abigone.

Magnus got back to his feet. 'No one deserves what my brother would have done to her.'

'I want to ask you something, Magnus,' said Abigone. 'Will you try to prevent me from killing Ragnvald and your father?'

'Is that what you plan to do?'

'Yes. The horrors your father and brothers have unleashed upon Steppen should be brought to a swift and brutal end. Masters like Ragnvald and the Whalebone King are the reason why the Sanctians hate us so much. If I see them, I will kill them, and I suspect Raewyn feels the same way.'

'I do,' said Raewyn. 'They are beasts.'

'This is the choice I face,' he said. 'Helping you doesn't simply mean that you will escape; it also means that you will destroy my family. I know they are evil, but they are all I have.'

'Apart from your mother,' said Abigone.

'If I hadn't helped you get out of the temple a few days ago,' he went on, 'I would have slowly turned into a younger imitation of Ragnvald. They were planning to test my loyalty by ordering me to hurt or murder my mother. If I had refused to do it, they would have killed me. If I had done it, there would be no going back.' He looked at the two young women. 'I will not stop you from killing them, but I'm not sure I'll be able to help you. I want to, but I might be too scared. Yes, I know you all think I'm a coward. I am a coward.'

'This might surprise you, Magnus,' said Abigone, 'but I happen to think that you are quite brave. I can't imagine many people being able to stand up to such cruelty, not after the life you have led. It would be so much easier to go along with whatever Ragnvald and the others suggest; and yet you haven't. You helped that Sanctian woman, for instance. And now you are helping us, when you know what the cost might be. It is natural to be scared; what is remarkable is that you have managed to overcome your fears.'

Magnus started to cry, and Raewyn rolled her eyes. Abigone walked forward and placed a hand onto his shoulder as he sobbed.

'Stop crying, Magnus,' she said. 'You have a job to do.'

He wiped his eyes. 'Follow me.'

They walked through the forest for hours. Every now and again, Magnus would adjust their direction, and Abigone realised that he was taking them round the southern edge of Steppen. The sun was directly behind them when they forded the River Ario at its shallowest point, then they plunged back into the thick forest. After another few minutes, Magnus stopped, and pointed at the way ahead.

'A large number of people passed this way a short while ago; perhaps yesterday.'

'Are we on the trail of mercenaries or allies?' said Abigone.

'The mercenaries are too frightened to go this far into the forest. Your friend Walter is responsible for that. We need to be very careful from this point onwards. If the Westlanders recognise me, they might attack without warning.'

'Were you cruel to them when they were slaves?' said Raewyn.

'Sometimes. I was never close to being as bad as the others, but I doubt the Westlanders will make a distinction.'

'How bad were you?' Raewyn went on. 'I need to know.'

'I hit them, now and again,' he said, unable to meet her gaze.

'And?'

'I once killed a Westlander who was trying to kill me,' he said. 'I stabbed him in the heart.'

'Was it self-defence?' said Abigone.

He nodded.

'Then I say this – if any Westlander tries to harm you, I will do all I can to protect you.'

'You shouldn't make promises like that, Abigone,' said Raewyn.

'And you should really start calling me Abbie,' she said. 'Let us follow the trail, Magnus. To find Walter, we must first find his Westlanders.'

Magnus looked uncertain, then he nodded and set off. Abigone and

Raewyn went after him, and they walked for another hour. Abigone was no tracker, but even she could see the line of trampled grass that Magnus was following.

'There's a stream along here somewhere,' Magnus said. 'I wonder if...?'

He fell silent as a huge Westlander stepped out from the trees in front of him, a long spear in his grasp. Magnus raised his right hand as though out of instinct, and Abigone walked forward.

'We are here to see Lord Walter of Upper Down,' she said to the Westlander. 'We are friends of his. Did Lothar get here? We have managed to escape from Steppen.'

The Westlander gazed down at her. 'You know Walter?'

'I have known him since I was a little girl,' she said.

The Westlander's eyes roved over Magnus and Raewyn, then he took hold of a wooden whistle that was attached to a length of string around his neck. He held it to his lips and emitted two sharp blasts.

'Are you calling for help?' said Abigone.

'You will see.'

Abigone made sure that she was standing a little ahead of Magnus, then she tried to relax, despite the presence of the huge warrior standing in front of her. She hadn't been as close to a Westlander since they had attacked the students in a clearing north of Klef Mordain, and it was difficult to shake her fundamental mistrust of them.

Three more warriors bounded through the forest, all armed with spears.

'What have we here?' said one, his eyes on Abigone.

The sentry gestured to her. 'This one says she knows Walter, and she mentioned Lothar.'

The other Westlander nodded, then his eyes tightened. He pointed his spear at Magnus.

'Spies!' he cried. 'He's a son of the Whalebone King, and a Master! Kill him.'

Abigone raised her arms to shield Magnus. 'No,' she shouted. 'He has changed sides. He helped us. Let me speak to Walter.'

'Get out of the way,' said a Westlander, his spear pointing towards Abigone. 'I want the little bastard's head.'

'We will only defeat the king if we have a Master with us,' said Abigone, standing her ground. 'Let us ask Walter. I will abide by his decision.'

Raewyn raised her hand. 'Do as she says. I am a Maker, and I could end this in two seconds.'

'We share the same goals,' said Abigone. 'We all want the so-called king to fall. Send someone to fetch Lord Walter.'

'Tell him Princess Abigone is here,' said Raewyn.

One of the Westlanders nodded to the sentry, who turned and raced off through the trees.

'If any of you harm Walter,' the Westlander said, 'your heads will be decorating the forest.'

'And he's a duke, not a lord,' said another.

Abigone raised an eyebrow. She suppressed her fears and tried to project a confident air.

'Walter has become a duke?' she said. 'Tell me; does he still enjoy a whisky or two?'

One of them laughed. 'There's no whisky down here, girl, but the boss likes his brandy.'

'That doesn't surprise me,' Abigone went on. 'I assume Lothar made contact with him?'

'Lothar's here. Eshia, too. That girl's been working her arse off to make us stuff. See this spear? She made it.'

Abigone smiled. 'I'm glad to hear it. I also intend to lend my assistance to your cause.'

'Stop making friends with her,' said the tallest Westlander. 'She's protecting a son of the Whalebone King.'

A large group emerged from the forest. A few of them cried out at the sight of Magnus, their anger rising, then Walter appeared in their midst, his gaze never leaving Abigone.

'Your Highness,' he said, his features transforming into a smile. 'Of all the places to meet. Everything I have done here has been for you.'

'Thank you,' she said; 'and I hear you are a duke?'

'Killie insisted,' he said. 'She couldn't marry a lord.'

'You married my sister?'

'I'm sorry we didn't invite you to the wedding,' he said. 'You were busy. How did you escape?'

She gestured towards Magnus.

'He's one of the Whalebone King's sons, boss,' said a Westlander.

'Is that true?' said Walter.

'It is,' said Abigone. 'He has turned. His family's depravity has pushed him into our arms. I ask that you allow him to join us, Walter.'

'Is he a Master?'

'He is the best young Master I have ever witnessed,' said Abigone.

Walter eyed Magnus. 'Are you prepared to fight by our side, against your father and brothers?'

Magnus seemed to shrink a little.

'Well?' said Walter. 'Answer me.'

'I will fight,' said Magnus.

'This could be a trick,' said a Westlander. 'We cannot trust him, boss.'

'We'll hold him securely for a while,' said Walter, 'until we better understand his intentions. Bind his wrists.'

Two Westlanders walked forward, and Abigone stood to the side. She didn't want Magnus's hands to be bound, but it was too early to question Walter's leadership.

'Don't worry,' she said to Magnus. 'You will not be harmed.'

Magnus gazed at the ground as the Westlanders pulled his arms behind his back and tied cords around his wrists.

Walter gestured in the other direction, and everyone bar the sentry began to follow the trail through the forest.

'This is Raewyn,' Abigone said to Walter. 'She is a Maker, and she and I will help in the next attack. There are still five students being held in Steppen; three in the temple, and two in the shanty town.'

Walter nodded. 'I'm going to embarrass you as soon as we get to the camp,' he said. 'Don't hold it against me.'

Abigone frowned. 'What do you mean?'

'Just play along, Your Highness. The Westlanders will need to witness what I do.'

They came into a large clearing in the forest, where dozens of Westlanders were sitting or working. More were appearing through the trees, having heard the sentry's whistle earlier.

Walter brought the others to a halt, then he walked out in front of Abigone. He faced the Westlanders, and raised a hand. They quietened, and turned their attention towards him.

Walter said nothing, then he turned and knelt before Abigone, his head bowed and his hands raised in supplication.

'Your Royal Highness, Princess Abigone of the free realm of Upper Down,' he said in a loud, clear voice, 'I humbly pledge my loyalty to you, my liege lady, my beloved princess; and I ask that you accept me into your service. It was for you that I ventured into the Great Forest, and my heart rejoices to see you again. I am yours to command.'

Abigone's cheeks flushed. Never had Walter spoken to her in such a tone, and his words had caught her off guard.

'You may rise, Walter,' she said. 'I accept your pledge.'

He took her hand and kissed it, as the Westlanders watched in silence, then he got to his feet and smiled at her.

'Sorry about that, Abbie,' he whispered, 'but it had to be done.'

'Please don't ever do it again,' she whispered back.

Walter turned to face the growing crowd. 'Tonight's attack has been postponed to tomorrow evening,' he said. 'The arrival of the princess and her friend means that we have two more Makers on our side; two more Makers to help us bring down the Whalebone King. I'll need time to re-think our plan, so everyone can rest tonight. Spread out through the camp, and tell everyone what you heard here.'

He turned to Abigone. 'There are a few people I think you will like to see, Your Highness.'

'Is Lothar in the camp?'

'Not at the moment,' said Walter. 'He's visiting someone that he's been taking care of since she also escaped from the temple.'

Abigone frowned. 'Who? She wouldn't happen to be a Sanctian, would she?'

'How did you know that?'

She gestured towards Magnus, who was being guarded by four Westlanders. 'I think she might be the woman Magnus saved. Does she have a broken leg?'

Walter eyed Magnus. 'She does.' He glanced at the Westlander guards. 'Take him to the isolated shelter to the east of the camp and hold him there. Let no one approach him. He is not to escape, but neither is he to be harmed.'

Magnus's eyes widened, and he stared at Raewyn and Abigone.

'I would be very upset if he is hurt,' Abigone said.

'He'll be fine,' said Walter. He nodded to the guards, and they led Magnus away. Walter gestured to Abigone and Raewyn. He escorted them through the busy camp, until they reached another clearing. In it, Eshia, Marlow and Aplin were hard at work. The two young Masters were converting heaps of earth and stones into metal, and Eshia was using the metal to summon all manner of objects, from spear heads to cooking pots.

'Aplin?' said Abigone. 'Does that mean...?'

Denny appeared from the darkness of the trees, and Abigone smiled as he hurried towards her. They embraced, and Abigone closed her eyes as she felt his arms around her.

'Betrothed to a Sanctian prince, eh?' said Walter. 'Just wait until Killie finds out.'

CHAPTER 30
THE CRUTCH

South-East of Steppen, Great Forest, Jallin, Central Provinces – 23rd Day of Quoma 108

Saffie hobbled about on her crutch in front of the shelter. A cold wind was gusting through the forest, and many of the trees were losing their leaves. Red, brown and orange foliage lay carpeting the ground covering the patches of grass, or was lying on top of the scraggly undergrowth. Saffie grunted, her left leg in pain as she exercised. Lothar had told her that it was too early to be up and about, but she had been unable to face another day of inactivity. Sixteen days had elapsed since her injury, and Saffie felt that it had been long enough; besides, trying out her new crutch had taken her mind off the other things pressing upon her mind.

Every Sanctian who had accompanied her to Steppen was dead. She had met Masters and a Maker and survived. She had lost her virginity; and, the most important thing of all – she had discovered that she was a Maker. There was nothing she could do about three of those things – they had happened and were in the past, but her entire sense of herself had been warped by the accidental summoning of a lump of misshapen wood.

No, she said to herself; don't think about it. Concentrate on staying upright, despite the agony her leg was causing her. Lothar had hurt her a couple of days before. He hadn't meant to, but he had leaned over her leg as though he had forgotten for a moment that she was injured, and the pain had been so severe that she had wept. Lothar's face had turned grey, and he had apologised several times, but she found it hard to stay angry with him. She liked the way things were going with the Mountain Ranger, and it was a pity he had found out that she was a Sanctian princess. She hoped it wouldn't change the way he acted towards her; the last thing she wanted was for it to ruin what they had.

Her thoughts went to Denny. She had been so happy to see her cousin when he had turned up at the shelter the day before with Walter, that she had overlooked the fact that he had been cagey with the answers to her questions.

She remembered what she had been told by Captain Zola before they had departed Elestia. The officer had informed her that Denny had last been seen in Klef Mordain in the company of a possible Maker, and that the possible Maker was rumoured to have been Princess Abigone of Upper Down. Zola had then asked her if there was any possibility that Denny might be a Master, and Saffie had thrown scorn at the idea. She hadn't told Denny any of this, preferring to listen to his explanations without him knowing what she knew, and that had made her feel dishonest. Denny would reject her as soon as he discovered her secret; unless, of course, the rumour about him was true. She needed to know, but how could she ask?

Saffie paused for a moment as sweat appeared on her brow. She was aching in a dozen different places after sitting or lying in the shelter for so long, but it was worth it to be up and about.

The sound of footsteps reached her. Her first instinct was to hobble back to her shelter, then she smiled as she imagined that it might be Lothar. She turned her head, and was only slightly disappointed when she saw Denny walking towards her.

'Hello,' she said, leaning on her crutch.

'Good evening, cousin,' he said. 'I wanted to talk to you, but I can't stay long.'

'The attack is happening tonight,' she said; 'I wasn't expecting to see you at all today.'

'The attack has been postponed until the same time tomorrow night,' he said. 'A few others have escaped from Steppen, and Walter wants to include them in his plans.' He smiled. 'You should have seen Walter last night. I don't think I've ever seen anyone get as drunk as that.'

'What's he like when he's drunk?'

'Loud,' said Denny; 'loud and boisterous. The Westlanders lap it up.'

'It could be worse, I suppose. Will you give me a hand to sit down?'

Denny walked over. He put an arm round her shoulder, and helped her to sit by the entrance of the shelter.

'Thank you,' she said.

'I assume Lothar usually helps you with these things?' he said.

Saffie shrugged.

'You seem quite close to him, cousin.'

'He saved my life.'

'Walter said something strange yesterday, about Lothar.'

'What did he say?'

Denny eyed her. 'He said that he thinks Lothar might be falling for you.'

Saffie suppressed a smile, but said nothing.

'I hope he hasn't been making any unwanted advances towards you, Saffie,' Denny went on. 'Would you like me to talk to him?'

'No, thank you.'

'Are you sure? I don't mind. I would hate to think that he's been making a pest of himself.'

'He has been nothing but kind, Denny; you needn't worry.'

'All right. Let me know if that changes.'

'So,' she said, 'who else has escaped from Steppen? More Masters and Makers?'

Denny lowered his gaze.

'I don't understand how you became associated with a group of Masters and Makers,' she went on. 'Where did you say you met them?'

'On the road,' he said. 'I didn't know they were Masters and Makers. My father and I were travelling through the Central Provinces, and it made sense to join a larger group. Safety in numbers, you know?'

Saffie eyed him. 'Once again, I am sorry about your father, Denny. I hope the Whalebone King gets what he deserves. You never did tell me exactly why you and your father left Sanctos.'

'It's complicated,' he said. 'Have you seen any of our other cousins recently?'

'Not really. I was serving with the Sanctian navy for a year before I joined the Offices of Purgation. I saw my brothers briefly, when the ship I was on docked for a few days. Cat was also there. They were all fine.'

'Cat was there at the same time as your brother Marcello? Didn't you tell me yesterday that they were betrothed?'

'That's right. The emperor is planning for three pairs of cousins to wed – me and Arturo, Cat and Marcello, and Erno and Marina. Cat and Marcello seemed embarrassed about it, and Allessandro was teasing them.'

'It seems strange,' said Denny, 'but I'm sure our grandfather has his reasons.'

'*Strange* is not how I would word it, Denny,' she said. 'The emperor is making a mistake. He put us all together as young children, and now he expects six of us to get married?'

'Yes, but he's the emperor. What can you do?'

Saffie bit her tongue. There was plenty more she could say regarding how she felt about the prospect of marrying Prince Arturo, but she knew she had to remain silent until she discovered more about Denny's situation.

'You were lucky you escaped in time,' she said; 'otherwise, it might have been you getting lined up with Cat.'

He smiled awkwardly.

'Have you met anyone on your travels?' she went on.

'I have met many people.'

'That's not what I meant. Have you met any girls you liked?'

Denny said nothing, then he looked away. 'Not really.'

'Where were you before you met up with the Masters and Makers?'

'We were in Campsie,' he said.

'And before that?'

Denny laughed. 'Why do I feel as though I am undergoing an interrogation?'

'I just want to know what happened to you. There was a rumour that you had gone to Geathan.'

'I have never been to Geathan.'

'Did your father want to take you there?'

'We didn't really discuss it.'

'Come on,' said Saffie, shaking her head; 'do you expect me to believe that?'

'Are you accusing me of lying?'

Saffie narrowed her eyes. Why was he keeping things from her? The only reason she could think of involved the rumours told to her by Captain Zola. She glanced at Denny, but he wouldn't meet her gaze. The two cousins had been good friends during their childhood; would she be risking that if she continued to press him?

'I have a confession to make,' she said.

Denny glanced up. 'Yes?'

'Lothar and I... we, well, we might have started something.'

'What? You and Lothar?'

'Is that so bad?' she said. 'I like him. He's not someone I would have imagined as being a possible imperial suitor; and I know that it probably won't go anywhere, but I am very fond of him.'

Denny narrowed his eyes. 'You were injured, and he was looking after you? Are you sure he hasn't pushed you into this?'

'Were you not listening before? I trust him. We don't agree on some things; I'll admit that – but am I not allowed to find a little companionship? He makes me... happy.'

'Are you sleeping with him?'

'That's none of your business.'

'I thought you wanted to wait until you were married?'

'That's what everyone told us in Sanctos, Denny. We had to be pure and virginal. I'm sorry to offend you, but I didn't feel like waiting.'

Denny said nothing.

'Do you think less of me now?' she said.

'No, Saffie; of course not. I remember all the lectures we received warning us not to sleep around before we were married, but I reckon at least half of the cousins have broken that rule at one time or another.'

'But not you?'

'I guess I'm saving myself for the right woman.'

'And have you found her?'

Denny hesitated.

'This is ridiculous, Denny,' she said. 'I have another confession to make. I was told that you were in Klef Mordain. You were seen entering the Sanctian embassy with a young woman, just minutes before the building was destroyed by that same woman. Why can't you be honest with me? According to reports, the woman was none other than Princess Abigone of Upper Down – the notorious Maker who destroyed Prince Valentino's cannon. Is it supposed to be a coincidence that Walter and Lothar also happen to be from Upper Down? How stupid do you think I am?'

Denny stared at her. 'You... already knew all that?'

'Yes.'

'Then why were you trying to trick me?'

'I wasn't; I was hoping you would tell me of your own volition. You are in a relationship with a Maker – admit it.'

Denny's eyes darkened into defiance. 'All right; I admit it. Abigone and I are betrothed, and I don't care what anyone on Sanctos thinks. I love her.'

Saffie smiled. 'At last. Was that so hard?

'Yes, it was hard. It was bloody hard. Abigone and I are wanted by the imperial authorities, and you, Saffie, work for those authorities. Are you surprised that I might have been a little reticent to reveal the truth to you?'

'But it's me, Denny. We've been friends since we could walk. I love you as I love my brothers.'

'I love you, too, Saffie; but you hate Masters and Makers. And I don't just mean in the way that most people on Sanctos vaguely dislike them – you loathe them with all of your being. Eshia told me that you would like to see her and Marlow executed; that they deserved to die. I presume you would also like to see Abigone being burnt at a stake?'

Saffie fell silent.

'I don't hear you denying it,' Denny went on. 'Perhaps I should go.'

'Wait,' she said. 'Why did you and Abigone kill those people in the embassy?'

'Because they wanted to kill us.'

'*Us*? Not just Abigone? They wanted to kill you, too?'

Denny shifted his gaze, his features troubled.

'Is there something else you aren't telling me?' she said.

Denny remained silent.

'I was told another rumour in Elestia,' she went on; 'one that I dismissed out of hand. Now I am not so sure.'

'What rumour?'

'That Abigone and you were among those attending a hidden school for Masters and Makers in Klef Mordain. Deny it, and I will believe you and never mention it again.'

Denny shook his head. 'And if I refuse to deny it?'

'Are you a Master, Denny?'

'Yes. I am, Saffie. I am one of those people you hate. That was why my father took me away from Sanctos. He found out, and he wanted to protect me. I wasn't abducted; I left willingly.'

Saffie sat in silence. She had won, in a way; she had forced Denny into revealing his secrets, and he had confirmed her suspicions.

'I won't be visiting you again,' Denny said. 'I know that you believe me to be a vile monster, and I wouldn't want to make you feel uncomfortable.'

'There was a reason I pressed you so hard,' she said.

'So you could report me to the Offices of Purgation? So that you could witness the look on the emperor's face when you tell him the truth about me?'

'I won't be doing either of those things, Denny.'

Denny laughed. 'Why not? Are you planning to blackmail me?'

'Do you know me at all, cousin?'

'I thought I did.'

'I had to squeeze the truth out of you, because that was the only way I would feel safe in telling you my own secret.'

'What secret? You already told me about Lothar.'

'It has nothing to do with Lothar. Well, that's not strictly true, as it was Lothar who led me to the truth.'

Denny narrowed his eyes.

'Four days ago,' she said, as her heart raced, 'I discovered something.'

'What?'

Her mouth almost froze. 'I... I am a Maker.'

Denny stared at her.

Saffie smiled. 'You would not believe the relief I feel in being able to tell you this, Denny,' she said. 'I am a Maker. I am one of the people that I have feared and hated my entire life.'

'No,' he said, shaking his head.

'It came as quite a shock to me, too,' she said. 'For over a year, I have had nightmares about being a Maker. I told Lothar about them, and he said that I should try to summon something, just to prove to myself that I wasn't cursed. After some persuasion, I relented. It worked. I summoned a lump of wood.' She laughed, then started to cry. 'A lump of fucking wood, Denny. That's all it was, and yet it represented something that I am still trying to understand. How did you cope when you found out? Did you think you had gone mad?'

'I... was just messing around one day,' he said. 'To be honest, I've known for a few years. I kept it a secret from everyone, but my father noticed, and he decided that we had to leave Sanctos at once. I was scared of being discovered, I guess. I'm not a very good Master. I had a year of study in the school in Klef Mordain, but I find it hard to clear the thoughts from my head.' He gazed at her. 'Four days? You must be going out of your mind. But what does it mean? Can there be Master and Maker blood in the imperial line? How could two of us have these abilities?'

'The emperor is to blame, though unwittingly – it's the only explanation,' she said. 'He married off his children to the foremost royal families of the Central Provinces, and those lands used to be ruled by Masters and Makers. Your father came from Geathan, and my mother is the daughter of a queen of Mylos. Without knowing it, the emperor was bringing Master and Maker blood into his own family.'

Denny laughed. 'When I came here today, I was worried about what I would say to you.'

'I was the same,' she said. 'I'm sorry for pestering you, but I had to be sure before I told you the truth about me.'

'What will you do next? I assume you will be leaving the Offices of Purgation?'

'I haven't decided anything yet,' she said. 'I am still struggling with my emotions. Sometimes, I think I should throw myself off a cliff, to rid the lands of a vile Maker. I had always assumed that every Master and Maker must be aware of their evil abilities, that it was impossible not to know; but I didn't know.'

'Abigone believes that Masters and Makers have been blessed by the spirits. The very opposite of what we were taught on Sanctos.'

'Do you believe that?'

'I don't know,' he said. 'Do the spirits love us, or do they hate us? Are the spirits good, bad, or are there some of both types? I don't know anything any more, so I try not to think about it.'

'I know what you mean. I haven't prayed in four days. I still believe, but what could I say to them?'

'If Abigone is right, then you should probably thank them.'

Saffie lapsed into silence.

'Shall we agree to keep each other's secrets from everyone on Sanctos?' said Denny.

'Yes,' she said. 'Only you and Lothar know about me. I know you must be very fond of Abigone, but please don't tell her, or any of the other Masters and Makers from the school you went to; and I won't tell anyone about you.'

'Agreed,' he said. He got to his feet. 'I'm going back to the camp now. Abigone wants to discuss tomorrow's plan with Walter and the other leaders, and I don't want to miss it.'

Saffie looked up at him. 'I will see you soon, cousin.'

Denny set off through the forest, and disappeared among the trees. Saffie tried to sort through her feelings. She felt less alone knowing that Denny was a Master, but she also felt a little annoyed that he had known for years and never told her. But why would he have told her? She knew how she would have reacted if he had confided in her while they were on Sanctos: she would have reported him to Aunt Isabella, the high priestess of their faith. Denny would have been interrogated and executed, and Mor Galthide would have been burned at the stake next to his son, to ensure that he could never father another Master or Maker.

Saffie gazed at the ground. No wonder Denny had fled.

'Blessed spirits,' she whispered; 'help me to know what I should do. Am I evil? I don't want to be. If I was born this way, then how can it be my fault? Should I hate myself? Help me.'

Lothar arrived late that evening, carrying a large bag over his shoulder as he emerged from the dark forest. Saffie had moved back into the shelter by that time, and had wrapped a thick blanket across her shoulders to keep out the chill. Lothar crouched by the entrance, but his eyes seemed distracted.

'Is something wrong?' she said.

'I wouldn't use the word *wrong*,' he said, as he entered the shelter. He kissed her, and she took his hand. 'Princess Abigone has assumed command of the entire shitshow, and she'll be leading tomorrow's attack on Steppen.'

'What about Walter?' she said.

Lothar laughed. 'He could hardly say *no*, not after publicly pledging his undying love and loyalty to her when she arrived in the camp earlier today. He wasn't expecting her to make a move like that, though; I could see it in his eyes. Do you fancy some dinner? I'll get a fire started, and...'

She put her arms round his neck. 'Dinner can wait,' she said.

He raised an eyebrow and smiled. For a flicker of a moment, she thought he was going to turn her down, and expose her insecurities. Why did she need him? Was it to distract her from the mess her life had become? She longed for human comfort, and she yearned to dispel the loneliness she felt while she sat by herself in the shelter all day. But there was more to it than that. Lothar accepted her for who she was; he understood her.

'I can hardly say no to that,' he said, putting the bag to one side.

'Take your time,' she said, as she gathered him up in her arms. 'I want every moment to last.'

An hour later, Saffie watched as Lothar got the fire going. He caught her gaze, and they shared a quiet smile.

'I told Denny the truth today,' she said.

'I thought you might,' he said. 'I noticed that he was looking extra thoughtful when he got back from seeing you. How did he take it?'

'I had to get him to admit that he was a Master before I was brave enough to tell him,' she said.

'That makes sense. If the emperor finds out that he has two grandchildren with these abilities he'll...' He paused, as he hung a pot of water over the fire. 'You know something; I have no clue what the emperor would do. I assume his head might explode.'

'You're not wrong,' she said. 'The news might cause him to keel over.'

'You're taking it very well, I think.'

'Am I? My entire worldview has been shattered. My faith is in tatters, and I haven't the faintest idea what I'm going to do with my life if we get out of this damn forest. What do you think you might do?'

'I will probably follow Walter to Sanctos.'

Saffie frowned. 'Why is he going to Sanctos?'

'To answer a summons from your dear old grandfather. The emperor isn't happy about the treaty with Upper Down, and he wants a regent from the realm to go to Sanctos to renegotiate it.'

'And Walter volunteered?'

'The only other regent in Upper Down is Princess Kilbride, Walter's wife, and she's pregnant. It had to be Walter.'

'Then Kilbride will be the sole ruler of Upper Down in his absence?'

'That's right. It's better that way. If Walter had been left alone in Upper Down without her, then he might have turned to the bottle, and the realm would have suffered. This way, at least Upper Down is being looked after properly.'

'In other words, Walter can't be trusted with his responsibilities?'

'It depends. Right now, Abigone is a restraining influence on him. Walter got very drunk last night, but that was before she arrived. Now that she's here, he's behaving himself again. Don't repeat this to anyone, but that's partly why I decided to go to Sanctos with him. Someone needs to be by his side, to remind him that it's not a good idea to negotiate with an emperor while drunk or hungover. If I do it, then maybe I can repay what I did to him when I was working for his brother.' He tipped a plateful of meat and vegetables into the pot and sat back against the tree. 'I don't suppose that you might fancy going to Sanctos as well?'

Saffie said nothing. She tried to imagine what it would be like to face the emperor and empress with the knowledge that she was a Maker. How would she cope with her Aunt Isabella? She would have to lie with every breath she took, and if she was discovered, she would be led to a stake and burned to death in front of a baying crowd.

Lothar nodded, but said nothing.

'Put yourself in my position,' she said. 'I am a Maker working for the

Offices of Purgation. If I go back to Sanctos, then I might be arrested and executed.'

'But only Denny and I know the truth about you,' he said, 'and I sure as fuck wouldn't say anything.'

'I know you wouldn't.'

'I wish you weren't a damn princess,' he said.

'There's another reason why I'm reluctant to return to Sanctos,' she said. 'My betrothed lives there.'

He narrowed his eyes. 'You're betrothed to someone? Why didn't you tell me?'

'I didn't want anything to spoil what we have, Lothar. I don't want to marry him; it was the emperor's idea. He has proposed that three pairs of the cousins intermarry, and I was chosen as one half of a pair. I'm supposed to marry Prince Arturo. He's nice, but...' She shuddered. 'He feels like a brother. If I return to Sanctos, then the emperor might decide to arrange our wedding.'

'How old is he?'

'Twenty-one.'

'Have you ever...?'

'I haven't seen him since I heard the announcement, Lothar, and we certainly didn't get up to anything before that. Aren't you being a little judgemental? I have never asked you about any women you might have been seeing over the years. There have been other women, I assume?'

'A few.'

'I have absolutely no interest in hearing anything about them. I want to live in the present, right here, with you.'

Lothar said nothing.

'Are you still thinking about Arturo?' she said.

'I'm thinking that we have no future,' he said. 'I understand why you wouldn't want to go back to Sanctos, but I have already promised Walter that I'll be going there with him. And I hadn't even considered that you might be part of an arranged marriage, even though it's fucking obvious. I mean, that's exactly what happened to the royalty in Upper Down. As far as I know, Walter and Kilbride are the only ones who have chosen to marry out of love, and that's because there was no one else around who could tell them what to do. We can never get married, even if we wanted to. I know that sounds as though I'm making assumptions about us, but even the tiniest flicker of hope for the future would go a long way. All right; I will try to live in the present.'

She watched as he stirred the contents of the pot. Had Walter been right – was Lothar falling for her? Part of her had assumed that he saw what they had as a temporary affair; something from which he would be able to walk away without any regrets. Did he want more from her?

If he did, she realised, he wasn't alone. She reached out for him, and he responded by wrapping his arms around her. He held her close, and she never wanted the feeling to end.

CHAPTER 31
ENTRUSTED

East of Steppen, Great Forest, Jallin, Central Provinces – 24th Day of Quoma 108

Magnus shivered in the damp shelter. It had rained during the night, but the cold wasn't the only thing that had kept him awake. The Westlanders guarding him had been muttering things in their own language while staring at him all night, and Magnus could guess exactly what they wanted to do to a son of the Whalebone King. Unable to get comfortable with his hands tied behind his back, he had sat miserably as the rain dripped down from the gaps in the roof of the shelter.

The rain had ceased at dawn, and the sun had risen over the steaming forest. Magnus needed to pee, but he was too scared to ask the Westlanders for permission. They would likely view it as an opportunity to humiliate him further, and he wondered if helping Abigone and Raewyn had been the right choice. Abigone had promised to protect him, but he had seen no sign of her since he had been led off to the eastern edge of the sprawling camp.

They were going to kill him. They knew he was a Master, and therefore too dangerous to be left alive. Walter would know this, and even if he didn't, then Magnus was sure that dozens of Westlanders would have reminded him. He wondered what Ragnvald was doing. Raewyn's slaughter of the mercenaries outside the temple would have been witnessed by many, and the king and his two remaining loyal sons would know that they were facing at least one belligerent Maker. Would they assume that Magnus would fight against them? It was strange to think that his rebellion had started when he had become slightly infatuated with Raewyn. How had a crush developed into a fight to the death? Neither side trusted him, and it was only a matter of time before he was murdered.

He gazed at the muddy ground, wishing he had never left the cave. At least his mother was safe, but for how long? As for Raewyn, it was clear that she loathed him. He had done the right thing by helping to save her and the others, but the price would be his life.

The Westlanders started talking again, then two figures approached the shelter. Magnus peered through the gloom – it was Walter and Abigone. They spoke to the Westlander guards, who moved back a little, then they walked up to the entrance of the shelter and crouched.

'Get it over with,' said Magnus. 'Please make it quick.'

Abigone raised an eyebrow. 'We are not here to kill you, Magnus.'

He frowned, not believing her.

'If we were going to execute you,' said Walter, 'we would have done it last night. Princess Abigone and I have been going over the plan for this evening's attack, and we are trying to finalise a few details. We've heard from some of the Westlanders that the Whalebone King's private rooms are on the top floor of the temple; is that right?'

'He lives in a large apartment up there,' said Magnus. 'We think it used to belong to the high priest of the temple, but no one knows for sure.'

Abigone narrowed her eyes. 'Look at him shivering. This shelter leaks, and he's been freezing in the rain all night.'

Walter turned to a Westlander. 'Bring some dry clothes and a few blankets,' he said. 'And some breakfast for the prisoner; and don't fucking spit in it.'

The Westlander rolled his eyes. 'Yes, boss.'

'I am sorry about the conditions in which you have been held here,' said Abigone, eyeing Magnus. 'Some food and dry clothes will make you feel a bit better.'

'We want to trust you,' said Walter. 'Should we?'

Magnus said nothing.

'Can you give us detailed directions on how to locate the quarters of the king, Ragnvald and Erling?' Walter went on.

'Are you going to kill my family?'

Walter half-smiled. 'We are certainly going to try.'

'You already knew this, Magnus,' said Abigone. 'I told you our intentions yesterday. If I remember correctly, you pledged not to stand in our way. Tell me – what do you want?'

Magnus hesitated. 'I don't understand.'

'It's a simple question,' said Abigone. 'Imagine that we are victorious, and that you are freed. What will you do? I mean, what would you like to do?'

'I, uh... I would like to join your new school.'

Abigone inclined her head slightly. 'Very well. If you help us defeat the so-called king, I will grant you this request.'

'But... but Raewyn said no. She hates me.'

'Raewyn is not Head Maker,' said Abigone. 'The decision is mine. Besides, if you prove your loyalty and worth this coming night, then the others will see that you have truly changed. Would you like to bring your mother along to the new school?'

'Could I do that? Would you allow her to come with us?'

'I would allow it. Annalise will be coming, and she isn't a Maker. We could find your mother a job within the school. Didn't she teach you how to read and write?'

'Yes.'

'Then she could help out with lessons, or some other role; that isn't important at the moment. What's important is that you are able to persuade us of your good intentions.'

'Will you kill me if you aren't persuaded?'

Abigone looked a little irritated. 'Let me make this perfectly clear,

Magnus – you risked your life to bring me, Raewyn and Stanza out of the temple. You killed four mercenaries in doing so. I do not forget those who have assisted me. When I told you yesterday that I would protect you, I meant it.'

'But you are not in charge,' Magnus said. 'Walter is.'

Walter gave him a wry smile. 'Certain things have recently changed around here,' he said. 'Princess Abigone has assumed command of the forces arrayed against Steppen. I take my orders from Her Highness now.'

'What?' said Magnus. 'But she... she's...'

'A woman?' said Abigone. 'I can tell that the concept of a woman in charge has confused you somewhat, Magnus. Not all places are like Steppen, praise the spirits. My sister rules in Upper Down, for instance; well, at least until little Alfie is old enough to become king in his own right.'

'But a woman cannot become queen,' he said; 'not unless she's married to a king.'

'Yes, I suppose that's right,' she said. 'However, as a princess, I hold the highest rank here. Duke Walter is now my senior military advisor and second-in-command, as he has far more experience than I do. There is but one reason why I assumed command. Tell him, Walter.'

'Princess Abigone pulled rank on me,' said Walter, 'when I told her that I wasn't going to allow her to fight on the front line tonight. She seemed to take exception to this, but I was only trying to protect her.'

Abigone smiled. 'Walter thought I would be content to remain here while he does all the work. Needless to say, I feel I will be of more use killing mercenaries than sitting in a camp with the injured and sick. The Westlander men allow their women to fight, so why can't we? Raewyn will be by my side during the attack. Your father will be facing two aggrieved Makers.'

'Raewyn will be fighting in the battle?' said Magnus.

'You have seen her kill,' said Abigone. 'Are you concerned for her safety?'

'Of course I am,' he said. 'I know she hates me, but...'

'Go on.'

'I... I can't stand the thought of her getting hurt.'

'I see. Would you be prepared to guard her while she goes about the business of slaughtering mercenaries?'

Magnus's eyes narrowed.

'That's why we're here,' said Walter. 'A Master could protect the flanks of our two Makers.'

'But you have other Masters.'

'None are as proficient as you,' said Abigone.

'But can we trust you?' said Walter.

'You have two choices,' said Abigone. 'If you help us, then you will have earned a place in my new school, and you might even be forgiven by Raewyn. You and your mother would have a new life, far from here, where you will be safe, and where you will have the chance to develop your abilities. It is sunny and warm in Geathan, or so I am told. It would be a good life. However, if you were to betray us, and we are defeated, then you would go back to your old life. Your mother would be re-enslaved, and your father and brothers would never trust you again. How long do you think you and your mother would survive under such conditions? A life of hope, or a life of fear; which do you choose?'

She paused as a Westlander arrived with clothes, blankets and a basket of food. He placed them on the ground in front of the shelter.

'Thank you,' said Abigone.

The Westlander eyed Magnus, then he backed away.

'Untie his hands, Walter,' said Abigone.

Walter reached behind Magnus and loosened the knots keeping his wrists together. The cords fell free and Magnus rubbed his hands together.

'Walter and I will leave you to eat and get changed, Magnus,' Abigone went on; 'that will give you time to reach a decision.'

'I've already decided,' he said. 'I want a new life; I want to be free. I will help you.'

Abigone smiled.

. . .

Magnus was left alone for much of the day. His wrists had been rebound after he had finished the food he had been brought but, despite that, Abigone had been right – his mood had improved after he had changed out of his damp clothes and had eaten something; and he had the wild dream of a bright future dangling in front of him. Could he allow himself to believe Abigone's promises? He tried not to allow his hopes to cloud his mind, but it was futile. The picture she had painted seemed unreal, and all he had to do to earn it was protect the two Makers. It was too good to be true, he told himself; there had to be a catch. Perhaps they would kill him as soon as he had served his purpose; women were like that, or so his father had always told him. They were fickle and capricious, which was why they were never allowed to hold any positions of power within the realm of the Whalebone King. They were there to cook and clean, and to gratify the desires of the men; and yet Walter, Lothar and the horde of savage Westlanders hadn't blinked when Abigone had taken over. Were they happy to obey her orders? Ragnvald would have laughed at the notion. Magnus wondered if killing Fyenna had been his father's biggest mistake. Prior to that, Abigone had been a quiet presence in the guest apartment, her role subservient to that of the older Head Maker. Now that she was free to lead, Abigone had taken control as though she had been born to it.

Dry, warm and fed, Magnus slipped into a light sleep. He was awoken at some point in the afternoon, when Lothar shook his shoulder.

'Wakey-wakey, Master-boy,' the Mountain Ranger said. 'Time to get up.'

Magnus rubbed his eyes and sat. Raewyn and Eshia were standing behind Lothar, along with several Westlanders armed with loaded crossbows.

Lothar took out a knife, and Magnus flinched away.

'Settle down,' said Lothar. 'I'm going to cut the cords binding your wrists; and this time, if you behave, they won't be put back in place again.'

'I object to this,' said Eshia. 'He will betray us.'

'I am aware of your feelings,' said Lothar, 'but Princess Abigone's in charge, not you.'

'He isn't going to protect Raewyn,' Eshia went on; 'he's going to kill her the first chance he gets.'

'I will not,' said Magnus.

'He's right,' said a huge Westlander, 'because if he tries, I will shoot the little fucker in the back of the head.'

'You're going to have a few Westlanders accompanying you,' said Lothar, as he reached round and cut through the cords binding Magnus's wrists together. 'Raewyn insisted.'

'It's a sensible precaution,' said Raewyn.

'I was with you for hours yesterday,' said Magnus, as he rubbed his freed wrists. 'Did I try to harm you?'

'Abigone and I were walking behind you for a reason,' said Raewyn.

Magnus glanced away. He was going to have to prove himself, while under the scrutiny of Westlanders who loathed him.

'All right,' he said.

Lothar extended a hand. Magnus took it, and the Mountain Ranger pulled him to his feet. He walked out of the shelter and stretched his limbs.

'I know none of you trust me,' he said, 'but this is the only chance I'll get to free myself of this place, and I'm not going to throw it away. Are my mother and the others still in the caves by the waterfall?'

'They were being moved here this morning,' said Lothar. 'They should be in the camp by now.'

'May I speak to my mother?'

'I don't see why not,' said Lothar. 'Come on.'

Magnus set off after the Mountain Ranger, noticing that the two Makers stayed behind him, no doubt so that they could kill him if he tried anything stupid. Magnus concentrated on keeping his hands by his side, aware that if he moved them in a way that looked suspicious, his body would be torn to shreds by Raewyn's powers.

They walked through the forest, and entered the main part of the camp. Dozens of Westlanders were preparing for battle, and they looked up as they saw Lothar approach with Magnus by his side. The muttering in their own language began, and a few made throat-slitting motions towards the son of the Whalebone King. Magnus did his best to ignore them, and he was led into a small clearing. His mother was sitting on a tree stump next to Annalise, and Magnus ran up to them.

Colette smiled. 'There you are, Magnus. I hear that you are joining tonight's attack.'

'Yes,' he said. 'Abigone trusts me, but I don't think anyone else does.'

'I trust you, son,' she said, taking his hand in hers. 'This is the opportunity you have awaited your entire life – a chance to show everyone what truly lies within your heart. I am very proud of you for getting this far, and I know you will not falter this night.'

'Sorry to interrupt, ma'am,' said Lothar, 'but the princess is waiting.'

Colette released her son's hand. 'Be brave.'

'I'll try,' said Magnus.

Lothar led him and the others out of the clearing and into a much larger one. Abigone was there, holding court amid the Masters and Makers rescued from Steppen, along with the officers of the Westlanders, Walter, and two other Mountain Rangers.

Magnus frowned as he gazed at the assembled crowd. 'Where are the other Mountain Rangers?' he said.

'What others?' said Lothar. 'There are only four of us here. Me, Walter, Otto and Dietar.'

'What? Do you mean that Walter attacked Steppen with only two men?'

Lothar smiled. 'What can I say? And now he has a fucking army.'

'Come closer,' said Abigone; 'Walter is about to go over tonight's plan.'

'Thank you, Your Highness,' said Walter. 'Here is the new plan – it's the same as the old plan. We are going to attack Steppen in the same manner that we did a few days ago, but with some little differences. The first difference is that part of Johan's job will be to prevent any freshly-escaped Westlanders from charging the temple. That's what screwed us last time. I'm not blaming anyone but myself for that; I might have reacted in exactly the same way if I'd just been freed from that shithole. The second difference is that we will have two Makers and two Masters accompanying us. All four will be in my team, lying in wait for any Master to emerge from the temple. The two Makers will kill anything that moves outside the doors of the temple, as soon as any Master appears; and the two Masters will each be protecting one Maker. Makers can kill a lot quicker than Masters, but Masters are more precise; they will pick off anyone who gets too close to Princess Abigone or Raewyn. The final difference is that we have more fighters available to us, so Johan will be getting thirty extra warriors to help him clear out the barracks. One more thing – we'll be attacking under the cover of darkness this time; but that shouldn't be a problem, as we all know the layout of Steppen by now. Think of the first attack as a practice run; and this time we'll finish the job. If no Masters are brave enough to come outside, we'll cut off the water supply to the temple and place it under siege. Any questions?'

Magnus raised his hand.

'Yes?' said Walter.

'Who is the other Master?'

Walter smiled. 'Prince Mor Dennahelm.'

'Who?'

'He means me,' said Denny, who was holding a shield and spear. 'I'll be defending Princess Abigone.'

Magnus glanced away, a little intimidated by the grim expression Denny had on his face.

'Does anyone else have a question?' said Walter.

'To be clear, boss,' said a Westlander, 'we kill Magnus if he disobeys orders?'

Walter glanced at Abigone.

'Yes,' she said, 'but it will not come to that. Treat Magnus as a friend and an ally unless he proves otherwise.'

'Any more questions?' said Walter. 'No?'

'Then we shall depart,' said Abigone. 'Fight well, and show no mercy to the enemy.'

Walter raised his arm. 'Move out!'

Lothar went to join the team he would be commanding, and Magnus followed Walter and Abigone to a large group of Westlanders armed with crossbows. Eshia and Raewyn embraced, then the younger Maker joined Magnus and the others, and they set off through the forest. The sun was descending over the trees to the west ahead of them, and it was growing dark within the forest.

'Why isn't Eshia coming with us?' said Magnus.

'She doesn't want to kill,' said Raewyn; 'but she's done so much for the army that no one minds.'

'Why isn't she the head maker?' said Magnus. 'She looks older than Abigone.'

'Abigone took the title without consulting Eshia,' said Raewyn; 'but she didn't care. Eshia has no desire to lead or fight.'

'Thank you for giving me the chance to protect you.'

She eyed him, and fell silent.

They moved through the forest at speed, forded the Ario River, then they turned north towards Steppen. They circled round the town, and approached from the west, Magnus knowing every path and track the party took. They came to a halt when they reached the edge of the forest, and Magnus peered out through the undergrowth. In front of him lay the western flank of the shanty town, while the temple was lit up by torches and lamps to its left.

'What now?' he said.

'Now we wait,' said Walter.

Magnus glanced over his shoulder, and saw two smiling Westlanders pointing crossbows at his head. Magnus took a breath, and turned back to face the shanty town.

'They won't shoot if you do as you're told,' said Raewyn. 'Will you?'

'I will do my job,' he said.

'Will you falter if Ragnvald appears? Will you run away?'

'I have been running away my whole life,' he said. 'That stops tonight.'

'Here comes Lothar,' whispered another Westlander.

Magnus watched as Lothar led his team of thirty Westlanders towards the south-western corner of the shanty town. They approached the tall fence, and two warriors got to work, opening up holes in the fence with their bolt-cutters. Enslaved Westlanders began to appear by the corner of the camp, watching the warriors work. As soon as the breach was big enough, they poured out through the gap. No spears were being handed out, and the released slaves were funnelled off to the south, away from the temple.

A whistle blasted. Mercenaries appeared on the road, then shouts erupted from the area of the barracks on the far side of the shanty town.

'Here we go again,' said Walter. 'Follow me.'

They moved off to the north, keeping to the edge of the forest as they drew closer to the temple. Whistles and horns were echoing up into the dark sky, then flames shot up from the other corner of the shanty town, followed by thick, billowing smoke. The flames spread rapidly, until the front of the temple was bathed in the reflective glow of flickering dark reds. Walter came to a halt when he was level with the road that ran in front of the towering structure, and he settled down to wait again. Abigone leaned over and whispered in his ear, and the two leaders held a quick conversation. Magnus crouched down by Raewyn's side, his gaze on the multiple entrances to the temple. He tried not to think about Ragnvald, and the terror his eldest brother induced in him. He told himself to focus only on Raewyn and doing the job he had been assigned.

A large door in the temple opened, and armed mercenaries began to stream outside.

'Where is that bastard?' muttered Walter. 'Does anyone see Ragnvald?'

'I can only see mercenaries, boss,' said a Westlander.

Magnus frowned. One of the mercenaries had a distinctive gait, and he was bearing himself in a manner different from the others.

'He's there!' Magnus cried, pointing. 'In the centre. He's dressed as a mercenary.'

Walter glanced at him. 'Good work. Let's go, everyone. Move.'

Walter raced out of the forest, and the rest of his team followed him. The mercenaries were gesturing at the flames and smoke, then Ragnvald walked up to the fence, and started to kill anyone within range. The slaves screamed, then other mercenaries threw lit brands over the fence and into the shanty town. The fires in the other corner of the slave encampment were roaring and spreading, and Magnus realised what was happening.

'They're burning the shanty town,' he cried.

Several mercenaries noticed the approach of Walter's group. They turned, their loaded bows aimed and ready. Raewyn and Abigone ran to the front of the group, with Denny and Magnus following them.

The two Makers raised their hands. 'Summon twenty horses.'

Over thirty mercenaries disintegrated, their flesh and bones ripped apart, and their crossbows clattering to the ground. Screams of panic rippled out from the others, and they started to flee. Some bolted along the road, while the rest fled back towards the temple, jostling and pushing each other to escape the carnage.

Raewyn raised her hand again, as she walked calmly onwards. 'Summon fifty horses.'

The last remaining mercenaries on the road between the temple and the shanty town were obliterated in an explosion of blood. The entrance to the temple was swung shut, and the road fell into silence.

'Did we get Ragnvald?' cried Walter.

'How the fuck are we supposed to tell, boss?' said a Westlander, as he gazed at the puddles and heaps of gore. 'The Makers haven't left us much to work with.'

'We aren't safe here,' Magnus shouted. 'There are crossbow loops in the doors of the temple.'

Several bolts spat out at them before anyone could react to Magnus's words. Three Westlanders fell, and Denny's shield was struck as he held it out next to Abigone. Magnus pushed his way in front of Raewyn, shielding her from the temple with his body.

'Pull back!' Walter cried. 'Back to our starting position.'

They began to withdraw from the road, hurrying towards the edge of the forest as more bolts were loosed at them from the interior of the temple. Another Westlander fell with a bolt in his neck. Magnus kept to Raewyn's right as they ran, then, just as they were reaching the corner of the temple, a bolt struck Magnus in his right leg and he went flying to the ground. He looked up, but the others were still running, not seeing him amid the darkness and smoke. He tried to crawl, then a door opened in the temple, and a small group rushed out. They grabbed hold of Magnus, and bundled him into the temple, his arms pulled behind his back. The door slammed shut as soon as they were inside, and Magnus was pushed to the floor, a boot on his back, and two crossbows aimed at his head.

Ragnvald approached, and crouched down next to his brother.

'I want you to know that it was me who shot you,' Ragnvald said. 'As soon as I saw you, I forgot about everything else.' He held a knife to his brother's throat. 'I was aiming for your head, you little prick,' Ragnvald went on, 'but this has worked out far better. Rather than giving the king the news of your death, I can give him his traitor son. I can only imagine what he's going to do to you.' He glanced at the mercenaries. 'Bind his hands and take him to the roof. Tell the king that I will remain here to lead the defence.'

More cord was affixed to Magnus's wrists, and he was dragged along the passageway by six mercenaries. He was hauled up several flights of stairs, his limbs hitting each step on the way up, and he almost passed out from the pain.

They reached the roof, and Magnus was carried to its highest point, where the Whalebone King was reclining on his favourite chair. Amid the pain, Magnus noticed that Nyli was absent from the roof, despite being the king's personal hostage.

'A gift from Ragnvald, boss,' said a mercenary, as Magnus was dropped onto the roof in front of him.

Hemming smiled, but the fury and hatred in his eyes was unmistakeable.

'The betrayer returns,' he said. 'Beg for forgiveness, and I shall make your end a quick one.'

Magnus whimpered, and he began to form the words in his head. Of course he would beg; what else could he do? He thought of Raewyn and Abigone, then his mother and Walter, and his mouth wouldn't open.

'Beg!' cried the king. 'I want to hear you plead for a merciful death.'

'No, Father,' said Magnus. 'I will not beg.'

'Bring him closer,' Hemming said to the soldiers.

The mercenaries dragged Magnus nearer to the king. Hemming leaned forward, and waggled the crossbow bolt protruding from Magnus's leg. Magnus closed his eyes as pain enveloped him.

'Does that tickle?' the king said. 'I heard that Ragnvald tutored you in the torture of Lord Matteo. Ragnvald is keen, but he is a crude amateur compared to what I learned on the high seas. Whenever we captured a ship, we would usually be short of a crewmate or two, but very few sailors ever wanted to join us. To get round this, I would select one of them at random, and torture him out on deck in front of everyone. By the time I was done, all I had to do was threaten the others with the same, and we'd have no shortage of volunteers. I'm going to cut the tips of your fingers off first; just the tips, then the tops of your ears. Snip, snip, all round your body. Start at the extremities, and work inwards.'

Magnus tried to concentrate, but his abilities were useless without the use of his hands, as Ragnvald had always told him that a Master needed to point at whatever they were attempting to transform. Was that correct? Magnus had managed to kill the two mercenaries on Lord Matteo's barge, and his hands had been bound at the time. Had Ragnvald been mistaken? If pointing directed the flow of Master abilities, what would happen if he neglected to do so?

The king continued to describe how he was going to torture

Magnus, while he twisted the bolt in his son's leg. Magnus had been in pain many times throughout his seventeen years of life. Regular beatings delivered by his father and brothers had been a fact of life, and he was able to clear his mind.

Magnus opened his eyes.

Hemming smiled at him. 'I'm ready to begin; are you?'

'Bone to wood.'

His father and the mercenaries cried out in pain as if each of them had been touched by the raw power emanating from Magnus. Several of them staggered, while two fell at once, writhing on the flat roof. His father remained on his chair, his eyes wide with shock and pain.

'Bone to silver,' Magnus gasped.

The last soldiers fell. None were dead, but all were convulsing in agony. Magnus saw a knife lying on the roof next to his father, and edged towards it. It was nothing, he thought, as he felt the cold blade cut his wrists and hands; he had done it before. The cut cords fell away covered in blood, and Magnus staggered to his feet. He gazed down at the mercenaries, then leaned over and began slicing through their necks one by one, feeling nothing as he ended their lives. When the last was dead, he turned back to the Whalebone King.

'Nothing to say, Father?' he said. 'Does it tickle?'

Hemming choked and gasped, but only flecks of blood appeared from his mouth.

Magnus picked up the bottle of whatever his father had been drinking, and took a long swig. It was brandy, but it was rancid. He leaned over and poured the rest into his father's mouth, as Hemming stared up at him helplessly. Magnus reached out, and took hold of one of his father's feet. He pulled him off the reclining chair, and hauled him over to the edge of the roof. Magnus gazed out over Steppen. The shanty town was burning, as were the mercenary barrack blocks, and the flames and smoke were rising to block out the stars and the Big Red Moon.

Magnus crouched down and prised off the yellowing whalebone

crown from his father's head, then, with his father watching, he snapped it in two.

'I guess that means you're not a king any more, Father,' he said. 'Goodbye.'

He reached out again, wedged his bleeding hands under his father, and rolled him off the side of the roof. The Whalebone King fell through the air, then he hit the gravel path with a crunch. Magnus watched as a pool of blood spread out from the motionless body, then he staggered back a few steps, the pain becoming too much for him. Magnus fell to his knees, then he toppled over, his eyes closing.

CHAPTER 32
A DIFFERING SET OF MORALS

Steppen, Great Forest, Jallin, Central Provinces – 24th Day of Quoma 108

Walter stopped running as soon as he was out of range of the cross-bows being loosed from within the temple. All around him, his team was retreating, and Walter tried to count how many were missing. The smoke was making it hard to see, despite the light from the flames devouring the shanty town. He caught sight of Abigone and Denny, his shield having taken two bolts, then he saw Raewyn.

'Where the fuck's Magnus?' he shouted.

Raewyn turned, her eyes scanning the road. 'He was right behind me,' she said.

'Can anyone see Magnus?' Walter cried.

'He was hit by a bolt, boss,' said a Westlander. 'I saw him go down.'

'He didn't run away,' Raewyn said. 'He got between me and the temple; he...'

'He was doing his job,' said Walter.

'We were right to trust him,' said Abigone.

'*You* were right,' said Raewyn; 'I was wrong. I thought he would panic and change sides. Is he dead? Who saw him get hit?'

'Me,' said the Westlander.

'Where was he struck?'

'In the leg, I think, miss. I was too busy running to get a proper look.'

'Then he might only be injured,' said Raewyn. 'I'm going to look for him.'

'No, you're not,' said Walter. 'Our immediate priority is now the Westlanders trapped inside the burning shanty town. If we don't get them out, then hundreds will burn.' He paused, remembering that he was no longer in command. 'Your Highness, do you agree?'

'Yes, Commander,' said Abigone. 'Proceed.'

'How will we get through the fence?' said a Westlander.

Walter patted a pocket. 'Bolt-cutters and brute strength. Follow me.'

He set off again, veering to the south to ensure that they didn't enter the range of the temple's crossbows. He glanced at the road as he ran. Bodies were littering the ground amid the heaps of summoned gore. One was moving – an injured Westlander. He was crawling towards the forest with a bolt embedded in his back, then two more bolts spat out from the temple. Both struck him, and the Westlander stopped moving.

'I couldn't see Magnus,' Walter said, as they reached the fence, 'but if he was injured, then he'll be dead by now; they're picking off the wounded.'

He glanced at the tall fence. Hundreds of Westlanders were trying get out of the shanty town, but the fires started by the mercenaries had targeted the breaches opened up by Lothar and the other team, and both ways out were blocked.

'Stand back,' said Abigone, her hand raised.

Walter blinked, then he moved aside for the princess.

'Summon for me an iron dragon,' cried Abigone.

Metal was ripped from the fence for over a distance of a dozen yards and, without its support, the beams began to topple over under the pressure from the trapped Westlanders. An entire stretch of fence collapsed, and the Westlanders poured out, streaming past Walter and the others to escape the flames. Their route took them past a large metal lump that had materialised a few yards from the breached fence, and several Westlanders stared at it in awe.

'Stay back from the temple,' Walter shouted at the escapees. 'Go south; south!'

Lothar appeared on the side road with his team, and hurried up to Walter and Abigone. He gazed at the huge breach in the fence, then at the fleeing Westlanders.

'I've opened up another two holes in the southern side of the fence, ma'am,' he said to Abigone, 'but the fires will be reaching there soon. I counted maybe three hundred Westlanders escaping from my section.' He gazed at the temple. 'Did we get any of the Masters?'

'The only one we know about is Magnus,' said Walter. 'He was hit by a crossbow bolt. Ragnvald came outside, but we don't know if we got him.'

'Magnus was hit, sir? What now?'

Walter glanced at Abigone.

'You are in operational command, Walter,' she said. 'I will abide by your advice.'

'Thank you, Your Highness.' He said, trying not to show any signs of disappointment or frustration on his face. 'We'll surround the temple and place it under siege. We have to assume that both enemy Masters are still inside, along with Nyli, Reath and Salus. We'll cut off their supply of fresh water and dig in for a few days. It shouldn't take any longer than that, unless they have wells or deep cisterns inside. I should have asked Magnus about that.'

'I think all their water comes from the channels that flow under the temple,' said Denny. 'They have no need for wells or cisterns; the temple wasn't built to withstand a siege.'

'Someone is up on the roof, boss,' shouted a Westlander, pointing up at the temple.

Walter peered through the flames and smoke, and saw the figure of a man by the edge of the roof.

'Is that Magnus?' said Raewyn.

'I can't see from here,' said Walter. 'Are you sure?'

'It's him,' said Denny. 'What is he doing up there?'

'The little shitebag has betrayed us,' said a Westlander, 'and now the Whalebone King knows our plans, and where our camp lies.'

The figure crouched down, then something fell from the roof. The object moved out of sight, falling behind the burning buildings of the shanty town; then the figure on the roof swayed and moved back, away from the edge. Moments later, mercenaries began fleeing in all directions, dropping their weapons and scattering. Some ran into the forest, while others held up their arms to surrender. A large group of them rushed down the road that ran by the side of the shanty town, their hands aloft.

'We surrender!' cried an officer.

The Westlanders tensed, as though they were ready to tear the mercenaries limb from limb with their bare hands. Walter walked forward, and raised his arm.

'Wait for it,' he told the Westlanders. He approached the crowd of surrendering mercenaries. 'Why now?' he said. 'Why are you surrendering?'

'The Whalebone King is dead!' cried the officer. 'His body fell from the roof. It's over, and we want no more part of this. Under the common law regarding mercenaries, you are obliged to take us into custody, unharmed.'

'You saw him?' said Abigone. 'You saw the so-called king?'

'I saw him,' said the officer. 'His body is splattered all over the fucking gravel.'

Walter eyed Abigone. She glanced at Denny, who didn't respond, then she turned back to Walter and gave him the slightest of nods. He faced the crowd of Westlanders.

'If you want revenge,' he said to them, 'take it.'

The massed crowd of Westlanders roared and surged forward, passing Walter as they charged at the surrendering mercenaries. Screams rose up from the road, as the mercenaries were kicked, stabbed and ripped to pieces. Denny lowered his gaze, his features betraying his unease. Walter also turned away from the massacre, and saw Raewyn gazing up at the roof of the temple.

'Magnus killed the Whalebone King,' she whispered. 'He didn't betray us.'

'I think you might be right,' said Lothar; 'and now he's stuck on the fucking roof. Did you see him stagger backwards? He's injured.'

'The bolt hit his leg,' said Walter.

'We should go in,' said Abigone. 'We should enter the temple as quickly as possible, before Ragnvald has time to respond.'

'I agree,' said Lothar. 'We should end this.'

'Reath, Nyli and Salus are still in there,' said Raewyn, 'as well as Magnus. We need to get them out.'

Walter stared at the temple for a moment. 'I suggest we do two things first,' he said. 'We'll need shields if we are going to force our way to one of the temple entrances; otherwise, we will be cut down by crossbow bolts, and we need to send Westlanders to surround the temple. There are probably back doors to the place, and the last thing we want is Ragnvald and Erling slipping out with a couple of hostages. Your Highness, could you and Raewyn take care of the shields? They don't need to be pretty. I'll organise the Westlanders.'

Abigone nodded. 'We can do that. And there are definitely back doors; some of them lead to the caverns behind the waterfalls. Come, Raewyn; let us get started.'

'Thank you,' said Walter. He watched as the two Makers walked over to a long stretch of surviving fence to gaze at the wooden beams, then he turned to Lothar and Denny, as the Westlanders finished off the last of the surrendering mercenaries.

'How many mercenaries are in the temple, do you reckon?' said Walter.

'A few dozen, sir, at least,' said Lothar.

'The king and his sons had their own personal guards to protect them,' said Denny, 'and all of them will still be inside.'

Walter walked forward to get the attention of the Westlanders on the road.

'The battle isn't over!' he cried. 'The temple is now under siege. Make your way round its flanks, and encircle it. There are back doors, and we don't want the bastards inside to escape. Let's go; shift your hairy arses.'

The Westlanders broke away from the carnage of the mercenaries, and began to move off towards the temple.

'At least they are still obeying me,' Walter said.

'For now, sir,' said Lothar.

A great shout came from behind them, and Walter and Lothar turned to see Johan leading another large contingent of Westlanders up the road towards them.

'Every Westlander has been freed, my friend,' Johan cried, his arms raised. 'From the old to the young, all of my people have been released from bondage. The Whalebone King is dead, and the mercenaries have been crushed. None remain – all have been slain, apart from a few cowards who fled like frightened children into the forest.' He reached Walter and embraced him. 'This is a glorious day, and you are the man who made it possible.' He lifted Walter's arm in the air. 'A cheer for our drunken champion!'

The Westlanders raised their weapons and roared out a cheer. Johan handed Walter a jug of something, and Walter took a drink, provoking another loud cheer. The Westlanders surrounded Walter on the road, slapping him on the back, and trying to pass him more jugs of alcohol.

'Sorry to be a prick,' said Lothar, pushing a few of the more enthusiastic Westlanders away from Walter, 'but we've got work to do. We can have our party later. Ragnvald and Erling are inside the temple, along with several hostages. Johan, we need you to send a few contingents of warriors round to the back of the temple, to make sure the bastards don't escape.'

Johan laughed. 'Did you hear that, lads!' he cried. 'Let us finish the job.' He pointed at a few of his officers. 'Take up positions around the temple. Let us repay Walter for what he has done for us.'

The officers gestured to their warriors, and several dozen moved off along the road. Johan remained where he was, his gaze going to Abigone and Raewyn, who had already summoned a small pile of wooden shields.

'Will you be storming the temple, Walter?' he said.

'That's the plan,' said Walter. 'The Makers are building shields for us.'

Johan nodded. 'I shall accompany you inside. When the battle is over, you and I will go our separate ways, and I shall lead the Westlanders out of the forest; but I will never forget what you have done for us. When we reach Upper Down, we shall spread the tale of your courage and cunning to your kinfolk, and to mine. Perhaps then, my people will view your tiny realm in a better light.'

'I couldn't have done it without you, Johan,' he said.

'Yes, I know,' said Johan. He frowned, as his gaze went to a small number of Westlanders hurrying back down the road towards them from the direction of the temple. In their midst was an old woman, her eyes wide as she was escorted towards Walter, Denny, Lothar, and the Westlander chief. She stared at the burning shanty town, and at the smoke rising into the night sky.

'This woman emerged from the temple, boss,' said a Westlander. 'She has a message from the wankers inside.'

Walter eyed the old woman. 'Have you seen our friends in the temple?' he said.

'I saw little Salus,' she said. 'Are you Walter?'

'I am.'

'Ragnvald sent me. He released me from the women's quarters, so long as I delivered a message to you. Ragnvald wishes to offer terms.'

'There will be no terms!' cried Johan.

'Wait,' said Walter; 'let's hear what he has to say. It'll give us an idea of what he's thinking.'

'Ragnvald will release every hostage,' the old woman said; 'that's what he told me. He will release Nyli, Reath and Salus, and every other slave held within the temple, if the Westlanders pull back to the east of the town, and allow him to escape down the Ario River. He will be taking Erling and the remaining mercenaries with him, and he wants a guarantee that they will be unharmed. If you refuse, he will start executing the hostages.'

'Did he mention Magnus?' said Walter.

'No,' said the old woman.

Abigone and Raewyn walked over.

'We have summoned forty shields,' Abigone said. 'Will that be enough?' Her eyes went to the old woman. 'I recognise you.'

'She has brought us Ragnvald's terms,' said Walter, 'and we need to discuss them.'

'What's to discuss?' said Johan. 'The vile Master is trapped inside the temple and we need to kill him, Erling, and his remaining mercenaries. There is nothing to discuss.'

'Princess Abigone is in command,' said Walter, 'and she needs to understand which choices are available. Let's move off the road for a few minutes.' He glanced at the old woman. 'Did Ragnvald provide a time for his deal?'

'He wants to see the Westlanders withdraw within the next hour,' said the woman, 'or the first hostage will die.'

Walter gestured to the others, and they walked away from the site of the slaughtered mercenaries. They went to an untouched stretch of lawn, and Walter turned to face Abigone.

'Tell me about his deal,' she said.

'We have an hour to pull the Westlanders out of Steppen, or Ragnvald will start killing those he has inside the temple,' Walter said. 'Ragnvald says that if we withdraw, the hostages will be released; and then he wants us to allow him and Erling to escape down the Ario. There was no mention of Magnus, but I don't know what that signifies.'

Abigone said nothing, her eyes dark.

'What are your views?' said Walter, his gaze roving over the others. 'I want to hear them.'

'You know my opinion,' said Johan. 'We cannot trust anything that serpent says. We should strike at the temple, at once.'

'And risk the lives of Nyli, Salus and Reath?' said Lothar. 'It's a tough call.'

'There is nothing hard about it,' said Johan. 'We cannot allow Ragnvald and Erling to flee. My people demand justice for what they have done to us. Hemming may have been king, but his sons were every inch as cruel and savage.'

'Apart from Magnus,' said Raewyn.

'I shall concede that,' said Johan. 'Magnus was too weak and young to be as vicious as the others, and he helped us this night; it is true.'

'Then we cannot abandon him to Ragnvald.'

'I agree, miss,' said the chief. 'That is why I utterly refute this deal. Ragnvald is a liar. For all we know, Magnus and the three little ones who remain inside the temple are already dead.'

Walter glanced at the old woman. 'How many are being held within the women's quarters?'

'There are twenty-three women living inside those quarters,' she said. 'Salus was also there. Ragnvald placed him with us when the attack began.'

'We should understand the consequences if we storm the temple,' said Denny. 'As soon as we set foot inside the building, Ragnvald and Erling will start killing the slaves and hostages. Twenty-three women, as well as Reath, Nyli and Salus.'

'There are other slaves in the temple,' the old woman went on. 'The men who keep the furnaces and boilers working, and personal slaves belonging to the king and his sons. Perhaps another forty, all told.'

'We should consider taking the deal,' said Denny.

Johan's eyes burned with fury.

'I am not suggesting that we allow Ragnvald and Erling to flee,' Denny went on. 'Their crimes demand justice; but could we not trick them? If we pull the Westlanders back, but position them to the south, rather than the east, then might we not be able to cut off their escape by the banks of the Ario? That way, we could see if Ragnvald is prepared to release the slaves and hostages.'

'You mean to deceive him?' said Johan. 'He might be expecting this, I think.'

'Ragnvald isn't stupid,' said Lothar. 'He'll keep a small number of the hostages with him, at least until he is certain of his escape. If he expects treachery, which he will, he might hold on to those hostages indefinitely. Are we prepared to allow Reath and the others to die in order to kill him and Erling?'

'But think how many he'll have to release in order to convince us that his intentions are sound,' said Denny. 'The more we save, the better.'

'But that risks allowing him to escape,' said Johan. 'I will not stand for that. The brothers must die.'

'This is what Ragnvald wants,' said Lothar; 'us fighting among ourselves. Whatever we decide, we have to remain united.'

'I want to speak to Princess Abigone and Denny alone for a moment,' said Walter. 'Could the others please take a few steps back?'

Johan narrowed his eyes, but he did as Walter said, and led the others back to the road.

'I need to know which way your thoughts are leading us, Your Highness,' said Walter.

Abigone lifted her chin. 'We should storm the temple.'

'No,' said Denny. 'There will be a bloodbath, and some of that blood will be on our hands.'

'The princess is in command,' said Walter.

Denny shook his head. 'I didn't want to have to do this, but if we are basing the leadership on Abigone's status as a princess of Upper Down, then, as a prince of Sanctos, I outrank her. You can't have it both ways, Walter. As you conceded authority to her, she should concede authority to me; and I say that we take the deal.'

Abigone's eyes widened for a split second, then her features grew dark.

'You would attempt to usurp my position, Denny?' she said.

'Did you not do the same to Walter?' he said.

'I did that so that I would not be left behind in the camp,' she said.

'And I am doing this to save the lives of dozens of slaves.'

'Ragnvald cannot be trusted,' said Abigone. 'His promises are empty, and I will not allow him to escape with his life.'

'No matter the cost?' said Denny. He eyed Walter. 'Instruct a messenger to inform Ragnvald that we accept his offer. Tell him that we will start withdrawing the Westlanders as soon as is practicable. Then, order the Westlanders to take up positions by the banks of the Ario.'

'I can't believe you are doing this, Denny,' said Abigone.

'I am doing it for you,' he said, 'to spare you the blood that will be on your conscience if you go ahead with an attack on the temple.'

'Don't patronise me,' she said. 'I know what will happen if we attack, and yet I still believe that it is the right thing to do. If we are quick, and ruthless, we can sweep through the temple before Ragnvald has a chance to slaughter the slaves.'

Denny narrowed his eyes. 'I gave you an order, Walter.'

Walter smiled. 'It's funny, but I don't recall ever swearing any oath to you, Mor Dennahelm of Sanctos. You can order me all you like, but my loyalty is to Upper Down, and to Princess Abigone. If you don't like that, well, I couldn't really give a shit.'

Denny frowned. 'But...'

'The only way I will obey you, Prince of Sanctos,' Walter went on, 'is if Princess Abigone commands me to. Your Highness, do you wish me to accept orders from this man?'

'I do not,' said Abigone.

Walter raised his palms. 'There you have it, Denny. If Princess Abigone orders me to storm the temple, then that is what we shall do. There will be consequences, but I honestly don't know if we will save more lives by attacking, or by accepting Ragnvald's deal. What I do know is that the Westlanders will not accept any deal that allows even the slightest chance of Ragnvald and Erling escaping with their lives. Therefore, I agree with the Princess. I would have followed her orders even if I disagreed, because that's how loyalty works. Are you prepared to do the same?'

'I cannot be a part of this,' said Denny. 'Innocents will die because of this decision.'

'And more will die if we allow Ragnvald and Erling to escape,' said Abigone. 'Will you not come with us, not even to protect me? Your shield stopped two crossbow bolts from striking us before; will you not do it once more?'

'You are changing in front of my eyes,' said Denny. 'You are becoming more ruthless with every day that passes. Where is the Abigone I met in Klef Mordain? I miss her.'

Abigone's eyes flashed with anger. 'Then go. If that is how you feel, then be gone from my sight. I have not come this far only to falter at the final hurdle. There will be plenty of Westlanders willing to shield me when I enter the temple; I do not need you.'

Walter watched as Denny and Abigone stared at each other, then the prince of Sanctos inclined his head a little, turned, and walked away. Abigone choked back a sob, then she hardened her features.

'He was right about one thing, Your Highness,' Walter said. 'You have changed. You are no longer the annoying little brat who adored King Alfgang the Great. Personally, I think it's an improvement.'

'You have also changed, Walter,' she said. 'What happened to the drunken oaf who always made a fool of himself? What you have achieved here in Steppen is little short of a miracle. I also prefer the new you.'

He gave her a half-smile. 'Denny will come round. I think he's the type who needs time to come to terms with the responsibilities of leadership.'

'He has questioned my ruthlessness before, Walter, after we assassinated the Sanctian ambassador in Klef Mordain. He said I was cold and heartless, and he called off our betrothal. This time, I am not sure I will take him back, if he does decide to reconcile. I need someone whose nerve doesn't give way every time there is a difficult decision to reach.'

'I don't think it's his nerves. I saw him defend you in the attack; he was brave and resolute. He's not a coward, but I think maybe he works to a differing set of moral principles.'

'Do you think I am cold and ruthless?'

'Sometimes, we need to be.' He glanced back at the road. 'Should we tell the others of our intentions, Your Highness?'

Abigone inclined her head, and they walked back to where Lothar and the others were waiting for them.

'I saw Denny walk off,' said Raewyn. 'Why?'

'We disagreed on the way ahead,' said Abigone. 'I told him to go.'

'Did you see where he went?' said Walter.

Lothar gestured along the road. 'He told us he was going back to the camp, sir.'

'Princess Abigone shall need a new protector to watch her back,' said Walter; 'as will Raewyn.'

'Does this mean we are attacking the temple?' said Johan.

'It does,' said Abigone. 'Prepare the warriors. Raewyn and I shall lead.'

Johan grinned. 'Let us bathe in the blood of our enemies.'

'And rescue as many slaves and hostages as possible,' said Abigone. 'Let's not forget that part.'

CHAPTER 33
HEAD MAKER

Steppen, Great Forest, Jallin, Central Provinces – 25th Day of Quoma 108

Raewyn eyed Abigone, as forty Westlanders picked up the shields summoned by the two young Makers. The fires in the shanty town were still raging, and with smoke blocking the view of the Big Red Moon, Abigone had no idea of the time.

'Is it over between you and Denny?' Raewyn said.

'I don't know. He agrees with your view of me, Raewyn. He believes me to be a ruthless killer.'

'Am I not also a ruthless killer?' said Raewyn. 'We have killed many over the past few days, and we are about to kill again.'

'Denny's heart differs from my own,' said Abigone. 'We knew it in Klef Mordain, but I thought we had worked through our disagreements.'

Raewyn shook her head. 'Perhaps you need a man who is as ruthless as you; a man who doesn't walk away when you need him.'

'He didn't walk away. I told him to leave, after he tried to assume control over Walter's army.'

'He did what?'

'He claimed that he outranked me. Walter was having none of it.'

Raewyn narrowed her eyes. 'Perhaps you are better off without him.'

'I told him I didn't need him,' said Abigone, 'but I was lying. I need him if we are to make our school a success in Geathan.'

'Is that all he means to you?'

'No. I do love him, but I'm tired of him thinking I'm a heartless beast.'

Lothar approached, a new shield on his left arm. 'We are ready, Your Highness. Do you have a preference about which door to attack?'

'The closest one will suffice,' said Abigone.

Lothar turned to a second group of Westlanders, who had assembled a few yards behind the forty bearing the new shields.

'Give us ten minutes after we get inside,' Lothar said, 'then follow us into the temple. Occupy the entire ground floor, and clear out any mercenaries you find. We shall be heading to the upper floors, and we don't want to get cut off.'

The officer in charge of the second group nodded. 'No problem, boss.'

The two Makers moved into the massed ranks of the leading group of Westlanders. Walter and Lothar kept close to them, and the group moved off down the road, with Johan at its head.

'Is it past midnight?' said Abigone.

'Most likely, Your Highness,' said Walter.

'I long for this night to be over.'

'Might I go over the arrangements, ma'am?' said Lothar. 'I will be protecting you, and Sergeant Otto will be defending Raewyn. Stick close to us when we enter the temple.'

'I thought we would be getting Westlanders to defend us,' said Raewyn.

'The Westlanders are better at attacking,' said Lothar. 'You need a Mountain Ranger to watch your back.'

Raewyn glanced at Otto, who was walking by her side with one of the new shields. 'Thank you, sergeant.'

'My pleasure, ma'am,' said Otto. 'Let me know if you intend to run off in a certain direction.'

'The same goes for you, Your Highness,' said Lothar. 'We're good, but we're not mind readers.'

The group halted just before they came into the range of the crossbows within the temple, and the forty Westlanders formed a solid line of shields along their front and flanks.

Walter gestured to Johan. 'Order the charge.'

The huge Westlander nodded. 'You heard the man,' he roared. 'Follow me!'

They set off at a run, and Abigone kept pace with them as they charged towards the westernmost entrance of the temple. They entered crossbow range, and the first bolts spat out, striking the shields held by the Westlanders in the first rank. One Westlander went down, a bolt hitting his leg below the knee, and the others jumped over him.

'You take care of the door,' said Abigone, as she and Raewyn reached the front of the group, 'and I'll deal with those behind it.'

Raewyn nodded and raised her right hand. She pointed at the large barred entrance. 'Summon a dining table.'

Wood exploded from the door, leaving only the metal braces and hinges.

Abigone raised her hand. 'Summon for me a dozen horses.'

The mercenaries who had been behind the door screamed for a split second, then their bodies were torn to shreds. The Westlanders swarmed round the upturned dining table and the heaps of gore and flesh that had appeared next to a narrow water channel, and they bounded into the temple, the two Makers in their midst.

'A dining table?' said Abigone.

'It was all I could think of,' said Raewyn. 'It was the last thing I was working on in Klef Mordain.'

A few mercenaries had been hiding to either side of the entrance, and the Westlanders butchered them in seconds.

'Do you have Saffie's map?' said Walter.

'I memorised it, sir,' said Lothar. 'Follow the passageway ahead. There should be stairs on our left.'

They raced along the dark passageway, then found the stairs leading up to the next floor. A few mercenaries were retreating before them, running at the sight of the forty Westlanders. Whistles sounded, then a horn echoed through the building, followed by screams.

'Turn right!' Lothar shouted. 'The old sanctuary should be there.'

Johan led his warriors on, their boots thumping over the stone floors.

'Careful ahead,' cried Lothar. 'This is where the Sanctians were slaughtered.' He gestured to Abigone as the Westlanders came to a halt, and the two of them edged forward. They peered round a corner, Lothar holding his shield out, and Abigone saw a large flight of stairs to their right.

'Ragnvald was standing at the top of those stairs when the Sanctians attacked,' Lothar whispered. 'There are only two ways into the upper floors, and this is one of them.'

'There's no one here now,' Abigone said.

'Lothar,' said Walter, 'you might want to see this.'

Abigone and Lothar turned. Walter and the others were gazing through the open doors of the sanctuary. Abigone walked up to the entrance. Inside, the bodies of over two dozen Westlander men were piled up along the wooden pews, each with their throats cut.

Lothar walked into the large chamber, and crouched by two of the bodies. 'They've been dead for a few hours,' he said.

'It is as we thought,' said Johan. 'Ragnvald began the slaughter of our people trapped inside the temple long before we attacked it. And to kill them in such a place as this – a house of prayer.'

'He probably gave the order at the same time he commanded the mercenaries to set fire to the shanty town,' said Walter.

Johan eyed Raewyn and Abigone. 'You may have to accept that we are here only for revenge; your friends might already be dead.'

'I will not give up hope; not yet,' said Abigone.

'Where next?' said Walter.

Lothar got back to his feet. 'We go up the stairs and turn right. The women's quarters are two floors above us, but this is as far as Saffie got.'

They regrouped outside the sanctuary, and climbed the stairs to the next level. There was no sign of any mercenaries at the top of the stairs, and they took a passageway that led off to the right, moving slowly through the darkness and shadows of the temple.

'I judge that to be about ten minutes,' Lothar whispered. 'The second team should be entering the temple around now.'

Walter nodded, then he gestured to a narrow spiral staircase. A Westlander took a few steps up it, and disappeared from sight. A few moments later, he fell back down the stairs, a crossbow bolt embedded in his left eye. The other Westlanders roared out in anger and started to run for the staircase.

'No,' said Walter. 'That's what they want us to do.' He gestured to Abigone. 'Destroy the stairs, and everyone hiding there.'

'Stand back,' said Abigone. She raised a hand. 'Summon for me two stone dragons.'

The spiral staircase buckled and collapsed as stone was torn from it. Screams echoed up, then they fell away as dust rose up from the destruction. At the same time, two monstrous lumps of dark stone appeared in the passageway. One rolled away, and fell down the main staircase by the old sanctuary, smashing the steps and ripping great gouges out of the floor.

Walter led them on, and they reached a set of wider stairs, which were empty. They climbed them, then they came to a row of doors. Walter nodded, and a Westlander opened the first one. Inside were two mercenaries, their wrists slashed. A bloody knife was lying on the floor next to where the bodies were lying slumped on their chairs.

The Westlander opened the next door, and he flinched away. 'Don't go in there,' he said.

'What is it?' said Abigone.

'You don't want to know.'

Two other Westlanders pushed past him and opened the door, then both spoke in their own language, their anger palpable. Abigone was ushered past by Lothar, and she caught the tiniest glimpse of a room full of dead Westlander women, before the door was closed again.

'We all know what we are fighting,' said Walter. 'Stay calm, and let's make the bastards pay.'

They carried on, then crossbow bolts spat out at them from a side corridor. One of them slammed into Lothar's shield as he protected Abigone, and another hit a Westlander in the throat. Six other Westlanders chased after the mercenary bowmen, charging down the corridor after them.

'Bring back one alive, if you can,' Abigone cried.

She glanced at Raewyn as they waited for the Westlanders to return.

'I hate this place,' Raewyn said.

'Will you help me destroy the temple when this is over?'

'I will. I understand why Magnus was so afraid all of the time; can you imagine being brought up here?'

'I don't want to,' Abigone said. 'People thought my father was evil, and he was, in a way, but he would never have done anything approaching this.'

'How could they behave like this?'

'Because they thought they could get away with it,' said Abigone. 'They were wrong.'

The six Westlanders returned, dragging one of the mercenaries by the ankles. The soldier had been punched in the face, but he was still conscious, and he stared at the towering Westlanders with tears in his eyes.

'Please!' he cried. 'I was only obeying orders.'

Abigone slipped the knife from Lothar's belt and approached him. 'Hold him down,' she said.

The Westlanders pressed down on the mercenary's arms and legs.

Abigone crouched next to him. 'Where are the women's quarters? Tell us how to get there.'

'Will you let me live?'

'Of course.'

'You keep going along this passageway, then take the second stairs on your right. Turn left at the top, and the women's quarters are right in front of you.'

'And what is waiting for us in there?' Abigone said. 'Have its occupants been slaughtered?'

'I don't know; I don't think so. We were told to kill every other slave in the temple, but I didn't hear any orders about the women's quarters. Don't hurt me, please.'

Abigone said nothing. She gazed down at the terrified, middle-aged mercenary, wondering if he had left behind a family in order to take the wages of the Whalebone King in Steppen. Had he been a decent, ordinary man back then? Did it matter? She pushed the tip of the knife into the mercenary's chest, and used both hands to drive it into his heart. The soldier convulsed, then fell still.

'You had me going for a moment there, miss,' said Johan. 'I thought you might actually let him go.'

'We are letting no one go,' said Abigone. She pulled the knife out, and wiped it on the man's uniform, then she stood. 'They all die.'

They followed the directions the mercenary had provided, and ascended another flight of stairs. Abigone glanced to the left when they reached the top, and saw a stout door ahead of them.

'Form up,' said Walter. 'Shields to the front, but leave two small gaps for the Makers.' He glanced at Abigone. 'If any hostages are in here, they might be between us and the enemy. If so, we'll have to do this the old fashioned way, with spears and blades.'

'I understand,' said Abigone. 'We will be careful.'

'What if Ragnvald is in there, boss?' said one of the Westlanders.

'I think you know the answer to that,' said Walter. 'If Ragnvald is inside the women's quarters, then he will start killing us one at a time. Do not let this knowledge defeat you. Johan selected each one of you, because you were the bravest warriors we have.'

'And if we die fighting,' said Johan, 'we shall join Prince Logar's eternal feast, forever blessed, forever honoured. We are ready, Walter.'

Walter nodded to Abigone. 'Take care of the door, Your Highness.'

Abigone raised her hand through one of the gaps in the wall of shields. 'Summon for me a wooden dragon.'

The doorway disintegrated, replaced by an enormous lump of twisted wood, then a hail of crossbow bolts were loosed at them. The Westlanders hunkered down behind their shields, and began to move forward, step by step, keeping the Makers in their midst.

Abigone peered through a narrow gap. A row of chairs had been lined up across the width of the chamber, and each had a slave or a hostage bound to it. The mercenaries were crouching behind the chairs, and were loosing from over the shoulders of the human shield. Salus and Nyli were there, tied to their chairs. Salus was gagged, but Nyli was screaming as the bolts raced out from behind her. Next to the mercenaries, Erling was in command. From his eyes, Abigone sensed that he knew he was beaten, but he continued to give the order to loose. Another team of mercenaries was located behind Erling, and they were busy reloading bows for the soldiers in the front lines.

The Westlanders took another few steps forward, then one was hit in the foot, and he fell. Another Westlander pushed forward, his shield replacing that of the one who had fallen.

'We're going to charge them,' said Walter, as a bolt sped past his face. 'Get ready; go!'

The Westlanders surged forward, their pace taking them into the chamber in seconds. Three fell as they ran, then another was hit before they reached the line of chairs. The huge Westlanders aimed down with their spears and drove them into the faces of the crouching mercenaries. Walter pulled two chairs to the side, their occupants screaming, and Westlanders poured through the gap. The mercenaries broke, scattering back, but the Westlanders were on them in seconds, their spears driving out. Erling took a knife and tried to ram it into Nyli, but Johan sprang at him, knocking the king's son to the ground, and sending the knife flying. Johan gripped Erling's neck, and squeezed.

'This is for my people,' Johan cried; 'this is for what you did to them.'

Erling's hands went to his throat, but the Westlander was far stronger than him. Erling choked and gasped, then Johan twisted his neck, breaking it. Johan staggered to his feet, tears coming from his eyes. Abigone tore her gaze from him, and ran towards Nyli. She used Lothar's knife to cut through the cords, then she passed it to Raewyn, who freed Salus from his chair. Abigone embraced Nyli.

'It's all right,' she said. 'You're safe. We're here. It's over.'

Walter came over, leading nearly two dozen older slave women from their rooms. They freed the others who had been tied to the line of chairs, and then the slaves watched as the last of the mercenaries in the women's quarters were slaughtered.

'Is Magnus here?' cried Raewyn. 'And Reath?'

'Neither one is here,' said one of the freed slave women.

'He killed the Whalebone King,' said another. 'I was on the roof; I saw it happen. Magnus killed Hemming, and all of the soldiers who were protecting the king.'

'What happened to Magnus after that?' said Abigone.

'I... I don't know,' the woman said. 'I ran away, and then the mercenaries took me here.'

'Ragnvald was here,' said the first woman; 'but when he learned of the king's death, he took hold of Reath – he's taken her up to the roof.'

Abigone eyed Walter. 'He is on the roof, cousin. Shall we?'

'We should get these people out of the temple first,' said Walter. 'Johan, could you...? Johan, are you all right?'

Abigone glanced at the weeping Westlander. The huge man wiped his eyes.

'I will be fine, Walter; what do you need me to do?'

'Send some of your men downstairs,' said Walter. 'Take the women, your injured comrades, and the two children. The rest of us will be going to the roof, as soon as someone tells us how to get there.'

'There are half a dozen ways up on to the roof,' said one of the freed slaves. 'The closest isn't far away.'

She rattled out a list of directions, and Walter nodded.

Johan gestured to one of his officers. 'Do as Walter commands; take ten warriors and get everyone to safety.'

The Westlanders began to lead the women from the chamber, while others picked up those who had been shot but not killed. Raewyn was holding on to Salus's hand, and Abigone eyed her.

'Go downstairs with them,' she said.

'Are you sure?' said Raewyn.

'I'm sure. Protect everyone. There may still be mercenaries hiding on the lower floors.'

With one hand still clutching Salus's, Raewyn put her arm over Nyli's shoulder, and joined the others.

Abigone watched as the Westlanders left the chamber with those they had freed. She glanced down at the bodies of the slaughtered mercenaries, suppressing any sympathy she felt for them, then her eyes went to Erling. For him, there was no struggle over her emotions – he had deserved to die.

Walter and Lothar gathered Johan and his remaining forces.

'You all know what we have to do,' Walter said. 'It will not be easy. Ragnvald will be desperate, and he likely has Reath as a hostage and human shield. Crossbows will be better than spears, so we'll take a minute to ensure that each of us has a loaded bow before we leave.'

'Get to it,' said Johan. 'One bow each, and make sure the fucking thing is loaded.'

The Westlanders picked up the bows from the dead mercenaries, and began loading them.

'Any advice, Your Highness?' said Walter, as they waited. 'How will we kill Ragnvald if he has Reath?'

'I need a distraction,' she said. 'If he has his back to me, I can strike.'

Walter gazed off into the distance. 'All right; I have an idea.'

'We are ready,' said Johan.

'Form up around our Maker,' Walter said. 'Lothar, you have one job – defend the princess at all costs.'

'Yes, sir.'

Walter set off, and the others followed him out of the women's quarters. They took the directions the freed slave had provided, and climbed another set of stairs to the top floor of the temple. They passed numerous doors but ignored them, and found themselves at the bottom of a spiral staircase.

Walter beckoned Abigone and Lothar forward, and the three of them crept up the dark steps, until the stairwell opened out into the smoke-filled night sky. Keeping low, Abigone gazed at the roof of the building. It was laid out on multiple levels, its carved stonework illuminated by the flames coming from the settlement below them.

'We're going to split up,' said Walter. 'Lothar, you and Abigone will circle round to the left, and I will take the Westlanders to the right. If you see Ragnvald, stay out of sight, and wait for us to attack him. We will draw his attention on to us, and then Abigone will strike. Go.'

'But we don't know where Ragnvald is,' said Abigone. 'I can't see him anywhere.'

'With six stairwells coming up onto the roof, he won't know which one to guard,' said Walter. 'The chances are that he's in a position where he can watch two or three of them at the same time; so he'll probably be somewhere central. Take care, Your Highness, and I will see you both when this is over.'

Walter disappeared back down the stairs to fetch the Westlanders, and Lothar turned to Abigone.

'Are you ready, ma'am?' he said. 'Stay low.'

They set off at a run, veering to the left and crouching as they raced over the roof. There were low walls and deep trench-like gaps criss-crossing the multi-levelled roof. Lothar and Abigone jumped over one of the trenches, then Abigone came to halt.

'Keep moving,' said Lothar.

'Wait,' said Abigone. She crouched by the trench. At the bottom, Magnus was lying on his side, his leg covered in blood.

'Magnus,' she said, 'can you hear me?'

'Raewyn?' he gasped.

'It's Abigone,' she said. 'You killed your father.'

'Yes. Raewyn... is she...?'

'She's fine, Magnus. I am very glad to see you alive.'

Magnus's gaze went to her. 'Thank you,' he said; 'thank you for trusting me.'

'We need to go, Your Highness,' said Lothar.

'We are going to leave you here, Magnus,' said Abigone. 'Ragnvald is on the roof, and he has Reath with him; but we will be back.'

Magnus closed his eyes. 'I know you will.'

Abigone and Lothar set off again. They clambered over a low wall and up onto a higher level, then hid behind a tall pinnacle of carved stone. Lothar peered round it, his shield covering them both, and his crossbow slung over his shoulder. He glanced around, then up at an even higher level.

'If I was Ragnvald,' he whispered to Abigone; 'then that's where I'd be. Up there.'

They edged out from behind the pinnacle, and raced to the base of the higher level. Lothar cupped his hands, and helped Abigone climb up, then he pulled himself onto the next level after her. They crawled over the uneven surface, and peered over a lip of rock. Ragnvald was crouching by the middle of the high platform, his right hand clutching a knife, and his left arm round Reath's shoulders. The girl had been gagged, and her hands were bound but, other than that, she appeared unharmed.

'Can you take him from here?' Lothar whispered.

Abigone shook her head, and they fell into silence, waiting.

'Are you ready to die, little Reath?' Ragnvald said, his gaze scanning the roof. 'This is the end, but if I fall, then you shall join me in death.' He laughed. 'Nothing to say for once? Your sister will be dead by now; I ordered Erling to cut her throat as soon as Walter broke into the women's quarters. It didn't have to be this way. Why did you come here? Everything was perfect before you arrived; the slaves knew their place, and we could live like fucking royalty. I was supposed to be the next Whalebone King; we should have killed you the moment you stepped off that fucking barge.'

A noise came from Ragnvald's left, and he turned his head.

'Here they come,' he said, placing the knife next to Reath's throat.

Walter and the Westlanders appeared, fifty yards from Ragnvald, their shields up, and their crossbows level.

'Take one more step,' Ragnvald cried out, 'and the girl dies.'

'It's over,' Walter shouted. 'Surrender, and we'll let you live.'

Ragnvald laughed. 'Do you think I'm fucking stupid? You're no Westlander, so you must be Walter.' He raised his free hand. 'Water to salt.'

A Westlander threw himself in front of Walter, who was pushed down to the roof. The Westlander screamed and choked, then fell silent.

'Charge!' cried Johan.

Lothar stared, his eyes wide. 'Shit.'

Abigone got to her feet. Ragnvald was crouching with his back to her, but if she summoned a horse, Reath would also die.

She lifted her hand, as the Westlanders rushed over the roof. 'Summon for me a rat.'

A chunk of flesh was torn from Ragnvald's back, and he let out a scream that ripped through the air. He dropped the knife and fell to his knees, as Abigone walked towards him.

She pointed at him. 'He's mine!' she cried. 'Summon for me a rat.'

More flesh was flayed from Ragnvald, and he collapsed onto the roof. Next to him, Reath stared up at Abigone, her eyes wide. Ragnvald was writhing on the roof, his back, legs and arms ragged and bleeding, with some bone showing through the open flesh.

'Summon for me a rat,' Abigone said for a third time; 'a rat from a rat, Ragnvald.'

The Westlanders arrived, forming a tight circle around them with their loaded crossbows aimed down. Walter pulled Reath away. He removed her gag, and loosened the cords binding her wrists. On the roof next to Ragnvald lay three small piles of gore, and Reath stared at them. Ragnvald tried to raise a hand, and a Westlander stamped down on it, breaking his fingers.

'Once more, Abigone,' said Walter. 'Finish him.'

Abigone took Lothar's knife from her belt.

'Please,' Ragnvald gasped; 'I'll do anything.'

'There is only one thing I need from you,' Abigone said, as she crouched next to him.

She pushed the tip of the knife into Ragnvald's neck, then drove it in up to the hilt. Abigone let go of the knife and stood, her gaze upon Ragnvald as he stopped moving.

Over to the east, the sky was getting lighter, and the morning chorus of birds in the forest was beginning. One of the Westlanders kicked Ragnvald to make sure he was dead, then the body was rolled over.

Abigone glanced at Walter. 'Magnus is alive,' she said. 'I would be obliged if you helped him to get out of the temple.'

'I know where he is, sir,' said Lothar. 'I can take you there.'

Walter nodded. 'Show me.'

Abigone watched as Lothar led Walter across the roof, then she turned back to the Westlanders, who were staring down at the body of Ragnvald.

'I'm taking his head,' said Johan. 'The others will need proof.'

Abigone took Reath's hand as Johan drew a stolen sword, and she walked with the girl over to the eastern edge of the roof.

'Let's watch the sunrise,' said Abigone.

Reath said nothing.

'Ragnvald was lying,' Abigone went on. 'Nyli is alive. We saved them all.'

'I knew you would come for us, Abigone,' said Reath. 'Nyli and Salus didn't believe me, but I knew. I wasn't sure about the others, but I knew *you* would come.'

Abigone said nothing as the sun split the trees ahead of them. She felt the warm rays touch her skin, and felt like crying, but she couldn't, not with Reath holding her hand. She had to be strong; she was Head Maker, and the others needed her.

'I will come with you to Geathan, Abigone,' said Reath. 'I will follow you wherever you go.'

Abigone gazed down at her. 'And I will protect you from the evil in this world.'

Reath raised her left arm, and pointed. 'Look,' she said; 'the cranes are moving. Up on the cliff; do you see?'

Abigone turned her gaze to the top of the easternmost waterfall. The four cranes were swinging their arms over the Antiago, and each was lifting a vessel into the air.

'The barges are here,' said Abigone. She smiled at Reath. 'And they won't be leaving without us.'

CHAPTER 34
THE MONSTER

East of Steppen, Great Forest, Jallin, Central Provinces – 25th Day of Quoma 108

Saffie paused for a break, her arms and shoulders aching, and her left leg as sore as it had been in days. She leaned against the trunk of a tall beech tree, her left hand grasping the crutch. She had been hobbling through the forest for hours, her sleep disturbed, and her worries driving her onwards. She gazed up, and saw the sky starting to brighten. She had probably missed the battle, but that was fine – what use would she be to anyone when she couldn't walk unassisted?

Her thoughts went back to Lothar.

'Please, spirits,' she whispered, 'let him be alive. Let me see him again, and I'll... I'll do whatever you want me to do. The dream I had; please tell me you didn't send it. If you did, then what does it mean?'

She closed her eyes, but heard no response from the spirits. Her Aunt Isabella, high priestess of Sanctos, had told the imperial cousins that the spirits always listened to their prayers; but Saffie had never heard them answer any of her pleas. She had assumed it was due to her being insufficiently pious, but perhaps it was because the spirits knew she was a Maker, and why would they wish to speak to a Maker?

With her eyes still closed, the nightmare replayed itself in her mind.

She had dreamed about being a Maker again, for the first time since her injury, only this time she had betrayed Lothar, and had summoned a creature to devour him. His body being torn apart and eaten had been the last thing she had seen before awakening, her brow covered in sweat. She had acted at once, pulling on her boots, picking up her crutch, and limping out of the shelter.

She steeled herself, wedged the crutch back under her left shoulder, and carried on, following the tracks left by so many Westlanders who had travelled back and forth to Steppen to raid and attack the settlement of the Whalebone King. The Westlanders might be barbaric, their backward moon religion repelling Saffie, but there was no doubting their martial prowess; just as there was no doubting Walter's tactical acumen. There was a leader who could be trusted; a man capable of taking advice and learning quickly from his mistakes; a man who didn't become disheartened by setbacks. If Captain Zola had possessed the same skills, then the Sanctians wouldn't have been needlessly sacrificed in their attack upon the temple. In his desire to make a martyr of Saffie, Zola had lost sight of their entire purpose in the forest – to eliminate the Master who had turned Steppen into a den of sadism and cruelty. In doing so, Zola had ignored the only factor that could have brought them victory – the enslaved Westlanders.

Saffie tried to keep her thoughts on Zola and Walter as she trudged and limped her way through the dark forest. She had avoided the large encampment where those who were too old, sick or injured to fight had remained, not wishing to have to explain herself before them. All she wanted to do, she told herself, was to make sure that Lothar was alive, and that the Whalebone King was dead. Then she could rest.

She stumbled into a clearing, and came face to face with over a dozen red-faced and panting mercenaries. They were arguing among themselves about what to do next, and it took them a few moments to realise that Saffie was at the edge of the clearing.

'Is she... a Sanctian?' gasped one, who seemed out of breath. 'Look at her uniform.'

'Are you lost, little lady?' said another, his crossbow clutched in his hands.

'I could ask the same about you,' said Saffie. 'I thought the servants of the Whalebone King were too frightened to enter the forest.'

'Kill her,' cried another, 'before she can tell the damn Westlanders that we're here.'

'Don't be fucking stupid,' said the one aiming the crossbow at Saffie. 'Look at her crutch; she's going nowhere. We'll take her as a hostage. We could use her to barter our way out of this shithole.'

'Why would you need to barter your way out?' said Saffie.

'The king is dead,' said one, 'and we're getting out of here.'

Saffie laughed. 'The Whalebone King is dead? Praise the spirits.' She wondered why she wasn't frightened as the mercenaries glared at her. Then it hit her – she was a Maker. She was terrified of what lay within her, but a few out-of-shape mercenaries didn't scare her. They were nothing – paid servants of the vile king.

'Who killed him?' she went on. 'Who do I need to congratulate?'

'You little bitch,' said one. 'Grab her, lads.'

Saffie raised her free arm as the mercenaries fanned out in an arc towards her. Lothar had told her that what she was about to try was impossible, but that wasn't going to stop her.

'Spirits,' she said, 'help me summon a giant spider to eat my enemies.'

Six of the dozen mercenaries disintegrated before her eyes, their flesh ripped from them, along with hair, bone and blood. The others screamed, as a gargantuan, monstrous creature materialised in the clearing next to them. The eight-legged beast reared up, its hideous shape terrifying to behold, then it opened its jaws and bit down on a mercenary, swallowing up his head and shoulders, and cutting him in half at the torso. Saffie watched, transfixed as the spider hunted down the others in the clearing, chasing them as they screamed and ran. They were quick, but the beast was quicker, and none could escape. The last mercenary tripped, then he crawled towards Saffie, who gazed down at him.

'Help me!' the man cried.

'No,' said Saffie.

The giant spider bounded over, and tore off one of the man's legs with its jaws, then it crouched over him and devoured the rest. When it had finished, the beast raised its huge head, its many eyes taking in the sight of Saffie standing before it.

Saffie gazed at it. What would it do, now that the mercenaries were dead? Would it try to attack her, or did she have some sort of power over it? It would be interesting to find out, but she knew she couldn't leave such a creature to roam the Great Forest, not when there was a camp full of the old and sick just a few miles behind her.

She raised her hand again, feeling a twinge of regret.

'Sorry,' she said. 'Spirits, please help me summon a giant dead spider.'

The body of her spider flung itself apart, and then it re-materialised a few yards away. Its legs were folded inwards, and its lifeless eyes were staring up at the lightening sky.

Lothar had been wrong, she thought; that hadn't been so hard. He had told her that summoning a living creature was too complicated, but Saffie had found it simple enough. Had her abilities somehow improved? She kept her hand raised.

'Spirits,' she said, 'help me summon a wooden chair.'

The closest tree creaked as wood was pulled from it, then a misshapen lump appeared a yard above the blood-soaked ground. It fell, and spilt apart upon landing, breaking into a dozen fragments. Saffie frowned. How could she summon a spider, when she was unable to create something as basic as a wooden chair? She wondered if Abigone held the answers. Perhaps it was time to find out more about what she could and couldn't do.

She limped through the clearing, drawing level with the body of the dead monster she had summoned. She gazed at it, feeling a little sorry that she had ended its life so quickly. It was ugly, a hideous monstrosity, but she had made it on her own, without any training, and it looked exactly the same as the beast she had seen so often in her dreams. She knew it was odd, but she couldn't help feeling a little fond of the creature.

Someone ran into the clearing, a drawn sword in his right hand, and he held out his other arm to shield Saffie from the dead spider.

'Denny?' she said. 'What are you doing here?'

'Never mind me,' he cried. 'What is that thing doing here? I heard screams.'

'It's dead, Denny; you don't need to be scared of it.'

'Did you kill it?' he said. He gazed around at the blood on the ground, and then at the assortment of items the spider had neglected to eat – a boot here, an arm there, a crossbow.

Saffie considered telling Denny the truth. As a Master, he might know more about how she had been able to summon the creature, but then she saw the look of horror and disgust on his face, and decided against it.

'I think it attacked some mercenaries,' she said. 'Perhaps they killed it.'

Denny stepped back, his gaze never leaving the spider. 'Do these... things live in the forest?'

'I wouldn't know,' she said. 'I've certainly never seen one before.'

He frowned. 'Why are you so calm? And where were you going?'

'I was hoping to discover some news about the attack on Steppen,' she said. 'Is the battle over?'

'I don't know.'

She narrowed her eyes. 'What do you mean you don't know? Why are you here? Where's Abigone?'

'She sent me away. I think our betrothal might be at an end.'

'Why did she send you away?'

'She wanted to use the Westlanders to storm the temple, but dozens of slaves and three of the students are still inside.'

'I heard that the Whalebone King was dead.'

'Yes, but Ragnvald is still inside. He offered us a deal, Saffie. He said that he would release the slaves and hostages if we let him go.'

'And Abigone refused this deal, I assume?'

'None of them would listen to me, so I tried to take Abigone's authority from her. Walter...'

'Walter told you that he was loyal to his princess?'

Denny glanced away.

'Oh Denny,' she said. 'You must have known that Walter would take her side over yours; and why would you believe a word that Ragnvald told you?'

'I wasn't going to let him escape. I wanted to move the Westlanders to the south, to cut him off, but Abigone insisted that we attack the temple. I was trying to save lives, Saffie. Ragnvald would execute everyone if we entered the temple. Abigone knew the risks, and yet she pressed on with ordering the attack. I couldn't stay to watch. Besides, Abigone told me that she no longer needed me.'

'Do you still love her?'

'Of course I do.'

'Then do you know what you need to do now?'

He eyed her.

'You need to go back to Steppen and apologise,' Saffie said; 'and hope that she forgives you.'

'I can't. She's changed. She was so sweet and innocent when I met her, but she has turned into a heartless killer.'

'She is trying to save her students,' said Saffie, 'and, it seems, she is determined to kill Ragnvald. She needs your support.'

'She doesn't; that's the thing. She doesn't need me any more.' He glanced at the body of the spider. 'Can we move away from this thing while we talk? It makes me feel sick.'

Saffie suppressed her anger at his words. Her spider had saved her life, and she didn't care for her cousin's tone.

'I am going to Steppen,' she said. 'If you wish, you may walk with me.'

She set off, limping through the clearing, not caring if Denny was with her. She heard his footsteps, and he caught up with her.

'Was Lothar alive when you last saw him?' she said.

'He was fine. All the slaves have been freed, apart from the ones inside the temple. Walter's forces were in complete control of the rest of the settlement.'

'Then the attack was a success?'

'I guess so.'

'Denny, the Whalebone King is dead. I think that counts as a great success.'

'But Ragnvald lives.'

'Maybe,' said Saffie. 'We shall see.'

They walked onwards, heading ever closer to the Ario River and the settlement. Saffie saw a cloud of smoke hanging over Steppen as the sky grew brighter, and she smiled, despite her exhaustion and the pain coming from her left leg. They followed the track until it reached the banks of the wide river, and Saffie gazed at the remnants of the barrack blocks where the mercenaries had lived. All of them had been destroyed, and some were still smouldering. Beyond, the slave settlement had also been burnt to the ground, and a light breeze was swirling clouds of ash around. Saffie turned to gaze at the temple, and her eyes widened. Half of it seemed to have collapsed, then, as she watched, another section crumbled and fell to the ground, as though it had been struck by an earthquake.

'A Maker is doing that,' said Denny, as they stared.

'A Maker?' said Saffie.

'She will be summoning objects made from rock, to rip chunks out of the building,' he said. 'It's what Abigone did to the Sanctian embassy in Klef Mordain.'

'What do you think it means?'

'I'm not sure. If Abigone's attack was a disaster, then Walter might have called for Eshia to destroy the building, with Ragnvald still inside.'

'Perhaps the attack was a success,' said Saffie, 'and Abigone is making sure that no Master ever takes control of it again. Still, it's a pity; it's a beautiful building.'

Denny eyed her. 'Are you feeling all right? You seem different today.'

'I will feel a lot better if I know that Lothar is fine, and that Ragnvald is dead.'

'That's twice you've mentioned Lothar. Are you in love with him?'

'I... I don't know. I will be heartbroken if he's dead, but he doesn't think that we have any future together.'

'He's right. If you go to Sanctos with him and Walter, the emperor will have you married to Arturo within weeks.'

They walked on, heading north along the western bank of the Ario. They passed a stand of trees and thick undergrowth, and the cranes by the waterfall came into view. Saffie and Denny came to another halt. Four barges were being lowered down from the cliffs, and another four were already berthed in the large basin that sat at the bottom.

'The barges are here,' cried Denny. He smiled at Saffie. 'Our way out has arrived.'

They pressed onwards, watching as the second batch of barges splashed into the water of the basin. Hundreds of Westlanders had gathered by the side of the basin, and they got to work, detaching the hooks and chains from the four new barges, so that the cranes could be raised again. Soldiers were also present, standing in large groups amid the crowds of Westlanders, but there was no tension between the two sides, and the Westlanders were in a victorious mood. Saffie and Denny reached a bridge, and began to cross. When they were halfway over, a tall figure in shining steel armour stepped off one of the barges and onto the wharf by the side of the basin. The crowd of Westlanders parted, and Walter appeared, leading another group. Walter and the armoured figure embraced, and the Westlanders let out a great cheer, their hands in the air. Saffie caught sight of Abigone standing next to Walter. With the princess were several others, including some children.

'Look,' said Saffie; 'are those the students who were in the temple? Did Abigone save them all?'

Denny said nothing for a moment, then he nodded.

'She did it,' said Saffie. 'You should have trusted her.'

Denny put a hand to his face, then he frowned. 'The man in the steel armour,' he said; 'is that Uncle Sebastian?'

'It can't be,' said Saffie. 'What would he be doing here?' She squinted, and her eyes widened. 'Sebastian!' she shouted, waving her free hand in the air. 'Over here! Sebastian!'

Walter and her uncle turned, and Sebastian's smile grew broader. The crowd surged towards the bridge, with Sebastian leading the way.

'Saffie!' he cried, then he swept her up in his arms. 'Denny, too,' he said. 'Let me look at both of you. Is your leg broken, Saffie?' He released her, and embraced Denny.

'What are you doing here, Uncle?' said Saffie 'And who are all those soldiers?'

'They are members of the Jallian militia,' said Sebastian. 'They cost me a fortune; let me tell you. The Jallian authorities had no interest in sending any soldiers down the Antiago, so I had to pay for them myself. And then I had to bribe at least a dozen Jallian officials to turn a blind eye to my activities.'

'But why?' she said. 'Why did you come here?'

'To assist Duke Walter,' he said. 'The more I discovered about Steppen, the more I realised that I couldn't wait until I had reached Elestia.' He glanced at Walter, then slapped him on the back. 'Of course, I needn't have worried. Duke Walter and Princess Abigone didn't require any damn help from me.'

'We appreciate it all the same, Sebastian,' said Walter.

Sebastian gazed at the smoking ruins of the settlement. 'What a mess you've made of the place. I trust that the Whalebone King has been taken care of?'

Walter nodded. 'And three of his sons.'

'Then who is going to look after the silver mine? The authorities in Jallin and Elestia will be rather upset if the flow of silver is interrupted.'

'There is no mine,' said a voice.

Sebastian turned, and eyed a young man on crutches with blood-stained bandages on his leg. 'And who is this fellow?'

'This is Magnus,' said Abigone; 'the fourth son of the Whalebone King. His help was essential to our success.'

Saffie narrowed her eyes. She had seen Magnus before, when the Sanctians had attacked the temple.

Abigone caught her glance. 'Magnus also saved your life, Princess Safina. He told Ragnvald that you were dead, and spared you from becoming his prisoner.'

'Is that true?' said Saffie.

Magnus lowered his gaze. 'I'm sorry I didn't do more for you.'

'Don't apologise, young man,' said Sebastian. 'If you saved my niece, then I will be forever in your debt. Now, back to the silver. What was that you were saying about the mine?'

'It doesn't exist,' Magnus said. 'It has never existed. My father and Ragnvald used their Master powers to transform rock into coins and bullion.'

Sebastian exhaled. 'I see. I wonder how the dear old Offices of Purgation will react when they discover that they have been handling money created by Masters, eh?'

'Why don't you ask Saffie, Uncle?' said Denny. 'That's who she works for.'

'Is it, indeed? I thought you were in the navy, Saffie?'

'I was, Uncle,' she said. 'I joined the Offices of Purgation in Elestia, and was sent to Steppen on my very first day. The others in my party were killed. I am the sole survivor.'

Sebastian nodded, then he turned and gazed around at the Westlanders.

'Have the first eight barges unloaded,' he said to a Jallian militiamen, 'and distribute the supplies to the people here.'

'Yes, my lord,' said the soldier.

Sebastian glanced back at Walter. 'There remain sufficient supplies on the four barges still up on the cliffs to take us all to Elestia. Who shall be coming along? Walter, I assume that you wish to continue onwards to Sanctos with me?'

'That's the plan,' said Walter. 'Otto and Dietar will be coming with us, naturally; and another Mountain Ranger you might remember from Upper Down.'

Lothar emerged from the crowd, but his gaze went to Saffie.

'I will also come to Sanctos,' she said. 'If that's all right, Uncle?'

'Of course it is,' said Sebastian, his gaze going from Lothar to his niece. 'I would be delighted to have you with us for the voyage. And what about the fair Princess Abigone? Shall you be returning to Upper Down?'

'I don't think so,' said Abigone. 'Might my friends and I travel on the barges as far as Yearl?'

'Yearl, eh?' he said. 'That won't be a problem, Your Highness. I am at your service. Denny, what say you?'

Saffie watched as Denny lowered his eyes, and she wondered if Sebastian suspected or knew that his nephew was a Master.

'I don't think I shall be returning to Sanctos, Uncle,' he said.

Saffie pushed him in the back, and Denny walked forward until he was standing in front of Abigone.

'I was wrong,' he said.

'You were,' said Abigone.

'Might we talk?'

Abigone said nothing for a moment, then she inclined her head. The crowd parted, and Denny and Abigone passed between them until they were out of sight.

'Might I inquire as to what all that was about?' Sebastian said.

'I should fill you in on a few details,' said Walter. 'Do you have any brandy?'

'Come now, Walter; do you think I would have travelled all this way without a little liquid refreshment? Come onto my barge, and we can talk.'

Saffie hobbled over to Lothar. 'I am glad you are alive,' she said. 'Very glad.'

He shook his head at her. 'Did you limp all the way here from the shelter?' he said. 'You're out of your mind; you could have set back your recovery.'

'Is that what you want to say to me?' she said.

'No,' he said, lowering his voice. 'I want to kiss you, but I have a feeling that we won't be doing any of that with your uncle around. Am I wrong?'

'You're not wrong,' she said, 'but that doesn't mean I don't want to be with you. Do you want me to come to Sanctos?'

'You know the answer to that,' he said, his eyes piercing her, 'but I will go mad if I have to watch you get married to someone else.'

'I will do what I can to have the wedding cancelled,' she whispered. 'We could be discreet, very discreet. No one else has to know about us. I need you.'

'What's all the whispering about?' said a teenage girl.

Lothar frowned. 'Saffie, this is Reath.'

'Hello,' said Reath. 'Are you coming with us on the barges?'

'Yes,' said Saffie. 'Is that all right with you?'

'Why would it not be all right?' said the girl.

'Be careful,' said Eshia, stepping forward. 'Saffie is a Sanctian who thinks Masters and Makers ought to be executed.'

Reath narrowed her eyes. 'Is that so?'

'My opinions might have changed in recent days,' said Saffie. 'You have Lothar to thank for that. He... has opened my mind to other possibilities.'

Reath laughed. 'That's a funny way to say that you've been shagging him.'

Saffie raised an eyebrow.

'Pay no attention to her,' said Lothar. 'Reath's main talent is annoying people.'

'I will make sure I am on a different barge from the Masters and Makers,' said Saffie. 'That way, neither of us will have to worry.'

'That suits us fine,' said Eshia.

'Right at this moment,' said Lothar, 'we are all on the same side. Could we not just enjoy the victory? Together, we defeated the Whalebone King and his sons, and we've freed nearly two thousand Westlanders. The bickering can wait.'

Reath stared at him. 'Do you know me at all?'

EPILOGUE

Great Forest, Northern Yearl, Central Provinces – 12th Day of Regula 108

Saffie sat on the deck of the barge next to Lothar, as the lead vessel pulled out of the Great Forest. On either side of the River Ario ahead of them were the fields and open countryside of northern Yearl, and Saffie felt her eyes well a little at the sight.

'We made it,' said Lothar.

She looked at him. 'We did.'

'I wonder if the Westlanders have reached the edge of the forest in Jallin by now,' Lothar went on. 'Do you think they'll be able to resist the temptation to raid the farms on the way north to their homeland?'

'I hope so,' she said. 'I heard Johan promise Walter that they would behave themselves on the journey.'

Lothar laughed. 'And when have you ever known a Westlander to behave?'

'I had never met any before Steppen, so I can't say.' She glanced over her shoulder, where Sebastian and Walter were talking. Only those going onwards to Sanctos were passengers on the lead barge, while Abigone and her students were on the next few along. 'Do you think my uncle suspects us?'

'Sebastian isn't stupid,' said Lothar, 'and Walter might have told him after a few brandies. The question is – will he do anything about it when we get to Sanctos? And will he tell the emperor that Denny is heading off to Geathan with a bunch of Masters and Makers? A lot depends upon your uncle, Saffie.'

'I know. It is just as well that he is a good man. He doesn't particularly hold to the view that Masters and Makers are inherently evil, which was something I always used to criticise about him. But now? Now I am very pleased that he isn't a fanatic. I do wish, though, that I had been given more of a chance to speak to Abigone on the journey down the river; there is much I would have liked to ask her about being a Maker.'

'You know what the others thought of that idea. Eshia has pretty much turned them all against you, and Abigone and the rest will be leaving us soon. I'll be sad to see Abigone go; we've been through a lot together since we left Upper Down, but it feels right being with Walter again.' He glanced at her. 'And it feels good to be with you, though I'd rather be open about what we're doing.'

'So would I,' she said.

They fell into silence as Walter and Sebastian approached the front of the barge.

'We shall stop for the night at the first town we come across,' said Sebastian. 'The Jallians are contracted to take us all the way to Elestia, but I feel the need to stretch my legs on dry ground again; and we should fill up on our supplies.'

Saffie smiled. 'How are you paying for all this, Uncle?'

'That's a little complicated, Saffie,' he said, 'but I shall sort it all out when we get to Sanctos. I may have to sell a small estate to cover the costs.'

'Abigone, Denny and the others will be leaving us when we stop for the night,' said Walter. 'Sebastian has loaned them money to hire a few carriages for their onward journey, and they felt it best to go their own way, now that we have left the forest behind.'

'Then we four, along with Otto and Dietar, shall proceed on to

Sanctos,' said Sebastian. 'By all the spirits, I am looking forward to seeing Carmen and the children again. Have you decided what you are going to do when we get home, Saffie? Will you be leaving your current employers?'

'I haven't decided anything yet, Uncle,' she said.

Sebastian gave her a look. 'You can do better than the Offices of Purgation.'

'I need more time to think it over.'

'Very well. I see no sense in harassing you on the subject, Saffie; you know my feelings.'

Walter gazed into the distance, a hand shielding his eyes from the sun. 'That looks like a village ahead of us. If it has a market and a tavern, we should stop there.'

'A splendid suggestion, my friend,' said Sebastian. 'Let us inform the Jallians on the other barges.'

Saffie and Lothar watched as the two men walked to the rear of the vessel.

'I'll have to watch that Sebastian,' Lothar said. 'He's going to lead Walter straight back to drink if I'm not careful, especially once Abigone leaves us.' He turned back to Saffie. 'Why would you not be sure about leaving the Offices of Purgation? I thought it would be an obvious choice.'

'I need to be very careful, Lothar,' she said. 'I told my Aunt Isabella that my ambition was to become a high-ranking agent in the Offices of Purgation, and it would look suspicious if she thinks I've given up after one operation. She would demand to know why, and I don't want to cross her. In her own way, my Aunt Isabella frightens me as much as the Whalebone King did.'

'You will have to teach me all about Sanctos before we get there,' said Lothar. 'The important things, you know – like, is it sunny and warm? What food do they eat, and are there fancy balls and parties to go to?'

Saffie smiled at him. 'Don't worry, Lothar,' she said; 'stick with me, and you'll be fine.'

AUTHOR'S NOTES

JANUARY 2025

Thank you for reading ***Whalebone King***, the third book of the Masters & Makers series. After two books in which Masters and Makers were portrayed sympathetically, I knew it was time to tell a story showing the darker side of what Masters and Makers could achieve. In many ways, ***Whalebone King*** is a grimmer book than the first two in the series, and this meant that I did not exactly find it a pleasant experience to write, although I had fun with Walter's story. I also liked introducing Saffie into the world of Masters & Makers, and I am looking forward to continuing her story as the series develops.

I hope you enjoyed it.

JOIN MY NEWSLETTER

Building a relationship with my readers is very important to me. Join my newsletter for information on new books and deals and to keep up to date on my writing progress.

www.ChristopherMitchellBooks.com/Masters

ABOUT THE AUTHOR

Christopher Mitchell is the author of the Magelands and Masters & Makers fantasy series.

For more information:

www.christophermitchellbooks.com
info@christophermitchellbooks.com

Printed in Great Britain
by Amazon

61284647R00292